THE PLAYGROUP

BY

JAMI WORTHINGTON

THE PLAYGROUP
Copyright © 2023 Jami Worthington
ALL RIGHTS RESERVED

No part of this book may be reproduced or transmitted in any form or by any means, electronic or mechanical, without permission in writing from the author. This book is a work of fiction. Names, characters, places and incidents are either products or the author's imagination or used fictitiously. Any resemblance to actual events, locales, or persons, living or dead, is entirely coincidental.

Formatted by: Brenda Wright, Formatting Done Wright

Follow on social media:
Instagram @jamiworthingtonbooks
Threads @jamiworthingtonbooks
Facebook: facebook.com/jamiworthingtonbooks

1

You're Invited to the Wyndham Preschool Potluck Picnic!

When: Saturday, September 1, 12:00 pm

Where: Wyndham Preschool Playground and Courtyard

Hello Wyndham Friends! The school year is almost upon us. Join us for a fun afternoon and get to know the 3's 4's family. Bring a favorite dish to share (Please no nuts. Gluten free preferred, and an assortment of vegan dishes are most welcome). Teachers Emily, Nora, and Kelly can't wait to see our old friends and meet our new ones!

Cleo

Cleo pulled into the Wyndham School parking lot and parked her BMW iX in between a Tesla and a Mercedes SUV. It seemed like every other car in Oak Valley was one of the two, with an occasional Porsche Cayenne or another BMW thrown in.

"You ready?" She unbuckled her seatbelt and turned to the back seat. Her daughter, Isabelle, secured in her car seat, stared at her with solemn eyes.

"I guess so." As always, Cleo's heart squeezed a little at her daughter's faint lisp.

"It's going to be fun, I promise." Already at three Izzy had mastered that, "oh really?" Face. *God help me when she's a teenager.*

Not that she could blame Izzy for her skepticism. Their lives had been turned upside down in just a few short months. Well, if she was being honest, Cleo had to admit *she* had turned their lives upside down. Though it was all for the better, she couldn't blame her daughter for feeling insecure.

She got out of the car and went around to the back seat to unbuckle Izzy. "Myself," Izzy insisted when Cleo went to lift her out of the carseat. As she awkwardly climbed out of the car, Cleo retrieved the fruit salad she had made from the floor of the passenger side. Cradling the salad in one arm, she reached for Izzy's hand with her free hand. She started toward the entrance, but paused as Izzy tugged at her.

"I don't wanna go."

Cleo's jaw clenched at her daughter's tone leaned towards a whine. She took a deep breath and bent to give Izzy a reassuring squeeze. Her irritation faded in a flood of warmth as Izzy's plump little arms wound around her neck. "Honey, there's going to be so many fun girls and boys. We're going to make so many new friends."

Izzy gave a rather dramatic sigh for a three year old, but allowed herself to be led towards the school.

As they approached, Cleo mentally compared Wyndham School to her faint memories of her own preschool. This beautiful, wood and glass structure couldn't be farther from the basement in a run down church where her mother had dropped her off for long days of playing with chipped wooden blocks and trying to avoid the boy with the biting problem.

Situated on a property that offered spectacular views of the Santa Cruz mountains, Wyndham was a state of the art, eco friendly masterpiece, whose teachers were tasked with molding the next generation of Silicon Valley superstars. Though the school was established in the seventies, the current building was only a few years old.

Apparently the parents decided that the converted nineteen fifties ranch house that had formerly housed the school wasn't good enough for their little princes and princesses. So millions of dollars were raised and spent so the poor underprivileged children of Oak Valley could finger paint and make mud pies in acceptable facilities.

How could anyone expect them to settle for less, especially in a town where the average net worth was over ten million dollars?

As she and Izzy walked through the breezeway between the classrooms and past the massive community hall, shrieks and laughter of toddlers mingled with the din of adult conversation. In addition to the expected play structure and sand box, Wyndham School featured a native garden with a chicken coop tucked into the back corner.

Of course.

Over the back fence, Cleo took in the stunning view of the rolling hills, unblemished by development thanks to the town's dedication to maintaining ample open space. This rural oasis in the heart of Silicon Valley was the last place Cleo would have ever imagined herself landing. But sometimes life took you in unexpected directions.

In any case, she couldn't deny the beauty of her surroundings.

As they got to the edge of the playground, Izzy once again hesitated. Cleo bit back a grimace of frustration and admonished herself to be patient. While she could understand Izzy's hesitation, she couldn't relate to it. Cleo had learned from a very early age to adapt to any social situation. She could walk into any room - or playground - and read every single person like a book. That meant she could control any interaction.

Well, almost any, she reminded herself. There were always a few wildcards. She had the scars to prove it.

Some might call her manipulative. She considered it a necessary survival skill.

She led Izzy out to the playground, taking in the scrum of three and four year olds littering the climbing structure and digging in the sandbox. Others stood shyly at their parents' sides, who gathered in gender segregated clumps around the courtyard.

The dads wore essentially the same uniform of polo shirts, many of them embossed with corporate logos, paired with khaki shorts or jeans. Sneakers or, ugh, flip flops completed the ensembles. When would men get the memo that no one wanted to see their callused, hairy feet?

The women were more interesting, wardrobe wise. While most wore either pre-distressed jeans and drapey tops or sundresses paired with flats or sandals, there were a few outliers. You could tell a lot about a woman by how she dressed. The mom in the hiking shorts and Keen sandals was probably still co-sleeping with her three year olds and made sure the teachers requested vegan options for today's potluck.

The one whose dress was just a little too short and tight, her wedge heels a little too high for a preschool function was still clinging to her youth. She did a lot of girls 'nights up in the city where she flirted with guys in their twenties as her tech bro husband cooled his heels at home.

Then there was the fashionista, who sported jeans that retailed at around $300 (Cleo would know. She owned three pair.), and had a pair of thousand dollar designer sunglasses perched on her nose.

She unconsciously smoothed her hand over the front of her shirt, pleased with the outfit she'd chosen for today. White twill shorts, short enough to show off her slim, toned legs, but not so short to imply thirst. They were paired with a black tank that skimmed her breasts and narrow waist, but whose neckline grazed the base of her throat. Other than her four carat emerald cut diamond ring, modest gold hoop earrings an Apple watch were her only jewelry. With her straight, dark hair pulled back in a sleek ponytail, her look was tasteful, polished, but not in any way attention seeking.

When entering a new crowd, Cleo found it best to stay out of the spotlight.

Her gaze locked on a woman who was talking to the fashionista and a tall, blonde woman in the ubiquitous distressed jeans and floral printed drapey top. With her dark hair piled on her head in a perfectly messy bun and her tall, curvy frame shown off perfectly by her boho maxi dress, there was something about her, a charisma, that drew Cleo's attention like a bee to honey.

Cleo wanted to believe the woman had spent hours in front of the mirror, trying to get her thick, wavy hair to look perfectly disheveled. But just then, a little girl in a green and white sundress and pink cowboy boots ran up and tugged at her hand. As the woman bent to her daughter, her hair came tumbling out of it sclip. Without missing a beat, she gave the long skein a few twists and secured it into a perfectly messy bun.

Cleo knew, with every fiber of her being, that this was a woman for whom everything fell effortlessly into place. She watched as the woman had a short exchange with her daughter and fetched her a juice box from the drink table. A beatific smile lit up her face as she watched her daughter skip off.

The very epitome of a loving, devoted mother.

"Do you want to put that over with the other food?" The hiking shorts wearing mom interrupted her study of the woman she was sure was the queen bee of this play ground. Cleo always figured out how to get in good with the queen bee.

"Oh, sure," Cleo smiled and tugged her hand free of Izzy's to offer it to the mom. "I'm Cleo Baird."

"Ellie Thompson," the woman replied and shook her hand firmly. "That doesn't have gluten or nuts in it, does it?" She cast a glance at the covered bowl in Cleo's hand.

Cleo suppressed an eye roll. "Last time I checked, fruit salad contained neither." She could tell the woman wasn't sure if she'd been insulted or not. It gave her a little thrill, throwing people off their footing, but today wasn't a day to lean into that. "It's lovely to meet you, Ellie. I'll just go put this down and get Izzy situated."

All the food was laid out on a long folding table covered with a blue and white checked table cloth. Note cards were propped in front of some, indicating taboo ingredients such as gluten or dairy. She set her bowl of mixed berries down with the rest of the salads. She marveled, as she often did, about the differences between how these kids were being raised and her own upbringing. If she ever had the audacity to refuse an ingredient, her mother was happy to let her starve. What's that you say, apples make your mouth itch? Tough shit.

"Izzy, are you hungry?"

Izzy shook her head mutely and clung tighter to her hand.

"Let's go get you a drink and see if we can find some new friends."

Izzy sipped at her juice and warily eyed the playground. "What about that girl," Cleo indicated the girl in the green and white sundress. The one with the perfect mother. "She looks nice."

"I like her boots," Izzy said softly.

"Why don't you go tell her? People love compliments."

She stroked Izzy's hair and urged her over to the edge of the sandbox where the little girl sat, studiously sifting sand through a plastic grate.

"Hi this is Izzy," Cleo squatted down to the girls 'eye level. "Izzy really likes your boots."

Izzy nodded.

"Thanks," the little girl replied, then launched into a long winded story about how the boots had been acquired. It involved going on an airplane to a place called Tana. Horses were involved, but not the big horses, because she could only ride the little horses… Cleo lost interest about ten seconds in.

Izzy, however, was captivated, as drawn to this little dark haired girl as Cleo was to her mother. As she nodded encouragingly at a three year old's discourse on fashion, she caught a movement out of the corner of her eye. It didn't take someone long to take the bait.

"Is this your daughter?" The woman asked.

Cleo stood up to greet her face to face. "Yes, this is Isabella - Izzy." She stuck out her hand. "And I'm Cleo."

"Cool name," the woman smiled and shook her hand. She had a timeless, sculpted kind of beauty, with strong cheekbones and a firm chin. Her heavily lashed green eyes sparkled with warmth. "I'm Alex. And that's Ava." She released Cleo's hand. "I actually love the name Isabella. It was on our list when we had Ava, but I let my husband overrule me."

Cleo gave her an arch look. "If you ask me, if you're the one squeezing a baby out of your vajajay, you've earned your naming rights."

Alex let out a hearty laugh. "You're funny."

Cleo shrugged. "I keep myself entertained." She saw the two women Alex had been talking to earlier sneaking glances over their way. No doubt looking to their leader for social cues.

"I need a refill," Alex said, gesturing with her empty disposable cup. Totally compostable, of course. "Can I offer you a glass of wine?" She gestured toward the adult drink table, with its ice buckets stocked with white and rose wine chilling in the late summer heat. Next to the table was a cooler full of beer for the menfolk.

"Always," Cleo replied.

Alex let out a little "phew" sound. "I thought so. You strike me as one of the funzie moms," she said with a wink. "You wouldn't believe how uptight some of these parents are."

Out of the corner of her eye, Cleo saw the hiking shorts mom flinch.

Confident that Ava and Izzy were engaged in their play, they started toward the table. Alex filled a cup of rose for Cleo and served herself a generous pour of Sauvignon Blanc.

"Come on," Alex gestured toward the two women who were trying not to be obvious about eyeing the newcomer. "I'll introduce you to some people.

2

Alex

"Hey guys, this is Cleo," Alex said to her two best friends in the world, Jenna Carver and Morgan Lambert. Though they were smiling, Alex knew them both well enough to see they were guarded. She gave them both a subtle "be nice" look as she ushered Cleo into their midst.

"Hi, I'm Morgan." Morgan reached out a perfectly manicured hand. "My son is over there." She pointed to her son, Jack, who was beating the side of the play structure with a large stick.

As always, Morgan was the epitome of chic, her hair blown out, dressed in white designer jeans and a silk blouse. Even the toddler handprint on her thigh couldn't deter from her sartorial perfection.

Alex fought the urge to check and see what was going on with her hair, which was ready to tumble out of its bun at the slightest disturbance. She'd hastily piled the thick mass back on her head and secured it without the use of the mirror. God knew what she was working with right now.

"Did you move here recently?" Morgan asked, her blue gaze sharp and intent. Sometimes Alex had to remind Morgan that she didn't have to interview every new acquaintance like she was the CEO of one of her potential venture investments.

Cleo didn't seem to notice, her manner relaxed. She didn't exhibit any of the new mom nervousness that many experienced when their children started at Wyndham. No furtive looking around, trying to figure out how to awkwardly insert herself into a conversation to introduce herself. When she first arrived, Alex's gaze was irresistibly drawn to her air of confidence and understated beauty. She'd been happy Ava had given her an excuse to break away from Morgan and Jenna long enough to approach her.

"We moved here in mid July," Cleo said.

"I think I've seen you and your daughter out." This was from Jenna, who held her six month old son, Noah, on her hip. She held out a hand to introduce herself. As she did, her shirt rode up several inches from the waistband of her jeans, offering a glimpse of an abdomen way too taut for someone who had just given birth six months ago.

Alex smoothed her palm over her own not taut abdomen, despite the fact that it had been over three years since she'd given birth. It did her no good to compare herself to Jenna, she reminded herself. Jenna, despite the fact that she was born in Oklahoma, was the quintessential California girl. Tousled blonde hair, bright blue eyes (albeit framed with dark circles), and an athletic, toned body that didn't seem to accumulate fat no matter what she ate. Of course, the fact that she hiked and ran several miles nearly everyday probably helped.

Alex, in contrast, was more… substantial. Not fat, but she'd never have veins in her biceps like Jenna did simply from hauling her baby and preschooler around.

"Do you live on Druid?" Jenna asked.

Cleo nodded. "We moved into the house two doors down from the corner, on the right."

Alex wondered if she noticed all of their eyebrows collectively popping up. Oak Valley had a lot of wealth, a decent amount of it held by the women in this small group. But if Cleo and her family had moved into *that* house, they were next level.

"Wow, that's quite a place," Morgan said.

"I know, it's a lot." She cast her eyes down sheepishly. "We're just renting for now. My husband's company made the arrangements, and that's where we ended up. We needed something furnished, and there weren't that many options," Cleo said with a wave of her slim hand. "Once we've settled in and my husband isn't traveling so much, we'll look to buy. Right now he's still spending half of his time in Singapore and it's all I can do to look after myself and Izzy," she gestured to where Izzy and Ava sat at the edge of the sandbox, staring raptly at the sand they were pouring from one bucket to another.

Morgan perked up at that. "I love Singapore. The shopping is fantastic."

Cleo nodded as she sipped her rose. "Even better, you can get a dead-on perfect knockoff of any designer gown hand made for less than a thousand dollars."

Alex wondered if Cleo noticed Morgan's subtle shudder at the word "knockoff."

"It must be quite the culture shock, coming here." Jenna jostled and swayed as Noah started to fuss.

"It is, but after years of living in the city, I'm loving all of this nature right out my front door. Maybe you guys could help me get familiar with the trails."

"That would be Jenna, out there with the double jogger every day," Morgan chuckled. "I prefer to work out in the comfort of my own gym."

"That must be why I don't see an ounce of baby weight on you," Cleo said as she eyed Jenna's enviably slim figure.

Alex fought the urge to fold her arms across her stomach.

Jenna shrugged and jostled Noah. "Honestly, it's less for my waistline and more for my sanity at this point. With Mark so busy and-" Noah let out a squawk and swung one tiny fist. It connected with Alex's cup of sauvignon blanc and sent it flying. "Fuck," she said harshly. The curse drew several pairs of censoring eyes. Worse, it startled Noah, who started screaming in earnest.

Alex fetched some napkins from a nearby table, and when she got back to the group Jenna was smiling gratefully as a man who epitomized tall, dark and handsome took Noah from her arms. Jenna took the napkins from Alex and blotted at her wine soaked shirt.

"This must be your husband," Cleo said, smiling. "I'm Cleo."

Jenna gave a startled laugh.

"Actually this is my husband, Ethan," Alex said.

Cleo's perfectly arched brows furrowed in confusion. "Sorry, I just assumed…"

"Don't worry," Morgan said. "Sometimes it feels like we're all a bunch of sister wives."

"Careful," Ethan said with a grin, "You go telling people stuff like that and then the rumors start."

"There was that group of swingers in Atherton," Jenna chuckled.

Alex felt her cheeks heat and gave Ethan's arm a little swat. "It's not like that. It's just that we're all so close, and in and out of each other's houses all of the time. It's certainly nothing sexual."

Ethan balanced a now calm Noah on his hip and reached a broad hand out to shake Cleo's. Alex didn't miss the way Cleo's nostrils flared or the darkening tint across her cheekbones.

Ethan had that effect on women. It wasn't just his good looks, though his thick head of dark hair, soulful brown eyes, and tall, athletic body were a magnet for female attention. He also had a natural charisma about him that drew people, especially women, like flies.

Alex felt a smug grin tease at her lips. Ethan was almost always the best looking guy in any room he walked into, and Alex never tired of being on his arm.

"Where's Mark?" Ethan asked Jenna as he released Cleo's hand.

Jenna sighed. "He's at work, of course. The boys haven't even seen him for the past two days." There was no mistaking the undercurrent of resentment in her voice.

Alex could relate, sort of. When Ethan had started his company right after they graduated from business school, he had worked night and day to get it off the ground. Then newlywed Alex had spent many an hour lamenting to Morgan that she hardly ever saw her husband.

Looking back, she realized that while it had been challenging, it was nothing compared to going through it with two small kids.

"David's here somewhere," Morgan said. "He's making sure Jack doesn't clobber anyone or throw sand in anyone's face."

Alex's gaze wandered over to David, stationed next to the play structure talking to another dad. He was good looking in a professorial sort of way, with his short salt and pepper hair and wire framed glasses. He looked trim and fit in his polo and khaki shorts, which stood to reason since he was semi-retired and spent most days tearing up the local trails on his mountain bike.

"I need to talk to him about our surf trip," Ethan said as he handed Noah back to Jenna.

"You're the best," Jenna said as she held Noah with one arm and hugged Ethan with the other.

Alex loved that her friends and their kids felt so close to Ethan. Lord knew, with Mark's crazy schedule not ending anytime soon, Jenna needed all the help she could get.

"Can I have everyone's attention?" Teacher Nora strained to be heard over the combined noise of adults conversing and children shrieking. "Hello?" She waved her hands, in the air trying and failing to capture everyone's attention.

Alex put her thumb and forefinger in her mouth and let out an ear piercing whistle that stopped everyone mid sentence.

"Miss Nora is trying to get our attention," she said.

Nora gave her a grateful smile and introduced the other two teachers, Miss Emily and Miss Kelly. Alex tuned her out as she went on to welcome the families and describe the school's teaching philosophy and expectations. This was her second year at Wyndham and she was president of the board, so she was more than familiar with the whole spiel. She tuned back in when Nora asked all of the parents to gather in a circle to introduce themselves and their child.

By the time introductions were over Ava was tugging impatiently at her skirt. "I'm stawving, Mama," she whined.

"Let's get something to eat," she grinned, enchanted as ever by the way she pronounced her r's. She took Ava's hand and led her over to the table laden with dishes. She grabbed a plate and got in line behind David, who had a plate in one hand while he tried to keep Jack from grabbing fistfuls of potato chips from a bowl.

Ava, in contrast, calmly pointed to platter of sushi and said, "Can I have some Cawifownia wolls please?" Not for the first time, she was grateful to have a calm (most of the time) sweet (most of the time) girl. Once Ava's plate was full, she led her over to where David, Morgan, Jenna, and Ethan were crowded around a picnic table. She looked around for Cleo and Izzy, and saw that they were sitting with Gareth and Rod Davis, dads of one of the few girls in their boy-dominated class. Satisfied Cleo wasn't lacking companionship, she took Ethan's seat on the bench as he got up to get food.

"Want anything?" He offered.

"Just a refill," she said and held out her wine cup. She already felt faintly buzzed after two glasses, but so what? It wasn't like she was driving or had anything important to do later.

"You're not going to eat anything?" Jenna asked. Alex looked enviously at her plate, piled high with a quinoa salad, an assortment of sushi, a half dozen chicken wings, and, as if to add insult to injury, a chocolate chip cookie the size of her head. Bitch would inhale as much as she could while her three year old, Liam, stayed occupied with his own plate and Noah sat quietly in her lap. And wouldn't see so much of an ounce of it reflected on her scale.

"I had a huge breakfast," Alex lied. In truth she'd had a hard boiled egg, two strips of bacon, and a handful of blueberries. Though she supposed her efforts at low carb dieting weren't helped much by her wine consumption. But she couldn't be expected to be perfect, could she? "Let me take Noah so you can eat," she said and stretched out her arms.

The kids finished eating in about five minutes and made a beeline back to the playground. The adults lingered as long as they could before a shriek of pain or a dispute over a tricycle called them away. Alex contemplated getting another glass of wine but then saw Ava yawning and rubbing her eyes. She checked her watch, and sure enough, nap time was fast approaching.

Other parents had done similar math, as everyone moved to wrangle their kids and gather up their leftovers.

Alex caught sight of Cleo, who was gathering up her things.

She started in Cleo's direction, determined to give her her number before she left. Though she considered herself to be friendly and social, it wasn't often that she was compelled to make yet another friend. But there was something about this newcomer. She couldn't put her finger on it. All she knew was she had potential.

Alex hesitated when she saw the petite woman with the no nonsense mud brown bob who Cleo was talking to. Tricia Newman. Alex held back a grimace. Tricia was on Wyndham's board with Alex, much to Alex's irritation. She was one of those insufferable types who, whenever they discussed anything related to the kids, started every sentence with, "As someone with a Master's in early childhood education…" Though she claimed to love Wyndham and everything about it, she complained to anyone who would listen about how the play-based curriculum wasn't nearly challenging enough for her "gifted" three year old, Matthew. Which was why she had him enrolled in after school Mandarin lessons and had hired a math tutor.

She wondered if Tricia noticed her little genius picking and eating his boogers over by the slide.

But her greatest offense, as far as Alex was concerned, was when she'd tried to convince the other parents that instead of having an adults only cocktail party and auction for the annual school fundraiser, they should have a kid friendly carnival with pony rides and a bouncy castle. Alex had pointed out that with all of the birthday parties the kids had, that was how parents, especially the moms, spent every weekend of their goddamn lives, thank you very much.

Tricia had snippily replied that Matthew must not be invited to the same parties Ava was.

Alex watched as she grew animated in conversation, reminding Alex as always of a nervous chicken clucking her way around the yard.

Over Trisha's shoulder, she could see Cleo's friendly smile strain at the corners, and took that as her clue to rescue her.

As she neared, she picked up snippets of their conversation. Unsurprisingly, Tricia was complaining. But for once it wasn't about Wyndham's curriculum.

"I hate to say it, but I've found the Wyndham parents to be a little cliquey."

"Everyone seems so nice and welcoming," Cleo said with a shrug.

"Oh, most of them are perfectly friendly when you see them, but there's a group that thinks of themselves as the 'cool moms,'" she raised her twig like fingers in air quotes, "who will never let you into their inner circle. Like-"

"Hi Alex!" Cleo said brightly before Tricia could start naming names.

Not that Alex didn't know that she was on the top of Tricia's shit list. If this were high school Tricia would have written a burn book about her. "Hi Tricia, how have you been doing?" She said, her tone corn syrup sweet.

"Good, Alex, and you?" Tricia's tight smile didn't reach her dark eyes.

"I've been great, thanks. I see you've met Cleo." She skirted around Tricia to move to Cleo's side. She reached out and put a hand on her arm. "I'm glad I caught you before you left. I wanted to make sure you have my number."

"Couldn't she just get it from the class list?" Tricia said, irritated.

"I suppose, but it's just as easy for me to give it to you now," Alex said. She turned to Cleo, effectively boxing Tricia out.

Cliquey, her ass. *Maybe if you got a sense of humor and bought your clothes somewhere besides Costco, people would invite you to happy hour, Tricia.* "Text me if you want to hang out sometime."

3

Cleo

Cleo parked her BMW in front of the old one room schoolhouse that still stood at the edge of Oak Valley's Redwood Park and Recreation Center. The park got its name from the towering trees that surrounded the baseball diamond, athletic fields, wood and glass buildings that housed the town hall, the library, and community hall. And of course, there was a perfect little fenced-in playground. Though she'd rather poke herself in the eye than spend another morning chasing Izzy through tan bark, this outing was a necessary next step.

She unbuckled Izzy from her carseat and grabbed her tote bag full of snacks, toys, and wet wipes.

As she walked toward the playground she spotted Alex and Jenna, sitting at a picnic table, deep in conversation. Liam, Jack, and Ava were all in the playground, hovered over by a Latina woman who looked to be in her forties and a woman with heavily streaked blond hair in her twenties. They were Alex's and Morgan's nannies, Cleo already knew from seeing them at pickup.

That was one of the main reasons she'd had to run Alex down at the park, because more often than not, Alex sent her nanny, Sylvia to pick up Ava rather than coming herself. To Cleo's irritation, that meant there had been few opportunities in the first two weeks of school to run into Alex organically to continue to build a connection.

Of course, she had Alex's number and could have reached out at any time. But whenever she reached for her phone to do so, her mother's voice echoed in her head. "Don't be pushy. Let people come to you. You never want to seem desperate or needy."

If this was going to work, it needed to happen naturally, with Alex just as invested in developing a friendship as Cleo was.

"Cleo, is that you?" Alex waved.

Cleo feigned surprise and waved back. "Oh, hey!" Of course she knew they would be here. Every Friday morning, Izzy, Jack, and

Liam went to Music and Me at the rec center. Afterwards Alex and Jenna hung out in the park while the kids played and had a snack.

It probably would have served her well to enroll Izzy in the class too. But the very idea of sitting on the floor with a bunch of three and four year olds banging on toy instruments was enough to give her a headache.

"Come join us," Alex called. "Ava will be so happy Izzy is here," Alex said as they approached. "Sometimes all the boy energy gets to be a lot." She cast a pointed look over at the playground. Jack stood in the sandbox holding a toy truck over his head. With a low roar, he threw it into the sand and yelled, "Hulk smash!" while Liam cracked up.

Ava was in a swing, looking supremely bored as Sylvia pushed her.

Izzy tugged at Cleo's hand. "Want to go swing with Ava!"

Cleo laughed and gave a little sigh. "I guess we're going to the swings."

"Just get her settled and come back. Sylvia and Irina can keep an eye on them."

She followed as Izzy dashed to the playground. "Open the gate, Mommy," she insisted when her chubby little fingers couldn't work the latch.

Cleo did as directed and trotted after her daughter to the swing set.

Sylvia greeted them with a broad smile. "Look who it is," Sylvia said in Spanish, "It's Izzy!"

Ava let out a delighted squeal as Cleo lifted Izzy into the swing next to her. "Do you mind keeping an eye on her while I catch up with Jenna and Alex?"

"Not at all," Sylvia replied with a shooing motion.

"How have you been?" Alex said with a welcoming smile as Cleo slid onto the bench next to her. Today Alex's hair was pulled into a ponytail with a few tendrils framing her face. Though she wore Lululemon camo print leggings and a black tank top, she somehow managed to look glamorous and put together.

Jenna, who was feeding Noah from a jar of pureed something as he sat in his stroller, also wore athletic wear. Her tight green tank top showed off her sinewy arms and her black running shorts revealed an expanse of legs sculpted by miles on the local trails.

Unlike Alex, she didn't look remotely put together. Her ponytail looked like she'd styled it in the dark, and a smear of whatever she was feeding Noah decorated the front of her shirt. Also unlike Alex, she didn't look exactly delighted to see her. Cleo took her tight smile that didn't quite make her eyes in stride, even as she made a mental note to find a way to get into her good graces. It would be harder for her to get close to Alex if one of her closest friends wanted to keep her out.

"I'm glad I ran into you," Alex said. "Ava has been talking about Izzy nonstop. I kept meaning to reach out and get the girls together, but these last couple of weeks have been a little nutty." She went on to explain that she sat on the board of a local non profit that offered services to children with learning differences and mental health issues. The start of the school year was a really busy time for them.

"That's wonderful that you give your time to support them," Cleo said, stifling an eye roll. Of course Alex was out there, ministering to the world's underprivileged.

"It's a great cause," Alex said, then leaned in as though to share a secret. "But I'm not going to lie. There are members of the board who are great business connections for Ethan."

"What exactly does he do?" Cleo asked as though she hadn't studied Ethan Drake's LinkedIn profile. Ethan was a tech entrepreneur who, right out of Stanford Business School, founded a company that had something to do with artificial intelligence and web algorithms. The company turned out to be a so-called unicorn, a startup whose valuation quickly grew to over a billion dollars. Within three years Google acquired the company, leaving Ethan, and of course his wife Alex, with enough money to last them several luxurious lifetimes. Now he worked with Morgan at Acorn Ventures as an entrepreneur in residence.

Which, from what Cleo knew of that world, meant that he was basically taking a paid sabbatical as he searched for his next opportunity at one of their portfolio companies.

"Mommy, I'm hungry," Ava called. She stood at the gate, waiting for Sylvia to undo the latch. She trotted over to the table, followed closely by Izzy, Sylvia trailing behind.

Alex reached into an insulated bag and started pulling out Tupperware. "Does Izzy like cantaloupe?"

"Izzy likes pretty much everything," Cleo said as she rose to help get Izzy settled on the bench next to her.

Alex served the girls small plastic bowls of melon. "Don't worry," she said quickly, "the plastic is BPA free."

Cleo wasn't worried. She said, "Great," as if she actually cared.

"God, I'm so jealous," Jenna said, watching over Noah's fuzzy head as Izzy shoved cubes of fruit in her mouth. "Liam's diet consists almost solely of chicken fingers, macaroni and cheese, and goldfish."

"I keep telling you, you need to hide the good stuff in with the bad," Alex said. "Have you tried that recipe for the butternut squash pasta bake that I sent you?"

"If I had time to cook a multistep recipe, I would." Jenna said this with a grin but there was no mistaking the strain in her tone.

Cleo watched as Jenna's gaze drifted to Sylvia as she gently coaxed Ava to eat more fruit. A flash of resentment, only noticeable to someone highly tuned to that sort of thing, appeared on her face.

Hmm.

"I think Izzy has such a good palate because we've lived internationally. Singapore has an amazing food culture, so she was exposed to a lot of flavors early on. And we were lucky that Scott's company paid for us to have a full time cook and housekeeper."

"God that sounds like heaven," Jenna said.

"It is and it isn't," Cleo said. "As much as I appreciated the help, sometimes it felt like we didn't have much privacy."

They talked a little more about how Cleo was adjusting from living abroad, and the culture shock from coming from such an urban environment to the relative sticks.

"It's a good change of scenery. And I love that Izzy is exposed to so much nature."

"It must be hard though, having your husband gone so much." Alex said.

"It sucks, but I'm used to it by now. Honestly Izzy and I get into such a routine that sometimes it's harder when he is around."

"I know exactly what you're talking about," Jenna said as she spread a blanket on the grass for Noah to sit. She grabbed several toys from her tote and put them in front of him. He promptly picked up an Olaf figurine and shoved it in his mouth. "Don't get me wrong, I love my husband, but he works. All. The. Time."

"What does he do again?" Cleo asked.

"He started his own company last year based on an innovative approach to cybersecurity. He's been working twenty-four seven for no money ever since."

"Startup life is hard," Alex said sympathetically. "I remember those days."

"And you didn't even have kids," Jenna said tartly.

Alex pressed her lips together and shifted on the bench. "It will all be worth it when it pays off."

"You say that as if it's a given." Jenna said with a shake of her head. "You know as well as I do that nine out of ten startups fail within five years. We can't all be married to unicorns." She heaved a tired sigh. "Anyway, when he's not traveling all over the place trying to raise money, he lives at the office. And then when he does come around he has all kinds of opinions about how things should go."

"Oh, my God, that is the most annoying thing. Scott was in town last week. One morning, I was getting Izzy ready for school and she was fighting with me about putting on her shoes. So I gave her a warning, like I always do, and told her if she didn't put on her shoes, she was going to get a time out. And he's all," she hunched up her shoulders and lowered her voice to approximate a blustery male, "'why do you even give her a warning? Just tell her to put on her shoes and if she doesn't listen, put her in time out.'" She laughed, felt a spurt of victory as Jenna smiled and rolled her eyes. The story might have been a complete lie, but it was enough to form a crack in Jenna's walls.

"There's nothing I like more than having Mark mansplain parenting to me. But then he'll take the boys out and completely ignore nap time, leaving me with a couple of lunatics to deal with."

"I still don't understand why you won't get any help, even for just a few hours a week," Alex said.

Jenna's jaw clenched. "And I keep telling you, I haven't found anyone I like yet."

"I don't have a nanny either," Cleo interjected. "From the moment I had Izzy, I couldn't imagine leaving her in someone else's care."

Alex opened her mouth to protest and Cleo hurriedly added, "It's not that I have anything against it or judge anyone. I'm happy to throw money at anything I don't want to do. I hired a housekeeper the first day we moved in."

"How nice for you," Jenna muttered under her breath.

Cleo pretended not to hear. "But I've always wanted to be as hands on as possible with her. It's my own baggage." She knew first hand how sideways things could go when a mother didn't look out for her daughter. She was all kinds of fucked up because of it. Unlike her own mother, Cleo loved Izzy way too much to put her daughter through anything close to what she went through.

"We all have our hang ups," Alex said.

Noah let out a whine from his blanket. Jenna sighed and looked at her phone. "That's my signal. Better get these guys home before we go full meltdown."

They all started packing up their stuff and Jenna asked Sylvia to retrieve Liam from the playground.

Neither Liam, nor Jack, who was trying to yank his hand from Irina's grip, were on board with the plan to go home.

Jenna handed Noah to Alex with a sigh and went to intervene.

"Come on, Izzy, Let's go check out the library." She reached for Izzy's hand.

"Can Ava come?" Izzy asked.

Cleo wanted to high five Izzy for her unintended brilliance. It would be great to get some one on one time with Alex. And if the kids initiated it, there was no risk of Cleo looking too desperate.

She felt a pang of disappointment as Alex's mouth pulled into a frown. "Unfortunately we can't today. I'm taking Ava and Jack over to Ethan's office so we can have lunch with him and Morgan."

"Sounds fun," Cleo said as Jenna rejoined them with a howling Liam in tow.

"Another time, though," Alex said as she stacked the plastic fruit bowls and put them in her tote. "You have my number. Text me if you want to get together."

"I'll do that," she said with a little wave and started towards the library.

"Hey wait," Alex called out after her. "You know, Jenna, Morgan and I have a standing playdate Wednesdays at 4. You should join us."

"I'd love that!" Cleo said, pretending not to notice Jenna's horrified expression.

"Next week is Jenna's turn. I'll text you her address."

Cleo smiled and thanked them both, and turned back to the library. *She was in.*

4

Jenna

Jenna's shoulders slumped as she looked around her kitchen, which opened up into a modest family room. She always tidied up when it was her turn to host playgroup, but this week she'd gone the extra mile. Not only had she swept the terracotta tiles in her kitchen, she'd taken the time to mop them. She'd vacuumed the carpet twice, wiped down the kitchen counters, and double checked that there was nothing repulsive going on in the powder room.

But no amount of mopping, vacuuming, or wiping up could hide the stains on the berber carpet in the family room. Nor could it hide the scratches on the second hand coffee table or the scuffs on the walls. Her father's voice echoed in her head. *You can't polish a turd.*

Of course, when they'd bought the house four years ago, it was with the intention of transforming the turd into a diamond. But then Mark's career had taken a sharp turn, the remodel plans were put indefinitely on hold.

Liam sat on the carpet playing with his train set while Noah squirmed on her hip. She looked at the clock and swore. It was already ten til four and she still hadn't put the snacks out. Thanks to Noah waking up early from his nap, she was forced to slice fruit and put together a charcuterie board one handed. At least she'd remembered to put the wine in the refrigerator in time for it to chill.

Normally, she would have thrown out a bunch of string cheese and goldfish crackers and called it good. Before Noah was born, Jenna had taken the time to put together elaborate spreads that rivaled those prepared by Alex and Morgan's nannies. But ever since Noah's birth, Jenna didn't have the time or the energy to bother. Besides, Alex was always dieting and Morgan seemed to have some new food restriction every other week, so it's not like they ate much anyway.

But though she hated to admit it, even to herself, she felt compelled to fancy things up a little bit for Cleo. She was so beautiful, confident, and goddamn it, charming, with her seemingly perfect life.

Even though rationally she knew it was stupid, Jenna didn't want to share with this newcomer just how much of a mess her life was.

Right, like overpriced charcuterie and triple creme brie are going to disguise the fact that your house was built in nineteen sixty and still has all of the original finishings.

She stifled a grimace at her countertops, with their terra cotta tiles and gray grout that matched the floor. It was like the kitchen equivalent of a Canadian tuxedo.

"Hellooo," she heard as the front door opened. It was Alex, entering in a cloud of orange blossom scented perfume. Jenna turned from her food prep with a smile that felt forced.

Alex reached out for a hug. Jenna returned it with one stiff arm and asked Alex to take Noah so she could finish up. "I tried putting him in the swing," she said, nodding at the electric swing that stood in one corner of the family room, "but he's extra grumpy today."

Alex took Noah and gave his cheek a nuzzle. "Do you think he's teething?"

"Who knows. All I know is he's in a pissy mood."

She retrieved a carton of goldfish from the pantry and shut the door with unnecessary force.

"Looks like he's not the only one. What is up with you?"

"What?" Jenna arched a brow at her as she poured the crackers into a bowl.

"You've been snippy with me for the last several days."

Jenna couldn't deny it. She lived in a state of constantly frayed nerves, and for some reason Alex's inclusion of Cleo into their group kicked her irritation up a notch. But to admit that would be exclusionary, and wasn't she always telling Liam to give everyone a chance? "Have you seen my life? Of course I'm snippy." She turned back to her charcuterie board and carefully laid out the sliced salami.

"If there's something you're upset about, I want you to tell me. We've been good friends for too long not to be honest when something's bugging us."

Jenna sighed and turned to face her friend. Alex was right. They'd been super close from the minute they met at their baby group three and a half years ago. She talked to Alex about the most intimate details of her life. But she was pathologically conflict avoidant by nature, and somehow talking about her prolapsed uterus after Noah's birth was easier than being honest about her irritation. Still, she knew if she didn't say something it would fester, and she couldn't bear the idea of that driving a wedge in their friendship.

She hadn't been kidding when she said she, Alex, and Morgan were like sister wives. They were each other's chosen family and support system. Jenna didn't just love them, she needed them, now more than ever.

"Okay, fine," she said. "It bugs me that you invited Cleo to join us without even asking me and Morgan first." Not to mention, when she Alex, and Morgan had met in mom and baby group, it had taken months for Alex to invite Jenna to her house. But Alex had no problem inviting Cleo into their inner circle within mere weeks.

Alex's perfectly threaded eyebrows scrunched with concern. "Don't you like her? I think she's really cool."

"I like her fine," Alex said. "But there's something about her, I don't know," she shrugged. "I just don't like that she's all, we're paying 25K in rent to give us time to find our dream home," she said in a sing-song tone. "I have a full time housekeeper so I can devote every second of my day to being mother of the year."

"I don't think she was saying that to brag," Alex chided. "Come on, Jenna, she just moved here. She doesn't know anyone and her husband is barely around. Can you imagine how lonely she must feel? Imagine how nuts we'd all be without each other."

Jenna's chest squeezed with guilt as Noah leaned out of Alex's hold to go back to his mom. She reached for her son, marveling at how Alex was so open and friendly to everyone. Everywhere she went, she was the social ambassador, welcoming everyone into the fold.

Jenna felt petty and small in comparison.

"Besides, it would be nice for Ava to have another girl. Ever since Jess and Ryan moved away, Ava's been missing Natalie." Ryan and Jess were another couple they'd gotten close to through their initial baby group. Unfortunately they had recently moved to Boston for Ryan's new job.

"I see your point," Jenna said. Nonetheless, her resentment didn't disappear entirely. She wasn't the most outgoing person in the best of times. These days she was running on fumes and didn't have any energy to make new friends.

Then she thought about how she, more than anyone, could understand how hard it was to be a de facto single parent due to her husband's job. It got lonely, even with a lot of hired help.

The doorbell rang and she went to answer, scolding herself for being over thirty and still acting like she was in high school. She resolved to give Cleo a fair chance as she opened the door to her smiling face.

5

Cleo

Cleo led Izzy over the threshold of Jenna's house, surprised when Jenna greeted her with a warm hug.

"I'm so glad you could join us," she said as she led Cleo down a short hallway, past a bathroom and into the kitchen. The kitchen opened up into a family room of sorts, and it was clear based on the toy bins lining the walls this was also the playroom. Cleo stifled the urge to wrinkle her nose at the dated terra cotta tile on the floor, and even worse, on the countertops. This was an older house, and other than maybe throwing up a fresh coat of paint, Jenna and Mark hadn't updated it at all.

Though the house hadn't aged gracefully, it stood on an amazing piece of property. Through the window over the kitchen sink, Cleo could see out to a flat lawn and beyond that, stunning views of the oak studded hills. Though Jenna's house was in one of the "more affordable" neighborhoods, according to her real estate agent, it would still sell for over three million dollars.

Because that was the kind of town Oak Valley was. Three million dollars got you a piece of land with a fifty year old shack on it.

She got Izzy settled with Ava and Liam and helped Alex pour water into sippy cups.

"Hello," Morgan called as she walked through the front door without knocking. Jack came screaming into the kitchen, waving a stuffed toy dog over his head.

"You brought Polly!" Polly, Cleo had learned, was the class mascot. Every week, a child was given the honor of taking Polly the Puppy home. The parents would write a story and take pictures to document Polly's adventures while at their house.

"Sorry I'm late," Morgan said as she hurried in behind him. "My meeting ran long and I wanted to change into something Jack can spill on."

"Only you would put on a pair of three hundred dollar jeans for Jack to spill on," Jenna grumbled.

As Morgan greeted everyone with a quick hug, Alex gathered four wine glasses from a cabinet, while Morgan went to the refrigerator and pulled out a bottle of wine.

"God I need this," Morgan said as she retrieved a corkscrew from a drawer.

Cleo observed both Alex and Morgan's familiarity with Jenna's kitchen, the way they found items as easily as if they were in their own homes. It was a level of intimacy that could take years to foster.

She needed to accelerate the process with Alex.

"Rough day at work?" Alex asked as Morgan gave each glass a generous pour.

"Work was fine," Morgan said as she handed each of them a glass of wine. "It's this fucking remodel that's making me crazy."

They moved to where the kids were playing. Alex and Jenna sat on the mushroom gray sectional that rested against one wall. There were two bean bags on the floor. Morgan sat on one of them, Cleo sat on the other.

"Morgan and Dave basically tore down their house," Jenna said.

"Shh," Morgan said as if they were being monitored. "As far as the town is concerned, it's a remodel." She took a long swallow of her wine. "Anyway, you know how we ordered all of those custom windows for the home gym?"

Alex and Jenna nodded.

"The contractor just told me they're on back order until March!"

"That sucks," Cleo said and took a small sip of her wine.

"I mean you'd think when you're paying ten thousand dollars for one stinking window, they could get them to you in less than five months?"

Jenna rolled her eyes. "Let me get out my tiny violin." She spread brie on a cracker and bit into it with more force than seemed necessary.

"Sorry," Morgan winced.

Cleo took another sip of her wine and gave them a wide eyed look over the rim of her glass.

Jenna finished her cracker and chased it with the last of her wine. "We were supposed to do a remodel last year. We had the architect hired, plans approved by the town, and then Mark decided that would be a good time to quit his job at Google to do a startup with a former classmate." She pushed up from the couch, went to the refrigerator and returned with the wine. She refilled everyone's but Cleo's. Dang, these ladies could drink. Cleo had barely had a third of her wine and they were already going for seconds.

"It's a really great product," Morgan said. "I know the company is going to be incredibly successful."

"Right, so that's why you invested millions of dollars into it."

Morgan's lips tightened into a flat line. "I told you, it's a conflict of interest. Acorn invested in a competitor six months before CarverLogic was even incorporated. My hands were tied."

"Yeah, well while you have your conflict of interest, and other investors are dragging their heels, Mark is barely making a salary. So not only is there no remodel, we're lucky we're paying the mortgage." She sat back with a heavy sigh.

Now this was interesting, Cleo thought as she resisted the urge to rub her hands together. She had already picked up on jealousy and insecurity on Jenna's part over Alex and Morgan's incredible wealth. But now there was an angle involving Jenna's husband and his business. She stashed this little tidbit away for later use.

"Could you go back to work?" Cleo offered as she helped herself to a slice of salami and a piece of Manchego cheese.

Jenna ate another cheese smeared cracker and gave her a deadpan look. "Yeah, that might be helpful if I had gotten a more practical degree than a master's in art therapy. Don't get me wrong, I loved working with kids, but it's not exactly a high paying field."

"Yeah, I remember you were planning to go back when we first met you at the mom and baby group," Alex said.

"That's where you all met?" Cleo asked.

"That's where Alex and I met Jenna," Morgan clarified. "Alex and I met in business school at Stanford."

"I didn't realize you had an MBA too," Cleo said, feigning surprise. Of course she knew about Alex's MBA. It was front and center on her LinkedIn profile.

"I do indeed," Alex said with a wry smile as she picked a slice of cheese from the board. "I had a pretty big job too, as a senior director of alliances at a software company."

So basically getting paid to schmooze, Cleo thought. "Sounds like something you'd be good at,"

"Oh, I was. I was on track to be a vice president. But then we started trying to get pregnant and Ethan - and I," she said with tight smile, "decided I should stop working to lower my stress levels."

Cleo didn't miss the slight hesitation. Clearly Alex hadn't led the decision to quit.

"And then by the time we had Ava, there was no need for me to earn a paycheck," she said with a laugh. Cleo wondered if anyone else noticed it sounded slightly hollow.

"But if you liked it, why wouldn't you go back, even part time?" Cleo asked.

"There is an immense amount of pressure around here to stay home if you can afford it," Morgan said. "No one will say it out loud, but if you have enough money for one parent to stay home, but both of you have big jobs that take you away from your kids, you will be judged."

"And unfortunately it's almost always the woman who gets pressured into scaling back or sacrificing her career entirely," Alex said.

"Not in your case," Cleo nodded to Morgan. "You've still got your big job."

"That doesn't mean people don't judge me. The only reason I'm not absolutely crucified is because David is practically a stay at home dad. No one can accuse me of letting the nanny raise my child."

"It sucks," Alex added. "Here we get these messages that as women we're supposed to lean in, but if we do, we're judged as being bad mothers."

Cleo took a sip of her wine as she struggled to keep the disgust she felt from showing on her face. Did these women have any clue how out of touch they sounded? Complaining that their husbands were too wealthy for them to pursue their careers? Even Jenna, in relative 'poverty' compared to Morgan and Alex, didn't have to worry about where she would sleep that night or how she was going to feed her children.

"I guess we all have our crosses to bear," Cleo said.

"And right now, my cross," Jenna paused as her mouth opened in a jaw cracking yawn, "is not sleeping for more than three hours a night."

"I'm sorry you're so exhausted," Alex said as she took the bottle of wine and drained the last of the chardonnay into her once again empty glass.

"I just wish Mark could be around more. It's not just taking care of the kids all of the time. I just miss his company."

Hmm. A wife who actually liked her husband. Cleo herself didn't have any experience with that.

"Ugh, I wish I had time to miss David's company," Morgan lamented.

"What are you talking about? You're at work all day."

"I know, and thank God I am because otherwise I'd be insane being with him in the house all day every day."

So that explained part of why Morgan still worked more than full time. Cleo had done a little googling of both Morgan and her husband. It was clear that whatever reason Morgan was busting her ass working her way up in the venture capital world, it wasn't for the money.

"David's great," Alex protested.

"I know, but he barely does anything. Sure, he sits on a couple of boards and has a couple consulting gigs, but that only takes up a few hours a week."

"I think it's great that he gets to spend so much time with Jack. I know he really regrets not being more involved when Simon and Lily were younger."

"Simon and Lily?" Cleo asked.

"David has two kids from his first marriage." Morgan offered.

"I didn't realize he'd been married before," Cleo lied. When she'd searched David she'd found photos of David and a wife who was definitely not Morgan. "How old are they?"

"Simon is fourteen, and Lily is sixteen."

Cleo gave a sympathetic wince. "That must be challenging."

Morgan gave her a deadpan look. "You have no idea. And you're right," she said, turning back to Alex. "It's great that he can be around for Jack and have kind of a do-over. But it's like, he's always there. The second I get home, he's in my face, asking questions about the remodel, wanting to show me his bike route for the day. When I get home, I want to have a glass of wine and chill for a minute. I swear, he needs more attention than Jack."

The other women were silent, but there was no mistaking the admonishing looks on Alex and Jenna's faces.

Morgan's blue eyes darted guilty at her friends. "I know, I know, David loves me, and I love him, and I'm lucky to be married to him." She gave a weary chuckle. "It's just that, when I married him, he wanted to go to movies and concerts, and take spontaneous weekend trips. And now, he's like an old dude who just wants to mountain bike and putter around the house all day."

"He's only forty six!" Alex said.

"Going on sixty five," Morgan muttered.

"Our husbands are gone too much," Cleo gestured at Jenna with her wine glass. "Your husband is around too much," she nodded at Morgan, then turned to Alex. "What's your deal?"

"Alex's situation is perfect," Jenna said, shaking her head. "Ethan is busy enough that he's not always in your business, but he's still around to help out a lot with Ava. Plus, he's not exactly hard to look at," she said with a sly grin.

Alex rolled her eyes. "No one's situation is perfect. We have our issues too." here was no mistaking the ever so slightly smug glint in her eye.

Alex, with her piles of money and hot, doting husband, knew she had it made. Cleo knew behind the modest facade, she enjoyed watching her friends seethe with envy.

Cleo was sure there were many people who would love to wipe that smug look off of Alex's face.

6

Morgan

Morgan drove through the wrought iron gate and pulled her Tesla into her driveway. The half mile long drive ended in a large, paved parking landing. Instead of turning right toward the main house, which was currently a construction zone, she turned left toward the guest house, where they were living while the main house was being remodeled. Her stomach clenched when she saw the white Jeep Cherokee parked out front.

Lily must have had a fight with her mom. Whenever she didn't like one of her mother's rules, she showed up at David and Morgan's regardless of the custody schedule.

Morgan pulled past the Jeep into the garage and saw that David's car was missing. She checked her phone and saw a text from him.

Picking up Simon from lacrosse. Hope it's ok if he stays with us tonight.

Morgan let out a groan and felt the pleasantly tipsy haze from the chardonnay disappear into the ether. The 2500 sqft, three bedroom guest house felt small enough when it was just the three of them. When David's moody teenagers were thrown in the mix, Morgan felt like the walls were closing in around her.

She closed her eyes, delaying as long as possible the moment she had to go inside. When had she started dreading coming home, even when Lily and Simon weren't with them?

"Want out!" Jack said.

"Just give mommy a minute, ok?" She closed her eyes and took several deep breaths.

"Want out!" Jack said again, louder, punctuating his request by hurling a sippy cup at the back of her head.

"Jack," she snapped, "how many times have I told you not to throw things at me."

She got out of the car and came around to the back. She opened the door, but didn't unstrap him from his seat. "Tell mommy you're sorry."

"Out, now!" He screamed loud enough to make her ears ring.

"Not until you say sorry."

He let out a sound that was in between a whine and wail and squirmed in his seat. The garage echoed in a cacophony of three year old rage while Morgan clenched her jaw, determined to win this battle. For once.

The door leading into the house flung open. "God, what's wrong with him?" Lily yelled over Jack's screams. "I have my noise canceling on," she pointed at the AirPod in her right ear, "and I can still hear him."

"We're just having a little disagreement." Morgan dodged Jack's flailing hand as he tried to smack her in the face.

"Well you need to settle it because I'm on a zoom with my tutor and I can barely focus." She folded her arms and gave Morgan a hard stare.

Fuck. She didn't want to give into either of these demanding assholes. But she also didn't want to spend the next hour in the garage, waiting for Jack to wear himself out.

If Lily hadn't been here, she would have gone into the house and poured herself another glass of wine and left Jack in the safety of his carseat to do what he needed to do.

But Lily wouldn't hesitate to narc her out to David.

"Fine," she snapped and pushed the button to release the three point harness on Jack's car seat. When Morgan reached out to help him down, he shoved her away and scrambled out of his seat.

With his tantrum forgotten now that he'd gotten what he wanted, he climbed out of the car and sprinted for the door. He paused and flung his arms around Lily's legs, left bare by her, in Morgan's opinion, far too short shorts. It didn't help that she'd paired them with an oversize gray hoodie, big enough to cover said shorts, leaving an observer to wonder if she was wearing any pants at all.

Morgan didn't think the idea of people speculating over whether or not a sixteen year old girl was wearing pants was so great. But when she'd broached the subject with David, he shrugged and said "that's what the kids are wearing. And it's not like she's a bad kid." Morgan wasn't so sure.

True, Lily was one of the top students at her highly competitive private school, and she wasn't a big partier. But over the years several pieces of jewelry had gone missing during the weeks Lily and Simon spent with them. And more than once Morgan had caught Lily looking at her with such contempt, it sent a shiver down her spine.

"You know he only acts like that because you're barely around to take care of him." Lily said with a swish of her long, blonde hair. "I don't even know why you had Jack, when you barely spend time with him."

"Thanks for the feedback," she snapped as she pushed past Lily into the house. She looked around anxiously for Jack. Even though he'd only been inside for a few seconds, she knew from experience that that was more than long enough for him to do some serious damage. "Jack gets plenty of attention from both of his parents." Ugh, since when was she reduced to defending herself to a bratty teenager? *Since the moment you got involved with their dad.* Then ten year old Lily had made her dislike for Morgan known immediately. No matter how hard Morgan tried over the years to win her over, nothing had changed.

"Jack?" She called as she entered the kitchen, which opened into a large family room. He wasn't there either. She started down the hallway to the bedrooms, ears peeled for the sound of whatever mischief he was no doubt making. Lily's door closed with unnecessary force behind her.

There it was. The sound of water running, coming from the master bedroom. One silver lining of living in the much smaller house was that she could hear most of what Jack was doing and could get from room to room very quickly. She rushed through their bedroom, with its California king bed and gray velvet couch at the foot, into the glass and marble bathroom.

Jack stood next to the jacuzzi tub, faucet running full blast, as he squeezed a bottle of fifty dollar shampoo from Morgan's hairdresser into the stream.

"Sweetie, what are you doing?" She hurried to his side and turned the water off, and tried to take the shampoo from his fist.

"Bubble bath." He jerked the bottle out of her reach.

"Honey, you can't start a bath on your own. Besides, it's not bath time yet. We need to have dinner first."

She glanced at her watch and grimaced. Shit. It was already six thirty. As often happened on Wednesdays, time flew when she was drinking chardonnay and bitching to her girlfriends. Now she would have to scramble to get Jack fed and bathed in time for his seven thirty bedtime.

"Bath!" He yelled. Her stomach clenched as his face screwed up in an all too familiar way. The last thing she wanted to deal with was another tantrum. But if she didn't get their routine back on track her night would be fucked.

"How about we have dinner first, and then you can have an extra long bubble bath in the big tub before bedtime?"

His brow was still furrowed and his bottom lip stuck out in a pout, but he didn't escalate.

"I'll make you Mac n cheese and Dino nuggies for dinner."

His eyes widened. "Dino nuggies? Tonight?"

In an effort to improve Jack's eating habits, she and David had decided that, along with screen time, the dinosaur shaped pieces of reconstituted chicken and the macaroni from a box were only allowed on weekends.

She nodded enthusiastically. "Just for tonight though."

To her relief, he took her hand when she reached for it, and allowed her to lead him into the kitchen. Another successful negotiation with the tiny terrorist.

She got Jack settled on the rug with his collection of trucks, then set a pot to boil on the stove. She retrieved the nuggets from the freezer and the Mac and cheese from the pantry, ignoring the pang of guilt as she saw mise en place that Irina had painstakingly prepared. Next to the bowls full of chopped veggies and aromatics was a printout for a recipe for a healthy chicken stir fry. *Chicken is marinating in the fridge and brown rice is in the rice cooker* was written in Irina's perfect printing.

At least the chicken nuggets and the Mac n cheese were the organic brand.

She got Jack settled in his booster seat with his dinner and was just pouring herself another glass of wine when she heard the garage door open.

She took a long sip and shoved away the feeling of dread that washed through her. As the door from the garage opened, she gave herself a little shake and put what she hoped was a pleasant expression on her face.

"Hi honey, hi Simon," she called as she rose from her chair to greet them.

"Hey," David greeted her with a wide smile and pulled her into his arms. He bent and kissed her tenderly. It was all Morgan could do not to wrench herself away when he lingered.

How fucked up was it that kissing her own husband felt so wrong?

Judging from the look on Simon's face when David finally came up for air, she wasn't the only one who found David's kiss mildly revolting.

"How was lacrosse?" Simon's blond, curly hair was damp around the hairline and his cheeks were flushed from exertion.

He shrugged and grunted something that sounded like, "ok," then muttered that he was going to take a shower.

"Dinner will be ready soon," David called after him, then frowned when he saw Irina's ingredients still sitting by the stove, untouched.

"Why didn't you get dinner started?" He looked over at Jack, whose face was coated in a thick layer of combined ketchup and cheese sauce. "Why is he eating that on a weeknight?"

Morgan sighed and went to retrieve her wine. "Playgroup ran late, and Jack was in a mood when we got home."

"I told you, you need to start having firmer boundaries with him. He doesn't act like that with me or Irina. He's only three years old and he already knows you're a pushover."

Her jaw clenched and her hackles raised. "Speaking of boundaries, if the kids hadn't arbitrarily changed the custody schedule, making it so that you had to pick up Simon, you could have started dinner."

David's mouth tightened and he ran his hand through hair that, albeit still thick, was starting to get a little heavy with the salt vs. the pepper. "Yeah, well obviously it's not convenient when they change things up, but you know I want to have them around as much as possible. Especially Lily. I only have a year and half left before she's off to college."

And Morgan was counting down every damn day.

"Well, congratulations to you and Irina for being parent and nanny of the year to Jack. I just don't have the fu-" she caught herself. They were all trying to be more careful about swearing in front of Jack, ever since he called another boy at the park a motherfucker.

Granted, the kid had kicked sand directly into Jack's face, but that didn't make his response any more appropriate. "I just didn't have the energy to argue with him tonight."

He shook his head and gave her a disappointed look but didn't say anything else.

She sipped at her wine and watched as David retrieved a saute pan from the cabinet and set it on the stove. He poured oil from the Italian ceramic carafe next to the stove and turned the burner on.

Uncomfortable with the silence, Morgan pulled the music app up on her phone. Soon, mellow electronic music was playing through the built-in speakers of their state of the art stereo system.

David paused as he pulled the marinated chicken out of the refrigerator. "This sounds like Ethan's music," he said, unable to keep his lip from curling. Unlike David, whose musical taste was stunted in high school, Alex's husband was a music buff who kept up with new music, particularly in techno and EDM. "Since when do you like that weird techno shi-" he glanced quickly at Jack, who thankfully was too enraptured with his forbidden dinner to notice the near slip-up.

"I find it relaxing." She gave him a look that dared him to ask her to change it.

He gave a shrug and turned back to the stove. He dumped the chicken in the oil, and Morgan's stomach rumbled as the scents of garlic and ginger filled the kitchen.

She took another sip of her wine and felt a pang of guilt that she was just sitting there while he cooked. "Can I do anything to help?"

He shook his head, attention still on the chicken. "You go ahead and relax. Sounds like you had a rough day."

She felt another stab of guilt, remembering the way she complained about him earlier. Who of them wouldn't be ecstatic if their husbands told them to relax and drink wine while he cooked dinner?

Cleo, whose husband was never around as far as Morgan could tell, would no doubt be delighted. Shit, Jenna would probably spontaneously orgasm.

Even Alex, with her almost too good to be true Ethan, would love to not be in charge of a meal sometimes.

And it wasn't even like David cooking dinner was an unusual occurrence, not now, anyway. During his first marriage, David had barely known where the silverware was kept, much less how to cook a family meal. However, after his divorce, he'd stepped away from his high pressure role as the CEO of one of Acorn's portfolio companies, determined to be there one hundred percent of the fifty percent of the time he had with his kids.

It was an ideal set up, especially because Morgan had no intention of stepping back from her career when they had kids.

But she missed that hard driving, intense entrepreneur she'd met when she'd been placed as a junior advisor to their board during her second year at Acorn. Her twenty seven year old self had been enraptured by all of that alpha male energy.

Now he was Mr. Mom, and as sexist and awful as it made her sound, she couldn't deny that it just wasn't as hot.

She sighed and tried to shove the thought out of her head. She had a great life, she reminded herself as she cleared Jack's plate and went to retrieve a damp cloth to wipe him down. Her husband adored her, she had a gorgeous little boy, and money would never be a problem.

Even if things don't work out, an insidious little voice reminded her. She smacked the thought out of her head before it was fully formed.

But it was true. She was making enough now that even with their prenup, she would be absolutely fine were they to split. She gave herself a mental shake. It was okay to use her work as an escape from her house, but not as an escape from her marriage.

As she walked past David he leaned down for a kiss. She offered up her cheek and gave him a light pat on the butt. "Thanks for making dinner."

She got Jack cleaned up and occupied with his trucks, then went to set the table. As David dished up the stir fry into a large, shallow bowl and spooned the rice into a smaller one, Morgan went to call the older kids for dinner.

"Dinner's ready," she said with a light rap on Lily's door. Several seconds passed with no response, so Morgan knocked again.

"Not hungry! God!" Was the exasperated reply.

Morgan opened and closed her mouth in an effort to unclench her jaw, then proceeded to Simon's door. "Simon, dinner's ready" Again, no response. She knocked again, harder this time. Finally the door opened and Simon's curly head appeared.

"What?"

"Dinner's ready."

He scowled and brought a hand up to his ear. "Huh?"

"Dinner," she snapped with a roll of her eyes. She hated how both Simon and Lily had their AirPods in twenty four seven, making it so that she and David had to repeat everything at least twice when trying to talk to them.

"Be out in a little bit," he mumbled, then shut the door in her face.

"Lily says she's not hungry, and Simon says he'll be out in a little bit."

Her heart squeezed a little at the look of disappointment that flashed across David's face. When she and David had first gotten together, it was clear he had a specific vision for his happy blended family. One where Morgan was a "bonus mom," whom the kids adored but whose relationship with them didn't threaten or undermine their relationship with their mother. One where they loved their little brother and loved the fact that they were forever connected to their step mother through him. One where they sat down for family dinners regularly to laugh and share about their days.

But that was a hard sell when a relationship started the way David and Morgan's had. Though there hadn't been a full blown affair, the fact that she and David started dating less than a month after he announced his separation raised some eyebrows, especially those of David's ex wife, Corrine. Though she was never able to find actual proof that David had been cheating on her with Morgan (because there was none to be found), that hadn't stopped her from raising her suspicions to anyone who would listen, including the kids.

Morgan fixed a plate of chicken and vegetables and took it to the table while David filled his plate with a sigh. By the time Simon came out of his room, they were more than halfway finished with their meal. Simon barely spared them a glance as he dumped what was left of the rice and the stir fry onto his plate. When he started to leave the kitchen, David said, "Aren't you going to eat with us?"

"Homework," Simon grunted and headed down the hall.

When Morgan had first moved in with David, she had tried to instill a "no eating anywhere but at the kitchen or dining room table," policy. It lasted about five minutes.

After they finished Morgan cleared the table, loaded the dishwasher and washed the pans while David moved into the family room with Jack. In theory, when David's kids were here they were supposed to help with the dishes.

In theory.

As she dried the saute pan she glanced at the clock mounted on the far wall of the dining area. "OK, Jack, time to do bedtime and jammies." She put the pan in the cabinet and walked over to the family room. David had reading glasses perched on his nose as he scrolled through his phone. Jack was performing some sort of demolition derby with his toy trucks.

"Come on, sweetie." She squatted down to his level.

Jack continued to make car motor and smashing sounds as if he hadn't heard a word she'd said.

"Jack," she said, sharper, "It's time to go have your bath." She reached for the truck he was about to smash into a tractor. He yanked it from her reach with a shriek.

"No!"

"Jack," David said in a warning tone. "Listen to Mommy."

"Don't wanna have a bath!"

Morgan closed her eyes, took a deep breath, and placed her hand gently on Jack's arm. "Sweetie, remember how you wanted to take a bubble bath in Mommy and Daddy's big tub?"

"I'm biddy," he scowled. Morgan ran a frustrated hand over her face.

"I know you're busy with your trucks, but it's time to put them away and have your bath now."

He started to whine. Morgan's jaw clenched and her hand involuntarily tightened around Jack's arm. "Jack come on," she rose and tried to pull him up with her. He went ragdoll and flopped to the floor.

"Noooooo! I don't want a bath!"

"I'm tired of this," she tried not to raise her voice and failed miserably. Keeping a firm grip on his arm, she started out of the room. She dragged Jack, literally kicking and screaming a few feet across the floor.

"Whoa whoa whoa," David jumped from the couch. He scooped Jack from the floor, cradling him like a baby and bouncing him around. Startled, Jack stopped wailing. "What's this about you not having a bath?" He pulled Jack's shirt up, buried his nose in his belly, and made loud sniffing noises. "You have to take a bath! You are so stinky!" Jack's giggles echoed off the ceiling as David poked his nose into Jack's armpit, then pretended to recoil in disgust.

"Stinky!" Jack guffawed as David carried him out of the room, bouncing and sniffing the entire way.

Morgan sank down on the couch, defeated. Even though she had had Jack fully aware of and seemingly fine with the fact that David would be more hands on in raising him, she hated the feeling of getting out-parented at every turn.

She sighed, pushed up from the couch and went to retrieve her laptop from her briefcase. She had business plans to review before a meeting the next day, and had to prep for an upcoming board meeting.

She sat down at the kitchen table and pulled up the documents. She forced herself to focus, which wasn't easy with the sounds of what sounded like Jack doing cannonballs into the Jacuzzi tub banging through the walls. Of the many reasons she was impatient to move back into the main house, having a proper office away from the rest of the house and a door she could shut and lock were at the top of the list.

She was about halfway through the first business plan when David poked his head in. "He's ready for stories and bedtime."

She followed him back to Jack's room, where he sat propped up against the pillows, his Paw Patrol themed comforter pulled up to his waist. She climbed on the bed and felt her heart melt as he snuggled up to her. No matter how difficult he could be, at the end of the day, when she felt that sturdy little body pressed into her side, she felt a rush of love that was unlike anything she'd ever experienced.

She might not be mom of the year, but damn, she loved her kid, she thought as she buried her nose in his damp curls.

David came over to kiss Jack on the cheek. "Night buddy."

"Night Daddy," Jack reached up to wrap his arms around David's neck. He squeezed Jack tight and met her eyes over the top of his head. In that moment, she felt connected with David in a way that was more and more rare lately.

David gave Jack another kiss on the cheek and gently unwrapped his arms from around his neck.

"What do you want to read tonight?"

She already knew the answer, and struggled not to roll her eyes when Jack crowed, "Wild things!"

Morgan propped the book in front of them and began to recite the book by memory. By the time she finished what felt like her thousandth reading about Max and the wild rumpus, Jack's head was heavy against her breast. She eased out from under him slowly and tucked his pillow under his head. She pulled his covers up to his chin and gave him a lingering kiss. How was it possible for her rough and tumble boy, full of fire and stubbornness, to have such impossibly soft cheeks?

"I love you, Jack," she whispered.

"Love you too, Mama," he murmured.

She turned off the light, leaving the room in the blue glow of his nightlight. She backed out and closed the door. She closed her eyes and leaned against the door, taking a moment to savor the feelings of peace and love rippling through her.

She heard the sound of a crowd cheering coming from the master bedroom. David must have been watching yet another rugby game. He'd become oddly obsessed with the sport in the past few years, and took every opportunity to pontificate on how and why it was far superior to the NFL.

Whatever. As long as she wasn't expected to participate in this passion, she was happy to have him occupied.

She sat back down at the table and opened up her laptop. She was so engrossed in her reading that she didn't realize David was in the kitchen until she felt the weight of his hands on her shoulders.

"What are you working on?"

"Business plan," she replied, shoulders instinctively stiffening under his touch. "Two guys out of Cal Tech have done some work with directed evolution of enzymes. It's pretty interesting stuff."

"I know something even more interesting," he bent down to kiss the top of her head and slid his hands from her shoulders, down her chest to cup her breasts. He bent his head to kiss her neck.

"I really need to read through this," she said, recoiling from his touch. "I'm meeting with them tomorrow for breakfast."

He sighed, removed his hands from her breasts and straightened up. "I thought we decided you were going to take a break from doing any new deals for a while. You're already sitting on half a dozen boards."

She spun in her chair to face him, anger and frustration burning a hole in her chest. "No, you decided I shouldn't take on any new deals. I never said I wouldn't."

"Your hours have gotten crazy lately," he complained. "On top of all of the travel. Half of the time you're not even here to put Jack to bed."

She stood from her chair and slammed her palm on the table. "That's not fair. When we got together, you knew damn well my career was important to me. And when we decided to have kids, I was very clear that I wasn't going to let a baby interrupt my career trajectory any more than any man would."

"I know, and that was all well and good in theory before we actually had Jack. But now I can see the detrimental effect it's having on your relationship with him. And I know because I made the same mistakes with my kids."

Her eyes burned with tears and her stomach roiled with nausea. "Are you implying I'm a bad mother because I choose to pursue a career I love and have worked my ass off to build?"

Frustration carved deep grooves in his face. "Of course I'm not saying you're a bad mother," he held his hands out in supplication.

"I'm just saying you can afford to pull back a little. Unlike when my kids were young, you don't have to work like crazy to support the family. In the famous words of Eddie Murphy, 'the ends are meeting like a mother fucker.'"

She swallowed down a scream of frustration. "Even more reason for me to keep working. You know how people called me a home wrecker and a gold digger when we first got together."

He waved his hand like he was shooing a fly. "That was just Corrine, stirring the pot."

"Yeah, well her pot stirring is still going on, and it's been six years," she snapped. "So when I hear people whispering behind my back, I like that I can rub the fact that I earned over five million last year in their faces."

"So you let the fact that people might think you're a gold digger keep you from spending time with your family?"

"You know it's not just that. I love what I do. And I love being successful at it. Given where I came from, it feels pretty fucking good to be named one of the Valley's forty under forty for three years in a row. So I guess in that sense, yes, I really do care what other people think of me."

"Fine. Go back to work then." He stomped out of the kitchen and retreated to the bedroom.

She returned to her computer, struggling to regain her focus as equal parts guilt and anger twisted her guts in knots. On the one hand, David was right. They had plenty of money combined, and even if she took a step back, the income from her existing portfolio companies was more than ample. There was no need for her to regularly work ten hour days and travel nearly half of the time. She had all of the resources to afford her a better work life balance, so why wasn't she using them?

Because you actually are a bad mother, a cruel voice that sounded suspiciously like her mother-in-law whispered in her head.

She gave herself a mental slap. Just because she chose to have a big career didn't make her a bad parent. All of the men in her firm worked just as much as she did, and no one questioned whether they were good fathers.

She worked for a couple more hours in the kitchen, until her back ached from the hard wooden chair and her eyes felt gritty. She shut down her laptop, poured herself a glass of water, and shut off the kitchen light.

She poked her head into Jack's room, and felt a rush of love at the sound of his slow, heavy breathing. She opened the door to her bedroom slowly, and breathed a sigh of relief when she saw that the room was dark. David was already asleep.

She changed into a satin nightshirt and went through her five step nighttime cleansing and moisturizing routine as quietly as possible. She tiptoed over to her side of the bed and slid under the covers, doing her best not to jostle the mattress. She rolled to her side facing away from David, closed her eyes, and tried to relax.

Beside her, David stirred, and she silently cursed as she felt his arm slide around her waist to pull her into his chest. It took all of her will not to shove him away.

"I'm sorry about before," he said and nuzzled at the nape of her neck. "I shouldn't give you a hard time about work."

"It's fine. I understand why you get irritated."

"No, it's not fine," he stroked the undersides of her breast with his thumb. "We both agreed to this arrangement, and it's not fair for me to try to change the rules on you. But a lot of why I get upset is because you're my favorite person and I wish I could spend more time with you."

Guilt formed a sour pit in her stomach, as once again David proved himself to be the epitome of a supportive, loving partner.

You should be so grateful. He loves you so much. All he wants is for you to be happy and to give you an amazing life.

Instead she lay there, her skin crawling as she felt the firmness of his erection against her ass. She steeled herself as he slid a hand up to cover her breast and teased her nipple through the satin. He was such a good guy, and he loved her so much. The least she could do was throw him a bone. Even though every cell in her body revolted, she gave into his advances.

She closed her eyes tight and conjured up the feel of another man's hands, another man's cock sliding into her from behind. Another man's fingers stroking her to climax.

She came out of her orgasmic haze to David pumping and heaving behind her. After a seeming eternity he came with a grunt followed by a heavy sigh.

"I love you," he whispered and kissed the side of her neck.

"I love you too," she replied, contemplating how devastated David would be to know that when she said it, she was thinking about someone else.

7

Cleo

"Oh my god, my abs are going to be killing me tomorrow." Alex raised her arms to the ceiling of the exercise studio and leaned back slightly to stretch her torso.

Cleo, who didn't think the pilates mat class offered at the Oakwood Swim and Tennis club was all that challenging, rubbed her flat stomach as though she was feeling the burn too.

"Thank you ladies for joining again today," said the instructor. She was a pretty bottle blonde in her early fifties with improbably large breasts bolted onto her lithe frame. "Don't forget to sign in, everyone."

They passed around a clipboard with the sign in sheet where everyone put down their name and membership number.

Alex quickly wrote down her info and passed the clipboard to Cleo. "You got off the waitlist!" Alex exclaimed as Cleo filled in her brand spanking new membership information.

"They just let me know this morning," Cleo said with a grin. "Now I don't have to mooch off of you guys anymore."

It had become clear very quickly that the Oakwood Swim and Tennis Club was the social nexus of sleepy Oak Valley. As such, Cleo had joined the waiting list when they had moved here over the summer.

"I'm happy to let you mooch," Alex said and gave her shoulder a squeeze. Fortunately, while Cleo had languished on the waitlist, Alex had been generous to a fault with her invitations to the club. Not only had she taken Cleo to pilates twice a week while the girls were in school, at least once a week she invited Cleo and Izzy to join her, Morgan's and Jenna's families for a casual, kid friendly dinner.

They put their mats away and slipped their bare feet into flip flops as they collected their things from the storage cubbies. Alex pulled a lavender fleece tunic over her black LuluLemon tights and tank top.

It wasn't cold enough to warrant fleece, Cleo noted as they exited the club's exercise studio into the open air. But she knew Alex was self conscious about the weight she carried around her middle and in her thighs. Though Cleo hated to admit it, the few extra pounds did nothing to dim the glory of Alex's stunning beauty. Even in her slightly disheveled post workout state, she was gorgeous.

"I don't know about you, but I could use some food after that. How about you?"

Cleo felt like she'd barely burned a calorie. "We only have fifteen minutes until pickup," she said as she glanced at her phone.

Alex dismissed her protest with a wave. "I'll have Sylvia pick up the girls and feed them lunch at my house."

"Ooh, a grown up lunch, I love it." Cleo followed Alex up the stairs that led to the club's deck. Several tables and chairs made up an outdoor dining area that overlooked the tennis courts. They sat at a table and Alex motioned one of the waiters to bring an umbrella over to provide shade. After he put the umbrella up, he went inside to retrieve menus and order chits.

"I don't know why I even bother to look at the menu when I always have the same thing," Alex mused as she wrote down her order for the club's Chinese chicken salad.

Cleo perused the menu wondering if it was possible for a menu to be any more basic. Finally she settled on a caesar salad with shrimp and felt very retro.

"What about drinks," Alex said, her pen poised above her chit. "Are we having wine?"

Over the past few weeks, Cleo had noticed that Alex would use any excuse for a glass of wine. Kidless lunch? Afternoon playdate? You stopped by to drop off Ava's sweater? Corks were popping. Since Jenna was nursing and Morgan wasn't around as much, Alex had quickly taken Cleo on as her drinking buddy. Or as Alex liked to say, they were partners in wine.

"Sure. I don't have anything this afternoon that requires much brain power." She wrote in an order for a glass of rose along with her salad and gave it to the waiter.

The wine was served almost immediately. One thing she would say about Oakwood: the menu might have been stuck in the last century, but the pours were very generous.

Alex held her glass up for a toast. "Cheers to a respite from the kids."

Cleo smiled and clinked Alex's glass, inwardly rolling her eyes. Alex had a full time nanny and a husband that worked reasonable hours. Why in the world would she need a respite?

She took a long sip and leaned back in her chair. "So what was up with Morgan and David this morning? They were practically making out in the parking lot." The school had invited parents to join the kids for donuts and cider to celebrate the beginning of fall. After it was over the parents filtered into the parking lot. David and Morgan said goodbye like teenage sweethearts leaving each other for summer break.

Alex sipped her chardonnay and waved one perfectly manicured hand. "Oh they're always like that."

Cleo frowned. "But she's always talking about how bored she is and can barely stand to have sex with him."

As Alex started to reply, the waiter appeared with their salads. "Thank you, Rodrigo," Alex said as he retreated. She leaned in. "It's purely performative. Morgan can't stand for anything to seem less than absolutely perfect. I mean, she'll open up to us, but it''s very important to her to maintain a flawless image to the rest of the world."

"That makes sense. I've never seen her without her hair and makeup fully done, dressed head to toe in designer wear."

Alex drained the last of her wine and signaled for another one. Cleo sipped at her still half full glass of rose. "She's always been a perfectionist. You should have seen her the first day in business school. All of us were dressed in jeans and sneakers, and she comes in wearing designer jeans, and a white button down shirt with a blazer. Instead of a backpack she had a Louis Vuitton computer bag. I hated her on sight and thought she was going to be a stuck up bitch. But one night out at the Dutch Goose proved me wrong. As perfectly put together as she is, Morgan knows how to have fun." Alex grinned as she lifted a forkful of salad to her mouth.

"Okay so I get appearances matter, but full on snogging in front of the preschool is a little much."

Alex shrugged. "It is over the top, but Morgan feels like she has a lot to compensate for."

"Compensate?"

Alex took another bite of her salad and leaned in. "Morgan doesn't like to talk about it, but her relationship with David didn't start out completely clean," she made air quotes with her fingers, "if you know what I mean."

"They had an affair," Cleo gasped as if that were the most scandalous thing she'd ever heard of.

"Well, she swears on the lives of her husband and child that nothing happened until David and his ex wife separated. But they were hot and heavy within a month of his wife moving out, and engaged within a year." She cocked an eyebrow and gave her a pointed look.

"So even if they didn't have sex…" Cleo trailed off.

"There was something going on between them," Alex finished. "Apparently it ended up being quite the town scandal at the time. David's ex had a lot of friends who shunned him and Morgan when she moved in."

"Why didn't he just move? Why would they want to stay in a town where everyone hated them?"

"It was a pride thing for him. He wasn't going to be run out of town when in his mind, he and Morgan hadn't done anything wrong." Alex took a sip from her freshened glass. "Then time passed, Ethan and I moved here too, so they had us. And when we had kids we made friends with other new parents and some of their families."

Conversation paused as they tucked into their salads.

"Hey Alex!"

Cleo looked up and saw a heavily pregnant brunette in her thirties beaming down at Alex.

"Oh my god, it's been ages," Alex said as she rose from her seat. She wrapped the woman in a warm hug, then placed one elegant hand on the woman's belly. "How much longer?"

"Four weeks, but I would be more than happy to get him out right now."

"I'm Cleo, by the way," Cleo rose from her seat when it was clear Alex had forgotten to introduce her.

"Sorry," Alex said, a little flustered. "Cleo, this is Marissa Travers. Marissa, this is Cleo Baird. Marissa and I used to work together." She turned back to Marissa, "And Cleo's daughter is in class with Ava."

They made small talk, asking after each others' husbands and Marissa's other kids.

"Do you want to join us?" Alex said, gesturing at an empty chair at their table. "We just got our food."

"I wish I could," Marissa said with a little pout, "But I have to get home to take Emma to speech therapy." They said their goodbyes and Marissa promised to call her soon to catch up.

As soon as her back was turned, Alex's smile gave way to sneer. "I hope to God she never calls me."

Cleo cocked an eyebrow.

"She's just so smug and fake," Alex said as she placed her napkin on her lap. "She's the kind of person who's so nice to your face, but then badmouths you to your manager as soon as your back is turned."

Thinking about Alex's enthusiastic greeting, warm hug, and seemingly sincere smile Cleo couldn't help but marvel at her complete obliviousness of her own hypocrisy.

"And I can't believe she's having another kid. This makes four in five years. I don't know what she and her husband are trying to prove, but the world does not need that woman's genes to be passed down."

"Wow, that sounds like a lot of wear and tear on your lady parts. As soon as I had Izzy, I was like, one and done."

Alex's expression turned wistful. "Not me. I'd probably have four myself by now if I had my way."

Cleo finished a bite of her salad, then said, "Ava's three. Seems like a good time to try for another."

Alex's mouth pulled down at the corners as her eyes flicked down. "I want to start, but Ethan wants to wait."

That seemed odd. It wasn't as though they didn't have the help and resources to raise another child. Alex must have picked up her thoughts from her expression.

"It wasn't easy getting pregnant with Ava," Alex said in a resigned tone. "We started trying a year after we got married, and tried for a long time before we finally figured out what was going on."

"That must have been so hard," Cleo reached across the table and gave Alex's hand a squeeze.

"It was awful. We almost split up."

"Wow."

"You know what it's like, when you go from having sex for fun to having sex when you're trying to have a baby."

Actually Cleo didn't know either part of that scenario. She'd never had much fun having sex, and Izzy's conception had been one hundred percent an accident.

"It all feels so clinical and forced. And then when we kept trying and not succeeding it just got worse. There were times," she lowered her voice, "when Ethan had trouble, you know…" she raised her eyebrows suggestively. "And then I felt like a failure, getting my period month after month. It was so depressing."

Cleo felt sympathy swelling in her chest and ruthlessly shoved it aside. Okay, so one thing in Alex's life hadn't gone perfectly smoothly. That didn't even begin to balance the scales. "Well you obviously made it through that rough patch and seem very happy together."

"We are. Honestly I think the whole experience made us stronger as a couple."

Cleo wanted to smack the slightly smug smile off of Alex's face. "Did you end up doing IVF?"

"Yes. We finally went to a fertility specialist after two and a half years with no success."

"Why didn't you go sooner?"

Alex drained the last of her wine and gave her a wry smile. "I was the one who resisted. I was in my late twenties when we started trying, for Christ's sake. I should have gotten pregnant as soon as we pulled the goalie!"

"You spend your whole early adulthood trying not to get pregnant, and then when you actually want to, you can't."

"Exactly! So part of it was me holding out hope that it would just happen eventually. And part of it was because I was afraid."

"Afraid of what?"

"That there was something seriously wrong with me that was keeping me from conceiving. I was afraid to find out that it was my fault somehow."

"There are lots of different solutions-"

"I know," Alex interjected. "But Ethan comes from a big family and from the very beginning he was adamant about having kids. If it turned out that I was the reason we couldn't have kids, I would have felt like I'd failed him."

"I'm sure he wouldn't have felt that way," Cleo admonished.

"Probably not. It's just that I feel so lucky that Ethan chose me, you know? I mean, look at him, he could have any woman he wants, and he picked me. I hated the idea of him feeling like he was stuck with a lemon."

Cleo inwardly sneered at the underlying desperation in Alex's words. "Hello, have you met yourself? You are a fucking catch. Ethan should feel lucky that *you* picked *him.*"

Alex's eyelashes fluttered demurely and she thanked her.

"So I take it there was no fatal flaw in your plumbing?" Cleo asked.

Alex shook her head. "Turns out Ethan has a very low sperm count. And the ones that he does have aren't very good swimmers. Turns out I married a lemon." Alex gasped and raised her hand to her mouth. "Shit, I shouldn't have said that. I've never told anyone about that."

"Not even Morgan or Jenna?"

Alex shook her head. "Ethan was very upset when he found out. He was raised on a ranch in Montana. To be seen as anything less than a real man in every way would be devastating for him."

"Wow, from the little I've hung out with Ethan, it doesn't seem like he would be insecure about anything."

Alex took the last bite of her salad and dabbed her mouth with her napkin. "That's what I thought too, when I first met him. He's so good looking and charismatic, and is so confident in many ways but…" she trailed off and looked at a point over Cleo's shoulders. "Everyone has insecurities, right?"

Cleo couldn't think of any of her own off the top of her head, but she nodded anyway.

"Anyway, please don't say anything to anyone about the sperm count or the ED issues. Ethan would be absolutely mortified if he knew I'd shared that with anyone."

Cleo mimed locking her mouth and throwing away the key. "I'm a vault." As long as it suited her to be.

"I don't know what made me tell you all of that," Alex said as they pushed back from the table and gathered up their bags. She placed a pair of oversize designer sunglasses on her nose.

Cleo had a pretty good idea. It was called two glasses of chardonnay in the course of an hour. "Sometimes it's easier to tell new friends your bigger secrets. We don't have as much history and it's not like my husband and Ethan are close like he is with David and Mark."

"I think it's more than that," Alex said as she hoisted her tote over her shoulder. She cocked her head and studied Cleo through her sunglasses. "Do you ever meet someone and feel like you've already known them for a long time? Like maybe you knew them in a past life or something?"

"Sure," Cleo said. "I felt that way the first time I met you."

"Same," Alex exclaimed. "It was like we just had this instant connection, right?"

Cleo nodded and smiled, inwardly gloating at how easily she'd gotten her hooks into Alex. *Yes, Alex. We're connected. I'm your new best friend and closest confidant. You can trust me.*

"I guess it sounds a little cheesy," Alex said with a laugh. "But I'm glad you moved here," she said and pulled her in for a perfume scented hug.

"Me too."

8

Cleo

Cleo and Izzy stood hand in hand on the edge of the chaos that was the Oakwood clubhouse on a Friday night. Friday night dinner at the club was a tradition for Alex, Morgan, Jenna and their families. After her first playdate with the group, Cleo and Izzy had been invited to join. It was a tradition for many other families as well, hence the cacophony of children of all ages milling around the club house while their parents sipped wine and cocktails and did their best to ignore them.

Alex had texted her a few minutes ago that she and Jenna were already there, having staked out one of the big tables that could accommodate their group. Cleo scanned the room, then spotted Alex in the far corner, talking to one of the other Wyndham moms named Kimberly. As usual, nearly all of Izzy's classmates were here with their parents. She and Izzy started toward Alex. It was a long process, since every two feet she ran into someone she knew and was forced to give a friendly greeting. Fortunately Izzy was hungry and in no mood, so Cleo had an easy way out of every attempted conversation.

She finally got to the table and dropped her purse into an empty chair next to Jenna. She greeted her with a quick hug as Alex turned from Kimberly to her.

"What are you drinking?" Alex said to Cleo as she held up her empty wineglass.

"I can get it," Cleo protested.

"Mommy, I'm stawving," Izzy said.

Alex waved her hand. "I'm going in for a refill anyway. Get Izzy sorted while I go order.

Cleo requested a glass of Pinot Noir and guided Izzy over to the buffet. This week was Mexican themed, one of Izzy's favorites. She piled her daughter's plate with chips, guacamole, a cheese quesadilla and some salad and headed back to the table. She sat Izzy next to Ava, who was playing a game on Alex's phone.

Cleo settled in next to Jenna, who held Noah on her lap with one arm as she sipped her Sauvignon Blanc.

"Where's Liam?" Cleo scanned the room for Jenna's oldest.

"He's over there," she indicated behind Cleo with her chin.

Cleo turned and saw Liam on one of the sofas that lined the wall. He had an iPad in his lap and was surrounded by four of his classmates.

"I know the other parents are going to hate me, but I just need a little break until Mark gets here."

Cleo raised her eyebrow. Mark was usually too busy to join them for Friday night dinners. "I thought he was out of town."

"He got home from London last night, thank God," Jenna let out an exhausted sigh and took another sip of her wine. "It's been hell this week. Noah is teething and Liam has been having night terrors."

Cleo noticed that the dark circles under Jenna's eyes were more pronounced than usual, even through a coating of concealer. Maybe she should invite Jenna to lunch followed by a trip to Sephora to help her find a product that offered fuller coverage.

"Hey, Cleo." She turned to see Tricia Newman standing to the left of her chair.

"Hi," Tricia gave her a tight smile and an awkward little wave. She was dressed in her usual outfit of baggy jeans, and a Patagonia fleece vest over a tee shirt.

"What's up?" Cleo prompted when Tricia continued to stand there.

"I wanted to know if you had a chance to read my email about the science class I'll be hosting starting next week."

Cleo had scanned, and immediately deleted, the email Tricia sent describing a parent/caregiver and child class (that was literally how she had described it, as the term "mommy and me" was deemed too exclusionary) in which they would spend two hours at Tricia's house once a week doing science experiments.

Cleo would sooner cover herself with honey and lay down next to an anthill.

"You know, I'm going to have to check my calendar and get back to you on that," Cleo replied, careful to keep the contempt off of her face.

Alex appeared behind her with a glass of wine in each hand. Since she was nearly a head taller than Tricia, Cleo saw Alex's lip curl in a sneer at the back of her head. She stifled a laugh and shared a sly look with Jenna.

"Hi Tricia," Alex said, her tone so sweet Cleo thought she might need to check her blood sugar.

"Alex, lovely to see you as ever," she said through clenched teeth. "Well, I better get back to my table. Cleo, you'll let me know soon, right? We want to limit it to no more than five kiddos and there are a couple of parents who are very interested. But I would really love it if you and Izzy could join."

"I'll let you know as soon as I can," Cleo replied as she took her wine from Alex.

"Let her know about what?"

"Izzy was invited to join the science class Tricia hosts at her house."

"You mean the Oak Valley Little Genius Club?" Her voice dripped with contempt. "You're not going to do it, are you?" Alex said as she lowered into a chair. Her eyes had a hard glint as she fixed Cleo with a stare. "It's ridiculous, how she thinks she can identify the 'gifted and talented 'among a bunch of three year olds."

Cleo settled back as Alex started on a familiar rant about Tricia and the private tutors she hired to conduct private classes in science, math, art, and language. Then she handpicked the kids she deemed the brightest and invited them to join. "It's so elitist and ridiculous at this age."

Cleo was pretty sure that the real reason Alex got so heated about the issue was because Ava had obviously not been seen as smart enough to garner an invitation. "I don't know, I think it would be fun for Izzy to have some exposure to science." She couldn't resist the urge to needle Alex a little.

"You're not seriously considering it." It was a statement, not a question. A challenge. A test of Cleo's loyalty.

That was something she'd learned very quickly about Alex. Underneath her warm extroversion and friendliness that she seemed to extend to everyone, if she hated someone, she expected her friends to hate them too. No Switzerland friends for Alex Drake.

Cleo's natural inclination would be to say fuck this high school bullshit; she could sign her daughter up for any damn class she wanted. But she knew the drill with women like Alex. She had to be a good little drone and go along with her queen.

Cleo shrugged and took a drink. "I thought it was worth some consideration, but obviously not if it's going to upset you so much."

"It wouldn't upset me," Alex got defensive just as Cleo knew she would.

Before she could protest further, Ethan walked up behind Alex and planted a kiss on her cheek.

"What wouldn't upset you?" He asked as he swooped Ava from her chair into a big bear hug.

"It's nothing." Alex gave Cleo a sheepish look. Even though Alex was absolutely prone to getting mired in petty mom drama, she didn't want anyone to know it.

Ethan greeted both her and Jenna with a hug and a kiss on the cheek. He nuzzled Noah's neck with a growly sound, earning him a baby belly laugh.

He headed to the bar for another drink. "Get me another chardonnay while you're there," Alex called after him.

A child's howl rose above the din. Cleo looked across the room and spotted Morgan, David, and Jack, who hadn't made it three feet into the clubhouse without going into a full meltdown.

"Jeez, this is going to be a fun night," Jenna grimaced.

They all watched as Morgan got down on her knees and put her hands on Jack's shoulders, her mouth moving as she tried to calm him down. Cleo could practically see the waves of tension emanating off of Morgan as she struggled to keep herself in check.

Whatever she said must not have sat well with Jack, because he hauled off and smacked her in the face.

Morgan's face turned beet red and David clenched his jaw so hard Cleo wouldn't be surprised if he cracked a molar. Morgan stood up as David said something. Jack threw himself to the floor and screamed bloody murder. Morgan held her hands out in the universal "I'm done," gesture. She picked her purse up from where it had fallen to the floor, turned her back on her shitshow of a son, and marched purposefully toward their table. David scooped up Jack and carried him through the doors that led to the pool deck.

She dropped her purse in a chair. "I'm going straight to the bar. Anyone need anything?"

Both Jenna and Cleo requested refills.

Morgan returned with their wine tailed by Ethan. She sank wearily into her chair and took a hearty gulp of red wine. "Oh, my God, that kid is going to be the death of me." Despite her frazzled state, Morgan looked as perfectly put together as ever. Not a hair was out of place, her manicure was flawless, and her silk top and designer jeans looked as though they were tailor made for her body.

"Jack is just spirited," Alex said with a reassuring pat on Morgan's hand.

"No, he's an asshole, and we all know it," Morgan took another sip of wine.

"All of our kids are assholes sometimes," Cleo said. The problem was that Jack was an asshole almost all of the time. That had to rankle Morgan, dedicated as she was to maintaining the facade of perfection in every other facet of her life.

"Well mine is a fucking embarrassment," gritted out as though she'd read Cleo's mind.

David appeared at the table with a now calm Jack. Jenna's husband Mark was right behind them, having just arrived.

"Hi," Jenna stood up, looking genuinely delighted to see her husband. At first Cleo thought it was because she could hand off Noah, whom she immediately shoved into her husband's arms. But the way they lingered as they kissed hello… Cleo felt like a voyeur.

Cleo wasn't the only one who noticed. "Get a room, you two," Morgan joked.

"Sorry," Mark said with a sheepish smile, "I've been on the road a lot in the past few weeks."

"Jenna and Mark are still super horny for each other," Morgan told Cleo in a low voice. "Last year at the preschool Halloween party, they snuck off and she blew him in Alex's powder room."

Cleo grimaced as she imagined Mark in a bathroom with his pants around his ankles, Jenna as she serviced him. "Good for them."

"I guess, but it makes the rest of us look bad," Morgan. "I mean, who's still regularly blowing their husband after seven years?"

"Certainly not me," Cleo said. Then again, her circumstances were markedly different.

"So where all have you been, Mark?" Ethan, who was seated next to Mark and David at the opposite end of the table from the women, asked.

Mark happily accepted a pint of beer from Jenna. "Where haven't I been?" He rubbed his eyes. "Last week it was Singapore, followed by Boston and New York. I got in last night from London."

"I'm sure there are a lot of people interested," David said.

Cleo knew from talking to Jenna that Mark was trying to raise a second round of venture funding to the tune of ten million dollars.

"Now that we have the proof of concept, there's definitely a lot of interest. The only problem is a lot of the top players are being cheap on the share price."

"You can't let them do that," Ethan said. "All those guys on Sand Hill Road, they think they can gouge you because of their names. When I was starting Ignosi, and that asshole at Rockland Ventures tried to convince me to give him a discount because of their 'reputation'," he lifted his his large hands and made air quotes, "I told him that if he really wanted a return on his investment, he would give us the money we needed to build a kickass product, and fuck their reputation." He turned to Alex with a smirk. "Remember that, Alex? That son of a bitch could have made twenty million dollars that day. Instead he got nothing."

Alex was looking at him with a doting smile that was a little blurry around the edges thanks to the two and a half glasses of chardonnay she'd consumed. "Oh, I remember. I was at that dinner and you made us walk out before the waiter brought my creme brûlée."

"You just need to stick to your guns. Don't let them steamroll you."

"Good advice," Mark said with a tight smile. Cleo watched as Mark looked at the back of Ethan's head, his lip curled in contempt.

Alex, who thought Ethan was God's gift, was oblivious to the fact that Mark disliked her husband.

Was it jealousy over Ethan's incredible success and equally impressive good looks? Who knew. But she tucked this new piece of knowledge away. She was sure it would be useful at some point.

"Mommy I'm hungry," Ava said, effectively diverting the conversation.

"I'll take her to get a plate." Ethan stood up and took Ava by the hand. "Want me to get stuff for the boys too?" He asked Jenna and Morgan.

"That would be great," Jenna said with a smile. "You know what they like."

By the time Ethan returned from the buffet with two plates piled high with quesadillas and tortilla chips, one of the club managers made the announcement that the weekly movie was about to begin.

Several parents of young children called out "Yay," and led the kids to the far side of the room, where couches and bean bags set up in front of the large flat screen TV.

"My favorite day of the week," Jenna said as she coaxed Liam to give up the iPad in favor of the TV. If they were lucky, the movie would hold their attention for the next hour and a half, allowing for more cocktails and mostly uninterrupted adult conversation.

Once the kids were settled, the adults went to get their plates. Cleo filled her plate with salad and some chicken fajita meat topped with salsa and guacamole.

"You're so good," Alex said as she placed a triangle of cheese and chicken quesadilla next to her mound of salad. "I just can't seem to resist the bad stuff," she lamented.

They returned to the table, where Morgan was picking at a salad and Jenna was already tucking into a tortilla filled with steak, cheese, and guacamole. A large pile of meat and vegetables remained on her plate, along with healthy scoops of beans, rice, and more guacamole.

"It's so unfair that you can eat all that and look like that," Alex said as she sank into her seat. "I shouldn't have even looked at this," she held up her quesadilla, "much less put it on my plate. I've probably already gained five pounds."

"All I've had today is coffee and an apple," Jenna said with a full mouth. "I'm starving.

"I saw you out running this morning," Ethan gestured to her with his beer. "How many miles today?"

Jenna swallowed the last bite of fajita, picked up another tortilla, and started building another. "Just six." She bit into her concoction and closed her eyes as if in ecstasy.

"Is that all?" Ethan rolled his eyes. He elbowed Alex in the arm. "If you got up and ran six miles every morning, you wouldn't have to worry about what you ate either."

Alex winced. "Are you telling me I need to worry about what I eat?"

Cleo somehow managed not to roll her eyes. Such classic passive aggressive bullshit for Alex to vocally complain about her weight, then get pissy with Ethan when he pointed out the obvious correlation between Jenna's activity level and her eating habits.

"Of course not," Ethan said and leaned in to kiss her on the cheek. "Just saying that Jenna's exercise routine is a little more hard core than the rest of ours, and that has its perks."

"Well, you've known me long enough to know that this," she gestured to herself, "isn't hauling out of bed at 6am and hitting the trails anytime soon. It's all I can do to make myself go to the gym and pilates class a few times a week."

"I know you don't believe me, but it's more for my mental health than anything else," Jenna said. "Since Mark started his company, I'm pretty sure it's the only thing that's kept me sane."

"We all have our ways of self medicating," Morgan said and raised her glass of chardonnay.

"Here, here," Alex clinked her glass enthusiastically. "Ethan's right though, I either need to step up the activity or start eating like you two skinny Minnies," she angled her head first at Morgan, then at Cleo. "I keep saying I never lost the baby weight, but Ava's three years old. This," she poked at one rounded hip, "Is officially mine."

"I think you look gorgeous," Ethan said as he slung an arm around her shoulders.

"That's because you're hoping to get lucky tonight," Alex said with a grin.

"I mean if praising your beauty gets me in your pants..." He leaned in and kissed her neck as Alex giggled like a teenager.

Morgan made a little choking sound next to her. Cleo turned to look. Her gaze was locked on Alex and Ethan, eyes narrowed, mouth tight. Being around the two loved up couples was definitely rubbing her the wrong way.

Her irritated glare disappeared before anyone else could notice. She made a big show of sliding her arm around David's shoulders and snuggling against his side.

A phone chimed loudly, breaking the spell. Jenna fished hers out of her diaper bag and looked at the screen. "It's from Chris," she glanced at Mark with a half smile. "He says he can meet us for dinner next Wednesday."

"Cool," Mark said around a mouthful of chips. "I'm looking forward to meeting him."

"I just can't believe you're so cool with her keeping in touch with her ex," Alex shook her head as she drained her wine.

"Chris is your ex?" Cleo said as she leaned forward. She'd heard Jenna talk in passing about how she had a friend coming into town next week, but she hadn't registered that it was an ex. "How did I miss that?"

Jenna shrugged and took Noah, who was beginning to fuss, out of Mark's hold. "I guess because we dated so long ago, I really just think of him as a friend now."

"It was college, so it wasn't that long ago," Alex protested.

"Uh, hello, I'm thirty two. So yeah it was pretty long ago."

"Still…" Alex said.

Mark waved her off. "He was just some guy she dated for a couple of years. Besides, what do I have to worry about when she gets to come home to all of this," he gestured to his body with a waggle of his eyebrows.

"True," Jenna chuckled and kissed him on the mouth.

"I don't think it's that weird," David interjected. "I'm still in touch with my college girlfriend and Morgan has no problem with it."

"Well, she does look to be about twenty pounds heavier than me," Morgan said with a sly grin. She leaned over to kiss him on the cheek. "And she's also fifteen years older."

Cleo wondered if anyone else noticed how she looked around to make sure people noticed the display of affection.

"Well that would never fly in our house," Alex said with a laugh.

"You've never been jealous of Ethan," Morgan scoffed.

"Oh, I'm not the jealous one," Alex took another sip of wine. "But Ethan is crazy."

"I'm not crazy," Ethan protested.

"Are you kidding? Remember that time you went completely nuts at my company Christmas party because Lorenzo joked about having a crush on me?"

"It wasn't that bad," Ethan's smiled, but there was no mistaking the tense set to his shoulders.

Alex let out a peal of laughter. "You threatened to kick his ass! And then you dragged me up to the hotel room. The sex was pretty hot though," she held one hand up to the side of her mouth.

"How come we've never heard this story?" Jenna asked.

"Because it wasn't my finest-"

"Oh, and I never told you about my cousin's wedding either, did I?" The word cousin sounded like coushin. She turned to face Ethan. "You flipped out that time too." She turned away to face the women. "There was a guy there who I'd hooked up with when I was like nineteen. Ethan found out about it and totally lost his mind."

"You told me you'd give me a head's up if I was ever going to run into one of your exes."

Cleo could see his arm shift as he placed his hand on Alex's thigh.

"I said it then and I'll say it again. He's not an ex. He's just a guy I made out with like a hundred years ago. He didn't even touch my boobs," she gestured to her full breasts.

"Even if it was just a hookup, I can see why he would want a head's up," Morgan said.

"Okay," Alex shrugged. "But I don't think that justified him storming out in a huff and accusing me of being unfaithful all of the time."

"And I don't think," Ethan said through a smile that was more a baring of teeth, "that you need anymore to drink tonight." He picked up Alex's glass and moved it out of her reach.

"Oh please," Alex started to reach for her glass. "Ow!" She turned to Ethan, who must have given her thigh a warning squeeze.

An uneasy silence descended on their table as everyone froze, eyebrows raised in a "what the fuck just happened" kind of way.

"Well, we all have our insecurities," Morgan finally filled the void. "What about you, Cleo? Your husband is away a lot. Do you ever worry about what he's getting up to?"

Cleo tore her attention from Alex and Ethan. Having Alex tell her about some of the cracks in her seemingly perfect marriage had warmed her to the tips of her toes. To witness the imperfections first hand made her positively giddy. "You know, I really don't. I mean, you travel a lot too," she said to Morgan, then shifted her gaze to David. "Do you worry about her at all?"

"Of course not," David said as though it was the most preposterous idea he'd ever heard. "We trust each other, and that's all there is to it."

"Same," Cleo said. "That was one of the things that made me fall in love with Scott. I knew, among other things, that I could trust him to be faithful. I knew he would never give me reason to worry about that."

It was true. Because it was impossible to worry about someone who didn't exist.

9

Alex

"Is everything ok?" Cleo asked as they walked out to the parking lot.

"Of course," Alex said, even as a wave of dread penetrated her three chardonnays haze. "Why wouldn't they be?"

Cleo shrugged. "Obviously I don't know Ethan that well, but he seemed like he was getting pissed."

Ethan had left the club rather abruptly, citing the need to get Ava home to bed, and said he would see Alex there.

Alex gave a little laugh as she dug through her purse for her keys. "He doesn't always like being the butt of the joke, but he's a good sport about it."

Cleo smiled and nodded, but the skepticism remained in her eyes. As Alex had gotten to know Cleo, she'd discovered that she was incredibly perceptive. She wasn't surprised she picked up on the anger seething under Ethan's forced laughter.

Alex drove home with a knot in her stomach, even as she held onto the hope that maybe Ethan wasn't all that pissed after all.

"There you are," Alex stood in the doorway of Ava's room, looking at what should have been a heartwarming scene of Ethan and Ava snuggled up on her princess bed as he read her The Very Hungry Caterpillar.

He looked up and she saw the all too familiar look in his eyes. A dead-eyed stare lacking any of the warmth, humor and charm he normally exuded. Shark eyes. The dread became a bowling ball in the pit of her stomach. She knew he wasn't going to be a good sport about it. He never was.

She entered the room, carefully avoiding Ethan's gaze as she went to the other side of Ava's bed and gave her a kiss goodnight. She retreated to the kitchen after promising to check in on Ava before she went to bed.

She contemplated pouring herself another glass of wine, but thought better of it. With Ethan in the mood he was in, she didn't want to give him any more ammunition. She poured herself a glass of seltzer and went to the family room to settle on the couch. She turned on the massive flat screen TV and tuned it to the cooking channel in an attempt to distract herself. From across the house she heard Ava's door close. Heavy footsteps on the hardwood floor made the hair prickle on the nape of her neck.

She heard bottles clinking as he detoured to the wet bar in the living room. He came into the family room carrying a glass half full of bourbon, neat. He settled onto the couch, pointedly leaving a good foot of space between them. He picked up the remote without a word and changed the channel to CNN.

Though he didn't say anything, she could feel the rage simmering in him. Part of her wished she could get up, go to bed, and have it all blow over it by the morning. But she knew from experience that if they didn't hash it out, if he didn't have the opportunity to tell her what she did wrong, he would carry on like this for days.

"You're upset with me," she said timidly. She hated how she felt so meek and small when he got like this.

He took a sip of his bourbon. "I just can't believe you could be so disrespectful." His gaze never moved from the TV.

Alex hated this feeling, like being called to the principal's office. When you knew that you had probably done something wrong, but you weren't exactly sure what, and you didn't know how bad the punishment would be.

At the same time, she resented the fact that once again, she would have to cater to his shockingly fragile ego. Not for the first time, she wondered how it had taken so long for her to realize how deeply insecure he was behind that charming alpha male facade.

"I wasn't being disrespectful," she protested. "I was just trying to share a funny story."

"A funny story?" He turned to face her then, and his stony expression made her want to disappear into the couch. "You think it's funny to make me sound like an insecure, jealous psycho?" He never raised his voice when he got like this, which was somehow worse than if he had yelled.

Perhaps if you didn't act like a jealous psycho, I wouldn't have stories to tell. Alex shoved the thought from her brain before it could fully form, as though he would be able to read the criticism on her face.

"You think it's funny to embarrass me in front of all of our friends? I would never talk trash about you just to get a laugh."

Her stomach twisted in a knot as the all too familiar combo of guilt and shame took root. She hated how whenever they had a disagreement, he somehow managed to land on some moral high ground. It wasn't just that she was wrong, or a jerk, but that she was in fact a worse person than he was. She'd spent enough hours with her therapist talking about it to know that it was a form of manipulation. But knowing that didn't stop her from feeling like dog shit every single time.

"I'm sorry, you're right," she reached out and put a hand on his thigh. She felt the muscles tense through his jeans, but he didn't jerk away. "I was just trying to add to the conversation. I didn't think about how it might make you look bad."

"There's been a lot of that lately."

Though her buzz was waning, she was still a little slow on the uptake. "A lot of what?"

"A lot of doing and saying things without thinking how it will make me feel."

Alex felt like she'd been punched in the chest. "How can you say that? Everything I do in life revolves around you and Ava and making you happy."

He shrugged. "Doesn't seem that way to me."

Tears burned her eyes as her jaw fell open. "How can you say that? I think about you when I decide what to make for dinner. I think of you when I plan vacations." If he thought going to a remote cabin in Montana was actually her idea of a fun vacation, he was nuts. But she knew better than to say that out loud because he couldn't stand the thought that one of his favorite places on the planet wasn't hers as well.

"You know what, I don't really want to talk about this right now," he snapped and turned up the volume on the news. "I don't see it being a productive conversation given how much you've had to drink."

The contempt in his voice cut her to the core. She wanted to keep going, to defend herself, to make him realize that he was the most important person in her life and she would never knowingly do something to hurt or embarrass him. But she knew when he was done talking, he was done. Now she would just have to wait until he was ready to get over it.

"Then I guess I'll go to bed." She rose from the couch and leaned over to give him a kiss. "I love you," she said, hating the imploring tone that crept into her voice.

A grunt was his only response.

She swallowed back tears. No mean feat with the baseball sized lump in her throat. As she walked through the kitchen, she paused to pour herself one more hearty glass of wine. If he was going to accuse her of drinking too much, she might as well prove him right.

She did her nighttime skincare routine and settled into bed. She took a deep drink of her chardonnay, waiting impatiently for it to take the edge off the anxiety holding her chest in its grip. She picked up her phone and prepared herself for a sleepless night.

That last chardonnay must have sent her over the edge because the next thing she knew, she woke up to the feel of a muscular arm wrapping around her waist.

There was no mistaking the bulge in his boxer briefs as he pulled her against him. His other hand tugged at the hem of her nightshirt, then pulled her panties down her legs.

She clenched her jaw and resisted the urge to shove him away. Didn't he know that telling her she was a thoughtless, disrespectful wife was not a great way to get her in the mood?

But there was no way she could turn him down. That, on top of her perceived slight to his ego, would make him go nuclear. Besides, with Ethan, as with most men, fucking him was the quickest way to put him in a better mood.

The next morning, she woke to find herself alone in their bed. She looked at the clock. Eight thirty. By some miracle he'd managed to keep Ava from jumping into her bed at the crack of dawn. She followed the scent of coffee and the sound of conversation.

Ava and Ethan were seated at the breakfast bar, he with a plate piled high with scrambled eggs, her with a bowl of oatmeal and some strawberries.

"Good morning," she said in a cheery tone, and went to pour herself a cup of coffee.

She went over to Ava and pressed a kiss to the top of her head. "Did you have good dreams?"

She glanced furtively at Ethan, trying to get a sense of his mood.

"Good morning," he said with a bland smile.

Her stomach flipped as she couldn't tell if it was a "I'm still really pissed but not going to fight in front of Ava," kind of smile, or a "I'm just going to pretend I didn't flip out on you last night and am back to business is usual," kind of a smile.

Once Ava was done with her breakfast and parked in front of the living room TV, Alex dared to scratch beneath the surface. "Do you want to talk more about what happened last night?" she asked. He got up from his barstool and took his plate and fork to the sink to rinse.

She waited with bated breath while he put the plate and fork in the dishwasher.

"I don't think we need to. I probably over reacted," he said with a sheepish grin. His dark eyes sparkled in the way that had made her stomach flutter the first time she'd laid eyes on him.

He held out his arms and she eagerly walked into them. She breathed a sigh of relief as he wrapped her in his muscular embrace. She wove her arms around his waist and clung for dear life.

The relief was so intense it brought tears to her eyes. "I'm sorry that I made you feel bad. You know I love you more than anyone on the planet and I would never want to hurt you."

"I know, and I love you too," he bent his head so his mouth could find hers.

It was a lot of tongue for nine a.m., but she kissed him back with all of the passion she could muster.

"So we're good?" She asked when he finally lifted his head.

"We're great." he chuckled. "Aren't we always great?" Suddenly his smile vanished and the shark eyes were back.

Alex cringed as though he had raised his fist. "Just don't make me look foolish in front of our friends again."

10

Jenna

Jenna pulled her Toyota Highlander into Cleo's driveway. Alex's Mercedes and Morgan's Tesla were already parked in front of the four car garage.

"Hang on," she said as Liam immediately started to unbuckle his car seat, ready to make a beeline for the front door.

She did a quick once over of her appearance, grimacing at the way her dark circles could still be detected beneath a generous application of concealer. At least she'd managed to wash her hair today. Of course, she hadn't had time to style it other than to pull it back into her customary ponytail. But at least it was clean. And so was her coral button down linen shirt and jeans, at least for now.

She swiped on another coat of lip gloss before retrieving the boys from their carseats. As she gathered up her diaper bag and slung it over her shoulder, she wondered what it said about her that she was so self conscious about her appearance when she was just going to hang out with the women who were her closest friends.

Well, at least two of them were. She was still on the fence about Cleo. While Jenna found her funny and interesting, sometimes Jenna caught her silently watching them in a way that made her uncomfortable. Like she was observing them all as part of a scientific study.

With Noah on her hip and Liam's hand tucked into hers, she started up the walkway to the front door. Was it any wonder she felt self conscious, even intimidated, walking into this house? Unlike the relic where she and Mark lived, this house was new construction, a veritable palace of wood and glass. The stonework leading up to the front door alone probably cost half a million dollars.

She rang the doorbell and was greeted by the familiar "ding ding ding" sound of Cleo's Ring doorbell. She would think that in a house like this, there would be a more elaborate security system.

The massive wooden door swung open to reveal Cleo. Through the entryway Jenna could see into the great room where Alex, Morgan, Ava, Izzy and Jack were gathered. As usual, Cleo, Alex and Morgan looked like they'd just finished a photo shoot. If her hands weren't full Jenna would have tried to smooth the wrinkles out of the shirt she hadn't had time to iron.

"Oh good, you're here." Cleo reached her arms out and pulled her in for a quick hug. "I was just about to do a quick tour. Clara," she called.

Her housekeeper, a Latina woman in her late forties, appeared in the doorway that led to the kitchen. "Si, Cleo?"

In rapid Spanish, Cleo asked Clara to keep an eye on the kids while she showed everyone around. "You can take them to the playroom."

Clara nodded eagerly, "Of course."

They encouraged the three year olds to follow Clara, who gestured for Jenna to hand over Noah.

"It's ok, he's a little shy -" she cut off mid sentence as Noah leaned towards Clara with outstretched arms. She handed him off with a shrug and stretched her blessedly empty arms above her head. "I've been dying to see inside this place. I run by here all of the time so I saw almost the entire building process." Jenna said as Cleo motioned them to follow her into the kitchen, "There was a ton of controversy around the construction."

She mouthed a silent "wow" as she took in the kitchen. Dominated by a massive marble island, the matching countertops contrasted beautifully with the gray cabinets. Wide plank wood floors stained to match the cabinets reflected the sunlight streaming through the massive windows. Beautiful wooden beams supported the high ceiling. All of the appliances were top of the line, especially the Le Cornue stove, imported from France. That alone cost around ten grand. Which she knew because she had heard Morgan go on endlessly about how backordered they were when they were ordering one to replace the stove in their guest house.

On top of the kitchen island was a metal bucket full of ice, where a bottle each of rose and chardonnay chilled. Next to it was a massive cheese and charcuterie board that looked like it could have been on the cover of Food and Wine.

Cleo poured them each a glass of wine before they continued their tour.

The kitchen flowed seamlessly into a family room area, which was exquisitely furnished with gray and white pieces arranged around a glass and wrought iron coffee table.

"Do you know the history of this place?" Jenna asked.

"Not really, just that the owners split up right as it was being finished."

"Apparently there was some huge controversy over the building plans," Jenna said as Cleo led them out of the kitchen. "The town design committee is always difficult to deal with," she continued as Cleo led them through the house, which in addition to six bedrooms and a dedicated playroom had a library, a movie theater, and a separate two bedroom guest house. "But in this case, it was the neighbors who were the problem. They didn't like the design, and claimed it obstructed their view. They recruited neighbors from several streets over to complain at the planning meetings. They didn't want to let the owners cut down several trees, even though they interfered with installation of the main sewage line. The owners finally had to file a lawsuit to get the plans approved." She took a sip of her wine and leaned in conspiratorially. "After that, one of the neighbors was caught on their security footage putting a bag of dog shit in their mailbox."

"How do you even know that?" Alex asked.

"It's all in the county court records," she shrugged. "I just looked up the case."

"Jenna's like our own private detective," Alex chuckled. "If you ever want dirt on anyone, get her on the case."

Cleo turned and looked at Jenna over her shoulder. Her lips quirked in a half smile as her eyes narrowed. "Good to know." She turned back to the tour.

"By the time the house was finished, their kids had gone off to college, and the wife filed for divorce." Alex said as she ran her hand reverently over the velvet cushion of the sofa in the library.

"I heard the husband was having an affair with one of the associates at his firm," Jenna said as they started up a wide staircase to the second floor. "Apparently it had been going on for at least a couple of years."

I don't understand why people are stupid enough to shit where they eat," Cleo said. "Having an affair is bad enough, but messing around with a co-worker just makes everything extra complicated."

"Where else are you going to meet someone to have an affair with, if you're working full-time?" Morgan said.

"What I don't understand," Jenna said as she followed Morgan onto the landing where the staircase jogged to the right, "is why, if your marriage was so bad that you were cheating on your wife, you would undertake a multimillion dollar, multi year construction project. I mean, clearly he had the money to cut bait, pay off the wife, and still have plenty leftover."

"Not everyone who has affairs wants to get out of their marriage," Cleo said. Her jaw clenched as she continued, "Some people get off on knowing they're getting one over on their partner. Some people just like to have their cake and eat it too."

Something in her demeanor made Jenna wonder if Cleo had had personal experience. She wondered if, despite Cleo's casual denial of ever being jealous of her husband, there was something more going on there.

"Well I just think it's really sad that they put all of that planning and effort into building their dream home and then never got to live in it," Alex said.

As they continued the tour through the upstairs bedrooms, something else began to bother her, something she couldn't quite put her finger on. It wasn't until they got to the massive master bedroom, including the closet that looked like a Neiman Marcus display, that she it clicked.

There was nothing personal to Cleo in that house. Sure, the clothes hanging in the closet and the shoes displayed on the shelves were things Jenna recognized. But there weren't that many of them. And as they walked through Cleo's husband's closet, Jenna saw that there were only a pair of running shoes and a pair of black oxfords. Only one suit and a couple of dress shirts hung from the clothing rod.

She knew Scott traveled a lot, but he didn't look to have enough clothes to sustain him for a weekend.

In addition to the lack of clothing, there were no family pictures to be seen anywhere. She knew Cleo was reluctant to settle in too much since the rental was temporary, but you'd think she'd have at least one picture of her husband and daughter hung somewhere.

Jenna was hoping to get an idea of what he looked like. So far her googling of Scott Baird had resulted in a commodities trader who lived in Chicago, and a bare bones, picture free LinkedIn profile for Scott Baird, Vice President of private equity at Sino Bank in Singapore. That had to be him, but a search for Sino Bank yielded nothing. What company in this day and age, especially a financial institution with international dealings, didn't have a web site?

She couldn't exactly ask Cleo about it, because she would have to admit to cyberstalking her husband.

Searching for Cleo herself didn't get her much farther. Unlike seemingly every sentient being on earth, Cleo didn't have a single social media account. Or any other sort of digital footprint to speak of.

"Don't you think that's weird?" She had asked Alex last week. They were at the park with the kids. Izzy had a doctor's appointment, so for the first time in weeks Cleo wasn't tagging along. It felt good, being just one on one with Alex. Cleo was good company, but she disrupted the easy going rhythm of Alex and Jenna's friendship.

Alex, as usual, shrugged it off. "Some people are more private. Or maybe it has to do with her husband's job. She's mentioned that a lot of his clients like to keep a low profile."

"Do you think he's doing something shady? Like laundering money for a drug cartel?"

Alex rolled her eyes. "I think you need to cut down on your true crime consumption."

She wasn't necessarily wrong, Jenna thought now as she contemplated Cleo's nearly empty closet and bare walls. Maybe she was viewing the world from a lens skewed by too much *Dateline* and *Dirty John.*

After a look at the master bath, a marble paradise complete with a steam shower and a soaking tub, Cleo showed them the remaining bedrooms.

"God I wish I had this kind of room when Ethan's family comes to visit," Alex sighed as Cleo pointed out the four simply furnished guest rooms.

"What are you talking about?" Jenna scoffed. "You have a full on guest house."

"That's fine when it's just his parents," Alex said. "But when his brothers and sisters and all of their families descend, we're packed to the gills."

Jenna supposed it was true, given that Ethan was the second oldest of six. But in addition to the guest house, there were two other spare rooms. When either Jenna's or Mark's parents came to visit, she and Mark gave them the master - such as it was - and slept on the fold out couch.

Tour concluded, they went down stairs. They did a quick check of the playroom, and satisfied that the kids were playing happily, they headed back to the kitchen. They refilled their wine and Cleo picked up the charcuterie board from the island.

"Let's sit outside," she said.

Jenna grabbed the wine as they all followed her out of the kitchen to the living room, where sliding glass doors opened up to the back yard and pool. The outside was as stunning as the inside, with a flagstone patio complete with a built-in barbecue and outdoor kitchen. Beyond that was a pool with a hot tub in one corner. To the left of that was a wide, immaculately maintained lawn. To the right were gorgeous flower beds and citrus trees. The fence was lined by manzanita bushes, giving a sense of being surrounded by nature while not obstructing the stunning views of the Santa Cruz mountains.

"It's gorgeous out here," Alex said as she wandered over toward the flowers. "I need to get the name of your gardener. My dianthus and mums are doing terribly this year," she said as she reached out towards a fat blossom. "My gardener says its because of climate change, but obviously that's not an issue for you."

"Oh, Ernesto only takes care of the lawn and the landscaping. I take care of the flowers myself."

"That sounds like a lot of work," Morgan said.

Cleo shrugged as she led them to a comfortable set of wicker outdoor furniture where they all took a seat. "Growing up, I spent a lot of time with my grandmother, who was a phenomenal gardener. I don't bother with vegetables or anything, but my love of growing flowers came from her. She also taught me how to grow all kinds of different herbs to make my own tea." She placed the meat and cheese board on the table in the center and went to retrieve some plates from the outdoor kitchen.

Jenna took a plate from the stack and eagerly piled it high with cured meats, cheese, and slices of French bread.

"Geez, Jenna, don't choke yourself," Morgan laughed.

Jenna could feel her cheeks flush as she paused, a piece of bread with a slice of Manchego topped with prosciutto halfway to her mouth. Of course, each of them had like one piece of salami and one cube of cheese sitting untouched on their plates. "Sorry. All I've had today is a banana and coffee, and I went on an hour and a half run this morning." Her head was spinning after only half a glass of wine.

"Eat up then while your hands are free," Cleo said and reached over to pat her on the leg.

Jenna smiled but made a concerted effort to take daintier bites and chew more thoroughly.

She was piling prosciutto and cheese on another slice of bread when Clara emerged from the sliding glass door, Noah on her hip.

So much for having her hands free. She stood up and went to retrieve Noah.

She was still a few feet away when it became clear why Clara had brought Noah out to her.

She wrinkled her nose as she took him in her arms. "Jesus, buddy, what did I feed you to make that happen?"

She excused herself to go change his diaper. She retrieved her diaper bag from the living room and took him to the powder room. The bathroom fan was no match for the odor that flooded the room as soon as she took off the diaper. She wadded it up, stuffed it into one of the plastic bags she carried for this purpose and tied it off. She contemplated leaving it in the brushed metal waste basket next to the fancy Japanese toilet, a petty urge to mess up Cleo's otherwise impeccable house. Scolding herself for her immaturity, she shoved the bag into her diaper bag and finished changing Noah.

When she went back out onto the patio, the other three women were deep in discussion. "What are we talking about?" She sat down, one arm holding Noah in her lap and one hand reaching for her wine glass.

"Halloween," Alex said.

Jenna inwardly groaned. For the second year in a row, Alex was hosting the preschool class Halloween party at her house. And for the second year, Jenna was supposed to be helping. "I'm sorry, I know I'm so far behind. I promise I'll send out the volunteer sign up sheet as soon as I get home tonight." God, she hoped she still had a copy from last year. There was no way she could remember every last detail from last year.

"Don't worry," Alex waved her off. "Cleo sent it out this morning."

"Oh," Jenna said, taken aback. "I haven't had a chance to check my email today."

"We were talking about the party yesterday after pilates," Cleo said.

Pilates class. One of the many activities Alex and Cleo did together. She took a sip of wine to wash the bitter taste from her mouth.

"And I was thinking since you're so overwhelmed, and I have some free time on my hands, I could take care of it. That way you don't have one more thing to worry about."

"Well that's great that it's actually done." Jenna smiled but it felt stiff. Why did she feel like this wasn't so much about Cleo doing her a favor, but trying to insert herself between Jenna and Alex?

11

Cleo

"Hi," Cleo called as she ushered Izzy through the side door of Alex and Ethan's sprawling Mediterranean style home. They walked down the short hallway that led into the kitchen and family room. Alex and Ethan were busy preparing food for the Halloween party later that afternoon.

Ava was on the couch in the family room, entranced by Paw Patrol.

"Hey," Alex started over to her. "I would hug you but I have hot dog hands," she said, waving her hands in the air. Instead she bent and pressed her cheek to Cleo's. Then she stood back and eyed Cleo and Izzy's costumes. "Oh, my God, you guys look so great. Ethan, don't they look great? We're waiting until just before everyone gets here to put ours on."

She and Alex had decided to dress as different types of sushi, since it was Izzy and Ava's favorite food. Cleo and Izzy were dressed as ahi nigiri and a California roll. Alex was going to go as a piece of salmon nigiri, Ava matched Izzy as a California roll, and Ethan was a bottle of soy sauce.

"They sure do." Ethan wiped his hands and treated them to his dazzling smile. He sauntered over and bent to give her his customary kiss on the cheek. "Let me take these," he reached for the box of cupcakes Cleo had picked up from the fancy bakery at the shopping center as Izzy made a beeline for Ava. "What can I get you to drink?"

"I'm having chardonnay," Alex volunteered.

It was only one o'clock and the party didn't start until three. If she started drinking now she'd be on the floor by then. "I'll just have sparkling water for now."

As Ethan retrieved a can of seltzer from the fridge, Alex went back to opening multiple packages of hotdogs and put them on a platter for Ethan to grill. "Do you mind opening the chicken and dumping it in the bowl with the marinade?" She gestured with her chin to packages of chicken breasts stacked on the counter next to a blue ceramic bowl.

Cleo did as she asked, inhaling the pleasant aromas of garlic, lemon, and oregano as she tossed the chicken in the marinade.

Alex paused in her unwrapping to take a sip of her wine and retrieve another plate from a cabinet. "So is Scott coming later, then?"

Cleo pasted a look of disappointment on her face. "I forgot to tell you. Something came up with one of his clients so now he has to stop in London for a couple of days."

"He'll miss Izzy's first time trick or treating!" Alex's face suggested that was among the worst tragedies to ever befall a child.

"I know, and he's super bummed." That was certainly true of the fictional Scott, who, despite his frequent absences, was a dedicated father. Izzy's real dad? Not so much.

Cleo gave the chicken one final toss. "What else can I do?"

"Let's see," Alex said as she finished piling another variety of sausages and hot dogs on a plate. "Sylvia's getting everything set up outside, so if you want to bring those bowls out to her that would be great."

Cleo retrieved the indicated shatter proof bowls, one containing goldfish crackers, the other potato chips, and walked through the French doors that led to Alex's backyard. Though she had been to Alex's house several times by that point, the view from her flagstone patio never failed to take her breath away.

On this gorgeous Northern California fall day, she could see all the way across the bay and up to San Francisco. Even without the views, Alex's backyard would have been delightful. A rolling lawn graduated into a series of terraces where Alex - well, more particularly Alex's gardeners - grew flowers and vegetables. Next to the pool was an open sided structure that offered shade and shelter when it rained. A large couch, loveseat and two arm chairs were arranged underneath.

In addition to the large metal and glass outdoor dining table, a folding table covered in a Halloween themed tablecloth held a stack of plates and disposable utensils. Sylvia was putting the final touches on an elaborate table scape that included fresh pumpkins of varying sizes, figurines of black cats and witches, and a bubbling cauldron full of "smoking" dry ice.

Cleo greeted her warmly. "The table looks beautiful," she said.

Sylvia thanked her with a modest smile and asked her to put the bowls of snacks at the end of the table.

She went back inside to find Alex pulling a series of gallon sized bags full of various items out of the refrigerator. "I almost forgot about the feel boxes," she said with a little laugh. "Can you get some bowls from the kid cabinet?"

Cleo went to the cabinet in question, which was full of plastic bowls, cups, and plates used for serving the kids. She retrieved several small bowls which would be filled by worms (damp noodles), eyeballs (peeled grapes), witches fingers (meat sticks), and teeth (popcorn kernels). The bowls were then placed in boxes decorated in Halloween themes. A hole big enough to fit a three year old's hand was cut in the top. Under Alex's direction, she placed them on the designated activities table, where the kids could get their faces painted and do Halloween themed crafts.

As they were finishing up, Alex took a look at her watch and grimaced. "Crap. It's almost three and we still have to get dressed. Ethan," she called to her husband, who was helping himself to a handful of chips from the kids 'food table, "can you get the grill ready and come put your costume on?"

"On it," he grinned and walked over to the propane grill tucked against the house.

"Oh, and can you finish the salad?" She asked Cleo as she started inside. "It's right here," she said, gesturing to a massive bowl full of leafy greens and avocados. "The dressing is already made." She went to the refrigerator, pulled out a jar of vinaigrette, and handed it to her.

She retreated to her bedroom, and Ethan followed her seconds later.

Cleo opened the jar of dressing, a concoction of lemon juice, olive oil and fresh herbs. She glanced over to the girls, whose attention was still fixed on Frozen. Sylvia sat next to them, staring at her phone as she scrolled.

Cleo retrieved her purse from where she had left it and pulled out a small glass bottle with a dropper dispenser. She took it over to the jar of salad dressing and squeezed the bulb at the top of the dropper to fill it with liquid. She would only need a few drops -

"Hi!"

Cleo jumped at the sound of Jenna's voice behind her and reflexively squeezed the entire dropperful into the dressing.

Well this was going to be even more interesting than expected. She hurriedly screwed the top back on the bottle and shoved it out of view. Jenna bustled into the kitchen with Noah on one hip, her giant diaper bag on her shoulder, Liam trailing behind. Cleo went over to give her a quick hug and pressed a kiss to Noah's sweet smelling head.

"You guys are early," Cleo said as she went back to the salad. She poured the dressing over the top and used Alex's wooden salad spoons to give it a thorough toss. Such a gorgeous salad, made with all organic produce and imported parmesan cheese. No one would ever suspect that eating it would make them terribly sick.

"We had to get out of the house," Jenna walked in and plopped her bag on one of the bar stools. "Liam was climbing up the walls, and Mark is trying to get some work done. I figured he could come here and jump on the trampoline. Work some energy out before he gets all jacked up on sugar."

"Good idea," Cleo said, inwardly breathing a sigh of relief as it became clear Jenna suspected nothing.

Liam, dressed as Spiderman, went bounding into the family room. "I'm Spiderman," he said, and made a flourish with his hand as though throwing a web.

Noah, in keeping with the superhero theme, was dressed as Ironman.

"I love your costume," Jenna said around a yawn. "This was the best I could come up with," she said, gesturing to her black miniskirt over tights that had a spiderweb pattern. The headband keeping her hair off of her face had cat ears.

"It's cute," Cleo said. "Do you want a drink? There's Chardonnay in the refrigerator and Rose, sparkling, and Sauvignon Blanc in the bucket outside."

"Sure," Jenna said, sounding a little uncertain.

Cleo was almost certain Jenna was not cool with Cleo acting as substitute hostess in Alex's home.

"Where are Alex and Ethan?" She said as she started outside. Cleo followed her with the salad.

"Helloooo," Morgan's familiar voice echoed from inside.

"Out here," Jenna and Cleo called in unison. Jenna caught her gaze, eyes narrowing almost imperceptibly.

Morgan, David, and Jack came through the French doors, dressed as Morticia and Gomez Addams. Morgan had obviously had her dramatic makeup professionally done, and her tight black dress glittered with intricate beading.

"Oh, my God, you look amazing," Cleo gushed.

"Thank you," Morgan said and did a little twirl.

"Where should we put the wine?" David asked, and hefted the box in his arms.

Cleo pointed him to the adult drink station Sylvia had set up. Jack took off for the trampoline, followed closely by Liam.

Ethan and Alex rejoined them on the patio, and Alex and Morgan took a moment to fawn over each others 'costumes.

Jenna, however, looked less than delighted. "I didn't realize you guys were coordinating."

Alex gave a little wince and shot Cleo a look. "We wanted to do something more original than princesses, so we thought it would be fun to dress as their favorite food."

"Cool," Jenna said through clenched teeth. She turned abruptly and headed for the bar.

Alex leaned in to Morgan and Cleo. "Why do you think she's so upset?"

"Don't worry about her," Morgan whispered back. "She's just got a lot going on."

Alex's brow creased with worry, but before she could go over to try to console Jenna, four kids and their parents arrived at the same time. Cleo helped Alex get everyone settled with drinks and snacks, and directed them to the activities table while Ethan started grilling. The rest of the class had arrived, and soon three spidermen were squaring off against superman and batman. Several princesses squealed as they blindly groped "eyeballs" and "guts" in the decorated boxes.

Most of the parents had dressed up as well, and it was interesting to see what some people considered appropriate for a kids Halloween party.

"Fishnet tights are an interesting choice," Morgan murmured, echoing Cleo's thoughts about Harley Quinn.

"And why in the world would you wear heels like that when you're going to be on grass?" Jenna observed as Katherine, the mother in question, stumbled and nearly fell as she tried to catch up with her son.

Cleo kept one eye on Izzy as she sipped her wine and chatted with the other parents. After about half an hour, Alex called out that it was time for the costume parade. She had all of the kids and parents line up next to the snack table, and had Sylvia film while everyone did a lap around the lawn. Shortly after, Ethan announced that the first round of hot dogs were ready for anyone who was hungry.

Several parents coaxed reluctant children over to line up for food. As Cleo hoped, most parents chose the fruit salad to accompany their kids 'hot dogs. She breathed a little sigh of relief. In the past, she had used this tincture of Senna plant only on adults. She had no idea how much more severe the effects would be on a smaller person.

"Are any of these vegetarian?"

Cleo's gaze narrowed on Tricia who pointed at the platters of hot dogs. She was dressed as Ruth Bader Ginsberg.

"The ones to your left are the veggie dogs and sausages," Ethan said.

Tricia thanked him and put one on Matthew's plate. "Do you have any gluten free buns?" she asked as she peered into the basket holding the buns.

"Oh, shi - oot," Alex caught herself before swearing. Impressive, Cleo thought, as she was already about a half bottle in. "I forgot to get any."

Tricia put her hand on her hip and gave Alex a peevish look. "This is the second year our kids have been in school together, Alex. You should know that Matthew is gluten intolerant by now."

Several parents exchanged pointed looks as they watched the women square off.

"Someone should tell her au pair," a mom named Kelly, who Cleo had hung out with at Oakwood a couple times, said to her in an aside. "Because I saw him at the club the other day taking down a soft pretzel like he hadn't eaten in weeks."

Cleo chuckled.

"I can have Sylvia run out and get some if you want," Alex said, smiling just a little too brightly.

"No, it's fine," Tricia replied, as she spooned fruit onto the plate in jerky motions. "Matthew will just have to make do."

"OOhkeee," Alex turned, eyebrows raised, and caught Cleo's eye. Cleo gave her a sympathetic grimace as Alex came to stand next to her.

"Seriously," Alex said under her breath, "I'm all about being a good hostess and accommodating your kid, but if he's the only one with dietary restrictions, maybe you should bring your own."

Cleo nodded, only half listening as she watched Tricia scoop a serving of green salad onto Matthew's plate. Any hope that she was getting it for herself was dashed when she said, "Look, Mattie, it's arugula. You love arugula!"

"Humblebrag, much?" Kelly said.

As Cleo steered Izzy through the food line, she tried not to think too much about what was in store for Matthew. There was collateral damage in every war.

"No, that's the lettuce you don't like," she said when Izzy pointed at the green salad. Thank god Izzy, unlike Matthew, hated arugula's peppery bite.

Once the kids were settled with their plates and started eating, the adults started through the line. Like ninety nine percent of the moms, Cleo loaded her plate with salad and a grilled chicken breast. She grimaced inwardly as she sat down across from Jenna. She didn't relish what was in store for her in the next twenty four hours. But it might be suspicious if she were to avoid eating the salad and the subsequent consequences. Sometimes, she thought as she forked a bite of arugula and avocado into her mouth, you had to suffer for the greater cause.

"Please," Jenna pleaded as she speared a slice of hot dog with her fork and offered it to Liam. She winced as Noah, who squirmed in her lap, tangled his hand in her hair and yanked it. "You need to eat a few bites of real food if you want to have a cupcake." Her own plate, full of salad, chicken, and a hot dog of her own, sat untouched.

As Cleo forced down a few more bites, she imagined Jenna several hours from now. She was barely able to manage the two boys under normal circumstances. How would she cope when she was chained to the bathroom?

"I'm going to get some water. Does anybody want anything?" She stood from her chair, and in the process managed to knock her nearly full glass of wine into Jenna's plate. "Oh, my God, I'm so sorry!" She grabbed a napkin and reached across the table to stanch the flow of wine before it dripped on Jenna's lap. She snatched up the wine soaked plate. "Let me get you more food."

She grabbed a fresh plate and placed another hot dog and chicken breast on it. Wouldn't you know, every last leaf of the salad had been consumed.

"Sorry, we ran out of salad," she said as she returned to the table and placed the plate in front of her. "I hope fruit is okay,"

"It's fine," Jenna said with a tired smile.

Cleo smiled back, patting herself on the back for the kind act. She didn't fool herself for a moment thinking she was a nice person. But she wasn't above showing mercy.

12

Alex

Alex woke up to the sound of the toilet flushing, followed by Ethan's groan echoing off of the marble walls of their bathroom. A slight sting of a headache told her she probably should have skipped that last glass of wine. She rolled over, grabbed her phone, and let out a groan of her own when she saw the time. Four twenty four a.m. Two and a half hours before Ava would come bopping into their room, never mind that it was a Sunday. She turned on her side and squeezed her eyes shut. She knew she probably wouldn't be able to fall back asleep but she was damn sure going to try.

"Oh fuck," Ethan's curse was followed by the slam of the door to the toilet chamber.

Alex flopped to her back. "Are you okay?" She called, doing her best to keep the irritation out of her voice.

She was met with silence, then another flush of the toilet. Ethan appeared in the doorway of their bathroom wearing his boxer briefs. He was backlit so she couldn't see his face, but she could see the way his broad shoulders hunched as he wrapped an arm around his stomach.

"I feel like everything I've ever eaten in my life just came out of my ass." He turned off the light and she heard him slowly shuffle over to the bed. The mattress shifted as he settled onto the bed.

"Do you think you have a stomach flu?" She reached over and put a hand on his forehead. No fever.

"Maybe-"he let out another loud curse and curled into himself. "Oh, my God, I feel like I have knives in my stomach," he panted. "I think I may need to go to the emergency room."

She was glad it was dark so he couldn't see her roll her eyes. For all that he was a tough Montanan, Ethan was an absolute wimp when it came to being sick. "I doubt it's that serious," she rubbed his bare shoulder. "Let me get you some Pepto."

She rose from bed, swaying a little as she got her equilibrium. She went to the bathroom and snapped on the light, wincing as the brightness made her wine headache give another stab. She reached for the drawer that held their medications, swearing under her breath as she fumbled with the child safety latch. She finally got it open, found the familiar pink bottle and pulled out the ibuprofen along with it. She threw three tablets in her mouth and drank directly from the tap to wash them down.

She picked up the bottle of Pepto and started back out to Ethan when he came staggering in, clutching his stomach. "Move!" She didn't have time to fully get out of the way as he practically body checked her into the vanity.

He closed himself in the toilet room once again. Even over the whir of the bathroom fan, she could hear the sounds of someone in extreme gastric distress. Nose wrinkling in disgust, she went back to bed and tried to scrub the experience from her memory.

Ethan showed no signs of leaving the bathroom any time soon, and Alex eventually fell back asleep. She didn't know how long she was dozing before she was awakened by a violent cramping in her stomach. She curled into a fetal position and tried to breathe through it, but the pain was so sharp she cried out.

And then….

Oh no. Ethan was still locked in their bathroom. The next closest bathroom was down the hall. The pain was so extreme she wasn't sure if she could move. But the heavy pressure building in her bowels meant that if she didn't, she was going to have an unholy mess to deal with. Cold sweat erupted all over her body at another wave of cramps. She willed herself to sit up and swung her feet to the floor. She didn't so much stand as hurl herself toward the bedroom door.

She staggered out into the hallway, panting as she dragged herself toward the powder room that felt like it was a mile away.

She was still a few feet shy of the bathroom when she felt it coming. She clenched her butt cheeks as tightly as she could, cursing herself for slacking off at the gym when that wasn't enough to keep the diarrhea at bay. She yanked up her nightgown and shoved her underwear down her legs as she staggered the last few steps, leaving a foul trail in her wake.

She sat on the toilet with a groan of relief, closed her eyes and gave over to whatever infestation had taken over her body.

She didn't know how long she sat there, enduring wave after wave of violent cramping followed by equally violent elimination. By the time it abated for a few minutes, she felt like her body was trying to turn itself inside out through her asshole.

She leaned back against the toilet, trying to muster the strength to clean herself up when she heard Ava calling for her.

"I'm in the bathroom, sweetie," she called weakly. A few seconds later the door to the powder room opened and Ava stepped inside.

Her sweet smile quickly morphed into a look of disgust. "Mommy, it smells yucky in here!"

Alex rolled her eyes. "I know honey. Daddy and I have upset tummies." At that moment her stomach cramped again, as though to punish her for describing their ailment in such benign terms. "Just go wait in the kitchen and I'll come out to make your breakfast."

It took several more minutes to get through the next surge. When she stood up she felt like a wrung out dish rag. Gagging, she picked up her soiled underwear off the floor and rinsed them in the sink. She got herself, as well as the mess she had made on the way to the bathroom, cleaned up, then joined Ava in the kitchen.

Once again, she gave thanks to the universe for blessing her with a sweet, biddable daughter who could be trusted to be alone for a few minutes without killing herself or destroying the house. Of course, sweet and biddable wouldn't work for her as an adult, but if Ava was anything like Alex, once she hit her teens she wouldn't have any issues with being more assertive.

"What do you want for breakfast, sweetie?" Alex asked as she retrieved a mug from the cabinet above the coffee maker. She poured a cup from the automatic brewer. She lifted it toward her lips, only to have her stomach heave at the strong aroma. Swallowing back bile, she poured the coffee down the drain.

"Cheesy eggs and toast," Ava said without looking up from her coloring.

Alex retrieved eggs and cheese from the refrigerator and grabbed a bottle of Pedialyte for good measure. She put two slices of bread in the toaster and unscrewed the bottle. She took a tentative sip of the sweet, electrolyte rich drink and waited several seconds to see what would happen. Satisfied it would stay down, she drank half the bottle before she went to work scrambling Ava's eggs.

Only to have it all come back up as soon as the smell of scrambled eggs hit the kitchen. She barely managed to get Ava's breakfast in front of her before she had to make another lengthy trip to the bathroom.

When she emerged, she found Ava's seat at the table empty, her half eaten plate of eggs and toast abandoned. She grabbed the bottle of Pedialyte off of the counter and headed towards the bedrooms, calling Ava's name.

She found her in their bed, snuggled up to Ethan, whose eyes were sunken into his skull. The TV was on, and the Bubble Guppies were bouncing across the screen. Ethan, who had absolutely no tolerance for what he called "this mind numbing crap," must have been feeling really shitty to tolerate this.

"I think I shit out my liver," he groaned as Alex settled back into her side of the bed.

Alex was too worn out to admonish him for his language. She passed him the bottle of

Pedialyte, settled back into her pillow, and closed her eyes.

When she woke again, late morning sun was streaming through the French doors that led out to the patio. Ethan's side of the bed was empty and Ava was nowhere to be found. She started to sit up, freezing when her stomach seized. Saliva pooled in her mouth as nausea roiled in her stomach. She desperately swallowed it back as she stumbled to the bathroom, barely making it as far as the sink before the meager contents of her stomach came spewing out.

She rinsed out her mouth, gagging at the taste of the water, then shuffled back to bed. She picked up her phone and saw that she had several missed texts.

From Jenna to Alex, Morgan, and Cleo:

Anyone up for a picnic in the park later today? Desperate to get my boys out of the house to burn up some energy.

Morgan replied:

> *I can't. David and I both came down with some horrible stomach bug. We've had it coming out of both ends since early this morning.*

From Cleo:

> *Me too!*

Alex's jumbled stomach twisted again, this time with dread. Had she inadvertently made everyone at the party sick?

> *Uh oh, guys. I'm sick too. So's Ethan. But Ava's fine. How are your kiddos?*

She crossed her fingers and prayed she didn't make the kids sick too.

From Morgan:

> *Jack is fine. But thank God Irina is here because David and I can't get out of the bathroom.*

From Cleo:

> *Izzy seems fine so far.*

From Alex:

> *Phew. It's still awful. everyone is sick, but at least none of the kids got it.*

From Jenna:

> *How is it possible that I'm the only one who didn't get sick?*

They went through a quick inventory of everything they and their kids had eaten.

> *It had to be the salad, Cleo wrote. Jenna's not sick because I accidentally knocked my wine into her plate.*

From Jenna:

And to think I was so pissed you ruined it. I ended up going home and having goldfish crackers and string cheese for dinner.

From Cleo:

Happy to help.

From Morgan:

Look on the bright side. We've probably all lost a few pounds.

From Alex:

You all know how I love a good purge.

They exchanged a few more messages and came to the conclusion that the lettuce must have been contaminated.

I'll call the grocery store tomorrow, Alex wrote.
I'm going to go weigh myself and go find out what Ava and Ethan are doing.

She went to the bathroom, dragged out the scale and stripped to her underwear. She got on the scale, disappointed to discover that she'd only lost a pound and a half.

As the day progressed several other parents messaged her, letting her know about their own stomach woes. Even though it was completely unintentional, the story about the time Alex Drake gave the entire '3s and 4's class the shits would follow her through Ava's entire academic career in Oak Valley. The odor in her powder room might dissipate, but this stink was on her to stay.

Rather than reply to everyone individually, she wrote a group email to the parents. She apologized profusely, and let them know that she thought that the salad was the most likely culprit. When the replies started flooding her inbox, she slammed her laptop shut. She'd already dealt with enough shit today.

Literally.

The next morning, despite a few lingering cramps, Alex dragged herself out of bed. Ethan lingered, saying he didn't think he could get out of bed yet.

Pussy.

She got Ava up, fed her breakfast, and managed to drink a cup of coffee without incident. She checked in with Cleo and Morgan, happy to hear that they were also mostly recovered. As the time for preschool drop-off approached, dread mingled with the lingering effects of food poisoning and set her stomach rumbling. Even though most of the parents replied to her email saying they understood it was an accident and could have happened to any of them, Alex wasn't relishing seeing them face to face. Could you ever really apologize enough for making people spend their Sunday shitting their guts out?

She looked at the clock on her phone and cursed herself for not asking Sylvia to come in early today. Whatever faint hope she had that Ethan might be able to swing drop off was dashed when she went back to the bedroom to get dressed. Ethan was in the bathroom in his boxer briefs, hands braced on the bathroom counter as though struggling to hold himself upright.

"I almost passed out when I got up to go to the bathroom," he offered before Alex could ask how he was feeling. "Do you think we have e.coli?"

Alex shrugged and continued into her closet to get dressed. "That's my best guess. Either that or salmonella."

As she pulled on a sports bra, leggings, and a tunic top, she heard Ethan dry heave behind her. "Whatever it is, it's hitting me really hard. Do you think you can take me to urgent care after drop off? I think I'm too sick to drive."

She was glad her back was turned so he couldn't see her jaw clench and her eyes roll. She adored her husband, she really did, but this thing where whenever they both got sick, somehow his case was a medical emergency while she was expected to take care of him, had become increasingly annoying over the course of their relationship. Particularly after they'd had Ava.

"Sure," she pasted a smile on her face. She kissed him on her way out and went to Ava's room to help her get dressed.

Five minutes later, she pulled into the Wyndham parking lot. She got Ava from her carseat and led her to the classroom where a group of moms, including Jenna and Cleo, were lingering just outside the door. She could tell from the sidelong glances and the way conversation halted as she approached that she was the subject of discussion.

She wanted nothing more than to hand Ava off to Teacher Nora and rush back to her car, but Alex Drake was never one to retreat with her tail between her legs.

She kissed Ava goodbye and turned to the group. "Morning," she said and moved closer to Cleo and Jenna. Even though the other parents weren't waving pitch forks, she felt the need for reinforcements.

"I'm really sorry about what happened everyone. I hope no one got too sick."

"Speaking for myself, I was over it within a few hours. But if you ask my husband, he's dying," Melanie Parker chuckled.

Alex reached out and grabbed her arm with a laugh. "Oh, my God, Ethan wants me to take him to urgent care after this!"

Several other women chimed in about what babies their husbands were when they got sick.

"The man cold is real," Cleo laughed in reference to the viral video.

"I can't believe you're all laughing about this," a shrill voice rose above the rest. "She made us all sick, and you think it's funny?"

"Tricia, I said, I'm sorry," Alex said as Tricia pushed her way over to Alex. "It wasn't like I made everyone sick on purpose."

"I don't care. It still isn't funny. Matthew was so sick he needed IV fluids!"

Alex apologized again, and noticed the other parents exchanging awkward glances, hoping to stay out of the fray. She felt a wave of vulnerability. She rarely had a problem holding her own, but she didn't like the way no one rose to her defense as Tricia publicly chewed her out.

"I would be within my rights to sue you," Tricia continued.

"Okay, okay," Cleo put herself between Tricia and Alex. "Matthew is ok, and no one is going to sue anyone."

"She served us contaminated food," Tricia protested.

Cleo put a hand up. "She bought contaminated lettuce from a grocery store where we all shop. This literally could have happened to any of us. I'm sure Alex feels terrible enough without you laying into her. And look at it this way," she put a comforting hand on

Tricia's arm, "the only reason Matthew got sick is because you've raised him to be such a healthy eater. Do you realize he's the only kid from the entire class who ate salad at that party?"

Tricia gave a little chuckle. "I guess there is that silver lining." She gave Alex one last glare as she took her leave.

"Wow, that was impressive," Alex said as she, Cleo, and Jenna, started towards the parking lot.

"Have you ever thought of being a diplomat?" Jenna asked.

Cleo smoothed a hand down her ponytail and gave them a coy smile. "You just have to figure out what people want. Tricia clearly feels out of place among all of us. She just wants to feel seen and included."

Alex felt a pang of guilt, considering how she hadn't given Tricia much of a chance, how that might have hurt the other woman's feelings.

"But really, what kind of loser three year old is eating fucking arugula salad?" Cleo continued.

"Our kids are way too cool for arugula," Alex laughed. She reached out and gave Cleo a quick hug. "Thanks for stepping in and having my back. I was feeling kind of abandoned out there."

She flicked a quick glance at Jenna and saw the stricken look flash across her face.

She hadn't meant it as a reprimand against Jenna, but considering thee way her supposed best friend hadn't uttered a peep, perhaps she deserved as much.

She turned back to Cleo and smiled. After her husband and her daughter, the most important thing to Alex was knowing she had friends she could depend on.

13

Cleo

"Aww, Liam says he's thankful for his baby brother," Jenna said with a little sniff. Halloween was in the rearview mirror, and now the holiday season loomed on the horizon.

They were gathered at Morgan's house for their weekly playdate. Cleo sipped at her rose, still marveling at the fact that Morgan's guest house could have easily fit two of her childhood homes inside.

Regardless of how many years she'd spent among ridiculously wealthy people, she was still occasionally struck by the stark contrast between how she grew up and how she lived now.

While the kids played in Jack's bedroom under Irina's watchful eye, she, Morgan, Alex, and Jenna sipped wine in the living room as they looked through the kids 'latest preschool projects. In honor of Thanksgiving coming up the following week, the teachers had helped the kids draw a turkey by tracing their hands, then gluing construction paper feathers onto the body. Then the teachers had asked each child what he or she was thankful for and wrote it below the turkey.

"Izzy says she's thankful for her friend Ava," Cleo said clinking her glass against Alex's.

"And Ava and I are thankful for you," Alex said.

Cleo didn't miss the way Jenna's shoulders stiffened.

"However," Alex continued, "Ava says she's thankful for chocolate ice cream."

They all chuckled. "What did Jack say?" Alex asked.

Morgan took a sip of wine and pressed her lips into a tight smile. "He says he's thankful for Irina because she makes him Mac 'n cheese. Never mind that her Mac 'n cheese is the same fucking Annie's Natural's that I make on the weekends which he then refuses to eat because I 'don't do it right.'" Her voice broke on the last syllable.

Cleo slid over and put her arm around Morgan's shoulders. "Is everything okay?"

"I'm sorry," Morgan placed her glass on the coffee table. She blinked rapidly against the tears flooding her eyes. "I'm just under a lot of pressure right now. I've got a big deal at work I'm trying to close, and we have this stupid Hawaii trip next week-"

"Oh the torture of having to go to your mansion in Wailea," Jenna snarked.

Morgan gave a little huff. "Look, I don't mean to sound ungrateful, but it's not exactly going to be relaxing. Lily, Simon, and David's parents are coming, and they're going to spend the whole time taking digs at me for working too much."

"At least if you're working you can avoid them," Alex pointed out.

"True," Morgan said with a sigh.

"You don't get along with your in-laws?" Cleo asked.

"That would be an understatement." Morgan reached for the bottle of chardonnay chilling in a bucket on the table and topped off both her and Alex's glasses. "It's not like we're actively fighting all of the time. More that they take constant passive aggressive jabs at me."

"They were very close to David's first wife," Alex said.

"Did I tell you that they're going to Vail with her and the kids over New Year's?" Morgan said.

"Well, Corrine and David were married for a decade. Just because his relationship with her changed doesn't mean it's fair for him to expect everyone else's relationship to change too," Cleo said.

"It would be one thing if they made an effort to have a good relationship with me too," Morgan snapped. "But they never miss an opportunity to rub my face in the fact that they wish David had never married me."

Cleo could relate to that, as it sounded like the way she would treat an unwanted in law. However, she was also pretty sure that David's first wife was, in fact, a much nicer, more down to earth person than Morgan. "Well, hopefully you can all get along well enough to enjoy your time in Maui. What's everyone else doing for Thanksgiving?"

"We're going to Bozeman to visit Ethan's family," Alex said.

"Lucky," Jenna said.

"I know, I can't wait," Alex said with a grin. "A whole week where I won't have to lift a finger."

It wasn't as though Alex was here toiling away like Cinderella. Cleo drained her glass of rose and set it on the table. "How does that work when you have a three year old?"

"Alex's mother in law is amazing," Jenna said before Alex could answer.

"She really is. Whenever we stay with them, she spoils us rotten. She makes all of our favorite food, spends hours and hours with Ava, does our laundry…"

"And unlike my mom," Jenna interjected, "she does it all without acting like a martyr."

"She's also really cool and funny," Morgan said. "Last time she came to town she had us howling over stories about how she and her sisters used to torment their aunts."

"I can't wait to meet her some day," Cleo smiled.

"What are you doing next week?" Jenna asked Cleo.

"Since Scott is in Singapore until the end of this week, Izzy and I are going to meet him in Tahiti."

"That doesn't suck," Jenna's expression was pinched as she reached for the bottle of rose.

"Yeah, well, since both of us have lost our parents, we don't really like to dwell on holiday traditions."

A wave of hushed "I'm so sorries," echoed through the room.

"It's okay. My dad died when I was very young, and my mom passed right after I had Izzy."

"Oh, that's so hard," Alex placed a hand on Cleo's arm as her eyes teared in sympathy. "Things are never the same after you lose a parent."

Cleo gave her a sad smile and summoned up tears of her own. *Oh, Alex, you have no fucking idea how true that is.*

Truth be told, Thanksgiving, or any other holiday for that matter, had never been a cozy warm family bonding sort of occasion. Holidays were a time of heightened emotions and fraught with expectations. To say that was an environment in which Cleo's mother did not thrive was a massive understatement.

Thanksgiving when she was fifteen, stood out in particular focus.

The fight started, as always, over something innocuous. They were all gathered around the dining room table at Dean, her mother's boyfriend of nearly a year's house. They had moved in with him and his eight year old son, Toby, at the end of the summer. Thanksgiving was their first big celebration as a blended family. Cleo knew that her mother, Stella, wanted to make everything perfect. She'd spent the last three days preparing, insisting on doing everything herself.

The turkey sat centerstage, roasted to a perfect mahogany brown. Mashed potatoes, green beans made with freshly sautéed mushrooms and fried shallots ("none of that canned soup trash food for my man," her mother had said to Cleo proudly when Cleo had snuck in to grab a snack), cranberry sauce, and cornbread stuffing made from Cleo's grandmother's recipe rounded out the meal.

She watched her mother watching as they placed slices of turkey and scoops of the sides on their plates. Her stomach knotted as she recognized her mother's expression. She knew that look, knew the tension humming through her mother's body as she waited for someone to say something that could be perceived as even the slightest bit critical.

As everyone started to eat, praising Stella's skill as they tasted every dish, Cleo felt the knot in her stomach uncoil enough for her to swallow a few bites of food. "Everything is so delicious, Mom," Cleo said and meant it. Her mother didn't cook much, but when she did she had serious skills.

Her mother beamed as she watched them all tuck in. The phrase "she had a smile that could light up a room" was such a cliche, but in Stella's case it was true. Her mother had the kind of smile that when she turned it on you, you felt like you were bathed in golden light. It was the kind of smile that made you want to lay the world at her feet. It was the smile that made Dean - and many other men over the years - fall in love at first sight.

Even Cleo wasn't immune to its power as she smiled back, relief coursing through her.

"Huh," Dean said with a thoughtful look on his face.

"What?" Stella said sharply, a forkful of turkey frozen halfway to her mouth.

Cleo's mouthful of mashed potatoes turned to paste in her mouth as a fist squeezed at her chest.

"The green beans," Dean said and dabbed his mouth with his napkin. "They're different."

Stella lowered her fork. "If by different, you mean they're made with fresh ingredients instead of that canned garbage, then yes, they are."

Tell her they're amazing. Tell her they're the most delicious green beans you've ever tasted, Cleo silently pleaded.

He chuckled and shrugged. "I guess I just like that canned garbage."

The words were barely out of his mouth before her mother was on her feet and hurling the casserole full of green beans in Dean's direction. It hit him square on the front of his blue Oxford shirt, the one Stella had told him to wear because it matched his beautiful blue eyes.

He shot to his feet, shouting "What the fuck," as he frantically wiped his shirt.

"I slaved away in the kitchen for three goddamn days," Stella shouted, "And now you fucking criticize me?" Her tone grew more shrill with every syllable. She picked up the bowl of potatoes and smashed it on the floor. The bowl shattered, leaving the potatoes in a thick puddle on the hardwood floor.

Dean stared, mouth agape.

Cleo was familiar with the expression. She'd seen it on the faces of several men who watched the woman they knew as kind, loving, and solicitous turn into a raging harpy in a matter of seconds.

"Mom, stop," Cleo yelled. "He didn't say anything bad." She knew it wouldn't do anything to diffuse the situation. Once the switch was flipped, her mom was defcon ten until she burned herself out. The best thing anyone could do was to get out of her way until you could come back and assess the damage.

"How dare you defend him," she reached for the bowl of stuffing.

Dean snapped out of his stunned state and grabbed her from behind before she could get to it.

He pinned her arms to her side, lifted her off her feet and moved her forcibly from the table. "Stella, you need to calm down."

"Don't you tell me to calm down," she raged. "I worked my ass off to put this meal together, and you don't even appreciate it. You don't appreciate anything about me." Her shouting ended with sob.

She was now transitioning from the rage stage to the self pity stage, Cleo knew.

Toby sat, wide eyed, at his father restraining his sobbing girlfriend.

Cleo went over to him and urged him out of his seat. "Come on," she urged. "You don't need to see this." She took his plate in case he was still hungry and followed him to the den. She got him settled in front of the TV. Thankfully one of the basic cable channels was playing a Harry Potter marathon, so he was easily distracted from the muffled sound of the fight leaking through the closed door.

Cleo left after a few minutes with a promise to bring dessert. At least the pies had been spared her mother's rampage. They were still cooling on the kitchen counter.

She cut a slice from the pumpkin pie and found the whipped cream her mother had made in the refrigerator. She plopped a generous dollop on the pie and set it in front of Toby.

Satisfied that he was sufficiently distracted, she left him in the den to eavesdrop.

"You don't care about me at all," Stella was sobbing.

The few bites of Cleo's meal that she'd managed to swallow congealed in her stomach.

"Of course I care about you," Dean sounded equal parts baffled and exasperated. Cleo could imagine him running his hands through his hair like he did when Toby refused to go to bed.

"You don't." Stella's screech was followed by the sound of something breaking. Dean had made the mistake of letting her go. "You just use me."

"How?" Dean said.

"You use me for sex, you use me as a baby sitter, your cook, your maid-"

"Stella, what the hell has gotten into you? This is crazy," Dean yelled.

Cleo closed her eyes. Her shoulders slumped. If there had been any chance to pull her mother back from the edge, Dean had obliterated it with a single word.

"Don't you dare call me crazy!"

"I didn't call you crazy, I said this is crazy," Dean said through what sounded like clenched teeth. There was a moment of silence, then, "Ow! That hit me right in the fucking eye, you bitch!"

It was surreal, hearing Dean, who was so easy going, swearing at her mother and calling her a bitch.

But that was Stella's superpower. Turning the nicest, most mild mannered men on the planet into red faced rage monsters. Sometimes it only took a few weeks. Sometimes it took months.

With Dean it had taken almost a year. Cleo had started to let herself hope that maybe this time could be different.

Cleo felt a wave of nausea surge in her throat as tears stung her eyes. God, she didn't want to move again. And not just because she loved Dean's house, with its fire pit on the patio and the extra comfy sectional in front of the gigantic flat screen. Not even because she finally had her own room, with sheets she'd been allowed to pick out herself and walls she was able to decorate.

She actually really liked Dean. He was nice and funny, and he had a way of talking to her like he wasn't trying too hard like some of her mother's previous boyfriends. He didn't try to boss her around and try to be her dad. She liked Toby too, even though she didn't have much in common with him. But he thought she was pretty cool, and liked to follow her around, showing her his toy cars and sharing his encyclopedic knowledge of dinosaurs. It felt kind of good to have an admirer.

And even more than Cleo, Toby loved Stella. Unlike her past boyfriends 'kids, many of whom took a snotty, "you're not my mom and therefore I don't want you anywhere near me," attitude, Toby was won over the first time they met, when Stella gave him a Tupperware full of chocolate chip cookies and a book about his favorite dinosaur. Cleo had really hoped that between Dean's calming energy and Toby's adoration, her mother would find a way to keep her anger under control. She'd hoped that this time it would last.

"You need to get out of my house," Dean said. He was no longer yelling, but his low voice had a steely undertone that was somehow scarier.

"Fine! I don't want to stay with an asshole who just uses me anyway! Cleo!"

Cleo sighed and came around the corner. She started at the sight of her mother. Even after all of these years, she was always taken aback at how Stella's rages transformed her. Her beautiful mother disappeared, all of the ugliness inside of her surging to the surface.

Dean's face was flushed. Blood dripped from a cut on his forehead. A broken picture frame lay at his feet. His jaw was clenched, eyes burning with fury. As he turned his attention to Cleo, the fury morphed into sadness.

"Get your stuff, we're going," Stella shoved past Dean and marched up the stairs.

Cleo started to follow. Dean stopped her with a gentle hand on her arm. She paused, staring at the patterns in the hardwood floor, trying not to cry.

"I'm sorry," he said. "I really am."

"It's okay." Her voice sounded odd and thin. "I understand."

He hooked a finger under her chin and forced her to meet his gaze. "I love your mother, and I care about you too, but I won't have Toby exposed to that kind of behavior."

Cleo nodded as he pulled her in for a hug. She hugged him back, cherishing for the last time the feeling of safety and comfort his strong arms and solid chest elicited.

"Will you be okay? She seems like she's in a bad way."

She shrugged and reluctantly pulled away. "She'll calm down eventually. She always does. Until the next time."

His brown eyes welled up, and the pitying look he gave her made her stomach lurch with shame.

"Cleo!" Her mother snapped as she charged down the stairs with her purse and an overflowing tote bag slung haphazardly over her shoulder. "Get out to the car, now!" Her mother took her forearm in a claw-like grip and yanked her toward the front door.

She yanked against her mother's grip. "At least let me get my backpack and some clothes."

"You better be quick or you'll pay for it." She slammed out the door as Cleo hurried up to the room that was briefly hers. She grabbed her backpack from the floor and made sure she had all of her schoolbooks inside. She took one of the duffle bags she'd moved in with and stuffed it with clothes from the dresser. Since they moved so much, Cleo didn't accumulate much stuff, so she didn't have to leave much behind.

The blare of a car horn pierced the silence, Cleo's cue to get a move on. She took one last look at the double bed with the butterfly print bedspread, at the framed print of Monet's Water Lilies on the wall. She swallowed back the sob bubbling up in her throat. Crying didn't help unless it was to get a reaction out of someone.

Dean waited for her at the bottom of the stairs. "Are you safe to go with her? Do you want to stay here with us until we can figure something out?"

She gave him a sad smile. "Thanks, but I'll be okay. I've been living with this ever since my grandmother died. I know how to handle her." Her mind started to drift back to the day her grandmother died. The day that any semblance of unconditional love and stability vanished from her life. She quickly shoved the memory down. Her life was her life. There was no use wishing she could go back to the past.

"If you need help, you can call me-"

The horn ripped through the air again, followed by her mother screaming.

Cleo gave him one last quick hug and asked him to say sorry and goodbye to Toby for her. They both knew she was never going to call him.

She slid into the passenger seat of her mother's Volvo station wagon and could barely get the door closed before her mother peeled out of Dean's driveway. She sped down the street, and Cleo was grateful it was Thanksgiving so most people were inside and out of danger.

They drove for more than an hour with Stella alternately sobbing at her plight and raging against Dean and his many imagined insults. Cleo stewed silently, resentment growing with every mile.

When it started to get dark, Cleo broke her silence long enough to ask where they were going to stay that night. She wanted to get off the road as soon as possible. Her mother's erratic driving had her fearing death at every curve when the sun was out. No way was she letting her mother drive through the night when she was having one of her episodes.

"There's a Best Western off the next exit," Cleo pointed to a road sign. She breathed a small sigh of relief when her mother took the off ramp. They could see the hotel a few blocks down, but Stella took a detour into the parking lot of a liquor store. She checked her reflection in the rearview mirror, wincing at her tear reddened eyes and blotchy face. She fumbled for her purse and pulled out a compact and lipstick, fixed her face, and then climbed out of the car.

She emerged from the store a few minutes later with a bag in her hand. Cleo didn't have to look inside to know that it held a large bottle of Pinot Grigio.

They checked into the hotel, which thankfully had vacancy despite the holiday weekend. Her mother had no sooner closed the door before she cracked open the screw top on the wine and poured a generous amount into a plastic cup provided by housekeeping. She gulped it down like it was water and quickly poured more.

"Can you actually believe he kicked us out?" she said for about the hundredth time since they'd left the house. "One little argument, and he just ends it."

Cleo turned on the TV in an attempt to drown her mother out.

"He obviously didn't really love me, if he could end things so quickly and easily." The tears started again. "I mean couples should be able to fight and make up," she slurred. "But why does every man in my life find it so easy to just dump me? I can't understand it. One day they adore me, and the next thing I know they want nothing to do with me. It all started with your father. He was so madly in love with me, and the next thing I know he's left me pregnant and broke-"

Suddenly a rage like nothing Cleo had ever felt before surged through her. "Shut up! Just shut up!"

"Don't you dare tell me to shut up," she said and took a menacing step toward her.

Rather than shrinking away or trying to diffuse her mother's anger, Cleo stood up and moved until she was inches from her mother. "I'm not going to shut up. I'm sick of how you ruin everything all of the time."

The crack of her mother's hand across her cheek echoed through the room. Her face stung and she could taste blood where her cheek scraped against her teeth.

"Apologize" her mother said, eyes glittering with fury.

"Why should I apologize when it's true? You ruin every relationship you're in. Everything can be fine, and then you pick a stupid fight and lose your fucking mind." She ignored Stella's gasp at her language. "If you treated my dad like you treat everyone else, then leaving you was the best fucking decision he ever made."

Cleo didn't so much as flinch when her mother slapped her again, then again, before bursting into tears and sinking to the floor. "How can you possibly defend him when he abandoned us the way he did? The way he used me and threw me away like trash so he could go spend all of his money on his other family?"

Resentment burned in her chest as she thought of her nameless, faceless father. It was bad enough he had turned his back on his unborn child without a thought. But even worse was that he had left her with a mother like Stella.

She left her mother sobbing on the floor and fished a bathing suit out of her duffle bag. She changed into it and grabbed a towel from the bathroom. "I'm going to the hot tub." She ignored her mother's protests as she walked out the door. With any luck, by the time she got back her mother would have passed out.

A dad in his forties watched from the side of the indoor pool as his kids splashed around. She didn't miss the way he gave her body a thorough once over. She shot him an icy glare and he dropped his gaze as blood crept up his neck.

She slid into the hot water and closed her eyes as it bubbled around her. As some of the tension uncoiled from her back and shoulders, she once again came to grips with the uncertainty of her future. She had no idea what tomorrow held or where she and her mother would go.

But she did know one thing. She was never, ever, going to allow a man to break her heart. She was never going to love anyone so much that losing them would make her crazy.

14

Morgan

"Do you guys want to take the kids up to the city to look at the tree in Union Square next week?" Morgan asked as she poured the last of the rose into her glass.

"I'm free all week," Jenna said, "but Cleo and Alex have their special mom's and daughter's tea party," Jenna said snippily. She stood from the couch and grabbed the empty bottle. "I'll go get more."

Morgan turned to Alex, eyes wide. "Is she still all butt hurt about not being invited?"

Ava's birthday was at the beginning of December, and this year Alex had decided that in addition to having a party at their house with all of their families, she was going to throw a tea party for Ava and all of the girls in her class.

Alex rolled her eyes. "It's not like I'm purposely excluding her and Liam, but I can't see him enjoying this sort of thing."

"No kidding," Morgan chuckled. "He and Jack are animals. They have no business being anywhere near a tea set."

Alex shrugged and reached for a slice of prosciutto from the charcuterie board. "You know how Jenna gets if she feels like she's being excluded."

Morgan rolled her eyes. She was thirty three years old and closing multimillion dollar deals. How was she still getting caught up in this high school bullshit? "I hope you're having the party catered this time," Morgan said with a sly smile. "You don't want those little girls shitting all over their princess dresses.'

"Nothing will be homemade. I'll even make sure Sylvia is the one to put the tea sandwiches out," Alex chuckled, but Morgan could tell by the color surging up her neck that she had gotten under her skin.

She felt a stab of satisfaction. Call her petty, but part of her enjoyed seeing Alex fuck up. It was nice to see evidence that Alex had a flaw.

The Playgroup | 111

Morgan had been drawn to Alex from the first day they met in business school eight years ago, and her attachment to her had deepened over the years. Still, sometimes she found it hard to be Alex's friend. With her easy charm and outgoing personality, she was almost universally liked.

In contrast, Morgan knew that she often came off as abrasive. But she couldn't survive in her business without developing a thick skin and hard edges.

Jenna returned holding a fresh bottle of rose by the neck. Her expression was still pissy.

"I don't know why you're upset about the tea party," Morgan said. "Jack didn't get invited either. We can't always be invited to everything."

"I don't expect to be invited everywhere," Jenna said, looking hurt. "But in the three years since we've known each other, we've never done gender exclusive things for the kids. It just doesn't feel good to have one of my best friends leave us out."

Morgan suppressed an eye roll.

"But Jenna, you guys are invited next Saturday. That's when we're doing the pony rides and petting zoo. The boys will enjoy that a hell of a lot more than a tea party," Alex said.

"It's not about whether or not Liam would like a tea party, it's the fact that you didn't invite him in the first place."

"I get it," Cleo reached out and put her hand on Jenna's arm. "It's the principle of the thing. But to be fair to Alex, I was the one who had the idea to have a separate party for just the girls. Our class is so boy-heavy, I just thought all of the girls and their moms would enjoy dressing up and being princesses for the day."

Jenna nodded and swiped her thumbs under her eyes. "I get it. I'm sorry I made such a big deal out of it. I'm just feeling really overwhelmed right now, and I haven't slept in like, a month," she said with a watery chuckle.

Everyone, including Morgan, leaned in to give her a hug, but Morgan couldn't shake her annoyance at the whole situation. She had big things, enormous things, going on in her life. She didn't have time for stupid mommy drama.

Clearly Morgan needed to work on her poker face, because Cleo leaned over and said so only she could hear, "I bet this all seems pretty stupid to you."

"Why would you say that?" Morgan feigned ignorance. Her gaze flicked to Alex and Jenna. Alex had her arm wrapped tightly around Jenna's shoulders as she reassured her of how much she loved her and valued her friendship.

Cleo shrugged and took a sip of her wine. "You've got a demanding job and a lot on your plate. I can see why you wouldn't have the patience to deal with these imagined slights."

Morgan gave her a wry smile. "Is it that obvious?"

"I'm pretty good at reading people. I can tell you don't have a lot of patience for people's insecurities."

Morgan raised her glass and clinked it with Cleo's. "Especially not my own."

15

Jenna

"Damn it," Jenna cursed as her curling iron sizzled against her earlobe. The instrument clattered to the counter of her vanity as she assessed the damage.

"Everything ok?" Mark appeared in the doorway of the bathroom, Noah on his hip.

"I'm fine," she said and picked up the curling iron. She wrapped a strand of hair around the barrel and curled it away from her face, held it for a few seconds, then released. Her lips pursed at the result. No matter how many times Alex showed her how to use the curling iron to get loose, beachy waves, somehow Jenna always ended up looking like Little Orphan Annie. "Fuck it," she muttered. She ran her brush under the faucet to get it damp, then pulled it through her curls. She was wearing a hat anyway so it didn't really matter what her hair looked like.

"I like the shirt," Mark said. "You'll be the hottest cowgirl at the party."

Jenna shot him a grin. Tonight was Wyndham's annual fundraiser, and this year they were going with a hoedown theme. Jenna had her mother send her an old shirt from her rodeo queen days. It was ice blue satin, studded with rhinestones, and decorated with fringe. It was fabulously ugly and Jenna loved every inch of it. She completed the look with skin tight jeans and the hand tooled cowboy boots she'd gotten for her eighteenth birthday. She was ready to give any buckle bunny a run for their money, if she did say so herself.

"Ugh, I don't even feel like going," she said as she checked the mirror to make sure her foundation was properly blended. She was happy to note that the silicone patches she'd applied earlier had reduced the bags under eyes to a more manageable size. "First Alex ices me out of the Halloween party planning, then doesn't invite me to Ava's birthday party, and now for the fundraiser I'm demoted from co-chair to bartender."

Alex had dropped that bomb right before she left town for Thanksgiving. Naturally, Cleo, Alex's fucking shadow, had replaced Jenna as co-chair.

Mark reached out with his free hand and wrapped it around her shoulders. "What are you talking about? I went to Ava's birthday party with you."

"I'm talking about the other one, the tea party. I know I told you about that!"

He gave her a befuddled look. "Yeah, but you said that was all girls. Of course you and Liam weren't invited."

Usually Jenna appreciated Mark's measured, logical approach to life. But sometimes his ability to compartmentalize really pissed her off. "It still hurts my feelings," she said. "And so does booting me out of the co-chair position for the fundraiser."

"I don't think you should take it as a slight," Mark said as he tried to rub some of the tension out of her shoulders. "You've got your hands full, and we just don't have the flexibility right now to pay for a babysitter so you can do volunteer work."

And whose fault is that? She thought with a stab of resentment. Last year, Liam's first year at Wyndham, the cost of babysitting had been a non issue. Last year, Mark was drawing a very nice salary plus stock options as a senior software developer at Google.

But he also felt miserable and stifled, and came home in a foul mood most days. Since starting his own company, he may have been working twice as much for less than half the money, but at least his mood had improved. She would do well to focus on that and be grateful.

"The last time she put Cleo in charge, everyone got the shits. Who knows what will happen this time," she chuckled. "Speaking of babysitting, thanks for staying in with the boys tonight. "

"I don't mind," he pressed a kiss to her cheek. "As much as I'd like to do some two stepping with my sexy cowgirl," he slid his free hand down to give her butt a squeeze, "I'm looking forward to some father son time."

She finished with her makeup and grabbed a straw cowboy hat from the closet shelf. She and Mark went to the kitchen where she showed him the pan of lasagna ready to go into the oven. She looked at her phone, wincing at the time. "I need to go. I promised Alex I'd get there early to help set up." She kissed everyone good bye and hurried out.

When she pulled up to Wyndham ten minutes later, she saw Alex's Mercedes and Cleo's BMW parked along with a few other committee members' vehicles. They'd started decorating the family hall earlier that afternoon with hay bales. Tables were set up with red and white checkered tablecloths. There was even a temporary wooden bar set up to make it look like an old time saloon.

She said hello to Tricia Newman, Melanie Parker, and Kimberly Schoenfeld, who were busy placing folding chairs around the tables. Jenna spotted Alex and Cleo over by the tables set up for the buffet. They wore matching fringed leather skirts and vests that they had no doubt rented from a costume store.

Jenna swallowed against the bitterness welling up in her throat as she wondered how she'd once again missed the memo on the matching outfits. As she got closer, she could see that Alex was on her phone, visibly upset. Beside her, Cleo wrung her hands, her brow furrowed with concern under the brim of her black cowboy hat.

"That's impossible." Alex snapped, then paused for the person on the other line to respond. "There's no way I did that." Another pause. "What the hell am I supposed to do? I have seventy five people coming in an hour." Her mouth tightened further at whatever the person said. "That's just great. You've been so incredibly helpful," her voice dripped with sarcasm. "I'll be sure to tell everyone I know about your unbelievable customer service."

"What's going on?" Jenna asked.

"That was the caterer," Alex said, her voice high and strained. "I called to ask why they're not here yet, and they told me that they received a call from me two days ago canceling the order."

Cleo let out a gasp.

Tricia, who was setting up chairs at a table nearby, called out, "Well at least if there's no food, no one can get sick."

"Thank you Tricia, that's very helpful," Cleo snapped.

"Did you?" Jenna said in a low voice.

Alex gave her an offended glare. "Of course I didn't. Why would you even ask that?"

Jenna shrugged. "Well, there was that time you took an Ambien after too many chardonnays and you-"

Jenna snapped her mouth shut as Alex's eyes went wide and she drew her finger across her mouth in "zip it" motion.

"Nevermind," Jenna mumbled.

"Okay, that's a story I definitely need to hear another time," Cleo chuckled. "In the meantime, what are we going to do?"

Alex took off her straw hat and ran a frustrated hand through her perfectly bouncy brown waves. "Hell if I know. The caterers said since I canceled the order two days ago, they didn't even buy all of the food. Not to mention, since its barbecue they would have had to start prepping hours ago."

Jenna's mind raced as she scrambled to figure out how to get food for seventy five people in less than an hour. "I could call Andale's and order a bunch of burritos with chips and guac."

Alex gave her a withering look. "People paid a hundred dollars a head for this party. We are not feeding them burritos from the overpriced taqueria where they already eat four times a week."

Jenna tried not to sink into herself and reminded herself that just because she wasn't as wealthy as her best friends, she wasn't exactly low rent.

Cleo held up a finger. "I have an idea." She rushed away in search of her purse as Alex and Jenna trailed after.

They listened to her side of the conversation. "Hey, Lauren, this is Cleo Baird. I met you last week at my daughter's swim lesson. Listen, I'm here at the Wyndham fundraiser and we've found ourselves in quite a bind."

Over the course of the next two minutes, Cleo got Lauren to agree to convince her brother to drive his very popular barbecue food truck over to Wyndham. Though he was initially resistant, Cleo sealed the deal when she promised to pay him double what he usually made on a good night.

When Alex heard that number she winced. "Cleo, that's way over our food budget."

Cleo waved her off. "Don't worry, I'm covering it. Consider it part of my donation."

"You're a lifesaver," Alex said as she threw her arms around Cleo.

Jenna pasted a smile on her face and tried not to dwell on how it must feel to be able to throw down a few thousand dollars without a single thought. "Yeah, that's really awesome. City Smoke's food is way better than the caterer's would have been anyway."

"Ok, now that that's sorted," Alex said, "We should go set up the bar."

The three of them started for the table stacked with cases of wine and boxes of rented wine glasses. Alex was called over by Melanie, who wanted her opinion on how she'd arranged the sign up sheets for all of the auction parties. Jenna and Cleo busied themselves lining up several rows of wine glasses and uncorking a few bottles.

By the time they were finished setting up, people were starting to arrive. It was mostly Wyndham families, but there were a handful of older parents whose children had graduated from the preschool program. Cleo and Jenna were instantly inundated with dozens of people looking to fill their glasses.

"Hey ladies," Jenna looked up and smiled at the sound of Ethan's voice. He was accompanied by David. Over their shoulders, she could see Alex and Morgan in a group of moms.

Ethan leaned over the table and kissed them both on the cheek as was his custom.

"Love the outfits," Cleo said. Ethan wore wrangler jeans, cowboy boots, a pearl snap shirt, and a black stetson hat. David's outfit was similar. "You're practically twins."

David laughed. "The big difference is that this guy actually had this in his closet," he pointed at Ethan. "Morgan ordered mine off Amazon earlier this week."

"Must be fun to bust out your ranching duds once in a while," Cleo said as she filled a glass of red wine for him.

Ethan shrugged. "It's funny to me how my childhood work attire is someone else's costume. Can I get a glass of that for Alex?" He pointed to the chardonnay.

"And I'll take one for Morgan," David said.

A few minutes after they left to deliver the wine, Cleo excused herself to take a phone call. "It's my babysitter," she said apologetically.

"Of course," Jenna shooed her away. "I can handle this."

Ethan reappeared at the front of the line, glass outstretched. "For Alex," he said.

She gave him a harried smile as she refilled it with. He left but returned moments later with his glass of red in hand. This time he joined her behind the table.

"Looks like you can use a hand," he said and refilled Tricia's proffered glass.

"You don't have to help me," she protested. "Go hang out, have fun."

"I don't mind. Alex is swarmed, as usual," he gestured with his chin to where Alex stood, surrounded. Cleo stood next to her, grinning like a proper sycophant. So much for that phone call. "And I'm not feeling that social tonight anyway."

"Really?" Jenna paused to refill a glass. Alex and Ethan were the life of every party. "That doesn't sound like you."

He shrugged. "I'm just feeling a little worn down. There's some stuff going on, and I'm feeling a little overwhelmed."

Jenna bit back a sound of surprise. In the three and a half years that she had known Ethan, she had never known him to be anywhere close to overwhelmed. She leaned forward to fill yet another glass. "Overwhelmed? Tell me about it."

He grinned, and as he did she noticed that the creases around his eyes seemed a little deeper than usual. "Oh, man, I can't even imagine." He wrapped his arm around her shoulders and pulled her in for a hug. "I remember how crazy the early days of Ignosi were, and Alex and I didn't even have kids."

She sighed and leaned into him. "Yeah, leave it to Mark to time the launch of his startup with the birth of our second kid. I mean, just being here for a couple hours kid free feels like a vacation."

"It'll get better, I promise." He gave her a brotherly kiss on the cheek. "And from what I know of Mark's product, it's going to be a game changer. Mark my words, in a couple of years, people are going to be banging on his door, asking *him* to invest in *their* ideas."

"From your mouth to God's ears." She stepped from his embrace and bent to grab a few more bottles of red from a box. Say what you would about the Wyndham parents, they were no teetotalers.

As she stood, she caught Cleo's gaze honed in on her and Ethan. She looked away as Jenna caught her eye and turned back to Alex with a serene smile.

The line for the bar had finally thinned out, so Jenna took the opportunity to pour herself a glass of Pinot Noir. She took a sip and sighed, "Goddamn that's good. I never get to drink red wine."

Ethan quirked a curious brow. "Do you have that thing where you're allergic to the histamines?"

Jenna shook her head and savored another delicious sip. "Have you met my children? If I drank red wine around them, every item of clothing I owned would look tie dyed. It's bad enough I almost always have a bodily fluid of some sort that's not mine smeared somewhere."

Ethan tilted his head back and laughed. Jenna chuckled as she looked out into the crowd. Once again, Cleo was watching them intently. Once again, she looked away as soon as Jenna noticed.

"What do you think of Cleo?"

Ethan shrugged. "Seems fine. Can't say that I feel like I know her very well. Alex is certainly enamored. Why?"

Jenna shrugged. "There's something about her that just feels kind of off to me. I can't put my finger on it. It's like she's-"

"Attention everyone! Can I please have your attention!" Alex's voice over the PA system prevented her from continuing. "If you haven't checked out the food yet, I encourage you to go now. The City Smoke truck will only be here for another half an hour, and the auction will begin promptly at 8:30."

Jenna and Ethan decided that people could pour their own wine and went to retrieve plates of food. They joined Alex, Cleo, and David at a table. Morgan joined them shortly after, having swiped a bottle each of pinot noir and chardonnay from the bar. Jenna attacked her plate of brisket, Cole slaw and cornbread with gusto, grateful for once to eat a plate of food without having grubby little hands reaching for it. She started to wave off Ethan when he went to refill her glass, then decided why not. Enough people here lived in her direction she could catch a ride home if she drank too much.

Their table quickly went through the two bottles of wine and Alex went to retrieve two more. Soon those were empty too and Jenna was feeling decidedly buzzed.

"What do you guys think of bidding on the Gilbert's house in Northstar?" Morgan gestured with her copy of the auction catalog. Every year several families offered up stays at their second homes in places like Tahoe, Hawaii, and Mexico, for the Wyndham party goers to bid on.

Jenna read the description of the 6 bedroom house in one of the most exclusive areas of the Northstar ski area. Even if they split it four ways, the starting bid alone was enough to make Jenna blanche.

"Ooh, definitely," Morgan said.

"Sounds awesome," Cleo said. "I also want to do this winemaker's dinner," she said, pointing to her catalog. She looked at Jenna expectantly.

Jenna took a swig of her wine and pasted a smile on her face. "Mark and I didn't have a chance to talk about our auction budget before I left, so I can't commit right now." She didn't have to ask Mark to know that a $500 per head dinner plus the cost of babysitting wasn't in their budget right now.

"Speaking of bidding, I better get up there," Alex said as she stood. She paused for a moment, swaying a little on her feet.

"Are you ok?" Jenna asked.

Alex shook her head and smoothed the front of her shirt. "I'm fine. I must have stood up too fast."

She caught Ethan's skeptical look as he eyed Alex's empty wine glass. Alex had only had a couple of glasses. Jenna knew from years of experience that she could drink more wine than that before she showed any signs of inebriation.

Alex made her way to the small stage that had been erected at the front of the hall and once again took to the microphone.

"Hello again everyone! I hope you enjoyed the food."

Murmurs of approval rippled through the crowd.

"You can all thank Cleo for saving our asses when the catering fell through."

Jenna felt a spike of alarm as the word "asses" came out more like "ashes."

"Now, if you'll give us your atten-" Alex paused, once again swaying on her feet. "Your atteshon," she clutched the microphone and staggered back a few steps.

"She's so drunk she can barely talk," Jenna heard someone whisper.

"What the hell," Ethan said through clenched teeth as he stood from his chair.

More mutterings rose from the crowd as Alex tried to regain her composure. "Sorry, everyone I'm jusht feeling a lil funny." A loud gasp erupted as Alex pitched to the side and went crashing down on the stage.

Ethan ran to her, followed closely by David. Katrina Sutherland, who was a doctor, quickly joined them. Once Katrina was satisfied that Alex hadn't sustained a head or neck injury, Ethan and David carried a conscious but still incoherent Alex out of the family hall. Jenna, Cleo and Morgan trailed after them as they carried her into the school lobby.

Through the closed door, she could hear Tricia on the microphone telling everyone to quiet down so they could get back to the auction.

Good old Tricia, keeping everyone on task.

Ethan and David carried Alex to the couch, where she slumped bonelessly in the corner.

"Alex, are you ok?" Cleo knelt in front of her and grabbed her hand.

Alex answered with a nonsensical mumble.

"She's fine, she's just wasted," Ethan said tightly.

"Are you sure?" Cleo said, eyes wide with concern. "I don't think she had any more to drink than normal."

"But if you mix wine with other stuff, anything can happen," Ethan snapped. He hefted Alex to her feet and hoisted her over his shoulder in a fireman's carry.

Jenna's brow furrowed as they all followed him out to his Range Rover. She knew Alex had struggled with insomnia, hence the Ambien prescription. But she'd never known her to take any other pills. "If she's mixed wine with something, shouldn't she go to the hospital?"

Ethan gestured for Cleo to open the passenger door and poured Alex into the seat. "She just needs to sleep it off," he snapped.

"But isn't that how, like, every celebrity dies?" Jenna protested.

"I'm not too worried about that," Ethan said. "But I'll keep an eye on her." He slammed the passenger door with more force than necessary, then climbed into the driver's seat. As he peeled out of the parking lot, Jenna wondered how many other secrets Alex might be keeping from her.

16

Alex

Alex woke up the next morning with a pounding headache and a mouth that felt stuffed full of cotton. The other side of the bed was not only empty, but the sheets and bedspread were still pulled tight. Where had Ethan slept? Had they had a fight? She dragged herself to the bathroom, gulped down water from the tap, then splashed cold water on her face. As she looked at her ruddy face and bloodshot eyes, she tried to think back to the prior evening.

A wave of panic surged to her chest as she realized she couldn't remember anything after she sat down to eat.

She went back to her bedside table to retrieve her phone. She already had a dozen messages and several missed calls. Her alarm increased when she saw that all of the messages were in the vein of, "are you ok?" "Do you know what happened?" "Did you go to the ER?"

"Ethan? Are you here?" When he didn't answer, she went looking and found him in their home gym. Ava sat on a weight bench while he grunted his way through a set of shoulder presses.

"Hey," she said, waving to get his attention as his AirPods pumped music into his ears.

Her stomach dropped to her feet at the stony expression that overtook his face when he noticed her.

"What happened last night?"

He finished his set, ignoring her. When he was done, he set the weights back on the rack and clicked the stem of his AirPods to pause the music. "We'll talk about it later. Right now you need to get Ava fed and ready for school."

"But I need to know what happened-"

He raised a hand, cutting her off. "You embarrassed the hell out of us, that's what happened. But I don't want to go into details in front of Ava. So if you would leave me to finish my work out in peace, I would appreciate it."

"It was weird," Cleo, who she called immediately after getting Ava settled in her booster and putting a plate of eggs and toast in front of her, said. "One minute you were fine, and then you were completely out of it. You seriously don't remember anything?"

Alex swallowed hard around the lump in her throat. "The last thing I remember was sitting down to eat. Did I really drink that much?"

"No more than usual that I could tell. But when you got up to go on stage, you were weaving a little. And when you got up there, it was clear you were fucked up as soon as you started talking."

"I got up on stage?" Her head felt like it was going to spontaneously combust from embarrassment. The feeling only grew as Cleo detailed how she had keeled over in front of everyone.

First she gave everyone food poisoning, then she appeared to be completely inebriated at a preschool function. No matter what happened from hereon out, she was forever going to be known as *that mom*.

Ethan finished his workout and came into the kitchen. Without sparing her even a glance, he took out a canister of protein powder and a shaker from the cabinet. He mixed the protein powder with water and stood at the sink, his back to her as the sound of the shaker filled the kitchen. Alex told Cleo she had to go and ended the call.

"I'm done," Ava said and tried to rise up from her booster as she fumbled at the clasp.

"Eat a few more bites of your eggs," Alex urged as she snuck a glance at her husband.

Ava started to fuss in earnest. Alex, too tired and out of sorts to do battle, relented and unclipped her from the booster.

She told Ava to go into her room to pick out an outfit and took the plastic plate full of her half-eaten breakfast over to the sink. Ethan pointedly stepped away as she came up beside him.

She let out a frustrated sigh. "Ethan, I get that you're upset with me, but think about how I feel."

He finally looked at her, dark eyes full of disdain. "Why should I care how you feel when you fucking humiliated our family in front of the whole goddamn school! Those aren't just our friends. They're also my work colleagues and contacts."

Alex brought a hand to her chest as though that could soothe the ache of the blow his words delivered. She passed out for seemingly no reason, and all he could focus on was his embarrassment? "Ethan, don't you think I'm humiliated too? And not just that, I'm scared. I mean, I fainted out of nowhere and have no memory-"

"Oh really, you fainted out of nowhere?" He threw his empty shaker into the sink, hard enough to send the last dregs of his shake splattering across the porcelain. "Bullshit. You don't deserve to be scared when you did this to yourself."

He turned and stomped out of the kitchen. She followed him, sputtering. "What are you even talking about? What do you mean I did this to myself?"

He ignored her, continuing his march down the hall, through their bedroom and into the bathroom. He opened the middle drawer of the vanity and fumbled through the collection of medications they stored there. He withdrew a bottle and held it up. "This is what I'm talking about."

He threw the bottle at her but she was so stunned it bounced off her chest before she could catch it. She bent to pick it up from the floor. It was Xanax. Alex had initially obtained the prescription from her primary care doctor when she'd developed anxiety while she and Ethan were going through IVF.

"I told you Alex, after the last time, I'm not going to put up with this kind of thing."

Alex's face went hot as she remembered the incident in question. It was the day after their second egg retrieval, and they still hadn't heard back from the doctor how many, if any, would be viable for fertilization. Work was also particularly stressful as her company prepared for a major product launch. The prospect of dinner with the chairman of Ethan's board was the last straw that sent her spiraling.

Before she met Ethan, she stopped home and took one pill. When that didn't seem to help, she took another and chased it with a generous glass of chardonnay. Sure, she knew that mixing benzos and alcohol was risky, but she was a substantial woman with a high tolerance.

Much like this morning, she woke up the next morning with no memory after that first sip of wine. The difference was that instead of waking up in her own bed, that time she woke up in the hospital. Ethan sat at her bedside, his eyes watery and complexion wan after what must have been a sleepless night. A psychiatrist was called in to evaluate her and make sure this was indeed an accident. Shortly after that Alex was cleared to go home.

Though Ethan had been the epitome of the solicitous husband in front of the nurses and the doctor who discharged her, she'd barely closed the car door before he laid into her.

"How could you be so stupid? Mixing Xanax with alcohol? That's how people die, Alex!"

"I only had one glass of wine," she fought to get the words out through lips that still felt a little rubbery. "I didn't think it would hit me that hard."

"And there I am, sitting alone like an asshole with Mitchell and his wife, making awkward conversation as it becomes increasingly clear my wife is standing us up."

"I'm sorry," she said meekly. "I promise it won't happen again."

"It better not," he replied. "I'm not going to spend thousands of dollars conceiving children with someone who has a pill problem."

Tears poured down Alex's cheeks as she absorbed the blow.

"Fuck," Ethan muttered as he reached over to grab her hand. "I'm sorry. I don't mean that."

"You sure about that?" Alex tried and failed to hold back a sob.

Ethan pulled his Audi sedan over to the side of the road and put it into park. "I love you, Alex, more than anything. I'm sorry I'm lashing out, but I was so fucking scared." All of the anger left his face, replaced by fear. "I was already worried when I left the restaurant, but when I walked in and saw you on the couch," he paused as his voice caught, "and then when you didn't respond-" his eyes flooded with tears and his breath jerked in his chest.

They reached for each other simultaneously. The seatbelts hampered their progress. Their watery chuckles filled the car as they unclipped themselves.

Alex practically flung herself over the center console, not caring that the steering wheel dug into her side as he pulled her to him.

She closed her eyes and snuggled against his chest. She breathed in his familiar scent of Tom Ford cologne, clean laundry and his own particular musk, a little sharper after a sleepless night in the ER.

"I'm so sorry I scared you," she murmured.

"It's just that I love you so much," his arms tightened around her and she felt the press of his lips against the top of her head. "The idea that I could lose you…" His voice trailed off as his body shuddered at the thought. He was silent a few moments, then drew back so he could look at her face. "Were you telling the truth? When you told the doctor this was a complete accident?"

"Of course I was telling the truth." She leaned up to land a tender kiss on his mouth. "I promise you, I'm not suicidal. I was just really stressed about the retrieval, and work. Then I started freaking out and couldn't stop and knew that I wouldn't be able to act normal at dinner. I just wanted to take the edge off."

His mouth pulled into a grin. "You did more than take the edge off. You turned yourself into a nerf ball." It was then that Ethan told her he thought she should quit her job. Clearly she wasn't capable of handling the stress on top of the IVF process. She tried to protest, but in the end she couldn't deny what had just happened.

When they got home, he tucked her into bed, then stripped off his clothes and joined her. Before long they were ignoring the doctor's admonition to take it easy.

Looking at Ethan's face now, Alex knew today's incident would not have such a romantic ending.

"Ethan, I swear, it wasn't like that this time. I don't know what happened. I must have had a bad reaction to the wine. Or maybe I didn't eat enough-"

He glowered and held his hand up. "Cut the bullshit, Alex. Are you going to tell me, if I make you pee in a cup, you won't test positive for benzos?"

Alex dropped her gaze to the floor. After her learning her lesson not to overdo it, Alex had kept her prescription current. She usually limited herself to half a Xanax at a time, never more than one. The lead up to the auction had her more stressed than usual, so she'd been taking a pill nearly every day. Certainly not enough to have her keeling over, even after a few glasses of wine.

But enough to show up on a drug test.

"That's what I thought. Now if you don't mind, I'd like some privacy so I can shower before I take Ava to school."

Her brow furrowed in confusion. Unless there was a special event, Ethan never took Ava because it was in the opposite direction of his office.

"Why-"

"I don't think I want you driving my daughter around," he snapped before she could even form her question. "I don't trust you to be safe."

As she reeled from that blow, he took her by the shoulders and guided her out of the bathroom.

"Get Ava dressed. I'm leaving in fifteen minutes."

He slammed the door in her face. The click of the lock echoed through her closet like a gunshot.

17

Cleo

"Thank you everyone, for meeting on such short notice. But in light of what happened last Thursday, it's of utmost importance that we address the issue as soon as possible." It was the Monday after the fundraiser, and the issue Tricia was referring to was to boot Alex off of the Wyndham board before she further embarrassed herself and the school.

Cleo sat next to Alex, who looked uncharacteristically unkempt. Her hair was in its usual messy bun, but instead of looking fashionably tousled, today it looked like a rat's nest piled on her head. Dark circles ringed her eyes, and there was a smear of what might have been egg yolk on her overpriced yoga pants.

Cleo could feel the tension radiating off of her body as Tricia made a formal motion to have Alex removed as the president of the Wyndham board. "All of those in favor?"

Of the eight board members, only Alex, Jenna, and Cleo voted no.

"You must understand why this needs to happen," Tricia said, oozing faux sympathy. For all that she pretended to be devastated on behalf of Alex, it was clear she was reveling in watching the queen bee's downfall.

"Honestly, I don't," Alex said, unable to keep the quiver out of her voice. "I've been under a lot of stress lately and not sleeping well, which made my usual consumption of my prescription anti anxiety medication and a few glasses of wine hit a lot harder than usual. It could have happened to any one of us."

Actually, it really couldn't have, because Alex's was the only glass of wine Cleo had spiked.

She watched as Alex looked at the other board members, blinking back tears as, one by one, they dropped their gazes, unable to look her in the eye.

Jenna, who sat on Alex's other side, reached over and gave her arm a squeeze. She didn't always attend meetings due to childcare issues, but she had showed up today to provide Alex with extra support.

She was a true friend to Alex. Which was why Cleo needed to work harder at getting her out of Alex's life.

"Alex, you were visibly, obnoxiously intoxicated in front of school families and community members. It would be embarrassing enough to have a member of the school community behaving that way. But the president of our board? Right before we go into enrollment season? You're drunken antics are not they kind of publicity we need."

A deep red flush crept up Alex's neck and bloomed in her cheeks. "After everything I've done for this school, all of the financial support we've given, you're kicking me off because of one little mistake?" Her voice broke at last, and she collapsed into heaving sobs.

Cleo and Jenna put their arms around her shoulders while everyone else looked on in discomfort. She almost felt sorry for Alex in that moment, knowing how humiliated she must feel. But she was taking too much pleasure from watching Alex fray at the seams to have any sympathy.

"I'm sorry, Alex. The board has voted." She gestured at the other women seated around the table. This time there was a hint of sincerity in her sympathetic expression. She adjourned the meeting and everyone stood and started for the door. Several people approached Alex and offered awkward words of comfort. Alex stood there, stoic, nodding or offering a tight smile in response.

As everyone started for the parking lot, Cleo and Jenna hung back with Alex.

"I can't believe this," Alex fumed. "I can't believe that fucking bitch-"

Alex snapped her mouth closed as Tricia appeared in the doorway. It was clear she had heard Alex start to rave and knew exactly who Alex was calling a bitch.

Nevertheless, she pasted a look of concern on her face as she approached. "I'm sorry to interrupt," she began as they gave her their attention, "but I just wanted to say, if you decide you want to get help, I know of an amazing facility in Pennsylvania."

She reached out and put a hand on Alex's forearm. Cleo could feel Alex fighting not to shake it off.

"They literally saved my sister's life." She removed her hand from Alex's arm and took her phone out of her pocket. "I'm texting you the website right now." Alex's phone chimed in confirmation.

"Thank you Tricia, that's very kind," Alex all but snarled. Tricia nodded and left them with a little wave.

As soon as Tricia was out of sight, Alex leaned toward them and said in a harsh whisper, "Can you fucking believe her?"

"She's just trying to be helpful," Jenna offered. "If you think you have a problem, it might be a good place to get help."

Alex's bloodshot eyes narrowed into a glare. "Are you kidding me, Jenna? Do you actually think I have a drug and alcohol problem? Does everyone think I'm a junkie?"

"Of course not," Cleo said, "certainly not *everyone*." Alex's eyes widened and Cleo had to fight to suppress a smile at her visible distress.

"Who? Who else thinks I'm an addict?"

"It doesn't matter," Jenna said and shot a look at Cleo that said she should have kept her mouth shut.

Cleo pulled her face into a grimace and mouthed a silent apology.

"Why can't anyone just believe that I had a bad reaction to medication that I'm normally able to handle? I had one Xanax at four o'clock, and didn't even have my first glass of wine until after six. That shouldn't be enough to knock me over, but for some reason that night it did."

Actually, Cleo thought, Alex had ingested a dose of GHB at around seven. That's when Cleo had spiked her chardonnay with enough of the drug to knock someone Ethan's size on his ass. Alex could have drunk less than half of that glass and still wouldn't have stood a chance.

"And yeah, I was drinking," Alex continued, "but it wasn't any more than any other festive night."

"Sometimes if I'm not paying attention and my glass just keeps getting topped off, it's easy for me to lose track of how much I've had," Jenna said, one eyebrow cocked.

"Even so, that shouldn't have been enough to make you black out," Cleo protested.

"I don't know," Jenna said with a shrug. "All I know is it was an insane night. I'm so sorry you have to go through this." She reached out and gave Alex a firm hug. As she pulled away, she glanced at her phone and grimaced. "Crap, I told the babysitter I'd be back by noon."

Cleo looked at her phone and saw that it was already five past. As Jenna hurried out, Cleo asked Alex if she wanted to have lunch.

"Sure," Alex said without enthusiasm. "But I can't go to the club. I can't deal with running into people right now."

In the end they decided Cleo would pick up food to go and bring it back to Alex's. Alex requested the nicoise salad and an order of onion rings. "I've got a lot of feelings I need to eat," she said with a feeble laugh.

Cleo ordered over the internet, choosing the club's Thai crunch salad for herself. She left Alex to go pick up their food. When she returned she found Alex sitting at the kitchen table, a wineglass full of chardonnay in front of her.

"Don't judge," she said tightly. She took the bag of food from Cleo and grabbed the container of onion rings. She retrieved a bottle of ketchup from the refrigerator, took it back to the table and sat down. The aroma of fried onions made Cleo's stomach growl as Alex opened the cardboard container and squirted a hefty amount of ketchup into it. She took an onion, dipped it in the ketchup, and bit into it with a pleasured sigh. As she chased it with a healthy gulp of Chardonnay, Cleo retrieved forks and bowls for their salads. Alex might not be in a good place, but there was no reason to eat straight out of the to-go containers like a couple of animals.

"How are you holding up?" She placed a bowl and a fork in front of Alex, along with her box of salad, then took a seat across from her. She opened her salad and poured half of it into her bowl, then dressed it from the plastic container that had come with the salad.

"Honestly, I feel like I'm losing my grip," she said as she dropped an onion ring, half eaten, back into the box. "I don't know what's happening, but it's like everything is spinning out of control."

Cleo took a bite of her salad and nodded sympathetically as Alex continued. "First there was the Halloween catastrophe. Then on Thursday that whole thing with the caterers." She shook her head, dropped her gaze to the table, and was silent for several moments. When she once again met Cleo's eyes, her gaze was troubled. "If I tell you something, will you promise not to tell another soul?"

Cleo put down her fork, sat up, and nodded. "You know I'm a vault." Well, until it was time to weaponize whatever secret Alex was about to divulge.

Alex leaned over the table, and even though they were the only ones in the house, when she spoke, her voice was barely over a whisper. "You know how the caterer said I called to cancel the order?"

Cleo nodded.

"I looked through my email, and there's a thread where I confirmed again last Monday. Just to prove them wrong, I decided to check my call log. According to it, I called them on Wednesday afternoon." She placed her palms on the table and raised her eyebrows. "I have no memory of making that call."

Of course she didn't, because Cleo had made the call when she and Izzy were over on Wednesday afternoon. Alex had left her phone in the family room while she went to the bathroom. She really was quite careless when entering her passcode.

"That's...concerning," Cleo said, and conjured up her very best worried face. "But you were making so many calls, handling all of the details for the party, you wouldn't necessarily remember all of them."

"That may be true, but you'd think if I called the caterer to cancel, that one would stick out more than most." Alex sighed, opened her salad, and poured the entire contents into her bowl. She poured the vinaigrette over the top and gave it a stir. She forked a bite of tuna and greens into her mouth and chewed like she was choking down a bite of hardtack. "And there's stuff going on with Ethan lately."

"What kind of stuff?"

Alex put down her fork and slumped in her chair. "I don't know, he's just been being kind of mean to me."

Cleo cocked a curious eyebrow, barely able to contain her glee. "Ethan? I can't imagine him being mean to you." That was a lie. She knew guys like Ethan, so handsome, charming and charismatic, seeming to dote on their wives and families. But under that perfect surface was a black hole of insecurity. The minute you didn't give a guy like Ethan exactly what he thought he deserved, or threatened his ego in any way, he would turn on you.

"Well first of all, he wasn't even worried that something might be wrong. He was just really, really angry at me for humiliating myself, and therefore him." She reached for her glass and drained the last of her wine. "I literally collapsed. You would think he'd be a little concerned."

"So he thinks it's your fault for mixing Xanax with alcohol."

Alex nodded, her face downcast. "And did I tell you he wouldn't let me drive Ava to school Friday because he wasn't sure I was safe?" She raised her hands to make air quotes. "As if I would ever drive Ava while I was impaired in any way."

All of the wine consumed at their weekly playdates would suggest otherwise. Cleo pulled her face into a sympathetic grimace. "Yikes. That had to sting. Have you guys made up?" She took a bite of salad as she waited for Alex to answer.

Alex shook her head. "Not really. He's barely talked to me since Friday. He puts on a good act for Ava, but if she's not around and I walk into a room he pretends I'm not there."

"Wow, that is mean," Cleo said. It took everything she had to keep the snark out of her tone. *Really Alex? You think a lack of concern for your seemingly drunk ass and giving you the silent treatment is mean? Mean is your husband slapping you so hard your ears ring because you made a joke about his ugly ass Hawaiian shirt. Mean is him forcing you to have sex with two of his "business associates" while he watches. Mean is him slamming you against a wall and choking you until you pass out in front of your two year old daughter.*

Cleo had put up with plenty of meanness at the hands of Izzy's father. But in the end, Cleo had given him the ending he deserved.

She let none of the bitterness seething in her gut show on her face as she reached over to give Alex's shoulder a squeeze. "I'm sure he'll get over it soon. There's no way he'll stay mad at you forever."

"I hope not," Alex said with a heavy sigh. "But maybe he will. He's never acted like this before."

"What are you talking about? Ethan adores you. You guys have, like, the perfect marriage."

Alex let out a sound that was half laugh, half sob and stood from her chair. "That's what I thought," she said as she went to the refrigerator to retrieve more wine. She refilled her glass and gestured the bottle to Cleo.

Cleo waved her off.

Alex plonked the bottle on the table and sat back down. "Honestly, something's been off with Ethan for the past few months."

"How so?" Cleo asked, careful not to sound too eager to hear about all of the cracks in Alex's seemingly perfect marriage.

"It's hard to put my finger on, but there's a distance between us, and I can't quite figure out how it formed."

"That's very common when we have kids. A lot of the attention we used to give our husbands goes to the kids."

"Yeah, but Ava's three and we've been fine up until recently. Believe me, I'm very aware of how much attention Ethan needs and I make sure to give it to him. But it's not just the distance. He's on edge and irritable. He's definitely been like that in the past, but that was when he was first starting his company and then when we were going through IVF. It was a lot of stress for both of us. But now?" She paused to take a sip of wine. "We're golden." She gestured around her state of the art kitchen. "We're completely set financially, we have a beautiful daughter and his job is basically like a hobby he gets paid for. We have an amazing life. There's nothing for him to be stressed about."

Of course, Alex couldn't entertain the idea of having a life that was anything less than perfect. How could she, when everything she wanted had always just fallen into her lap?

"Do you think maybe, there might be something else going on?"

Alex's brow furrowed. "Such as?"

"In the past, with some of my friends, when their husbands started acting weird or distant," Cleo spoke slowly, as though she were choosing her words carefully, "often it was because there was someone else in the picture."

Alex sat up straight at that, offended at the thought. "No. Absolutely not. Ethan would never, ever cheat on me."

Cleo held her hands up, palms out. "I'm sorry. I'm not saying that I think he actually is, just that I've had friends whose husbands started acting like Ethan. And it turned out it was because their husbands were cheating on them."

"Well, it's ridiculous to even think that Ethan would do that. You haven't known Ethan that long, but if you did, you'd know that he is one of the most straight up, ethical people you will ever meet. I mean, when Morgan and I first met him in business school we nicknamed him Dudley Doright."

Cleo nodded as though she agreed. "Okay, okay I hear you. And I'm glad you're so sure about his fidelity." She fell silent and played around with the salad left in her bowl while Alex picked at her own. She made a show of starting to say something, then stopping herself, until finally Alex took the bait.

"What is it?" Alex asked sharply.

Cleo dropped her fork with a clang. "I don't even know if I should say anything."

"About what?" Alex said through clenched teeth.

"Look, I know I'm new to this group, and I don't fully understand the dynamics between all of you but…." She paused and took a deep breath, as though bracing herself for Alex's reaction. "Do you ever worry about Ethan and Jenna?"

Alex started as though she'd been zapped with a cattle prod. "Are you crazy? No! We're all just good friends, and Jenna would never do that to me. And neither would Ethan, for that matter!"

"I'm sorry, I shouldn't have said anything. It's just that sometimes when we've hung out, I thought I sensed a certain vibe between them."

"Well you're wrong," Alex stood up, grabbed her bowl, and carried it to the sink. "There is no 'vibe.' Ethan thinks of Jenna as his sister."

Cleo knew she was walking a fine line. Depending on how she handled this, Alex would either see her as a good friend and would value her honesty, or she would see her as a shit stirrer trying to create drama with Jenna. "I'm sorry, I must have misread the situation. Honestly, I haven't had male friends for so long, it's hard for me to not to read any sort of affection as romantic interest. I'm really sorry I even had the thought, much less put it out there."

Alex turned and gave her a tight smile. "I'm sorry I got angry. I know you were just saying it out of concern. It's funny, I feel so close to you that sometimes I forget we only met a few months ago."

"Yeah, and even though I feel like I know you so well, I'm still trying to figure out Jenna and everyone else." She picked up her bowl and carried it to the sink. She turned to Alex and gave her a reassuring hug. "I'm sure everything will sort itself out with Ethan. He obviously adores you. Just give him time. And extra blowjobs."

"The way to every man's heart," Alex chuckled.

Despite her laugh, Cleo could see the flash of doubt in her eyes. The seed was planted. And no matter how hard Alex tried, she'd never be able to uproot it. It would linger, festering, spreading its poison to everything she held dear. Casting an inescapable shadow on her seemingly perfect life.

18

Alex

As they got deeper into December and the holiday craze took over their lives, Alex, Morgan, Jenna, and Cleo scattered to different corners of the country (or in Cleo's case, to a resort in Thailand).

Unlike last year, when the friends had all gone in on a house in Tahoe for the week between Christmas and New Years, this year Alex and Ethan rented a house in Maui and invited Ethan's parents, his six siblings, and their families to join. Anyone observing them would have thought it was idyllic. All the little cousins frolicked on the beach under the watchful eyes of the two babysitters they had hired. The adults relaxed with umbrella cocktails, laughing and enjoying each others 'company.

Ethan would reach over periodically to take Alex's hand and kiss it, or give her back a little rub as he walked by. The vacation sex was, as always, a little more frequent and interesting. Maybe because of it, or specifically because Alex had followed Cleo's advice and offered up some bonus blow jobs, Ethan was softer and less irritable, more like his usual self.

And yet, no matter how hard she tried, she couldn't get what Cleo said out of her head. She could be having a perfect moment with her husband and his family, and suddenly her brain would zoom in on the possibility of Ethan having an affair with one of her best friends. It was like when you had a sore in your mouth and you couldn't keep your tongue from it.

The worst part was, she couldn't really talk to anyone except for Cleo, and she was seventeen hours ahead of her.

The thought nagged at her all through the trip, as she found herself on high alert every time Ethan got a call or a text. By the time they got back home she couldn't take it anymore. Even though she never imagined she would ever do such a thing, in an act of desperation she waited until he was asleep one night to do a deep dive into his phone.

To her relief, the only texts from Jenna were all group chats in which Alex was included as well. Any texts from any other women appeared to be work related.

It's entirely possible he has another phone, a nasty little voice whispered. Unable to silence it, she went into the phone settings and set it so he was sharing his location with her.

She placed the phone carefully back on his nightstand and crawled into bed with him, stomach churning against the idea that her husband could be cheating on her.

As school started again and they settled back into their routines, she checked Ethan's location several times a day. If Ethan and Jenna were around each other, she eyed them carefully, trying to pick up on any kind of sexual vibe. Did Ethan's lips linger a little too long when he gave her his customary kiss on the cheek? Was his hand on her back just a little too intimate?

She couldn't pick up on anything. And yet… Then, in the second week of January, Ethan said he would be home late because he had a business dinner. That in itself wasn't unusual. But when she checked his location, she saw that he was at a hotel in Menlo Park.

Her stomach dropped to her ankles and she let out an audible gasp. She tried to call him, but it went to voicemail. *It's not unusual for him to have his phone on do not disturb during a meeting,* she reminded herself. "Hey, just wondering when you'll be home. I was going to start that new Netflix show but I'll wait to watch it with you if you're going to be home early enough." Lame, but it was all she could come up with as her mind spun out of control.

By the time he got home a little after ten, Alex felt like she was coming out of her skin. At the first scrape of his key in the lock, she was up and moving to the front door.

"Hey," he said, a little surprised to find her right in front of him. "I thought you'd be in bed already."

Were you hoping not to have to look me in the eye right after you were with another woman?

She shoved the thought out of her head as he pulled her in his arms and gave her a lingering kiss. She leaned into him, and when he lifted his head she buried her face against his chest and took a deep inhale.

He smelled like his usual self. No unfamiliar perfume or women's shampoo could be detected.

"How was the dinner?" She asked as she pulled away and walked toward the kitchen.

"It was fine," he answered behind her.

"Who was it with?"

He stared at her blankly for a half second. The knot in her stomach tightened as she wondered if he was scrambling for a cover story. "It was with the co-founders of Synquest." He went to the bar and poured himself a bourbon.

Though she didn't need any more to drink, Alex took that as her cue to open another bottle of chardonnay. "Yeah? What do they do?"

"It's actually pretty cool." Alex's brain couldn't take in any information about the company's bleeding edge technology as it was too busy buzzing with the question of why he would be meeting with two tech nerds at a hotel.

Finally she couldn't take it any more, and when Ethan took a pause, she blurted, "Why did you meet them at the Standard Hotel?"

Ethan took a sip of his drink and frowned. "We had dinner at Oak and Violet, the new restaurant that just opened there. It's nice. We should go sometime." He started to move to the couch then stopped, his eyes narrowing as they landed on her face. "Wait, why would you think I was at the hotel? How did you even know I was there in the first place?"

Alex took a bracing sip of wine and set the glass on the counter. She felt equal parts stupid and guilty as she confessed, "I snooped through your phone and turned on the location sharing."

"Why would you snoop through my phone?" He sounded genuinely offended.

She swallowed hard. "I was worried you were having an affair." She didn't bother mentioning Jenna specifically. He would never be able to hang out with her and Mark again without it being awkward.

"What? That's insane. Why would you ever think I was having an affair?" His tone suggested that it was the most foolish notion she could possibly dream up.

Alex wanted to sink into the floor. "I don't know, you've just been different the last few months. You're short tempered and even though you seem to have gotten over your anger about the fundraiser, you still seem irritated with me a lot of the time. And it would be really easy to use all of your business dinners as cover..." she trailed off, unable to bear how lame it sounded. Did she really believe that just because he was in a bad mood he was cheating on her?

"Come here," He set down his glass and reached for her. Alex practically flung herself into his arms, a wave of relief washing through her as he held her tightly. "Honey, I'm not cheating on you, I promise."

"I know. I'm sorry I went there." She closed her eyes and burrowed against his chest.

"I know with your history, it's hard for you to trust. But I love you, I love our family, and I love our life. I would never in a million years do anything to risk losing all of that." He pressed a kiss to the top of her head. Then he cupped her cheek in his hand, tilted her face up to his. "You're the only woman I want to have sex with."

"Promise?"

"Promise." Of course that wasn't true. No matter how in love two people were, they always thought about having sex with other people. But as long as he didn't act on it, she had nothing to worry about.

She leaned up to plant a lusty kiss on his mouth. "Then prove it."

19

Morgan

Morgan tapped the keycard against the door lock. The lock flashed green and clicked as it unlocked. She pushed open the heavy door and stepped into the hotel room. It wasn't anything special, just a king bed, a dresser with a flat screen tv perched on top, and some generic art on the walls. But it was clean, and more importantly, close enough to her office to be convenient, but far enough out of her regular orbit to mitigate the risk of running into anyone she knew.

She was glad she was a few minutes early, giving her a chance to touch up her makeup and smooth her hair. Not that it wouldn't look like she'd been through a hurricane when all was said and done, but she liked to start out looking nice.

Her body hummed with anticipation, as though it had been weeks instead of just a few days since they'd been able to sneak away. A memory of the other night flooded her brain, making her instantly wet.

There was a soft tap on the door. Lust curled in her belly as she went to answer. She barely got it open before he had her pinned against the wall, his mouth hungry on hers. One hand tangled in her hair while the other hooked her knee over his hip so he could grind himself against her. She let out a gasp at the firm pressure as her fingers fumbled with the buttons of his shirt.

"You're so fucking hot," he groaned as he reached around to unzip her red sheath dress. He shoved it down her shoulders, leaving her in only her la Perla bra and panties and nude Prada heels. Normally she would have snatched the dress up and hung it neatly in the closet, but such was her lust for Ethan that she didn't care that her eight hundred dollar dress was crumpled at her feet.

"Do you know how crazy you drive me," he said, kissing her and running his hands over her body as he steered her toward the bed, "prancing around the office in your tight dresses and high heels?" He urged her onto the bed, where she lay on her back while he paused to shove his shirt from his shoulders and unfasten his slacks. "Do you have any idea how many times I wanted to bend you over a desk and fuck your brains out?"

He shoved his pants and boxers down his legs and proceeded to do exactly that.

After he came with a loud bellow and rolled off of her, he wrapped his arm around her shoulders and tucked her against his side. This was a relatively newer part of their routine. The first time they'd had sex, it was in a hotel in San Francisco. They were staying in the city for an investment banking conference. The hour had gone late, the alcohol had flowed, and somehow they ended up back in her room with yet another bottle of wine reminiscing about their business school days. Somewhere in all of that, Morgan confessed that she'd always had a little bit of a crush on him.

She'd never intended to sleep with Ethan. He was not only her best friend's husband but also her coworker. But she had, and she couldn't unring that bell. But they'd tried. That night, it was as though their orgasms were like buckets of cold water, sobering them up instantaneously. Ethan leapt from the bed as though he'd been electrocuted, scrambled for his clothes, and left mumbling something about how they needed to act like it never happened.

The next time he left just as quickly, and the next time after that. But eventually he had started lingering like this, holding her snuggled to his side. Now they spent as much time cuddling and talking as they did fucking.

She sighed and rested her head against his shoulder, her body pleasantly achy. Fucking Ethan always left her like she'd just done a cross fit workout. She ran her hand over his chest, appreciating the thick mat of hair and heavy muscles. So different from David's smooth chest and lean frame. Ethan was rugged power while David was refined sophistication. Objectively David was the more skilled lover, one who devoted a lot of time and technique in pursuit of his partner's pleasure.

But there was something about Ethan's big, strong body and his almost brutish approach that turned her on in a way that she hadn't been in years.

His phone buzzed, indicating an incoming call. He leaned over her to reach for his pants where they lay in a pile on the floor. He tugged the phone out of his pocket, hit the accept button and put it to his ear. "Hey sweet cheeks, what's up?"

Morgan stared at the ceiling as she listened to Ethan tell Alex that he was having a lunch meeting with a Phd out of Stanford who was working on a new idea for CRISPR technology use in agriculture." There was absolutely no hitch, no hesitation in his voice as he fabricated not just a business lunch, but also a person and a technology that didn't exist.

"Yeah, I'll definitely be home in time for dinner. Okay. I love you too."

Morgan told herself it was the fact that she was naked in bed next to Ethan while he talked to Alex, and not hearing Ethan tell Alex that he loved her, that made her stomach clench.

He ended the call, then placed the phone face down on the bedside table. "We're going to need to be more careful," he sighed as he leaned back against the pillows. "Her radar is up, so she snooped in my phone and is tracking my location. The other night she asked me why I was at The Standard and if I was having an affair."

Morgan sat up, sheet clutched to her chest. "Did she suspect anything about me?" Her stomach churned as she remembered the pictures she occasionally sent, the sexually charged messages. Sure, she sent most of them to his other phone, the one Alex didn't know about, but a couple of times she'd slipped up and sent them to his main number.

He shook his head. "I denied everything, of course."

"And she believes you?"

His wide shoulders lifted in a shrug. "As far as I can tell. Even so, we need to be careful. I can't turn off the tracking on my phone without making her more suspicious. So we need to make sure to meet at places where I could plausibly have a business lunch or dinner."

"Where are you 'having lunch 'today?" She asked. Though there were several restaurants nearby, the hotel restaurant at the Courtyard by Marriott was no place Ethan would take someone he wanted to impress.

"The taco truck parked out front. The guy who's doing the research says they're the best he's had since moving from San Diego."

Morgan settled back against his side, relieved Ethan had been able to allay Alex's suspicions. Mostly, anyway. As much as she was relieved, there was a small part of her that wanted to blow this whole thing wide open. To hurl the truth in everyone's faces and let the pieces scatter where they may.

When they first hooked up at that conference, Morgan told herself that it was just wish fulfillment from business school. She had met Ethan her first day of Finance I class, and like nearly every straight woman on the planet, she was dazzled. When she ran into him later that week at the local dive bar, he seemed like he was a little dazzled by her.

Then Alex, who Morgan had invited along with a couple other people from their Data Analysis and Decision Making Class, arrived on the scene. Just like that, any chance Morgan may have had to capture and keep Ethan's attention was extinguished like a candle in a hurricane. They were like two supernovas joining forces, outshining every other person in any room they entered.

Morgan had accepted it and turned her attention elsewhere, and she and Morgan had gone on to become best friends, their lives intertwining as they both moved to Oak Valley and had babies within months of each other.

As guilty as she'd felt at first for betraying her friend, the super competitive side of Morgan's nature reveled in taking back what Alex had unknowingly stolen from her. She told herself that was all this was about, that and the fact that she was bored out of her mind with her husband. It was an ego boost and a fun diversion, nothing more. She figured it would fizzle out on it's own after a few stolen moments.

But every time they were together, it made her want him more and more. The sex got better, the secrecy became more thrilling. Whenever Alex and Ethan were affectionate with each other, she had to remind herself she had no right to feel the jealousy burning like acid in her veins. They both maintained from the very beginning that this was nothing serious, that it was just sex, and that neither of them had any intention of leaving their spouses.

But the longer this went on, the more it became something bigger than sex and petty revenge. For Morgan, anyway. She knew it was dangerous. She knew if they got caught it would be like a nuclear bomb blowing up both of their lives. But she was a moth and Ethan was her flame. She couldn't stop herself from flying to it. She could only pray it wouldn't burn her alive.

20

Cleo

"Everyone is wearing a swim diaper, right?" Gail, the head of the swim program asked. It was an unusually warm January Sunday, and Cleo, Alex, Jenna, and Morgan had brought the kids to Oakwood to splash around in the kiddie pool.

"Yes, everyone's contained," Jenna said, rolling her eyes at Gail's back as she walked away. "Jeez, your kid has one accident in his life and now they're policing me forever." Jenna, dressed in a sporty bikini, sat in the baby pool with Noah on her lap while the bigger kids splashed and squealed as a sprinkler fountain erupted in the middle of the pool.

"To be fair, it wasn't just an accident," Morgan, who sat next to Alex on the side of the pool wearing a giant hat, designer sunglasses, and a stylish cover up said. "It was explosive diarrhea in the training pool during the Fourth of July Barbecue."

Cleo, who wore a high cut one piece and sat with her feet in the water let out a sound of disgust.

Jenna shot her a glare. "It wasn't my fault. He was wearing a swim diaper and rubber pants and everything. He just couldn't be contained, poor little guy." She pulled a little frown and looked at Liam, jumping and laughing a few feet away."

"Liam's certainly not the only toddler who's caused the pool to be shut down." Alex looked effortlessly glamorous in her embroidered caftan, oversized sunglasses and broad brimmed hat. She kicked her feet in the water and leaned back on her palms, face tilted up to the sky. "God, I love these warm winter days when we can just throw the kids in the pool and enjoy an afternoon cocktail." She picked up the margarita next to her and took a sip.

"Amen to that," Cleo said, raising her own drink in a toast.

"Speaking of day drinking," Morgan said, taking a pull off of her own drink, "I am counting the days until we get to Cabo. Life has been absolutely insane lately and I'm desperate for a break."

"God, me too," Alex said. "Ethan has been crazy busy lately too." She turned to Morgan, "I thought this entrepreneur in residence gig was supposed to be cushy."

Morgan shrugged. "It usually is, but there's been a lot of opportunities coming through lately."

"Well anyway," Alex said, "I'll just be happy to have him in one place for a week so Ava and I can actually see him." She gave a little grimace and turned to Cleo. "Sorry, we shouldn't be talking about this when you can't go."

"No worries," Cleo waved her off. For the past two years, Alex, Morgan, Jenna, and their families had gone to a high end, all inclusive resort in Cabo San Lucas. Unfortunately for Cleo, by the time Alex had thought to invite her, the resort was sold out for the week in February when the group had reservations. "Izzy and I are going to find some fun things to do around here. We haven't even been to the Monterey Aquarium yet."

"The only thing I'm not looking forward to is being in a bathing suit next to this one," Alex used her drink to gesture towards Jenna. "I am not anywhere near bikini ready."

It was true Jenna was blessed with a naturally lean form and enviable abs after giving birth to two babies. Still, Cleo couldn't help but think that if Alex cut back to one bottle of chardonnay a day and stopped eating Ava's unfinished chicken tenders and fries, she might see more of the results she wanted.

"Well, it doesn't look like you're going to have to worry about that this year," Jenna said, dodging as Noah swung at her face with a wet fist. "Mark and I aren't going to be able to make it."

"We've had this on the calendar for a year," Morgan protested. "It won't be the same without you guys. Who's going to win the hula hoop contest?"

Jenna shrugged and cast her eyes down with a little laugh. "Mark's about to close an important partnership deal, and he just can't swing the time off. Someone else is going to have to win us a bottle of tequila."

"Then come by yourself," Alex said. "If Mark's going to be working the entire time, there's no reason you shouldn't have some fun."

"Me on vacation alone with a three year old and an almost one year old doesn't sound fun," Jenna scoffed.

"Hello, they have childcare, and we'll all be around to help, ' Alex said.

Jenna's mouth tightened into a narrow line. "I don't feel right about going without Mark. I just don't think it's in the cards for us this year."

Cleo suspected that Jenna's decision had more to do with their financial circumstances than Mark's work schedule.

Alex must have reached the same conclusion, because she blurted, "If it's a money thing, you know Ethan and I are happy to-"

Jenna held up her hand. "It's not the money." They all fell into an awkward silence for a few moments, then Jenna said. "Look, the decision isn't set in stone. I'm going to talk to Mark before the cancellation deadline to see if there's a way he can make it work."

"I have an idea," Alex said, perking up. "If Jenna and Mark can't go, Cleo can take their spot."

Out of the corner of her eye, Cleo saw Jenna flinch as though she'd been slapped. It was shocking how someone seemingly so warm, so caring, as Alex could be so incredibly tone deaf.

"Let's let Jenna get her situation sorted out before I try to take dibs on her room," Cleo said, earning her a grateful look from Jenna.

"If you did go," Morgan asked, "Will Scott join you?"

Cleo looked up at the sky, pretending to ponder the matter. "What are the dates again?"

Alex told her.

She quirked her mouth in feigned uncertainty. "I think he has to be in Hong Kong that week, but I'll check the calendar to be sure."

Morgan let out a little laugh. "How is it that you've lived here for over six months, and we've still never met your husband?"

Cleo made sure no one noticed her hackles raising. "You all know how it is to be married to a man with a big career or have a big career yourself," she looked pointedly at Morgan. "Family time is often a secondary priority."

"You sound like you don't even care that you and Izzy barely see him," Jenna said. "I hate how Mark starting this company is affecting our family."

Cleo smiled and waved at Izzy over Jenna's shoulder. "It's what's necessary at this stage. I can rail against the fact that right now, we don't get to spend a lot of time with Scott, or I can accept what is and be grateful for the perks his career provides."

"I wish I could be that zen about it," Jenna said with a heavy sigh as she shifted Noah's weight on her lap. "But maybe part of my problem is that I don't get enough of the perks," she said with a hollow laugh.

"I don't know," Morgan said, fueled by two of Oakwood's notoriously strong skinny margaritas, "If I didn't know better, I'd think Scott was made up."

Cleo, Morgan, and Alex laughed at that. So did Jenna, but Cleo didn't miss her speculative stare. Alex had shared some of Jenna's theories about Scott, his lack of an internet presence, and the true nature of his business. She wondered how deeply Jenna was inclined to dig. A google search on Scott Baird got you thousands of hits. Which was why Cleo had chosen such a generic name for her fictional husband. But anyone who really wanted to drill down could discover that there was no Scott Baird who worked for Sino Bank in Singapore. Especially since said bank didn't exist either.

She made a mental note to lay some more digital bread crumbs. Nothing that would come up on the initial searches Jenna had already done, but an obscure link here and there that would provide some evidence of his existence.

What no one would ever be able to discover was the identity of Cleo's real husband. No one would ever be able to connect her with the reclusive widow of Paul Vanderpool, whose vast trust fund allowed him to party his life away in exotic locales all over the world.

When she'd first met him at a club in Mykonos, he'd seemed like the perfect mark. By the age of twenty four, Cleo had been on what felt like hundreds of trips to places like Greece, Ibiza, the south of France, anywhere filthy rich men hung out on their yachts looking for beautiful young women to party with. Paul had seemed different to her, vulnerable in a way most of the other mega rich fuck boys and their billionaire daddies weren't.

He wasn't particularly good looking, with a short pudgy body and unremarkable features. But money more than compensated for a lack of looks. A guy could be a complete troll, but if he was a

The Playgroup

billionaire he walked through the world like he was entitled to everything in it.

But Paul seemed different. He came off as shy and self effacing. He was up front about acknowledging that a girl who looked like Cleo wouldn't have given him the time of day if not for his money. Instead of sounding angry or resentful about it, he sounded genuinely sad. As though he had lived his entire life only wanting to be loved and liked for who he was, instead of what he had.

Right then and there, Cleo knew she had to take a different approach. She put aside the usual ego stroking and overt sexuality, and made a concerted effort to engage with Paul on a deeper level.

That night, after securing an invitation to Paul's yacht the next day, she stayed up until sunrise learning everything she could about him. That afternoon on the yacht, instead of prancing around in nothing but bikini bottoms and deciding who was most likely to give her the best handbag in exchange for a blowjob, she asked Paul all about the independent movies he'd produced, and the book he'd co-written on some obscure French director from the seventies. By the end of the evening he was eating out of the palm of her hand and inviting her to sail the Croatian coast.

As the summer went on, he proved himself to be exactly what she wanted. He was head over heels in love with her, easily manipulated, and just enough of a recreational drug user to not be bothering her for sex all of the time. With his wealth, she would finally have the lifestyle she deserved. One a hundred times more lavish than her father ever could have provided.

That's all she cared about. Not love, or companionship, or any of that other bullshit.

When he proposed, she knew she had won the lottery. On the day of their wedding, she enthusiastically said her vows, confident from that day forward she would live the life of her dreams. And she would only have to suck one dick to earn it.

He was crafty, she'd give him that. He'd waited until they were married and he had her isolated from the rest of the world before he showed his true colors. That's when the abuse started, both verbal and physical. He liked to say that he owned her, and to prove it, he'd force her to fuck his friends while he watched.

She told herself she could endure it, as long as he left her alone most of the time. Which he did, especially as his addiction to cocaine and opiates spiraled farther and farther out of control. When she unintentionally got pregnant her first instinct was to have an abortion. Then she realized a child of Paul's offered an additional layer of financial security depending on what the future held.

But when her daughter, who they'd named Elizabeth, after Paul's mother, was born, Cleo was overwhelmed by the force of the love she felt for her.

Lizzy became her entire world and keeping her safe and loved was the only thing she cared about. Cleo knew putting up with Paul's abuse was the only way to keep Lizzy's future secure. But as Lizzy grew older, the things Cleo initially chose to suffer in order to maintain her billionaire lifestyle became more and more intolerable. Cleo was able to keep Lizzy away from her father and his nastiness most of the time. Even so, as she grew older, no matter how hard Cleo worked to protect her, she would start to notice things. Children always noticed things.

She was tortured thinking about how her daughter would view Cleo and the kind of abuse she put up with. What would she think of a mother who let her husband rage at her, hit her, and force her to sleep with other men?

Cleo was really good at compartmentalizing, but she wasn't so dead inside that the idea didn't cut her to the very core. That's when she started thinking about what it might take to escape.

But it wasn't until Paul choked her into unconsciousness in front of then eighteen month old Lizzy that the plan came into razor sharp focus. No amount of money, no luxurious lifestyle, was worth letting her daughter grow up with this monster. She was not going to allow her to see her mother mistreated, or god forbid, be mistreated herself.

It was only a little over a year ago that she put that plan into action. Thanks to Paul's heavy drug use, his death was the easiest part. One batch of fentanyl laced coke took care of that. The money was harder to get to, since most of it was in his trust. The iron clad new identities were also no joke. But Cleo was nothing if not determined, and resourceful as hell. She'd spent her entire life figuring out how to get what she wanted. She certainly wasn't going to stop when her life, and more importantly her daughter's life, were at stake.

21

Jenna

"Liam, please just have one more bite of your toast," Jenna said wearily. From his high chair, Noah discovered he was out of strawberries and let out a scream.

"Just a second, I'll get you some more," she said as Noah wailed and held up his sticky, empty hands. She hurried to the kitchen counter, where the nearly empty container of fruit sat next to the cutting board and cut the berries into bite size pieces. "Fu—uudge," she yelled as the paring knife sliced her knuckle. She scooped up the pieces, blood and all, and dumped them on Noah's tray. His wails mercifully ceased as he shoved a fistful into his mouth.

Liam took that as his cue to whine, "I'm done. I want down."

She looked at the barely touched breakfast on his plate, and knew that if he didn't eat more there would be a low blood sugar meltdown in her near future. "Eat two more bites of toast and a couple of strawberries. And finish your milk."

Liam's response was to hurl the sippy cup across the table at her and yell, "I'm done!"

"Liam!" She yelled. "That is not ok! You are going to time out." She went over to him, unclipped his booster, and carried him, writhing and screaming over to the corner.

She set her watch for three minutes and attempted to drown out his wailing as she wondered how in the hell was she going to survive the next week. It was the second week of February, and like most schools Wyndham was closed for winter break. Many families took off for the mountains, but others, like Alex, Morgan, and in previous years, Jenna, took the opportunity to head to the beach. So not only was Jenna deprived of the small break that Liam's preschool offered, her closest friends were gone as well, leaving her alone with her children, struggling to keep them occupied and herself sane.

And to add insult to injury, Cleo Baird had taken her place in Cabo.

Mark walked into the kitchen then and Jenna felt a little spurt of relief, thinking she could hand off one kid if only for a few minutes. "Hey can you-" he held his hand up to cut her off, and pointed to his ear to indicate he was on a call.

"Uh huh," he said to whomever was on the other line. "We can definitely get those metrics up."

She watched, seething, as he continued on his call and helped himself to a cup of coffee.

When they decided to cancel their vacation, Mark had generously offered to work as much as he could from home, the theory being that he would be able to help out more. Instead, his presence taunted her, offering the possibility of relief without it ever coming to fruition. She glared at his back as he took his coffee and retreated to the office. Jenna got a damp dish towel to wipe down Noah's face and hands. She took him out of his high chair and set him on the floor while she retrieved Liam from time out. His wails had quieted to sniffles and his cheeks were smeared with tears and snot.

She knelt in front of him. "Do you understand why I put you in time out?"

"Because I dinnit eat my toast and I frew my cup at you," he said with a sniff.

"That's right," she nodded. "It's not okay to throw stuff at people."

"Sorry mommy." Even through her frustration, she felt a little curl of warmth as he wrapped his sturdy arms around her neck and nuzzled her shoulder. She didn't even mind the smear of mucus he left behind on her t-shirt.

Which reminded her she needed to do laundry. She sat the kids in front of Sesame Street and made sure Noah was secure in his exersaucer before she hurried to the boys 'room to retrieve their hamper. Once the laundry was started, she went back to the family room. The boys stared, enraptured by Elmo and his antics. She ignored the guilt as she remembered all of the articles she read that said children shouldn't be exposed to screens of any kind before the age of two.

Usually, she limited their at home viewing to a few hours on weekends. But all bets were off, this, of all weeks. It was vacation, she rationalized.

Some vacation, she fumed as she surveyed her disaster of a kitchen. Right about now, the Mexico crew would be making their way to breakfast. They would choose from a sumptuous buffet that included eggs Benedict, pancakes, waffles, and a stunning array of tropical fruit. Alex would no doubt be starting her day with a Bloody Mary while Morgan sipped at a mimosa.

She wondered what Cleo would have, she thought as she tossed the pan Mark had used to cook himself eggs into the sink with more force than necessary. As usual, he hadn't used enough butter, so there was a stubborn layer of cooked egg stuck on the bottom. She turned on the faucet and grabbed the sponge, mentally cursing him as she scrubbed.

"Hey," she jumped when she felt a hand on her ass. The faucet had drowned out the sound of Mark's approach.

"Hey," she said, deadpan, and forced herself not to recoil when he went to kiss her cheek. She finished cleaning the pan and set it on the dish rack to dry, then started on the pot from last night's spaghetti. "Did you need something?"

"No, I just have a minute between calls and I wanted to see what you're up to."

"Living my best life, as always," she said with a snarl thinly disguised as a smile.

"Is it okay for the kids to be watching TV? I thought we only did that on weekends."

The rage simmering in her gut bubbled up to her throat. "Oh really, Mark," she let the pot clatter against the sink as she turned to glare at him. "You're going to lock yourself in your office for twelve hours a day and then just randomly pop out with some parenting advice?"

He frowned and held up a hand in defense. "You're the one who made that rule. I was just asking-"

"You're right, I am the one who made that rule. I'm the one who has to make all of the rules. But this morning, goddammit, I'm reserving my right to break the rule! So fuck off!"

Mark actually took a step back, he was so shocked. Later, when Jenna looked back on this fight, she would understand why. In the course of their six year relationship, they had never yelled at each other. Not to mention, Jenna rarely swore, and she couldn't remember a time when she'd told someone to fuck off. Not to their face, anyway.

"Watch it!" He snapped, gesturing to the boys.

Jenna was too engulfed in the red haze of rage to care what the boys might have overheard. "Don't tell me to watch it! How about you don't come in here offering parenting tips when I'm the one who does all of the parenting? You want me to come into your office and tell you how to build a better firewall?"

He shook his head, frowning, and leaned back against the counter. "What's going on with you? Why are you so angry all of the sudden?"

"Why am I angry?" She held out her arms and pulled her shoulders into an exaggerated shrug? "Maybe because while I'm here trying to keep the kids distracted long enough so I can wash your fucking breakfast dishes, my two best friends are lounging around a pool in Mexico while someone else watches their kids."

"Why are you so mad at me?" Mark said, voice straining as he struggled to keep it down. "You were the one who insisted we cancel."

"You'd rather we go and face yet another massive credit card bill? Do you have any idea how much - make that how little - we have in our bank account right now? And you were too proud to take Alex up on her offer to pay for us!"

A red flush crept up his neck. "I'm not going to give that pompous asshole one more thing to hold over me! "

"Daddy?" Even Elmo couldn't hold Liam's attention over the extremely rare occurrence of his parents yelling at each other.

"It's fine, sweetie," Jenna said. "Daddy and I are just having a discussion." She opened the sliding glass door that led from the family room to the patio and motioned for Mark to follow her. She closed the door, positioning herself so she could keep an eye on the boys. "Since when is Alex a pompous asshole?" She asked, shivering against the February chill. "I thought you liked her."

Mark raked his hand through his hair. "Not Alex. Ethan. There's no way in hell I'm going to take a handout from that fucker. Honestly, even though I know you hate to miss the Mexico trip, I'm happy that I don't have to spend an entire week with that douchelord."

Jenna gaped at him, shocked. "Since when do you not like Ethan?"

"Since the first time we went over to their house for that barbecue."

Jenna went back through her memories of all of the times they'd hung out as families, when Mark had returned from a guys ' night, the previous trips to Mexico. Not once had she ever picked up that Mark didn't like Ethan. "How am I just learning this?"

He shrugged. "When you first met Alex, you liked her so much. You were struggling and really worried about making mom friends. I didn't want to ruin that for you."

She grimaced, remembering how insecure she'd felt, walking into that mom and baby group for the first time. Alex and Morgan had walked in together, Alex glowing like a Madonna as she cradled Ava in her arms, Morgan with a fresh blowout and dressed in a flowy maxi dress. Unshowered, her sweatshirt stained with breast milk and god knew what else, Jenna felt like a troll next to them. But incredibly, Alex had sat next to Jenna and struck up a conversation. By some miracle, by the end of the meeting, Alex liked her enough to ask for her phone number.

Soon they were all sitting together, along with another woman, Jess, who was part of their group before she and her husband moved away. A few weeks later, they started getting coffee or lunch together. When, after a few months, Alex had invited her and Mark along with Morgan and Jess's families over for a barbecue she'd been both nervous and excited. When all of the guys seemed to get along, she was over the moon. It was one thing to make girlfriends. Making couples friends were an entirely different beast. She felt like she'd hit the jackpot.

"How can you not like Ethan?" And really, how had years gone by without her even picking up a hint of Mark's true feelings? A curl of unease took root in her stomach. If he was so good at hiding his feelings about Ethan from her, what else was he capable of hiding?

Now that the truth was out, Mark didn't hold back. "He's an overbearing know it all. I swear to God, if I have to hear one more piece of advice or one more story about when he was starting Ignosi, I'm going to stab myself in the ear."

She stared at him, dumbfounded, wondering how someone she thought she knew as well as herself could have a completely different opinion than she did. What he read as pompous and overbearing, Jenna took as confidence. Sure, Ethan tended to take up more space in the room, but with his good looks and charisma, he naturally drew people's attention. Whereas Mark, who she had no doubt was smarter than all of them put together, tended to sit back and observe.

"Honestly, I think there's a part of you that's jealous of Ethan," she blurted before she considered the consequences of her words.

"Jealous?" He hissed. "You think I'm jealous of Ethan?"

Jenna shrugged. "He's really successful, not to mention ridiculously good looking."

His eyes narrowed and his fists clenched at his sides. "Is that what you want? Someone more like Ethan?"

In all honesty the answer to that question was sometimes yes. Yes, it would be nice to wake up next to someone who bore a not insignificant resemblance to Henry Cavill. It would be nice to have a partner who was able to be more helpful with the kids. And call her shallow, but goddamn if it wouldn't be nice to have a few of Ethan's zeros in their bank account.

But she didn't let a single hint of that show on her face. Even in her unhinged state, she knew that if she crossed that line she could never go back. "No. I'm just pointing out that some of your negativity towards Ethan might due to jealousy."

"Like you're jealous of Cleo and how close she's gotten to Alex?"

Jenna felt her cheeks heat as Mark's arrow hit home. Of course she was jealous of Cleo, with her flawless beauty, immaculate home, and a seemingly bottomless bank account. But Mark was right. She was most jealous of how Cleo had so quickly insinuated herself into Alex's life, becoming Alex's go to companion and leaving Jenna to feel like the constant third wheel. But she wasn't going to let herself come off like a twelve year old indulging in mean girl shit, not even to her husband. "I'm just worried that we don't know her very well. I don't want to see Alex get hurt."

Mark's mouth pulled into an uncharacteristic sneer. "Bullshit. You're worried that she's coming between you and Alex. You know you can get a little… intense about some of your relationships."

She stood there, speechless from the force of the blow. Mark knew that she had to learn the hard way not to dive so intensely into her friendships. Sometimes people saw her as clingy and pulled away. In college, there had been one relationship that had been particularly toxic at a time when Jenna was struggling with her mental health that had resulted in the other woman seeking a restraining order against Jenna. For Mark to casually throw it in her face felt exceptionally cruel.

"Fuck off," she snarled, too wounded to think of a more clever rebuttal. She yanked open the sliding glass door and went inside. She went to the bedroom to change into workout gear, her entire body vibrating with rage as she yanked on a sports bra and leggings. When she returned to the family room, Mark was on the couch, staring at his phone. He looked up, his face awash with guilt.

"Jenna-"

"I don't want to talk to you right now," she snapped. Ignoring their protests, she scooped the boys up and carried them out to the garage and strapped them into the double stroller. She put in her AirPods and cranked up a murder podcast to try to drown out the boys 'wails at being ripped away from Elmo.

She steered the stroller to the trail that ran in front of her house and charged up the first hill. Today not even the heart pounding hill or the bracing air was enough to keep her thoughts from racing. As her legs ate up the miles, she couldn't focus on the podcast, her brain too busy ruminating about Cleo. Who was this beautiful, enigmatic woman who had infiltrated every aspect of Jenna's social life? After six months, Jenna still didn't have a sense for who she really was.

All she knew was that she couldn't shake the feeling that she was trying to push Jenna out. Call her paranoid, but her gut was screaming at her that taking her place in Mexico was only the beginning. She needed to know more about Cleo Baird. Maybe then she could understand what her real intentions were.

She slowed to a jog, then to a walk. By now, the boys were mercifully quiet in the stroller. Through the clear plastic window in the stroller's canopy she could see them idly taking in the scenery as

The Playgroup

they bumped along the trail. When her breath slowed down, she took her phone out of her pocket and dialed.

Her brother answered on the second ring. "What's up in hempville?"

Though Jeremy was a detective in the comparatively liberal Austin, Texas, he never missed a chance to rib her about her choice to go live among the bleeding hearts of California. Probably because their family had never forgiven him for going to UT instead of OSU, and he needed something to pin on her to distract them.

"Oh, you know, taxed to hell and praying my house won't burn down this summer. The usual. Do you have a sec? I'm hoping you can help me with something."

"Yeah?"

"There's a new mom this year at the preschool who joined our playgroup. I need you to do some digging on her. I tried all of the internet databases, but I'm not coming up with anything."

"Why are you snooping around about someone from preschool?"

Jenna shrugged even though he couldn't see her. "I don't know, there's just something off about her, like she's hiding something."

"Maybe what she wants to hide is her business."

She let out a frustrating sigh. "Or maybe she's lying to us because she has, as Nana used to say, malicious intentions."

"Is this like the time you were convinced your neighbor was secretly in the CIA?"

"It all added up," she protested. "He was ex military, worked in tech in both China and the middle east, and when Mark asked him what his company did Mark said he didn't seem to know as much as he should for someone at his level."

"And then it turned out he really was just a telecom executive who moved back to California to be near his parents."

"Fine, but remember that time in high school. I knew something was off about the new art teacher and no one wanted to believe me. Next thing you know, she was sleeping with Anthony Gerard."

"Yeah, it was weird that the co-captain of the football team was suddenly into ceramics."

"So will you help me?"

His sigh echoed over the line. "Sure. But it might take a while. I'm pretty backed up on all of my cases right now."

She shoved down a surge of impatience. "That's fine. When I get home I'll send you an email with all of the information I have so far. And I'll see if I can get, like her driver's license and social security number in the next few days."

"Okay, Nancy Drew. Love you," he said as he rang off.

"Love you too."

As frustrating as it was to have to wait for more information, at least knowing her brother was on the case kept her from obsessing about Cleo as she turned the stroller home. Instead she obsessed about the fact that while her friends were day drinking and having hotel sex with their husbands while their children were off in the kid's club, she had to go home and figure out how to make up with Mark.

22

Alex

"Let's not wake mommy," Alex heard Ethan whisper. She cracked her eyes to see him with Ava in his arms, with her little pink backpack slung over his shoulder. She closed her eyes, feigning sleep, more than happy to let Ethan take her to breakfast and drop her off at the resort's kids 'club.

She rolled over and dozed for another half hour before she finally gave up on sleep. She checked her phone. There were new messages in the group chat between Alex, Morgan, and Cleo discussing activities for the day. They had spa appointments later this afternoon, but nothing planned before then. Alex replied that she was just getting up and would meet them at the main pool. Then she sent a quick text to Jenna. *Miss you guys! How's everything back in Oak Valley?*

She climbed out of the luxurious king size bed and went to the bathroom. When she was finished she pulled on a one piece bathing suit that sucked in her stomach and highlighted her cleavage, and topped it with a gauzy cover up. She pulled her hair into a loose braid, and stowed her wide brimmed sun hat and Oliver Peeples sunglasses in a tote. She was just sliding her feet into her flip flops when the door opened.

"Good morning," Ethan greeted her with a warm smile. "I brought you some coffee," He said, indicating the mug in his hand.

"Thank you," she set her tote down and reached for the cup. But instead of handing it to her, he set it on the table in the entryway.

"You look nice," he said, his eyes locked on her cleavage as he approached. He settled one hand in the curve of her waist, while he reached up with the other to trace the deep neckline of her bathing suit. "Is this new?"

"It is." She felt a shimmer of desire at the feel of his fingers against her skin. "I'm glad you like it."

"It highlights some of your best features." He grinned wolfishly and bent to press his lips to the plump curves of her breasts. She wove her fingers in his hair and let him steer her back over to the bed.

Afterward, as she lay flushed and breathless with him on his back panting beside her, she marveled that she ever suspected he was having an affair. In the three days since they'd arrived in Mexico, they'd had sex seven times. She was no expert on cheating husbands, but she doubted they wanted to fuck their wives several times a day.

Unless of course, with his affair partner unavailable for the next week, he was just making do.

She shoved the thought aside. Obviously they just needed some time away from their daily routines to relax and reconnect.

Her phone dinged, indicating an incoming text. It was from Jenna.

Living the dream. Both Liam and Noah have colds, so I'm covered in mucus and no one is sleeping. Have a margarita or 40 for me.

Alex felt a stab of guilt, thinking of Jenna stuck at home with her boys while they were all reveling in Mexico. Then she reminded herself that she offered to treat them several times before Jenna transferred the reservation to Cleo. If Jenna wanted to be a martyr, that was her business.

After a quick shower, she pulled her bathing suit back on as Ethan pulled on his trunks and a t-shirt.

She sipped the coffee he had brought her, wincing at the now lukewarm temperature. On the way to the pool they stopped in the dining room where she got a fresh cup. The aromas of bacon, eggs, and the resort's signature chorizo breakfast tacos made her stomach growl. But after the indulgences of the last few days, Alex felt compelled to skip a meal or two before she turned into Jabba the Hutt. A poolside Bloody Mary would help tide her over until lunch.

She and Ethan arrived at the pool to find Morgan reclining in a lounger. There was an empty lounger next to her, no doubt reserved for David. She looked like she was ready for a photo shoot in a coral bikini with metal accents, oversize Gucci sunglasses, and a fedora.

"Good morning," she waved just as a waiter appeared at her side. She smiled and took what looked like a rum punch from the tray.

"I would have ordered for you but I wasn't sure when you were coming down."

"It's okay," Alex replied as Ethan asked the attendant to set up their loungers next to Morgan and David's. "I need to get some coffee and more water in me before I start drinking."

As they settled into their loungers and rubbed sunscreen on each other's backs, David arrived, looking flustered.

"How did it go?" Morgan asked warily. Jack was not on board for the kids 'club program. The first morning, he'd only lasted an hour before someone had to come find Morgan and David. Apparently they weren't going to let him cry for several hours straight. Yesterday had been a little better. He'd made it an hour and a half before having a full blown melt down and biting a five year old boy.

"Better this morning," David said with a sigh as he settled next to Morgan. "I think the ice cream last night made a very big impression. I may have implied that he could expect more today."

Alex spotted Cleo headed for the pool in a suit that was very different from the simple black tank suit she'd worn a few times to Oakwood. She looked stunning in a royal blue high cut one piece which clung to her lithe figure and made her legs look miles long. The neckline plunged almost to her navel, but was lined with a mesh insert that offered only a glimpse at the inner curves of her breasts. Alex shifted and tried to rearrange herself on her lounger so her stomach didn't stick out as much and her cellulite didn't squish out to the sides.

She wasn't the only one who noticed how incredible Cleo looked. Both David and Ethan stared, looking slightly dazed.

"Good morning everyone," Cleo sang, seemingly oblivious to the admiration. She signaled to an attendant and asked him to set up a lounger for her.

A spurt of jealousy seized Alex's stomach as she saw Ethan's eyes dart from Cleo's breasts, to her legs, and back again. Was it possible that Cleo made the accusation about Jenna to cover her own tracks?

She rolled her eyes behind her glasses and gave herself a mental slap. She and Ethan had had sex less than an hour ago. She had nothing to worry about. "There's the karaoke queen!" Alex called.

Cleo gave a little laugh. Last night, after an early dinner with the kids, they dropped them off at the kids 'club so they could hit the resort's karaoke bar. Alex and Morgan did a mostly on key rendition of That Don't Impress Me Much, followed by Ethan doing his go to number, Friends In Low Places. Then Cleo had stunned them all by absolutely killing it with Bad Romance by Lady Gaga.

"Seriously," Ethan said admiringly, "who would have known you had those pipes?"

Cleo set her tote down and stretched out on the lounger the attendant had pulled up next to Alex's. "My mother was a Vegas lounge singer. I guess I get it from her."

"Seriously?" Morgan asked.

Alex sat up a little, curious as well. Cleo very rarely talked about either of her parents.

"No," Cleo waved them off with a laugh. "That just sounds more interesting than saying she was an admin at an insurance company."

"Really though," Alex probed. "You must have had some professional training."

"Not really," Cleo said. "I mean, I was in jazz choir in high school. And I get a lot of practice in the car and the shower."

A waiter came by to take their drink orders. Alex ordered her Bloody Mary with extra olives, hoping that would take the edge off of her hunger. Ethan and David ordered Corona Lights and Morgan ordered a refill on her rum punch. Cleo asked for a seltzer with lime.

"Seltzer? Again?" Morgan ribbed.

"I'll have something later," Cleo said as she pulled her kindle out of her bag. "If I start drinking now, I'll just fall asleep."

"Isn't that the point when you're on vacation? Drink, sleep it off, then drink some more." Morgan chuckled and toasted with her nearly empty cup.

"I want to work out after lunch," Cleo shrugged. "If I start drinking now that will never happen."

Alex felt a surge of self disgust. In the years they had been coming to Grand Velas, she had never seen the inside of the gym. When she was here, her somewhat regular workout routine went right out the window.

Cleo, on the other hand, had worked out every day since they'd arrived. Just yesterday Ethan came back from the gym, marveling at what great shape she was in. Laying next to her on the lounger, Alex felt like a beached whale.

The waiter arrived with their drinks. Alex took a long sip of her cocktail, hoping the vodka would dull the edges of her insecurity.

Ethan sat up suddenly, his fingers on his neck as he looked at his watch.

Alex put a concerned hand on his leg. "How high is it?" A couple of years ago Ethan had been diagnosed with a heart condition that occasionally caused an elevated heart rate. *Maybe staring at Cleo in her sexy swimsuit sent his heart rate soaring.*

He took a few moments to answer. "It's ninety. A little elevated, but not too bad."

"You need to go see the cardiologist when we get back."

"Cardiologist?" Cleo asked, sounding worried. "Are you okay?"

"I have something called intermittent atrial fibrillation," Ethan said. "Occasionally my heart rate spikes or becomes irregular." He removed his fingers from his neck. "It's not that serious, just something I need to monitor."

Alex tightened her grip on his thigh. "Considering it can cause blood clots to form in your heart, I would say that it's pretty serious. You need to go to the doctor when we get back."

"Okay, nurse Nancy," he said with a grin. "I'll have my assistant make an appointment." He leaned over and gave her a lingering kiss. "But right now, I'm going to jump in." He got up from his lounger and dove smoothly into the pool.

Any worries about what kind of attention he might be paying to Cleo or any other woman dissipated in the face of Ethan's overt affection throughout the morning. Every few minutes there was touch to her thighs, a stroke of her arm, a kiss on her neck as he reapplied sunscreen to her back.

She wasn't the only one who took note.

"Wow, I was completely wrong about Ethan," Cleo said later that afternoon. She, Alex, and Morgan were all waiting for treatments in the resort's spa. Dressed in thin cotton robes, they curled up on downy soft couches in the sweetly scented waiting room. "He is all over you."

"What about Ethan?" Morgan asked.

"She thought he might be having an affair," Alex said. "With Jenna."

Morgan's eyes widened and her mouth gaped. "You think Jenna and Ethan are sleeping together?" She laughed in disbelief.

Cleo shook her head and held her hands up. "I know, I know. It's completely ridiculous. I can't even believe I thought it, much less mentioned it out loud."

"Yeah, I really wish you hadn't," Alex felt a stab of irritation. "Even though I know it's crazy, it's been hard to get the thought out of my head."

Cleo leaned over and took her hand. "I know, I'm sorry. It's just that I've seen a lot over the years. I've had friends who were married to really good looking, successful guys, and as soon as they started having kids, and their husbands weren't the center of attention…" She trailed off.

"That might be the case with some couples," Morgan scoffed. "But that's not true about Alex and Ethan. He's obviously still madly in love with her." She sounded a little angry about it. "You just haven't known us long enough to understand our dynamic. We've all become so close, we're practically family."

Cleo's eyes narrowed a bit at that. "You're right. I projected my past experience onto the situation, and I'm sorry for that."

Alex sipped at her drink, reassured that any doubts she had about Ethan's fidelity were completely unfounded. Yet there was a new source of unease as she wondered if Cleo's motivation in voicing her suspicions were out of genuine concern for Alex.

As Morgan pointed out, they hadn't known Cleo all that long and still didn't know a whole lot about her. And Cleo certainly didn't know them, if she thought there was any possibility that her husband would betray her with one of her best friends. Anyone who really knew them would know the truth. Anyone who knew them would never sow doubt.

23

Cleo

Cleo felt a subtle shift in Alex's energy at Morgan's reminder that Cleo was a relative newcomer to their group. She kept her expression composed, showing no sign of her irritation at Morgan for undermining her. She knew it was a risk to voice her suspicions to Alex. It was a fine line to walk, forming a wedge between Alex and her friends, taking the risk that Alex would turn on her instead.

An aesthetician called Alex in for her treatment, leaving Cleo and Morgan alone.

"Did you seriously think there was something going on between Ethan and Jenna?" Morgan kept her voice low even though there was no one around to overhear.

Cleo shrugged. "I mistook their friendship and misread their body language. I should have kept my mouth shut."

"If Ethan were to cheat, he wouldn't be doing it with Jenna."

"Really? I think Jenna's very attractive."

"Oh, she's gorgeous. But she's always with her kids. She wouldn't have the time."

Interesting that she was backing off of her "Ethan would never" stance. It wasn't that she thought Ethan would never cross the line, it was about whether Jenna would be both willing and available.

Cleo didn't disagree. Even if Ethan wasn't sleeping with Jenna, Cleo hadn't missed the way Ethan had been eying her at the pool these last few days. Alex could tell herself Ethan would never until she was blue in the face, but Cleo knew that look. Sure, David took a good look too, but his demeanor was as though he was admiring a piece of art. Ethan's look was not just sexual, it was downright predatory. It was a look she'd seen too many times in too many men's eyes to mistake it.

It would be so easy to seduce him, and such an obvious way to absolutely eviscerate Alex. But seducing someone's husband was like using a BB gun when she had access to a nuclear arsenal. Her goal wasn't just to wound Alex. She wanted to destroy her life as she knew it. She would settle for nothing less than blowing Alex's entire life to smithereens.

Alex quickly got over her irritation at Cleo, and the next morning she invited her and Izzy to join her and Ava for mani pedis at the spa. By the time they were finished it was lunch time, and they went to the poolside restaurant where they found David alone with Jack.

"Where's Ethan?" Alex asked as she settled Ava in a seat and sat down next to her. Cleo sat Izzy on Ava's other side and took a seat between Izzy and David.

"He and Morgan went back to our suite to do a call," he said as he gently urged Jack to sit on his butt. "Just once," he said, "I'd like to go on vacation where Morgan doesn't spend half of it working."

"She hasn't been that bad this trip," Alex chided. "Not like last year when she barely made it out of the room before three every day. It's weird that Ethan's on a call," she paused as a waiter came over to take their order.

"Why is it weird he's on a call?" Cleo asked.

Alex shrugged. "He's usually pretty good about clearing his calendar on vacation. It was an agreement we made after he sold his company and he had a lot more flexibility in his schedule. I was sick of going on trips where I hung out by myself while he spent the whole day on the phone."

"They're talking to the CEO of one of Morgan's companies. They're considering putting Ethan on the board," David said.

"Well I don't see why that couldn't wait a week," Alex groused. "And I like how he didn't tell me about it because he knew I'd be pissed." She quirked her mouth and thanked the waiter as he brought their food and drinks.

"Better to ask forgiveness than permission," Cleo said as she scooped some ceviche onto a tortilla chip. She took a moment to revel in the crisp saltiness of the chip, the acidic bite of the lime marinade on the fresh fish. While the Grand Velas was nice, it was far from the most luxurious place she had ever stayed. But they did have some of the best food. "I'm sure he won't be too long."

Alex stabbed at her salad. "That's not really the point though. After I put up with all of the time he took away from me when he was starting his company, I expect him to prioritize family time. Especially when we're on vacation."

Cleo let out a little laugh. "Sorry if I don't have a ton of sympathy. You're talking to the girl whose husband couldn't even come on vacation."

Alex winced with guilt just as Cleo knew she would. "I'm sorry. I feel like an as-" she caught herself before she said "asshole" - "a jerk."

"Don't," Cleo said as she spooned up a bite of gazpacho. "I accept that Scott's work doesn't allow him to spend a lot of time with us. You and Ethan have a different agreement."

"Compared to Scott, Morgan is practically a housewife," David said wryly.

"Is there any sense of when that's going to change?" Alex asked.

Cleo suppressed a smile at Alex's frown of genuine concern for someone who didn't exist. "He keeps saying things will calm down in six months, a year tops."

"I hope that's the case. I know you have help, but it must suck for him to be gone so much." She turned to Izzy, "You must miss your daddy so much!"

Izzy swallowed a bite of her quesadilla, leaving a smear of sour cream in the corner of her rosebud mouth. "Daddy goed away," she stared solemnly at Alex.

Cleo felt a knot in her stomach as Alex cocked her head. "That's right," she said as she wiped Izzy's mouth. "Unfortunately Daddy *goes* away a lot. Lucky for us, we get to keep each other company." Since Izzy was only two when her father died, she didn't have many memories of him. She so rarely talked or asked about him, Cleo was surprised she even mentioned him now. She snuck a glance at Alex, reassured when it was apparent that Alex hadn't read anything darker into Izzy's words.

As they finished their lunch and talked about their plans for later that afternoon, David chuckled and pointed at Izzy. "Rough night for that one?"

Cleo had been so absorbed in conversation with Alex that she hadn't noticed that Izzy had fallen asleep in her seat. "I guess before we do anything, a nap is in order," she whispered.

"I should take Ava back for a rest too," Alex said as she and Cleo rose from their chairs.

David sighed and looked at his watch. "Hopefully Ethan and Morgan will wrap things up soon so we can go back to our room."

"I don't want a nap," Jack pouted. He rubbed his eyes with his fists, betraying the fact that whether he wanted a nap or not, he definitely needed one.

Cleo slung her tote over her shoulder and lifted Izzy from her chair. Izzy stirred long enough to wrap her sturdy legs around her waist and buried her head against her shoulder. She pressed a kiss to her daughter's soft curls and inhaled the scent of sunscreen and chlorine that clung to her skin.

Alex picked up Ava and they walked together until their paths to their rooms diverged. They agreed to text each other when the kids woke up from their naps to make a plan. Cleo was rounding a low wall covered with bougainvillea when she saw the door to David and Morgan's villa, which was three units from the one she shared with Izzy, swing open.

Morgan stepped out, followed by Ethan. Cleo was about to wave hello when Ethan took Morgan's hand and lifted it to his lips.

Cleo froze, then ducked behind the wall and peaked around the edge.

Morgan said something she couldn't hear, looking around furtively as she tried to tug her hand away.

Ethan murmured something in reply and looked up and down the pathway. Oblivious to their observer, he pulled Morgan to him, took her mouth in a deep kiss, and slid one big hand down to her ass.

Cleo's mouth curled in a satisfied grin. So much for Alex's near perfect, hopelessly devoted husband. Cleo loved it when she was right.

24

Morgan

Morgan reached for her phone to silence the alarm. Next to her, David stirred and reached across the pillow for her.

"Why are you up so early?"

She forced herself not to flinch as he caressed her arm.

"Sunrise yoga." She leaned over to give him a peck on the cheek, hiding a grimace as she caught a whiff of his morning breath, tinged with the bourbon he and Ethan had sipped the night before.

"Just be back in time to take Jack to breakfast and kids club," he muttered as he burrowed back into his pillow. "Ethan and I have a nine am tee time."

She reassured him she would be back in plenty of time and retreated to the bathroom. She did a quick rinse in the shower, hoping David wouldn't find it odd that she was showering before a yoga class.

Fortunately he was snoring softly when she stepped out of the bathroom. Just in case, she dressed as though she was going to yoga in a stretchy tank with a built in bra and capri length leggings. She stepped out of the bedroom and crept quietly past a sleeping Jack. The air conditioning was set to arctic. Goose bumps broke out on her bare arms as she leaned over to give him a kiss and pulled the comforter up to his chin. Asleep, with his long lashes shadowing his round cheeks, his plump lips parted, was when she felt the greatest surge of maternal love. When he was at rest, she didn't have to cope with all of the aggression and frenetic energy that she didn't know how to manage. She pressed a kiss to his curls.

As she straightened, she noticed something stuck between the upper right corner of the fold out mattress and the couch's armrest. She picked it up, her stomach flipping as she realized it was a pair of men's underwear. Ethan's underwear, to be specific. Her cheeks heated with a rush of guilt over what she and Ethan had done on the same couch where her child slept.

It was immediately followed by a surge of relief that she had been the one to find Ethan's underwear. Unlike Ethan, who wore form fitting boxer briefs, David wore old school boxers. "So my boys can have some freedom," he'd told her when they'd first started dating and she'd attempted to upgrade his underwear game. At the time, it had made her laugh. Now the thought of her husband's balls bouncing around under his boxers made her cringe.

If David had found the boxers, he would know immediately that they belonged to someone else. Morgan balled them up in her fist, relieved to have dodged that bullet.

She stepped outside of their villa, breathing in the salt air. Dawn was just beginning to turn the sky pink, and as she made her way through the resort, she only saw a couple of the staff, hosing off the walkways and getting the resort ready for the day. As she passed the main pool, the gym with its wooden yoga platform out front was up a few stairs to her left. It was empty, as the sunrise yoga class wouldn't start for another forty five minutes.

Her pulse thrummed and her skin tightened with awareness as she walked past it and continued down to the beach. She and Ethan had to be more clever in their trysts this week. Sure, it had been easy enough to make up a work call yesterday to give them an excuse to be alone together. But thanks to Alex's strict no work on vacation rules for Ethan, they wouldn't be able to get away with that again.

How stupid Alex was, to think she could control him. Annoyance stiffened her shoulders as she thought of her friend. Or more specifically, as she thought of the over the top affection Ethan displayed towards her.

Several cabanas lined the edge of the stone patio that abutted the beach. She saw Ethan waiting for her in front of the fourth one from the end.

"You're late," he said as he reached for her.

She felt a rush of moisture between her thighs at the impressive erection tenting out the front of his shorts. Then a wave of bitterness at the memory of Alex crowing about how much sex she and Ethan were having. *It's a miracle he even has the energy left over to fuck me.*

The Playgroup | 175

"You're lucky I'm here at all," she said as he wrapped his arms around her and pulled her against him. She kept her own arms by her sides.

"David?" He ignored her prickliness and pulled her hips in so he could grind against her lower belly.

"No," she snapped. "But speaking of, we could have had a serious problem if he'd found these." She dangled the boxer briefs in front of him.

"Oh shit, where were those?"

"They were in the couch. I found them this morning, practically on Jack's head."

He gave a surprised laugh. "I didn't even realize I didn't put them back on."

What kind of grown man didn't notice whether or not he was wearing underwear? "It's not funny. If David had found them he would have known they weren't his."

Ethan shrugged. "You could just say they must be from the last guest."

"Huh. I didn't think of that." Ethan's ability to conjure a plausible explanation to cover up his deception really was impressive.

"What about Alex? Did she have any issues?"

"She didn't even twitch when I got out of bed. Thanks to the bottle of chardonnay she drank after dinner, I don't think she'll be moving for several more hours." There was no mistaking the contempt in his voice.

And yet, he could still muster the desire to, if Alex was to be believed, fuck this woman he had such contempt for twice a day nearly every day since they'd arrived. She stiffened as irritation mixed with unwanted jealousy twisted in her stomach.

"What's wrong?" He sounded more exasperated than concerned.

"I don't know. Maybe watching you and Alex make out by the pool and listening to her brag about how you're fucking around the clock makes me a little less horny for you."

He took a step back, his eyes stony as they stared into hers. She held his gaze, undaunted in the face of his glare.

"Really?" He drew out the word, his voice dripping with derision. "You're jealous of my wife, meanwhile you're here with your husband. If you're going to start pulling shit like this, maybe we should just cut it off now. I don't want to deal with the fallout if you start to catch feelings."

Too late, she thought, as she realized that while she had indeed caught feelings, to him this was still purely physical. Though she was old enough and more than smart enough to recognize the folly in continuing to see him without an equal emotional investment, neither age nor intellect would prevail.

Lust, combined with what she was beginning to fear was unrequited love, were much more powerful forces. "Of course I'm not catching feelings. And I'm not jealous," she rolled her eyes. "I just don't love seeing the two of you all over each other."

He reached out and rested his hands on her hips. Her nipples tightened at the feel of his strong fingers pressing into her flesh. "It's all for show."

She wanted to point out that fucking behind closed doors was hardly for show. But arguing would only delay the pleasure her body was clamoring for. "Oh yeah?" She said and slid her hands up his arms to rest on his shoulders.

"If I can't keep my hands off of her, she has no reason to suspect anything is going on. If I didn't want to have sex with her, it would seem weird."

Morgan's mouth tightened. "I get what you're saying, but twice a day seems excessive."

He pulled her tight against him, crushing her breasts against his chest. One hand came up to cradle the back of her head as he bent to her.

"You know me, and my… big appetites."

Her body shuddered with need as he pressed his mouth to hers. He parted her lips with his tongue and she moaned as it slid against hers. She offered no resistance as he raised one of the canvas flaps and backed her into the cabana.

25

Cleo

"Seriously, neither of you are going to join me for pilates?" Morgan said, exasperated. She, Cleo, and Alex were gathered around the pool while Ethan and David played golf.

"I worked out this morning," Cleo said as she stretched in her lounge chair. "Thanks again Alex for letting Izzy stay with you last night. I love when I can get exercise out of the way first thing in the morning."

"And I think lifting this is all the workout I need today," Alex grinned as she lifted her margarita to her lips.

"Fine, I guess it's just me then," Morgan huffed as she gathered up her things. "Are we at least still on for the spa this afternoon?"

"Of course," Alex said. "You know I'll never say no to a massage."

As Morgan walked away, Alex leaned towards Cleo and asked, "Is it just me, or is Morgan acting a little weird?"

Of course she's acting weird. Just a few hours ago she was fucking your husband. Cleo knew this because when she got up at six thirty to go to the gym, she happened to see Morgan walk past her room. Curious, she followed her, not terribly surprised when instead of heading for the gym or to get a cup of coffee, she instead went down to the adults only pool. Once there, she made a beeline for one of the cabanas that opened up to face the ocean. At this hour of the morning, the pool was deserted.

Except for one person.

As Cleo furtively crept around the edges of the pool, keeping hidden behind the decorative hedges that rimmed it, she could see Ethan step out from behind the canvas sides to pull Morgan into his arms.

She watched, first stunned, then delighted, as Ethan shoved his tongue halfway down her throat. They withdrew into the cabana, and soon Cleo heard the rhythmic thumping of a lounge chair and the moans and groans they couldn't quite stifle.

Cleo kept all of this to herself, of course, and said mildly, "Weird how?"

"I don't know," Alex shrugged, causing her ample cleavage to quiver precariously over the neckline of her one piece. "She just seems kind of irritable and snippy with me. Can you think of anything I might have done to make her mad?"

Nothing other than being married to the guy she's fucking every chance she can get. "It sounds like work is kind of stressful. And, you would know this better than I do, but it seems like she doesn't like spending tons of time with David."

"You're right about that. She doesn't really do down time that well. Every year that we've come here, after a few days she's ready to get back to work and away from her family. This year it seems like it's even worse."

"That's kind of sad, that she doesn't want to spend time with her husband and kid."

Alex shrugged again and took a sip of her drink. "It's not that she doesn't want to spend time with them, but I think she gets bored pretty quickly She's always been like that, super career focused. If she were a guy, no one would judge her for it." She looked over the rims of her sunglasses pointedly. "I mean, no one, including you, is bashing Scott for missing your vacation entirely."

"Touche," Cleo said with a smile. "You're right, I don't know Morgan as well, so who am I to judge? And David seems like a very hands on dad."

"True. David is an amazing husband and father. And honestly, I think Morgan totally takes him for granted."

You have no idea.

"Hopefully she'll be in a better mood by the time we meet up this afternoon," Alex continued.

"You know, maybe it would be a good idea for me to sit this afternoon out," Cleo offered. "When was the last time you and Morgan did something where it was just the two of you?"

"God, it's been months," Alex said. "You're right, it would be good for us to have some time together. Thanks for being so thoughtful."

Oh that's me, bringing friends together. It was so strange, this world, where women were as invested in their female friendships as they were in their marriages. "You're welcome. While you're doing that I'll take Izzy for ice cream or something. I feel a little guilty about all of the hours in the kids 'club."

Alex made a scoffing sound. "Oh please, she's having a ball. And you deserve a break every once in a while. We all do."

Cleo fought to keep her lip from curling into a sneer. As though Alex was slaving away the rest of the time. As though she'd ever known what it was to have to work hard and sacrifice to earn her rest and relaxation. "I suppose you're right."

Later, she and Izzy ran into Alex and Morgan on their way back from the spa. Both had tousled hair and wore similar dreamy, relaxed expressions courtesy of the skilled masseuses employed by the resort.

"How was it?" Cleo asked after Morgan peeled off to return to her room.

"Really good," Alex smiled. "I mean, the massage was great, but it was also good to talk to Morgan one on one. I really feel like we reconnected."

"I'm so glad," Cleo smiled.

"Me too. Between that and how great things are going with me and Ethan, I feel like this vacation has been kind of a Godsend." She excused herself to go back to her room to shower.

As Cleo watched her retreat, she couldn't stifle a grin. She almost felt sorry for Alex. The poor woman had no idea that her dear friend and her beloved husband were betraying her right under her nose. She had no clue that her seemingly perfect world was about to come crashing down.

26

Alex

"Mexico was fun, but Jenna, it just wasn't the same without you," Alex said. Alex, Morgan, and Cleo were back from Mexico and had resumed their weekly ritual of drinking wine and sharing secrets while the kids played around them.

"I'm sure that's not true," Jenna said as she unceremoniously dumped a basket full of laundry onto the floor.

Jenna had been prickly all week, and as soon as Alex walked in the door, it was obvious her mood wasn't improving. Alex exchanged a look with both Cleo and Morgan, who shrugged and sipped at their wine.

She bit back an exasperated sigh. On the one hand, she understood Jenna was disappointed she couldn't join them this year and felt left out. On the other hand, it was what it was, and as an adult she had to get past it. Still, she made a conscious choice to lean into the more compassionate side of her nature.

"Of course it's true," Morgan piped in. "And not only did we miss you, Jack missed Liam," she gestured at the two boys, who were playing on one side of the family room, separate from the girls.

"Thanks," Jenna said tightly and picked up a onesie from the pile of laundry.

"Do you want some help?" Alex offered.

Jenna shook her head and chuckled. "I know we're close, but I'm not going to ask you to handle my family's underwear." She held up a faded pair of mens 'boxer briefs to demonstrate. "Sorry to do this right now, but our dryer was on the fritz until yesterday and I'm catching up on several days worth." She pulled another garment from the pile. Alex gave a little snicker at the faded purple women's briefs that looked like they belonged to someone twice Jenna's size.

"What?" Jenna asked.

Alex laughed harder. "I'm sorry, but Jenna, you have to up your underwear game."

"What's wrong with my underwear?"

"Two words," Morgan said. "Granny panties."

Jenna's bold cheekbones flushed with color. "They're comfortable. And I don't have a ton of time, not to mention money, these days to go shop for fancy underwear." She folded the pair in quick motions and set it aside.

"I'm sorry," Alex said, annoyed at herself for further pissing off her already annoyed friend. "But you have such a rocking body. If I had a rig like yours I'd be prancing around in push up bras and g-strings."

"I'm sure Mark would appreciate that," Cleo, who was seated next to her on the couch, raised her glass to her lips. "Ooh, maybe you should get a little outfit for your trip next week!" Cleo said. "Neiman's is having its big sale right now and they have a ton of stuff."

Jenna paused in folding the tee shirt she was holding as her shoulders sagged. "Yeah, that would be great, if we were actually going."

"Wait, why aren't you going?" Alex asked. Jenna had told them earlier in the week that since Mark knew how disappointed she was to miss the Mexico trip, he had planned a three day weekend for them in Carmel by the Sea. His parents were coming into town to take care of the kids.

"Unfortunately, Mark was invited to the Midas Summit, which happens to be in Boston next Friday and Saturday."

"Yeah, that's kind of a big deal," Morgan said, grimacing. "When you're at Mark's stage of company building, you can't really turn that down."

Alex's eyebrows shot up. "Ethan tried to get invited for three years. He still has never been."

Jenna sighed and continued folding. "I know, and I'm super proud and excited for him…"

"But of course you're disappointed," Cleo said, expression awash in sympathy.

"Yeah," Jenna said with a humorless laugh. "I guess you can relate. So now, not only are we not going, I'll be stuck entertaining his parents for three days."

Cleo nodded, then cocked her head. "If his parents are coming anyway, there's no reason you can't go by yourself."

Jenna shook her head. "I can't do that. It's too much money to spend on just myself."

Cleo gave Alex a look, telling her to chime in. "Jenna, if anyone deserves a night or two alone in a hotel room, it's you. Just imagine, sleeping as long as you want. Eating whatever you want, whenever you want. Going on a long run and not have to push a double jogger."

Jenna leaned her head back and closed her eyes. "That sounds like heaven." She put the last onesie on a pile of several others and started stacking the folded laundry back into the basket. "I don't know, it seems so extravagant. We have until Tuesday to cancel our reservation for a full refund..."

She stood up, picked up the basket of laundry, and carried it down the hall.

Alex shook her head and gave an exasperated sigh. "I swear, she's got to stop doing this martyrdom thing." She pulled out her phone as Cleo and Morgan nodded in agreement. By the time Jenna returned to the family room, Alex had Mark on speakerphone.

"Hey Alex, what's up?"

"Why are you calling Mark?" Jenna said as she rushed over to the couch.

Alex held her finger up to silence her. "Hey Mark, we're all here at your house for a playdate, and Jenna just told us that you won't be able to make it down to Carmel next week."

"Yeah, it's really unfortunate timing-"

"Congratulations on being invited to the Midas Summit by the way," Morgan chimed in.

"Yeah, I was just telling everyone that Ethan was never able to wrangle an invitation," Alex said. "Anyway, we firmly believe Jenna needs a break and should go by herself.

"Honey, don't listen to them," Jenna protested. "We can go together another time."

"I think that's a fantastic idea," Mark enthused.

"I'm glad you agree," Alex started.

"It's too much money to spend for just me," Jenna interjected.

"Honey, I wouldn't have booked it if we couldn't afford it," Mark said. "You deserve the break more than anyone I know."

Jenna bent over the phone, wringing her hands. "I don't know…"

"Honestly, I'd feel better if you went," he said. "I know my parents aren't always easy to be around, and this way I don't have to worry about whether or not you're getting along."

Alex could tell from Jenna's face that she was coming around. "Well, maybe I could go for a night or two…"

"At least," Mark said.

They said goodbye and hung up.

Alex reached for the bottle of chardonnay chilling in a bucket on the coffee table and topped off her glass. "Hey, aren't you and Ethan going to be down in that area next week too?" she asked Morgan.

Morgan nodded. "Yeah, at the Visicare company retreat. But I'm only going Thursday and coming back Friday." She looked at Jenna. "I'd say we should meet up, but my schedule's pretty slammed."

"Well Ethan will be there until Saturday afternoon," Alex said. "If he has time maybe you two could meet for a drink or something." She met Cleo's gaze, as if to underscore how over the idea of Jenna and Ethan having an affair she was.

"Why don't you and Ava come and keep me company?" Jenna suggested.

Alex laughed and shook her head. "Just what you need, someone else's kid on what's supposed to be your relaxing weekend. Besides, I have too much to do to get ready for the Children's Wellness Council spring gala that's coming up. Ava will be with Sylvia most of next week."

Morgan looked at her apple watch and grimaced. "Crap. I need to get home for dinner. David's making tacos."

Everyone agreed it was time to wrap it up. Alex gathered her glass and Cleo's while Jenna picked up the cheese and charcuterie board they'd been snacking from. As she stood, Alex felt a wave of dizziness and wavered on her feet.

"You okay?" Cleo asked.

Alex shook off the vertigo. "I'm fine, I just stood up too fast."

"Are you sure?" Alex's jaw tightened as Cleo's gaze flicked to the empty wine glasses in her hands. "I can give you and Ava a ride."

Alex did a mental tally of her wine consumption. It wasn't any more than usual. "It's fine."

Cleo shrugged and excused herself to go to the bathroom.

Alex gathered up Ava and all of her gear, as the others did the same. They gathered in the foyer to hug each other good bye.

"Ping me in the morning about hiking," Cleo said to Jenna.

Alex felt a ridiculous little pang at the idea of them making plans without her. But she hated hiking and they knew it, so why would they invite her?

Her car was parked in by both Morgan and Cleo, so she was the last one to leave. She followed Cleo down the long, narrow driveway, then turned right to head towards home. Though the road was curvy and unlit, Alex drove quickly, confidently, knowing these roads so well after driving them for years. As she approached the stop sign at the intersection, a small shoe landed in her lap. Ava immediately squawked for its return. It was a new game Ava had learned from Jack earlier this week. Alex didn't find it at all amusing.

"Ava, I've asked you several times not to throw your shoe." She twisted her body to hand the shoe back to the carseat, and snuck a look at her daughter. She was grinning and clapping her hands like it was the funniest damn thing on the planet.

Alex fixed her attention back on the road to find she'd drifted a little over the centerline. She gave a whisper of thanks that no one was coming from the other side, and pulled to a stop at the stop sign.

She turned right at the intersection, and was just about to turn onto her street when she saw the flashing lights in her rearview mirror. There were no other cars around. The flashing lights could only be for her. Her stomach flipped as she realized she was being pulled over.

As the officer approached, she retrieved her license and registration. The wine's sour aftertaste lingered on her tongue and she wished she had gum or a mint. She could only pray that the garlic and spices from the salami she'd consumed would cover the odor.

She dutifully rolled down the window when he tapped on it. "License and registration."

She held both up to show she was prepared.

He shined his flashlight on them, taking what felt like an eternity to examine them. "Do you know why I pulled you over?"

"I honestly can't say that I do," she replied, trying to keep the nervous quiver out of her voice.

"Back there, before you turned onto Meadow Road, you swerved over the double yellow line."

She forced out a breezy laugh. "I'm so sorry officer. My daughter has this fun new game where she throws her shoe at me from her car seat. I was handing it back to her."

The cop flicked his flashlight to the back seat. In the rearview mirror, Alex could see Ava squint against the bright beam.

"Have you had anything to drink tonight?"

Alex swallowed hard, as her brain scrambled for the correct answer. "Why - why would you ask?" She finally stuttered.

The bright beam of his flashlight hit her square in the face. She forced herself not to recoil. Finally, after what felt like hours, he spoke. "I'm going to need to you to step out of the car."

27

Cleo

"Should we just do the dish loop?" Jenna asked as she stooped down to shove Liam's backpack in his designated cubby at school. As she did so, Noah launched himself from her hip and took off at a speedy crawl. Fortunately one of the teachers scooped him up before he could put anything in his mouth.

The dish loop was a paved trail that led to a giant satellite dish on the nearby Stanford campus. "That's the easiest with the stroller." Frankly, Cleo didn't care where they hiked. She just wanted to work up a sweat and see if she could get any useful information out of Jenna.

"You know me, I don't mind off-roading," she said with a chuckle. Then she paused, looking over Cleo's shoulder towards the door.

Cleo turned to see Ethan leading Ava in by the hand. "I wonder what's going on," Jenna said in a low voice. "He almost never drops Ava off."

Cleo had a pretty good idea. She crossed her fingers, hoping it was true.

They both called hello and waved. Ethan gave them a nod as he took Ava's backpack from her. She ran to join Izzy at the sensory table and he came over to join them by the cubbies.

"Where's Alex?" Jenna asked.

"Car trouble," he replied curtly. "And Sylvia called in sick, of all fucking days."

"Oh no, what happened?" Cleo asked, all ignorance and innocence.

This morning Ethan's charming, easy going demeanor was nowhere to be found. Instead, his brow was furrowed and his jaw had a hard set.

"Not sure," he said as he stuffed Ava's backpack into her cubby. "She just can't drive it. Speaking of, can either of you give

Ava a ride home today?" He looked at his watch. "I better get to the office." He hurried out of the classroom without even pausing to say goodbye to Ava.

"I wonder what's his problem this morning," Jenna said.

"Yeah, he's definitely in a sour mood." *And I'm taking that as a very good sign.* "We should get going if we want to have time for the full six miles."

Jenna nodded and went to say goodbye to Liam. She retrieved Noah, who was happily sitting in teacher Emma's lap, playing with her colorful beaded necklace.

Cleo went to the sensory table and knelt down to say goodbye to Izzy. She squeezed her tightly, kissed her soft cheek. "See you at story time." Izzy nodded and went back to her play.

As she and Jenna were heading for the door, their phones chimed simultaneously.

Cleo pulled hers from the side pocket of her leggings. "It's from Alex."

I know you guys were planning to hike, but is there any way you can come over here? Things are really fucked up right now."

Cleo met Jenna's wide eyed gaze with her own mask of concern. *What's going on?* She typed quickly.

I'll tell you when you get here.

"On our way," Jenna said as she typed.

"What do you think is going on? It sounds bad," Jenna said as they hurried to their cars.

Cleo was pretty sure it started with a D, followed by a U, and ending in an I. "I don't know. I just hope no one is hurt or anything."

Cleo followed Jenna to Alex's house. They parked their cars and Cleo went to the front door with a level of haste meant to convey deep concern as Jenna retrieved Noah from his carseat. Even though Alex was expecting them, it took her several moments to respond to the doorbell.

When Alex opened the door, Jenna let out a gasp.

Alex looked, in a word, awful. Her eyes were puffy and red rimmed, and her complexion had a grayish cast. Dark shadows haunted her eyes and she looked like she hadn't slept for a week. She was still dressed in her robe and pajamas and hadn't bothered to run a brush through her hair.

"Oh my God, what's wrong?" Cleo pushed through the doorway to wrap her arms around Alex. Alex draped her arms heavily over Cleo's shoulders, as though she didn't even have the strength to hug her back.

She could feel Alex's body shudder with a sob.

"What happened?" Cleo said again.

"Did someone die?" Jenna quivered as she placed a comforting hand on Alex's shoulder.

"No, thank God," Alex pulled out of her embrace and rubbed the back of her hand across her nose. "So I suppose it could be worse." She took a deep breath and closed her eyes. "Last night, on the way home from Jenna's, I got a DUI."

Cleo gave herself mental props for the shocked gasp that came from her throat. It sounded just as authentic as Jenna's.

"No!" Jenna said. Then, "How?"

Alex sighed and beckoned them back towards the kitchen and family room. She sat heavily on the sectional. Cleo and Jenna flanked her on either side. They listened as she explained how she had swerved handing Ava's shoe back to her. The sheriff's deputy who happened to be driving behind her on Eastridge witnessed and pulled her over.

Cleo gave an inward shout of triumph. When she'd hatched her plan, she knew it had a fifty fifty chance of coming to fruition. But Alex swerving over the double yellow line was a blessing from the universe that Cleo couldn't have planned any better herself.

Alex was summoned from the car. After administering a sobriety test, the officer arrested her on suspicion of driving under the influence.

"It was horrible, you guys." She closed her eyes as though trying to shut out the memory. "Of course Ava was in the car and she was getting upset. Can you imagine having the cops give you a sobriety test in front of your four year old? Or having her see the police put you into handcuffs?" Her voice cracked on a sob. "And then I had to call Ethan to come pick Ava up because they had to take me down to the police station. I had to spend the night in jail and they impounded my car." She scrubbed her eyes with the heels of her palms.

"What happens next?" Jenna asked softly.

Alex shrugged and sniffled. "I have a court date in a couple of months, and I'm meeting with an attorney tomorrow to talk about possible outcomes."

"You won't get jail time, will you?" However much pleasure Cleo felt at the idea of seeing Alex behind bars in prison orange, she knew she wouldn't be that lucky.

"I guess I can't say anything for sure before I talk to my attorney, but from the research I've done I'll most likely pay a fine and have some restrictions on my license."

"I'm just so glad no one was hurt," Cleo said and gave Alex's thigh a comforting pat. "Things could be so much worse." And for Alex, they would be, soon enough. The private investigator who she'd hired to tail Ethan and Morgan upon their return from Mexico would help ensure that. He'd taken several photos, as well as a few videos, that would absolutely gut Alex when she finally saw them.

"I don't understand how this happened," Jenna shook her head as she set Noah down at her feet. He immediately pulled himself up on the edge of the coffee table and began to cruise around.

"I had too many glasses of wine at your house, got pulled over, and blew a .10. What don't you understand?"

"I don't understand why there was a cop there in the first place. They're always hanging out at the intersection of Oak Valley Road and Willowbrook, but in the four years we've lived here I don't think I've ever seen a police car on Eastridge unless they were specifically called to a house."

Alex shrugged. "Who knows? Maybe someone did call him and he happened upon me on his way out."

Or maybe he was there because right before you left Jenna's, someone called the sheriff's dispatch with an anonymous tip about a suspected drunk driver.

Of course, once the call was placed, Cleo had no guarantee that they would act on it. She loved when the universe worked in her favor.

"I didn't feel I was in a position to ask him what he was doing there," Alex said.

"What was Ethan's reaction?" Cleo asked, though she had a pretty good guess based on his mood at drop off. "He was so angry about what happened at the fundraiser…"

Alex's already pale complexion went impossibly whiter. "He's so angry," she said in a quivering voice. "I don't think I've ever seen him this mad. I honestly don't know what's going to happen to us."

"Don't say that," Jenna admonished. "This is just a speed bump. He got over you passing out at the fund raiser. He'll calm down about this too."

Alex shook her head. "I don't know. You didn't see how he was this morning when I got home. He said he couldn't be married to someone so out of control."

Oh, like you control your dick, Ethan?

"He told me something like this would work in his favor if he ever wanted to go for full custody of Ava."

"That's such a low blow," Cleo said, as though stunned Ethan would go there. But men who fucked their wive's best friends weren't exactly known for taking the high road.

"I'm sure he didn't mean it," Jenna reassured her. "We all say things in anger we don't mean." She gave a little laugh. "I mean, you should have heard me and Mark last week." She paused, then, "I'm sure everything will be fine. You'll get through this together."

Tears welled in Alex's blue eyes. "God I hope so. I can't imagine losing him." She buried her face in her hands as her shoulders heaved.

Cleo felt a pang of sympathy and immediately shoved it away. She wasn't about to feel sorry for Alex just because she finally had to suffer a little bit in her life. She had no idea what it felt like to be truly hopeless. Now she was finally getting a small taste of what Cleo had endured her entire life. And Alex wasn't even close to enduring the worst of it.

"Thanks for picking me up. Even though I'm technically still allowed to drive until my court date, Ethan doesn't want me driving other than to and from preschool." She hadn't even been doing that. Instead she had Sylvia come early to take Ava. On the days Sylvia couldn't, Cleo picked Ava up on her way with Izzy.

"That sounds a bit controlling," Cleo said as Alex buckled herself into the passenger seat. It was just over a week ago that Alex had been arrested, and the first time Cleo had been able to coax her out of the house. "I take it he's still upset?"

Alex nodded. With her hair brushed, a light application of makeup, and dressed in her designer workout wear, she looked a thousand times better than she had the morning after her arrest. But the dark circles under her eyes told her that fallout from the DUI was taking its toll.

"He's still furious, still giving me the silent treatment." She turned in her seat to face Cleo. "He hasn't spoken to me in person for the last week. He only communicates by text."

Cleo backed out of the driveway and headed out towards Oakwood. "That's awful. Honestly, I would expect better from him."

Alex shrugged. "His parents have the same dynamic. They don't fight, they just go quiet."

"Just because our parents treated each other like crap doesn't give us the right to treat others in the same crappy way," Cleo snapped. She considered herself to be a case in point.

"I know," Alex sighed, "and we've talked about it. But it's never gone on for so long before." She was silent for a moment, then sniffed as though holding back tears. "The worst part of it is, it's not like he's just mad at me for making a mistake and doing a bad thing. He's treating me like I'm actually a bad person."

Well, you did drive over the legal limit with your four year old strapped in your car... Even so, it was quite the hypocrisy for Ethan to claim the moral high ground in their relationship.

By the time Alex composed herself she was pulling into the Oakwood parking lot. Cleo turned off the engine and unbuckled her seatbelt. Instead of following suit, Alex sat with her hands clenched tightly in her lap.

"I don't know if I can do this."

"Alex, it's a workout class. Everyone will be focused on their own thing."

"That's bullshit and you know it. I know everyone has been talking about me."

"How would you know since you haven't left the house?" Cleo said, even though Alex was one hundred percent right. Her DUI was the hottest topic since one of the other preschool moms had discovered that her husband was living part time with another woman in New York.

"She's always so put together," Kimberly said at pickup the other day. "You would never suspect she had a drinking problem."

"And to get pulled over at five thirty at night. I mean, how early does she start drinking?"

Although she very much enjoyed listening to everyone tear Alex off the pedestal they'd put her on, Cleo understood the importance of appearing to be Alex's good friend. "Oh please, Melanie," she interjected. "I saw you pour Bailey's in your coffee at Valentine's breakfast."

Melanie's cheeks flushed as several eyes turned in her direction. "But I didn't get hammered and drive around with my kid in the car," she snapped.

Now she reached over to cover Alex's hands with one of her own. They were ice cold under her palm. "Come on, it will be good for you to get some exercise."

Alex shook her head. "I can't. I can't deal right now."

Cleo stifled an exasperated sigh. It was a fucking pilates class, not the gauntlet. "You can't hide from the world forever. At some point you're going to need to face them. Might as well rip the band aid off."

Alex closed her eyes and took several deep breaths. When she opened her eyes, Cleo could detect fear, but also resolve. "Okay. Let's do this."

When they entered the studio, class was already in session. Cleo and Alex laid their mats out in the back of the class. Several people craned their heads, to look at them before the instructor reminded them about neck alignment.

As they moved through the workout, Cleo could feel anxiety emanating in waves from Alex. A few times she paused altogether to close her eyes and take several deep, shaky breaths. Cleo felt a begrudging respect for her as she pushed herself through the entire class, when it was clear she wanted to bolt.

As soon as class ended the buzzing began. Alex smiled at Cleo as though oblivious to the whispers and furtive stares. "Let's grab coffee at my house before pickup," she said brightly. She hurried out of the studio, nodding and smiling at the women whose expressions ranged from judgmental to sympathetic.

"At least that's over with," she sighed as she sank back in Cleo's passenger seat. "God, I thought it was bad after I passed out at the gala. At least that could be explained away as a medical issue."

Cleo reached over to give her a reassuring pat before backing out. "You know as well as I do that this will die down before you know it. In a few days someone's kid is going to bite someone or someone's going to accuse someone's kid of bullying their kid that'll be all they're talking about." *Or it will come out that someone's perfect marriage is anything but, and that will be the scandal of the decade.*

They were mostly silent on the way back to Alex's. When she pulled into the driveway, she asked, "Do you actually want me to come in for coffee, or was that just to make it look like we weren't fleeing the scene?"

"Definitely come in." Alex unclipped her seatbelt and opened her door. "With Ethan barely speaking to me before he went to Carmel and Morgan and Jenna out of town too, I've been feeling pretty isolated."

"I thought you were super busy working on the CWC event coming up."

Alex opened her front door with a tight smile. "Yes, well, someone very kindly let the chairwoman of the board know about my DUI."

"Who would do that?" Cleo asked. As though she didn't remember exactly what she said in the message she left over the weekend.

"Apparently they don't think it looks great for someone with a DUI to represent their cause, so they've asked me to step down."

"That's ridiculous," Cleo said as she followed Alex to the kitchen. "After all of the work you've done for them over the years." It was all Cleo could do not to cackle like an evil genius in a Bond movie. She knew how big of a blow losing her position on the board of such a prominent organization was for Alex. She might have given up her big corporate career for her family, but Cleo knew how important it was for Alex to be well known and well regarded in the community. She didn't want to be seen as "just" a stay at home mom.

Alex opened the top of her coffee maker and added several scoops of grounds to the reusable filter. "I know! Not to mention how much money we've donated." She filled the carafe with water, then poured it into the machine's reservoir. "And don't get me started on how many donations we've generated. The largest donors for the past three years were all recruited by me." She pushed the start button and leaned back against the counter. "Seriously, who gets fired from two volunteer jobs in the space of a few months?"

Someone who appears to be dealing with a worsening substance abuse problem?

"Well fuck them, and fuck the Wyndham board too." Cleo said. "I'm sure there are tons of great organizations that would be more than happy to have your help."

"Thanks," Alex said with a crooked smile. She reached out to give Cleo a hug. "I really appreciate what a great friend you've been to me."

Cleo smiled and returned her hug. "Of course. I'm just so grateful for how you've welcomed me into your life." *And I'm so grateful you have no idea how much you're going to regret that.* "It's not easy moving someplace new, and you've definitely made moving to Oak Valley much better than I expected."

"Aw, you're going to make me cry." Alex sniffed and ran her thumbs under her eyes.

The coffee maker beeped, signaling the pot was ready. Cleo went to retrieve two mugs from a cabinet while Alex took a carton of half and half from the refrigerator. Alex just started to pour coffee into one of the mugs when they heard the heavy front door open and slam shut.

Alex paused, her brow furrowed in concern. "Hello?" She called. "Who's there?"

Ethan's deep voice echoed from the entryway. "It's me."

"Isn't he supposed to be gone until tomorrow?" Cleo asked quietly.

Alex nodded and finished pouring. "You're home early," she said with a tight smile as he appeared in the doorway of the kitchen.

"Yep." He had his computer bag over his shoulder and a small duffel in one hand. It was clear he wasn't going to offer any explanation for his early return.

"Cleo and I are just having coffee." As though Ethan couldn't figure that out for himself.

Ethan nodded and flashed a tight smile at Cleo. The tension between them hung thick in the air. Cleo took it all in, feeding off that negative energy. "I should probably get going," she said. "Seems like you two might need a minute."

Ethan held up a big hand, stopping her as she started toward the entryway. "Don't leave on my account. I just came home to grab my extra phone charger and then I'm headed to the office." He set both his computer bag and the duffle on the kitchen island and headed down the hall to his office.

Alex flashed her a pained look. "See, it's like he hates me."

Cleo was too fixated on the duffle bag to concern herself with Ethan's hostility towards his wife. "Of course he doesn't hate you! Go talk to him. Tell him you understand why he's so upset, but the way he's treating you is unacceptable."

"I don't think that will fly with him right now."

"Well you have to do something. The longer this goes on, the worse it will get. You have to find a way to get him to soften up."

Alex didn't look totally convinced, but she left the kitchen to follow Ethan into his office. Cleo felt a surge of contempt. Alex was like a kicked dog, slinking back to her abuser to beg for crumbs of affection.

She retrieved her purse, marveling at yet another stroke of incredible luck. She listened carefully for any sound of their approach. She had been carrying around a piece of clothing for over a week, waiting for the perfect opportunity. Ethan, when he left his duffle bag unattended on the kitchen island, had just presented her with it.

She opened her purse and unzipped one of the interior pockets, from which she retrieved a pair of pink and white polka dot cotton granny panties. As she stuffed them into Ethan's bag, she wondered if Jenna had even noticed that they were missing.

28

Alex

"Okay, I'm off." Ethan came over to the kitchen table where Ava was finishing her breakfast while Alex sipped her coffee and checked emails. He bent to give Ava a noisy kiss on the cheek.

Then he turned to Alex and gave her a soft kiss on the lips. The tension had started melting between them a few days ago, but she still felt a wash of relief that he was no longer icing her out. Alex had learned over the years with him that no amount of cajoling, apologizing, or trying to force him to talk would work. She just needed to be patient and bide her time while he worked his way through his moods.

It wasn't the healthiest dynamic, but when Alex had once suggested they go to therapy to discuss it, along with some other issues, he had firmly shut it down.

"I'm from Montana. We don't do therapy."

She'd learned to live with it, especially since, until now, his moods had never lasted more than a day or two. This time, he'd kept up the silent treatment for three more days after he'd returned from Carmel. That, combined with his remarks about her DUI charge helping him in a custody battle, had her completely unraveling, terrified that this was something they could never come back from.

To her relief, a few days ago he had woken up and started treating her as though the past few days hadn't happened. Well, other than to ask about how her appointment with her DUI attorney had gone.

Now, she tipped her face up, cupped his cheek in her hand and returned his kiss enthusiastically. "You have a dinner tonight right?" She asked as he straightened.

He nodded and reached for the computer bag that he'd set on the kitchen island.

"What time do you think you'll be home? Should I wait up to watch Ozark with you?" Two years after the series finale, they were finally making their way through the Netflix drama.

"Actually, I was thinking I might just stay in the city tonight."

She frowned. "Your reservation is at seven. How late do you think it will go?"

"It's not just how late it goes. I was just thinking that if I'm going to be drinking it's probably a safer choice for me to stay in a hotel rather than drive."

"It's not like you're going to get hammered-"

He held up a hand. "Obviously not. But your arrest was a wake up call. It shows just how easy it is to just have one too many, but still think you're fine to drive. And even if I'm not over the limit, if I get in any kind of accident or anything like that, any alcohol in my system means more trouble."

It was on the tip of Alex's tongue to point out that he could choose not to drink at all. But their truce was so new and fresh she didn't feel safe rocking the boat. "Ok." She rose from her chair and went to give him a hug and another kiss. "I guess we'll see you tomorrow sometime?"

"I'll come home early so I can spend extra time with you two." He flashed her the grin that, after all of these years, never failed to make her toes curl and her skin feel tight.

Ethan came home early from the office the next afternoon as promised, and the three of them met up with Jenna, her boys, and Cleo and Izzy. Jack was there too, with Irina since Morgan was still at work.

"Looks like you guys have smoothed things over," Cleo remarked when Ethan took Ava to push her on the swings.

Alex gave a hollow laugh. "Yes, apparently he's decided he still wants to be married to me. Everything seems to be back to normal."

However, over the next week, Alex couldn't shake the feeling that something was still off between them. She tried to rationalize it by noting that Ethan's work schedule had dramatically intensified recently. Not only was he habitually working longer hours than ever since starting at Acorn, he had two more business dinners and subsequent hotel stays in the same week.

Then of course, there was the biggest elephant in the room: the fact that they hadn't had sex since she'd been arrested. She made a note to rectify that as soon as possible.

That evening when he came home she made a point to be extra affectionate. Once Ava was tucked into bed, she poured him a bourbon and joined him on the family room couch. He picked up the remote and pulled up the latest episode of Ozark as she snuggled against his side. She rested her hand on his thigh, and about halfway through the episode she began to inch it higher.

When it was next to his groin, he placed his hand on hers and interlaced their fingers. "Whatcha doing down there?"

"I don't know," she said, "I just thought I'd check and see if there's a package waiting for me." She tried to move her hand to cup him through his gym shorts. He held it fast.

"I really want to watch this," he nodded to the TV.

Despite the darkness the TV screen must have illuminated her face for him to see her dismay at his rejection. He lifted her hand up and pressed a lingering kiss to her palm. "Later, I promise."

She nodded and focused her attention back on Marty and Wendy Bird and their quest to buy a riverboat. But she couldn't shut out the voice in the back of her head that reminded her that in the seven years they had been together, not once had Ethan turned her down for sex.

By the time they finished three episodes, Ethan had consumed two more bourbons and it was after eleven. Unsurprisingly, Alex exited their bathroom after performing her nightly skin care routine, Ethan was sprawled against his pillow, a snore rumbling from his throat.

So much for later.

She turned out the light and nestled into her pillow. As she drifted off to sleep, a little voice that sounded remarkably like Cleo's whispered, "Maybe he's getting it somewhere else."

"I don't know what you're so worried about," Jenna said a couple of days later when everyone gathered at Alex's for the weekly playdate. "Mark and I have had some crazy dry spells." It was early March and spring was very much in the air. They opted to sit outside by the pool while Sylvia kept all of the kids entertained in the playroom.

"So have David and I," Morgan said. She reached for the bottle of Chardonnay and held it over Alex's empty glass with a questioning look.

Alex reluctantly shook her head and covered her glass with her palm. "I'm switching to seltzer." She pulled out the bottle of Pellegrino chilling in the bucket and filled her glass.

"Why does it matter?" Morgan said as she filled her own glass, then topped off Jenna's. "It's not like you're driving anywhere tonight."

She shrugged and sipped her water. "I know, but I made a commitment to myself and to Ethan that I would cut back. Even if I'm not driving, I don't need to be buzzed enough to blow over the limit at four thirty on a Wednesday afternoon."

"I guess that makes us the drunkards," Morgan said and clinked her glass against Jenna's.

"That's not what I meant and you know it," Alex sighed. She paused for a moment, unsure if she really wanted to say what she was about to say. Once she actually said it out loud, there would be even more of a spotlight on the issue.

But hell, these women were her best friends and she trusted them more than anyone in the world. "Look, it's no secret that I've had a tendency to drink more than you guys when we're hanging out. Normally I'd be on my third glass right now, while you two," she indicated Morgan and Jenna with her glass, "are only on your second. Cleo's barely halfway through her first. I've always rationalized it because I'm bigger and taller and therefore can tolerate more, but that's clearly not the case."

Jenna set her glass on the low table in front of the outdoor couch and leaned toward her. "Do you actually think you have a drinking problem?"

Alex paused before answering. She'd been thinking about this question before the DUI, even, if she was honest, before she passed out in front of everyone at the fundraisers. How many times had Ethan gotten upset with her for having a few glasses of wine and letting loose with a story that she found hilarious, but he found embarrassing or hurtful?

In the past, she'd brushed it off as his fragile male ego, patiently waited for him to have his pout, and continued business as usual until the next time.

"I wouldn't say I'm an alcoholic, but alcohol has been a factor in enough fights with Ethan and other problematic episodes in my life. I feel like it's important for me to take a serious look at my relationship with it."

The other three nodded sympathetically and contemplated their glasses. "I'm sure all of us have had times where we need to cut back or take a break entirely," Jenna said.

"Well I have no intention of cutting back any time soon," Morgan said tightly. "I've been under so much stress lately I feel like the wine is the only thing that keeps me from completely bouncing off of the walls. "

"Ethan's been really stressed lately too," Alex said. "Maybe that's part of why he's not up for it, so to speak."

"I'm sure that's part of it," Jenna said. "When Mark is super stressed, he's not interested at all. He's getting ready to raise another round of funding right now, and he's barely touched me lately."

Cleo leaned forward in her chair and rubbed her thumb and forefinger against each other. "Hello, here is the world's smallest violin playing for you. Have you forgotten that you're talking in front of a woman whose husband is gone so much, I cough and a cobweb shoots out of my cootch."

Alex choked on a sip of water as the others exploded in laughter. "I know, I know," she said when she could finally breathe. "But you don't understand, in all of the years Ethan and I have been together, this is the longest we've ever gone without having sex. Even when we were going through IVF and really struggling, we still did it once a week."

"Didn't you have to take a break after Ava was born?" Cleo asked.

Alex shrugged and sipped at her water. "He was getting blow jobs a week after we got home."

Cleo looked at her with a look of horror. "Your husband made you suck his dick when you had a newborn?"

"He didn't make me," Alex said, flustered. Cleo wasn't the first woman to sound appalled at the prospect. "My point is, he's always had an extremely high sex drive." So high that she'd felt compelled to satisfy it, even when her body was exhausted and sore and leaking milk. Alex had always been secretly proud, taking it as a point in her favor that she was so much more attentive to her husband in this way than her friends were.

"Having a high sex drive is one thing," Cleo said. "Expecting a blow job when your wife has just given birth is another."

Alex's shoulders tightened as she bristled at Cleo's judgment. "You once asked how I could be so sure Ethan would never cheat? A big part of that belief is because I know that he's not going to go looking if he's not lacking at home."

An uncomfortable silence settled over them as everyone came to the same conclusion.

Morgan was the first to voice it. "So you're worried that if he's not looking for it at home, he's getting it somewhere else."

"I guess so," Alex managed to squeeze around the knot in her throat.

"I'm sure that's not true," Jenna was quick to reassure her.

Too quick? Alex thought as Cleo's suspicions about the dynamic between Jenna and Ethan stabbed to the surface.

Jenna continued. "He's working a lot, he's stressed out. Then he comes home, has a drink or two, then, whoomp," she held up her index finger and let it go limp.

"It's just so weird, how it happened so suddenly," Alex protested.

"Everyone slows down eventually," Morgan said, an edge of irritation in her voice. "You think this is bad, try being married to a guy in his forties." She tossed back the rest of her wine and plunked it down on the table with more force than necessary.

"Mark and I just started putting it in the calendar," Jenna offered.

"That sounds awfully business-like," Alex said. "Isn't sex supposed to be spontaneous?"

Jenna shrugged. "Two little kids, no regular childcare, and a husband who works at least twelve hours a day does not leave room for spontaneous sex. Not with any regularity, anyway. So now we look at the calendar at the beginning of the week and make sure we have it in the calendar at least twice."

Morgan picked up her phone and. "Oh yes, here it is, 'fuck husband,' Monday at two fifteen," she mimed looking at her calendar.

"Make fun of it all you want," Jenna said as she reached for a piece of salami and a slice of Manchego. "But I think it's really helped our sex life. He knows he's going to get it, so he doesn't feel rejected if I'm not in the mood the rest of the week. And I don't feel pressured to do it when I don't feel like it or guilty if I turn him down."

"What if it comes time for your appointment and one of you isn't in the mood?" Cleo asked.

"So far that hasn't been an issue. It's like knowing we're going to have time for it helps me anticipate it more."

"It doesn't sound like the funnest approach," Alex said, "but at this point it's worth a try." However, she wasn't going to just settle for a random half hour on a week day. If she had to resort to scheduling sex with her husband, she was going to make it special.

That night, after they put Ava to bed, Alex curled up next to Ethan on the couch to watch their show. Before he could push play on the remote, she said, "I want to go away for a night this weekend."

"I guess that's ok," he said. "I can ask Sylvia to help out if I need it."

She laughed and gave him a light swat on his arm. "No, I want the two of us to go away for a night."

He frowned. "Are we celebrating something I forgot about?"

"No, it's just that you've been so busy lately, and it's been hard to… connect with you." She paused and rested her hand on his thigh. "If you know what I mean."

He nodded. "I do, and I'm sorry for that. A night away will be good for us." He leaned over and gave her a kiss on the cheek.

A combination of happiness and relief burst in her chest. "Awesome. I'll book a room at the Ritz and make sure Sylvia can stay with Ava. Which night is better?"

Ethan pulled up his calendar on his phone. She peered over his shoulder and saw that while Friday was jam packed with meetings until six, Saturday was completely clear.

"Saturday should work," he confirmed.

"Great. I'll see if Sylvia can come early so we can spend the day there."

Even though he didn't make a move on her that night or for the next two days, Alex comforted herself with the fact that Saturday and Sunday they would be loads of hotel sex. So much sex she'd be lucky if she didn't end up with a UTI.

Then Friday afternoon he came home earlier than expected. She knew something was wrong the moment she saw his face. "What's wrong?"

He dropped his computer bag on a kitchen chair. "I'm so sorry to do this, but I have to go to San Diego until Monday."

Disappointment stabbed at her gut. "For work?"

He nodded grimly.

"Why in the world would you have a work trip on the weekend?"

He ran an exasperated hand through his hair. "It's complicated, but the long and short of it is that we've been trying to schedule a meeting with Raj Patel for months now."

Alex recognized the name of the billionaire tech investor. "He's playing in a golf tournament this weekend and has agreed to see us if we go to him."

"That's ridiculous! Just do a zoom call!" Alex raged.

"This guy is… eccentric. He doesn't want to do anything online, because he thinks people will spy on him." He rolled his eyes.

"Even so, why do you have to go for the whole weekend? Can't you just meet him tomorrow morning and fly back?"

"Like I said, this guy is on his own program. He's agreed to meet with us sometime between tonight at eight pm and Sunday at two. But he won't tell us until thirty minutes before."

"These goddamn tech bros and their power plays," Alex fumed. "I thought you were done dealing with egos like this."

"As long as I'm in this business I'll be dealing with egos like this," he said with a weary chuckle.

"I was really looking forward to our night away," Alex pouted.

"Me too," he said and pulled her into his arms. "I'll make it up to you, I promise."

She wrapped her arms around his waist. She tipped her head back and gave him a sly smile. "Ava is still asleep. We could get in a quickie before she wakes up."

He grimaced and sucked in a breath through his teeth. "Unfortunately our flight leaves in an hour and a half. I have just enough time to pack and get to the airport."

Fifteen minutes later, she closed the door behind him, shoulders slumped. She looked at her watch. Four o'clock. A reasonable hour for her first glass of wine. As she started for the kitchen, she noticed his gym bag where he'd dropped it next to the entryway closet. She picked it up and took it to the bedroom to put it in his closet.

Whatever is in there probably needs to be washed, a little voice whispered. *You better take everything out and put it in the hamper for when the house keeper comes.*

She unzipped the bag, knowing full well it wasn't the dirty laundry she cared about. She pulled out a couple of crumpled t-shirts, a pair of shorts, and two socks. She put the faintly musty pile of clothes on the floor and saw that there were some scraps of paper underneath. They were receipts, she noticed. One for the hotel in Carmel where he'd stayed for the recent conference, another for a restaurant nearby.

Nothing out of the ordinary, she thought as she released a breath she didn't realize she'd been holding. Then she noticed the interior zipper pocket on the right side of the duffle's interior. She slid her hand inside, felt a scrap of fabric. She pulled it out and held it up in front of her.

Her vision tilted and her stomach bottomed out as every cell in her body tried to reject the reality of what she held in her hand.

Underwear. Women's underwear. More specifically, pink, cotton, utilitarian, granny panty, underwear.

The kind of underwear Alex had never worn a day in her adult life.

29

Alex

Alex felt as though she was freezing from the inside out, even as a film of sweat coated her body. Her heart raced and her breath came in sharp pants as she stared at the fabric in her hand.

There was a strange, high pitched sound echoing through the entryway. After a few moments she realized it was coming from her. She swallowed hard, trying to get her heart to stop beating against her ribcage, to get her hands to stop shaking as she desperately tried to deny what this meant.

Her mind raced with possibilities. Maybe they were Sylvia's. She stayed over with Ava occasionally. They could have gotten mixed up with their laundry. Just last week Ethan had gone to pull on a pair of gym shorts and found a pair of Alex's lace panties stuck to them.

But the last time Sylvia had stayed over had been months ago. What were the chances a random pair of her underwear would have gone unnoticed, only to appear months later in Ethan's gym bag?

Please God, please don't let this be true.

But there was no other explanation. Ethan was cheating on her. Even though she'd had her suspicions recently, as long as there was no concrete evidence to point to, she could continue to believe in his fidelity.

All it took was a few square inches of cheap cotton to shatter her faith.

Tears spilled down her cheeks as she slid to the floor. Her shoulders heaved in sobs as her mind spun out of control contemplating what the future might hold.

She didn't know how long she sat there, sobbing and shaking as her entire world tipped off its axis.

"Mommy?" Alex started at Ava's voice, calling from down the hall. Christ she'd all but forgotten that Ava was home napping. She pushed herself to her feet and swiped her fingers under her eyes.

"Coming sweetie," she called in a wobbling voice. She ducked into the powder room to blow her nose, splash cold water on her face, and wipe away the mascara streaming down her cheeks. She took several deep breaths. *Pull yourself together. If this is really happening, if he really is that guy, you are going have to stay strong for Ava's sake. You are going to do things differently. What happened to you will not happen to her.*

She patted her face dry with a hand towel and went down the hall to Ava's room. She was sitting up in bed, her arm curled around her stuffed panda. Her round cheeks were flushed and her hair was flattened on one side. Alex's heart swelled painfully in her chest. What would all of this mean for her sweet, innocent girl?

A sob rose in her throat as Ava lifted her arms. So trusting that her world was safe. So ignorant of the fact that her mother's world had just been shattered. Alex swallowed back the sob as she bent down to gather Ava in her arms. She lifted her from the bed, holding her like her life depended on it. She buried her face in the curve of Ava's neck, breathing in her sweet little girl scent. No matter what happened, she had her healthy, perfect girl to take care of.

"Ow, mommy, too tight." Ava squirmed.

Alex forced herself to loosen her arms as she carried Ava to the bathroom. "Sorry. Mommy just needed an extra big hug today." She sat Ava on the potty, then took her into the kitchen for a snack without any thought. Her brain could only focus on one thought: her husband was cheating on her.

She sat across from Ava, wanting to crawl out of her skin, wanting to teleport herself from this moment, this reality. She wanted a drink, a pill, anything to calm her down.

On the table, her phone pinged, announcing an incoming text. It was Jenna, texting to the thread that included Alex, Morgan, and Cleo. *What time are you guys headed to Oakwood? Liam is up from his nap and bouncing off the walls. Was thinking of having him swim before dinner. Join?*

"Fuck," Alex said before she could stop herself. Ava paused, a strawberry halfway to her mouth.

"What fuck mean?"

Alex bit back another curse and scrambled for an answer. "It's just something grown ups say sometimes when we're frustrated. But it's only for grown ups, ok?"

Ava nodded solemnly. She continued eating her strawberries as a wave of dread washed over Alex.

She couldn't possibly join everyone for dinner and act like none of this was happening. Especially since that style of underwear-

She cut the thought off abruptly. It was too much to even contemplate with everything that was happening. She could only survive one nuclear blast at a time.

She quickly replied, *Sorry not going to make it tonight. Ava's not feeling well.*

After Ava finished her snack, Alex sat her in front of the TV and started an episode of Bubble Guppies. She sank down on the couch and stared into space as she tried and failed to make sense of her world. She picked up her phone, started to dial Ethan's number, then stopped. She couldn't do this over the phone, especially with Ava sitting next to her. The conversation they needed to have was too big, too huge, too life altering.

She stared at her phone, wanting to talk to someone, anyone, to help her process what was happening. At the same time, once she told someone, there was no taking it back. Anyone who knew would have opinions about Ethan, opinions about her. Opinions about what decisions she would make about her marriage.

You know, infidelity is a deal breaker, right? She swallowed back a sob as her own words echoed in her head. They were still in business school, dating but not engaged yet. Ethan had just found out that his brother was having an affair, but he and his sister in law were determined to work it out.

I would never stay with you if you did that to me. I would be out of there so fast there would be skid marks.

But that was easy to say when you didn't have seven years of life and a child together.

I would never cheat. I know first hand how painful it is to be cheated on. At the time, she had no reason to doubt his word. He'd told her all about how his college girlfriend, who he was convinced he was going to marry, had cheated on him with one of his fraternity brothers.

She didn't doubt that he meant what he said at the time. She'd meant what she'd said too. But now, punched in the face with the reality of his betrayal, it wasn't nearly so cut and dried. Instead of setting his clothes on fire, or packing herself and Ava up and leaving without so much as a word, she was stunned into inaction. Caught in the limbo of before and after, incapable of determining the best way to move forward.

A little after five thirty, her phone chimed with another text. It was from Ethan. *At the airport. About to take off. Will call you when I land. Love you both.*

Her heart felt like it was collapsing on itself. How could he love her and do this to her? To them? The pain was so sharp she could barely breathe.

She got up from the couch and went to the refrigerator. She pulled out a bottle of chardonnay and retrieved a glass from the cabinet. While Ava watched episode after episode of Bubble Guppies, Alex worked her way through the bottle. When Ava got hungry, Alex heated up some chicken nuggets and let her eat them in front of the TV.

As Alex opened another bottle, it occurred to her that it might be a good idea for her to eat as well. She picked up a chicken nugget from Ava's plate and took a bite. She chewed it into a paste, and even then could barely swallow it.

Ava's bedtime came and went, but Alex was too wrapped up in her head to bother taking her to her room. Eventually Ava slumped over on the couch, fast asleep. Alex pushed herself up, swaying a little bit as she did so. She bent to pick up Ava and started to topple over. She caught herself on the back of the couch before she smothered her daughter under her weight. She took a moment to steady herself, then scooped Ava up from the cushions.

By some miracle, she got Ava to her room and tucked into her bed without dropping her. She thought about going to bed herself, but the thought of lying in the bed that she shared with Ethan made the bowling ball that had settled in her stomach swell to twice its size.

She went back to the family room and switched from Ava's show to the cooking channel. She didn't pay any more attention to Guy Fieri yammering on about some greasy spoon than she had to the adventures of Zooli, Nonny, and Deema. She went to pour another glass of wine, frowning when she realized the bottle was empty.

A tiny voice of common sense tried to convince her that two bottles was more than enough. She overrode it, rationalizing that extreme circumstances required extreme amounts of alcohol. She needed the wine to make her forget that the husband she adored was cheating on her.

At three forty four a.m. Alex woke up, face down on the couch. The glass of chardonnay she'd been holding had tipped over, leaving a sour smelling stain on the ultrasuede. Her mouth tasted like vinegar and felt like she'd been eating cotton balls.

Her mouth filled with saliva and her stomach seized in a cramp. She heaved herself off of the couch and hurled herself down the hallway towards the bathroom. She barely made it three steps before her stomach heaved. She sank to her knees as two and a half bottles worth of Chardonnay erupted onto the hardwood floor. She retched until there was nothing but bile left and slumped against the wall.

Her gaze snagged on a picture hanging on the wall. It was of the three of them. Ava, just over a year old, sat on Alex's lap as they grinned at each other. Ethan looked at Alex with such adoration it usually made Alex's heart swell.

Now she looked at it and felt like a shriveled, empty husk.

Who would have thought that the woman in the picture would end up drunk, despondent, sitting next to a pool of her own vomit?

She dragged herself from the floor and cleaned up the mess as best she could in her inebriated state. She went to the bedroom and changed into pajamas, but still couldn't bring herself to climb into their king size bed. Instead she went to Ava's room, lay down on the twin mattress and curled herself around her daughter.

She woke a few hours later to Ava whispering, "Mommy," and patting softly on her cheek.

She cracked open one sticky eyelid, then the next. For a few seconds she forgot why she was here instead of in her own bed. But it didn't take long before her hangover was joined by an overwhelming sense of dread.

Determined not to betray any of that to her daughter, she mustered up a smile and croaked a good morning.

Ava recoiled against her pillow. "Mommy, your breath is stinky!"

She could only imagine. "Then I better go brush my teeth."

They climbed out of bed and Ava followed her to the bathroom. She brushed her teeth while Ava used the toilet. They went to the kitchen where Alex downed several glasses of water and struggled not to gag at the smell of Ava's scrambled eggs cooking. She checked her phone and saw a missed call and voicemail from Ethan.

I'm here in San Diego on my way to the hotel. I was hoping to say goodnight to Ava before she goes to sleep. Love you both.

Her throat tightened and her eyes burned with fresh tears at the loving words, the seeming sincerity in his tone. She scrubbed at her eyes, determined not to fall apart in front of Ava.

As the morning went on and her hangover faded, Alex grew more and more restless. The knowledge of Ethan's affair was like a snake roiling around inside her, threatening to consume her from the inside out. She had to get it out, had to talk about it with somebody.

But everyone she would usually tell were close to Ethan or possibly involved in this hideous situation.

Except for one. She picked up her phone and texted Cleo. *Are you around? Can Ava and I come over?*

Thankfully her reply was immediate. *Sure. But I thought you and Ethan were headed out for your sex fest ;-)*

A mirthless laugh exploded from her throat. Had it only been yesterday afternoon that she'd been anticipating a romantic, sex filled, getaway with her husband? It felt like a hundred years ago.

Getaway is canceled. I'll explain when we get there.

30

Alex

"We're out in the garden," Cleo called to Alex as she helped Ava out of her carseat.

Alex took Ava by the hand and led her through the gate. She found Cleo crouched down in one of the flower beds pulling weeds from the ground while Izzy watched.

Cleo looked up at the sound of the gate closing. "What's going on?"

Alex's hand tightened around Ava's as she swallowed hard. Her throat constricted at the thought of telling Cleo what she'd found. "I'm always so impressed that you do all of this yourself."

Cleo gave her a confused smile. "You know gardening is my therapy."

Alex gave a mirthless laugh. "Maybe I should take it up." She reached out to touch a delicate white blossom.

Cleo grabbed her wrist. "Careful. That's called a tread softly. The bloom and the leaves are covered with tiny stinging hairs. If you so much as brush against it you'll get a terrible rash."

She dropped her hand to her side. "Did you hear that Ava? Don't touch that flower."

Cleo stood up. "Actually, all of the flowers in this bed are a little dicey. Izzy knows better than to touch anything, but we should move the girls away."

"Why would you plant flowers that aren't safe around Izzy?" She asked as Cleo led them over to a wrought iron table with a painted ceramic top and gestured for them to sit.

Cleo gave her a sly smile. "Sometimes the most dangerous things are the most beautiful."

Something niggled at the back of Alex's brain, a strange ping, a warning of sorts. Warning her of what, she couldn't identify.

The feeling vanished as Cleo sat down across from her and asked, "Are you going to tell me what's up? I know you didn't come over here to talk about gardening."

Panic washed over her, making her heart race and sweat bead on her upper lip. Her face felt oddly numb, her lips stiff as she struggled to form words. "It's bad," she finally managed. She darted a meaningful look at Ava, then at Izzy whispering nearby as they contemplated a bug.

Cleo understood immediately. "Izzy," she said and stood. "Why don't we go inside and ask Clara for a snack?"

As she led the girls inside, Alex stared blankly at the explosion of color that was Cleo's flower garden. How was it that such beauty could exist in the world when what was happening in her life right now was so ugly?

"They're settled," Cleo sat back down, a look of concern on her face. "Tell me what's going on."

She swallowed and tried to catch her breath. "It's bad," she repeated.

"No offense, but I can tell that by looking at you. You look like shit."

"I feel like shit." The last word came out as a sob. She bent her head as her shoulders and chest heaved. She was vaguely aware of Cleo's arms wrapping around her as she made soothing sounds.

It was several moments before Alex was able to speak. She dug a Kleenex from her purse, blew her nose, and wiped her eyes. She took a shaky breath, reached into her purse and pulled out the scrap of pink cotton that forever changed how she viewed her marriage. "I found these in Ethan's gym bag."

Cleo picked them up, eyes wide. "They're not yours, I assume?"

Alex shook her head and bit her lip as a tear rolled down her cheek. "I'm a Commando girl, all the way." Alex had been wearing the lingerie line's seamless bikini briefs for nearly a decade.

Cleo's brows furrowed and her eyes narrowed as she studied the pink cotton underwear more closely. "Those look like-"

"Don't say it." She cut her off. "I don't want to believe Jenna could do that to me."

Cleo put the underwear down and reached out to take Alex's hand. "We never really know what anyone is capable of."

"No, I guess we really don't," she said in a quavery voice. "Honestly, I don't know how she would even have time. She's always with her kids-" she stopped abruptly. Her gaze locked with Cleo's. She knew from her expression Cleo had just connected the same dots.

"Carmel," they said in unison.

"She was there the same weekend he had his conference." Alex felt a surge of nausea. She remembered how refreshed, almost glowing Jenna was when she returned from her weekend. When she had commented on it, Jenna gleefully chalked it up to two nights of uninterrupted sleep.

Apparently fucking your best friend's husband was positively rejuvenating.

"Do you think this has been going on for awhile?" Cleo asked.

Alex shrugged. "Who knows? I mean, you picked up on something the night of the auction. We've all been close for the past three years."

"I wonder if Mark should do a paternity test on Noah," Cleo said.

Just entertaining the possibility that Ethan might have been sleeping with Jenna long enough to have fathered her second child sent a tsunami of rage through her. She seized it with both hands, relieved for a moment to feel something other than devastating grief. "That fucking bitch. After all I've done for her, after what a good friend I've been to her, she goes and fucks my husband?"

She stood from the chair and paced angrily around the garden, kicking at the gravel that lined the pathway through the flower beds. "And that mother fucker. I got him through business school and set him up with his first investors in his company. I supported him until he got it off the ground, put my body through hell to have his child, and this is how he treats me? What did I do to deserve this?" She felt the rage drain from her as quickly as it had appeared, leaving her deflated.

Cleo pulled her into her arms and Alex fought not to crumple onto her smaller friend. "This isn't about you deserving it and you know it. It's all about them and their selfishness. They don't care if they hurt you as long as they get what they want."

"How could they not care about hurting me?" Ethan's face appeared in her head, smiling so tenderly on their wedding day. Looking at her with utter adoration as she cradled a newborn Ava. His expression morphed into that shark like look he got when he was angry. Dead eyed, soulless, utterly uncaring. It was easy to imagine that man not giving a shit about tearing her heart to bits. She clung to Cleo as sobs once more wracked her body. They made their way back over to the table where Alex all but collapsed into her chair.

Cleo excused herself to go to the bathroom. She returned with a box of Kleenex and a glass of ice water. Alex gratefully plucked a tissue from the box, blew her nose, and gulped down the water as Cleo assured her that the girls were still happily playing inside.

"What are you going to do?"

"Right now, putting on my Jimmy Choo stilettos and stomping on his balls sounds pretty good," she said. But she knew that wasn't what Cleo was really asking. "Honestly, I don't know. I always thought infidelity would be a deal breaker. I always said if he ever cheated on me, I would leave him, no question. But…"

"But it's different when it actually happens. It's not that black and white."

"Are you speaking from experience?"

"Not with Scott," Cleo said. "At least not that I know of. We're apart more than we're together, so it would be easy enough for him to get away with it." She shrugged. "But my last serious boyfriend cheated on me, and I stayed with him for two more years after I found out."

"What made you stay? It's not like you were married or had kids like we do now."

Cleo shrugged again. "I still loved him. And we'd been together for three years at that point. I thought I was going to marry him. I didn't want to throw all that away over something he convinced me was nothing more than a casual fling."

"I guess I need to ask myself the same question. I don't even know if it was a one night stand or if they're like, in love." Bitterness burned at the back of her throat as she wondered what was worse: Ethan risking their marriage for a meaningless fling, or risking it because he was in love with someone else. "I don't know what to do."

"You don't have to know right now. You don't have all of the information you need. But whatever you decide is best for you and your family, I will have your back, one hundred percent."

Alex gave her a shaky smile as gratitude pierced through the blanket of grief. Her life might be going to hell, but at least she knew she could count on Cleo. "Thanks for being such a great friend to me."

Cleo once again reached for her hand. "I'm here whenever and however you need me."

31

Jenna

Are we on for playgroup tomorrow? I know Morgan is out of town but I'm happy to host here.

Jenna hit the send button, then put her phone down to turn her attention back to the boys. Liam sat on his booster shoveling yogurt into his mouth while Noah gorged on cheerios and strawberries.

Her phone dinged.

From Alex: *Sorry. I have a lot going on this week.*

Cleo's reply quickly followed. *Izzy hasn't been napping very well this week. I think we'll lay low.*

Jenna's stomach clenched as she frowned at their replies. She momentarily considered suggesting that they meet another day, that way Morgan could be included. But the idea felt desperate and awkward. Which was a horrible way to feel when you were talking about an interaction with people who were supposedly your closest friends.

She hadn't seen Alex since before she flaked on Friday night dinner last week. When Jenna had reached out to her over the weekend, she waited hours for a response, only to be blown off. Alex had seemed similarly standoffish at school drop off and pick up yesterday, breezing quickly in and out with vague explanations about being in a hurry.

As Jenna drove out of the Wyndham parking lot, she noted that Alex was not so busy that she didn't have time for what looked to be an intense conversation with Cleo.

"What's with the face?" Mark's voice behind her pulled her out of her stewing. He bent to kiss her cheek, then her neck. Even through the distraction of potential friend drama, she felt a little shiver skate down her fine. After their fight, they'd had some long, productive discussions, as well as several scheduled sex dates.

Like she said to Alex, it was amazing how something like putting sex with your husband on the calendar worked wonders in helping them feel more connected.

"Alex is being weird," she said with a shrug.

"How so?" Mark went to the coffee pot, poured himself a cup, then topped her off.

As he sat down across from her and sipped his coffee, she explained the lack of response, the seeming evasiveness, and the vague excuses for canceling their regular playdate. "I get that things come up, but we've been meeting every week for over three years. You'd think if they both had to cancel, one or both of them would suggest another day to meet."

He set his mug on the table and pressed his lips together thoughtfully. "At the risk of hitting a sore spot, I think you might want to consider that you're reading too much into this."

She cocked an eyebrow at him, then turned to Liam, who held up his empty yogurt cup. "Mow yogut peese?"

"I got it," Mark jumped up and went to the refrigerator. "I forget, which flavor does he hate?"

"Peach," Jenna replied.

Mark returned to the table and placed the cup of strawberry yogurt in front of Liam. He happily shoveled a bite into his mouth. As drops of yogurt steamed over his wrist, she could hear their pediatrician scolding her for feeding him so much sugar, and cautioning her that so much dairy would make him constipated.

Shut up, Dr. Presad. I'll brush his teeth, slip him some prune juice, and call it good.

It was ridiculous how obsessed she was with her children's diets, considering how she'd survived her childhood drinking from a garden hose and binging on Spaghettios.

"I appreciate your diplomacy," she returned to the subject of Alex. "And you're right, I have a tendency to be over-reactive, some might even say paranoid."

Mark looked at her, his expression attentive but impassive. *Smart man.*

"But," she continued, "something about this feels weird. I can't shake the feeling that she's avoiding me, and that somehow she and Cleo are like, joining forces against me."

Mark pressed his lips into a small line, and she knew him well enough to know he was suppressing an eye roll.

She tamped down a spurt of frustration at his dismissiveness. "I get it, it sounds like I'm accusing a couple of thirty somethings of middle school crap."

"It does seem a little immature."

"I'm not saying it isn't, but believe me, if you hang around these moms enough, you will see some shit pulled straight from seventh grade. It's just that now usually kids are involved. I know it sounds silly to you, but my gut is telling me something weird is going on here. Alex is blowing me off, and I have no idea why."

With no additional insight to offer and a meeting to get to, Mark finished his coffee, kissed them all goodbye, and promised to be home by dinner time.

Jenna was in the process of wiping down Noah before pulling him out of his high chair when her phone rang. Her stomach flipped when she saw her brother's number on the display. It had been weeks since she'd asked him to see if he could find any information on Cleo.

While she and her brother were close, most of their regular communication was via text. It was highly unlikely he was calling just to shoot the shit.

She desperately wanted to answer, but Noah was fidgeting in the high chair, making increasingly loud sounds of frustration. Liam was fiddling with the clasp that strapped him to his booster seat, seconds away from painting the walls and furniture with strawberry yogurt.

She let the call go to voicemail, reminding herself that it would be better to talk to her brother when the kids were napping or otherwise occupied.

As she got the boys cleaned up and Noah dressed and packed for school, she listened to Jeremy's voice mail.

Hey, just wanted to let you know that I finally had a chance to look into your friend. There's not a lot there, but I found a couple things. Call me when you can.

Jenna's heart thudded in her chest and she felt light-headed with anticipation.

After dropping Liam off at school (and brusquely brushing past Alex), instead of strapping Noah into the jogging stroller for their usual run, she made a beeline for home.

Once she arrived, she put Noah in his exersaucer, dragged it in front of the TV, and turned on the Teletubbies. She pulled out her phone and dialed her brother's number.

Her brother's phone rang two, three, four times. Her jaw clenched in frustration. Of course, Jeremy was notoriously hard to get a hold of. Depending on his case load, it could take him days to call her back.

Miraculously, he picked up. "What's up, sis?"

"What did you find out? And go quickly because I probably only have about ten minutes before Noah decides that he's had it with the exersaucer."

He gave a little chuckle. "I hear you. I don't have a lot of time either. We had a body turn up in the park this morning and I'm supposed to meet the ME in thirty."

"Ok, shoot."

"Can you get on your computer? This will be easier if I can share my screen."

Confirming that Noah was still occupied, she darted down the hall to their office and retrieved her MacBook. She brushed the layer of dust from the top - it had been that long since she'd used it - grabbed the charger and went back to the kitchen table. She powered it up, keeping one eye on Noah in the family room to watch for signs of a meltdown.

She logged into the zoom link that he sent her and was greeted by her brother's smiling face. They shared similar blond haired blue eyed all American good looks. His nose was a little bit bolder and his jaw squarer. And, she noticed with a grimace as she looked at her own hi res image, he didn't have dark circles around his eyes so big they looked like she'd been in a bar fight.

"So what did you find?" She asked.

"Like you said, I wasn't able to find anything on Cleo Baird."

"Which is very unusual, for someone to have no digital footprint whatsoever," she interjected.

Derek grinned. "You're the one who should have been a cop. But yes, you're right. It's very strange in this day and age for there not to be a stray picture or a work bio of some sort. Now, I'm not going to tell you how I did it but I was able to get into her DMV records where I found something odd. Her car lease isn't in her name or her husband's. It's leased under an LLC based in the Cayman Islands."

Jenna frowned. "So she's like, a tax dodger?"

"Could be. In any case, it's strange. So then I called a buddy at the bureau and was able to get a copy of her tax records, and that's when I found something really strange. When I ran her social security number, it matched with a Cleo Baird from Alabama."

"She said she moved around a lot as a kid, so I don't know why that would be so strange."

"It's strange because Cleo Baird died in nineteen ninety one at the age of three.

Jenna sat back with a gasp. "Shut the front door. Cleo Baird is a fake identity?"

"It appears that way."

"I knew it," she crowed. "I knew she was hiding something." She didn't think it was as big as a false identity, but she was relieved to know her instincts weren't off. "Do you think she's in witness protection or something?"

"I suppose it's possible, but I doubt it. Most of the people in witness protection don't have glamorous backstories or end up living in multi million dollar houses."

"What if she turned on the mob or something but was able to hide a bunch of money in the Caymans first," Jenna said, her mind spinning with possibilities.

"Don't get carried away," he said with a chuckle. "There's more."

She sat back in her chair and motioned for him to go on.

"Once that big red flag was raised, I asked my buddy to put that picture you sent me through the facial recognition system."

"Wow, you called in a lot of favors for this," she said, impressed.

He shook his head, his expression a little sheepish. "I'm like you, once I start down the trail, I can't stop until I figure out what's going on. Now this is where it gets really interesting."

On the screen, her brother's face disappeared, replaced by a photo. It showed several middle aged men on what appeared to be a super yacht, surrounded by several bikini clad women who looked to be in their twenties. "See this woman, on the far right?" He used the cursor to indicate an enviably slim blonde woman in a bright pink bikini. Her face was partially in profile, but the angle of the jaw and line of the nose could be a match.

"Where is that?"

"This was taken off the coast of Thailand, but that's not the only place she pops up." Another picture appeared. "Here she is in the south of France." Another took its place. "And here she is in Barcelona."

In the last photo, there was no denying the resemblance to Cleo. "Who is she?"

"I wasn't able to find that out, but she shows up in a lot of different places with a lot of different men."

"So she was like, one of those girls who sleeps with rich older men for fancy trips and handbags?" She grimaced at the thought of letting one of those chubby, hairy men from the photos paw at her.

"I don't know the specific nature of her relationships with those men, but it's certainly not unheard of."

"Yeah, a podcaster I listen to calls it 'hooker-lite.' You're not a full blown prostitute, but it's understood that you put out." She gave a little shudder of disgust. Call her a prude, but in her opinion, no luxury vacation, designer bag, or any amount of money was worth what Cleo - or whatever her name was - was evidently willing to endure.

Another thought occurred to her. "Why would the FBI have all of these pictures? Why do they care about a bunch of rich men and their sugar babies?"

"Because some of them earn their money in unsavory ways, like drugs, human trafficking, arms dealing."

"Wow." She shook her head, trying to imagine how Cleo went from partying on mega yachts with arms dealers to being a stay at home mom in tiny little Oak Valley. "Do you think maybe she pissed someone off? Hence the fake identity?"

"Could be. Some of these guys are capable of things you can't even imagine."

"I wonder how she got all of her money."

"Apparently Saudi princes and Russian Oligarchs are extremely generous."

Jenna shook her head. "Or maybe she bamboozled one of the billionaires into marrying her and things went south. I still don't understand why she would come here, of all places. And if she's hiding from something, why would she go out of her way to make such a big splash in the community?"

"That I can't tell you, sis. But knowing you, eventually you're going to find out."

32

Alex

Even though Alex knew to expect Ethan home Wednesday evening, her heart still leapt to her throat when she heard the sound of his key. She was cuddled up in bed next to Ava, reading her a story as they waited for Ethan to come home and kiss her goodnight.

"We're back here," she called, hoping he didn't notice the quiver in her voice. Every cell in her body was on high alert, trembling in sick anticipation of the confrontation to come.

He walked in, his face breaking into a smile at the sight of them. "There are my girls."

The lump in her throat threatened to choke her as she wondered how he could look at them, at her, with such seeming adoration, then betray her in the most brutal way?

He climbed onto the bed on the other side of Ava, who eagerly threw her arms around his neck and snuggled close. "Oh, I've missed you," he said and gave her a smacking kiss on her cheek.

He lifted his head and leaned over to Alex. "I've missed you too," he said and bent his head to give her a lingering kiss.

Alex forced herself to return it like everything was normal. As though she hadn't found what she was certain was a pair of her best friend's panties in Ethan's gym bag. Call her sick, call her pathetic, but despite everything she felt a pulse of lust as he lightly traced her lips with his tongue.

Apparently after all of this time, it was hard wired in her to desire this man. When he lifted his head, he looked at her with eyes blurred with a passion she hadn't seen in weeks.

Confused, she turned to Ava to give her a kiss goodnight.

"I'll be out in a few minutes for you to welcome me home properly," he winked.

As she walked to the kitchen, a sliver of doubt worked its way into her brain. Could she be wrong about all of this? Could his lack of desire really be chalked up to his anger over her arrest compounded by stress at work?

She so desperately wanted it to be true that when he joined her in the kitchen and pulled her into his arms, she went willingly. She let him guide her down the hallway, kissing her all the while as he tugged her shirt out of her waistband.

She stretched across the bed, eagerly welcoming his weight on her as she slid her hands up the back of his shirt.

But as he pulled off her shirt and slid his hand inside her bra to cup her breast, an image assaulted her. One of him, his hands on Jenna's breasts, still so perfect and perky despite nursing two babies. Once it took root, it was joined by another, then another, until every shred of desire vanished as she couldn't think of anything but her husband fucking her best friend.

Suddenly his hands on her skin, his tongue in her mouth, were revolting. "Stop, I can't," she wriggled out from under him and sat on the side of the bed, gasping for air.

"What the hell?" He sounded equal parts pissed and confused.

"I can't do this right now." She reached for her shirt and pulled it back over her head.

"Why the hell not?" He flipped over and propped himself up against the pillows. "For the last few weeks you've bitched about me not wanting to have sex, and now that I do, you're freaking out?!"

She took a shaky breath and kept her back to him, her eyes downcast. She needed a pedicure, she thought as she noted a chip in the red nail polish adorning her big toenail. "I need to talk to you about something."

"Really? I just walked in the door and all I want to do is make love to my wife, and you need to talk?"

Her shoulders knotted and she felt like she had swallowed a bowling ball. What if she didn't say anything? What if she pretended it didn't exist, and she just fucked him like he wanted and made him happy?

Her skin crawled in revulsion. She needed to know the truth, even if that truth destroyed her life as she knew it.

She stood up and went to her closet. She opened her sock drawer and reached into the corner where she had stashed the offending garment. Bile choked her as she pulled it out.

She went back to the bedroom. His jaw was clenched and his arms were folded across his bare chest.

She held the underwear up for him to see. "I found these in your gym bag." Her heartbeat throbbed so loud she could barely hear herself speak. "Please tell me they don't mean what I think they mean."

His brow furrowed in confusion. "What are you talking about?" He sounded genuinely bewildered.

"I'm talking about finding a pair of women's underwear that doesn't belong to me in your gym bag."

His brows shot up his forehead and he held his palms up in defense. "I have no idea how they got in my bag. I've never seen those underwear in my life."

"Really, you expect me to believe that they snuck into your bag of their own volition while you were at that conference in Carmel? You're trying to tell me these don't belong to some whore you slept with while you were there?"

"I don't know what the hell you're talking about. I told you, I've never seen those underwear in my life."

Her conviction wavered at the utter sincerity in his expression. Was he telling the truth? Or was he really that much of an accomplished liar? "Do you swear on Ava's life that you have no idea how these got into your bag?"

He set his jaw as his eyes burned with fury. "I swear on Ava's life that I have never seen those before, and I have absolutely no clue how they got into my bag. The best explanation is that when I had my laundry done at the hotel, they got mixed in with my stuff."

Though far etched, it was a plausible explanation. Before she could fully ponder it, he turned on her in self righteous anger. "Fucking hell, Alex, I'm sick of all of the constant suspicion that I'm cheating on you!" He swung his legs over the side of the bed and stood up. Even though she was a tall woman, he still loomed over her, the muscles of his chest and shoulders bunched in fury. "Maybe at this point I should just do it. Is that what you want?"

"Of course not," she said in a voice thick with tears.

"Hell, if I'm going to be punished, I might as well commit the crime."

He flung his arms up over his head and Alex couldn't keep from flinching.

He lowered his arms and took a deep breath. "Don't act like I'm going to hit you. You know I'd never do that."

Honestly, she wasn't sure that she knew anything about anybody anymore, especially Ethan. Her breath choked on a sob. "I'm sorry. I don't want to believe that you would ever cheat on me. I just feel like everything is about to fall apart and I don't know how to stop it." She buried her face in her hands as sobs overtook her body.

She stiffened at the feel of his hands on her shoulders, pulling her close. Despite the alarms still ringing in her head, she found herself relaxing into him, instinctively reaching for him for comfort. She so desperately wanted to believe he was telling the truth.

Maybe he is. Just because people who were supposed to love and protect you betrayed you in the past, doesn't mean Ethan will too.

"You promise me you're not cheating?"

She could feel his breath against the top of her head as he let out another exasperated sigh. "For God's sake, yes I promise." His arms tightened around her until it was hard for her to breathe. "Get me a stack of bibles and I'll swear on them. But unless you actually find me with my dick inside another woman, I don't ever want to talk about this again."

She nodded in agreement.

He kissed her then, hard, his tongue thrusting deep as one hand fisted in her hair. Still discombobulated, she was more overwhelmed than aroused by his ardor. Still, she didn't resist when he steered her back to the bed, pulling at her clothes as he did. While he was always a vigorous lover, tonight he was even less tender than usual. She wasn't sure if his lack of finesse was a sign of overwhelming passion, or a result of his anger. But when he bent her over the side of the bed and took her roughly from behind, she didn't offer any resistance. She squeezed her eyes shut and feigned enjoyment, grateful that despite her greatest fears she was the only one he was doing this with.

He was soon snoring beside her. Alex stared into the darkness, unable to sleep. Despite Ethan's reassurances, adrenaline still pumped through her body, her reptilian brain sending the message that if she didn't do something her very life was in danger.

She slipped out of bed and went into the bathroom. For the first time since the disastrous holiday fundraiser, she pulled her bottle of Xanax out of the medicine cabinet and shook a pill into her palm. She washed it down, drinking directly from the faucet. She straightened and glanced guiltily around her as though Ethan might be lurking, waiting to catch her.

She padded back to bed and slid beneath the covers. As she drifted off to sleep, she wondered why she felt guilty, when it was Ethan who was the one acting shady.

When she woke up the next morning, the sun still hadn't fully risen. The other side of the bed was empty. Ethan's phone sat charging on the nightstand.

As though of its own accord, her hand reached for it and keyed in the passcode. The fact that he hadn't changed it since the last time she had snooped had to be a good sign, right? A voice in her head warned her that if Ethan caught her snooping, there would be hell to pay. But she couldn't stop, compelled by a force greater than common sense to scroll through his texts, search his emails.

Now, as the last time she'd snuck into his phone, there was nothing to raise suspicion. She knew there were apps that could hide secret accounts and messages, but Ethan had only the basic apps that came preinstalled with the phone, a fitness app, and rideshare apps. He didn't even have Instagram, so no way for anyone to slide into his DMs.

Not that you know of, anyway, a little voice whispered. She shoved it aside. She had to stop this. Not only had Ethan given his word that he had no idea where the underwear had come from and that he wasn't cheating, there was no evidence on his phone that contradicted him.

It was time to put her paranoia to bed and appreciate her husband for the amazing partner that he was.

She lay back on her pillow. She had over an hour before she needed to get Ava up and ready for school. She closed her eyes and tried to go back to sleep, but it was soon clear that wasn't going to happen. She got up, used the bathroom and pulled on workout gear, thinking she'd squeeze in a rare early morning workout.

She went into the kitchen to fuel up on water and coffee and found Ethan sitting at the kitchen island. He held his phone in his hand, his gaze focused on the screen as his thumbs moved across the keyboard.

Her stomach flipped and there was a hissing sound in her ears as the image of his phone, charging on his nightstand flashed in her head.

"Oh hey," he flashed her a smile and set his phone down on the countertop. Alex didn't miss the fact that he'd put it face down.

"You're up early," she managed. He must have grabbed his phone when she was in the bathroom. That had to be it.

"Just catching up on some emails. You going to workout?" He asked, taking in her attire.

"I figured I'd get it in before Ava gets up. That way I can get some work done while she's at school."

"Good idea," he said and pushed off of the barstool. "I made coffee," he said as he walked over to the pot. "Want some?"

"Sure," she said. In her head, her voice sounded like it was coming from several feet underwater. "I'll be right back. I left my AirPods on the dresser."

She forced herself to walk at a normal pace back to the bedroom, trying to control the panic that made her want to take off at a full sprint. She walked through the door, past her dresser, past the AirPods in their case sitting on top, her gaze laser focused on Ethan's bedside table. His phone sat, still charging, right where she'd left it.

33

Cleo

"Where is it?" Cleo had followed Alex home from Wyndham drop off. She had watched as a visibly upset Alex all but ignored Jenna's attempt to engage her, her mouth pulling into a grin as she took in Jenna's distressed expression. The wedge between those two was growing deeper by the day.

When Alex stopped her as she was getting into her car and said, "I found a phone," Cleo could only hope it would be yet another nail in that friendship's coffin.

"Here," Alex pulled an older generation iPhone out of her purse. She quickly keyed in the pass code and handed it to Cleo.

Cleo opened the messages and started scrolling through. "How did you figure out the passcode?"

A scoffing sound erupted from Alex's throat as she plopped onto a barstool at her kitchen island. "He's so fucking predictable. He uses some variation of Ava's name and her birthday for every passcode. It only took me three guesses."

Cleo looked up from her scrolling. "You'd think he'd be a little more careful."

Alex turned to her, eyes welling with tears. "I'd think he shouldn't have to be careful, because he shouldn't have anything to hide."

Cleo felt a surge of satisfaction at the crack in Alex's voice.

"So what do you think?" Alex wiped her nose on the sleeve of her sweatshirt.

Cleo read back through several messages. "They only go back a couple weeks, and there's not anything like, super sexual or dirty."

"Yeah, but a lot are to make plans to meet up and talk about how excited they are to see each other," Alex said shakily. "And he might be too dumb to think up a better passcode, but he's smart enough to go back and delete conversations."

Cleo sighed and set the phone down on the counter. "And then there's the fact that the messages are only between Ethan and whoever SB is." The initials were associated with a number Alex didn't recognize. "Do you think SB is Jenna?"

"Obviously that's not her number, but she could have a secret phone too. If you scroll back, there's a message where he tells her he gets off on sitting across from her husband at dinner. How many times have we all had dinner together in the past six months? Or however long this has been going on?" Once again tears spilled down her cheeks.

Cleo loved the fact that with her blotchy cheeks, puffy, red rimmed eyes, and contorted face, Alex was an ugly cryer.

Suddenly Alex sat up straight and grabbed the phone. "I'm going to call her."

Cleo reached out and stayed her with a hand on her wrist. "I don't think that's a good idea."

"Why not? Why shouldn't I call Jenna to tell her to leave my husband alone?"

Because I'm not ready for you to find out that the person on the other end isn't Jenna yet. "Because you don't want to tip your hand. You need to get your ducks in a row and figure out how you want to proceed as rationally and calmly as you can."

"And by how I want to proceed, you mean whether I stay with him and try to save this thing, or if I decide to leave him."

Cleo nodded. "If you call her and rage at her, it makes everything messier no matter what direction you choose. If you decide to leave, it makes you look overly emotional and unstable-"

"Which I think is understandable in this situation," Alex interjected.

"True, but that doesn't mean he couldn't potentially use it against you. God knows guys love to tell anyone who will listen about how they could have been great husbands if only their wives weren't batshit crazy."

"And if I decide to stay?" Alex asked in a strangled whisper.

If you decide to stay, nothing would give me more pleasure than imagining you spending the rest of your life miserably monitoring his every move, knowing that if you make one wrong move in his eyes, you risk pushing him into another woman's bed.

"If you stay, you don't want to do anything to add to the drama or bad feelings in the community. This is a small town, and the more people who know, the more people will judge. Him for fucking around in the first place, and you for putting up with it."

Alex's gaze dropped to her clenched hands resting on the countertop. "I don't know what to do."

Cleo placed a hand on her shoulder. "You don't have to yet. You're in shock. This isn't the time to make any major decisions about your and Ava's future."

Alex's phone chimed from inside of her purse. She pulled it out to read the incoming message.

"Jenna?" Cleo asked at the look of disgust that crossed Alex's face.

"'Can we get together? I really need to talk to you.'" She read in a sing songy voice. "I just bet you fucking do, you bitch. 'Sorry, busy'" she said as she typed.

Her phone chimed again. "'Please, it's really important.' Unless it's more important than the fact that my husband's dick has been inside your vagina, I don't need to hear it."

She put her phone on do not disturb and shoved it back in her purse. She stood and started pacing around the kitchen. "I feel like I'm going to lose my mind, sitting here waiting for the other shoe to drop. I need to get out of here."

Cleo stood and checked the time on her phone. They still had an hour and a half until pickup. "Let's go for a walk. Exercise and fresh air will help clear your head."

Alex shot her a glare and mumbled something about fresh air being overrated. But she retreated to her bedroom and reappeared wearing her running shoes. She shoved her phone in the side pocket of her leggings and headed for the front door, Cleo on her heels.

As they walked down the front steps, they froze at the sight of the driveway gate opening to allow Jenna's highlander to pull through. She roared up the driveway, parked in front of the garage, and quickly climbed out of the car. Through the open window, they could hear Noah fussing, but Jenna paid him no attention.

Alex folded her arms across her chest and met Jenna with a clenched jaw and hard stare. "What are you doing here Jenna?"

Jenna hesitated at Alex's obvious hostility. "I don't know what I've done to upset you or why you're avoiding me."

"Oh really?" Alex scoffed.

Cleo stifled a smile at Jenna's look of genuine bewilderment. "Yes, really, Alex. I've been trying to get a hold of you for days because I need to talk to you." She gave Cleo a look. "Alone."

"Anything you want to say to me, you can say in front of Cleo. God knows she's been a better friend to me in the eight months that I've known her than you ever have."

Jenna's hand went to her chest as though she'd been shot. "Alex, I don't have any idea why you're upset with me, but I need to tell you that she," she pointed at Cleo, "isn't the person you think she is."

Cleo's stomach clenched as she wondered exactly what Jenna had managed to uncover. She let none of her turmoil show on her face, furrowing her brow in seeming confusion. Before she could defend herself, Alex jumped in.

"How dare you come here a to trash talk Cleo to me -"

"I'm not coming to trash talk, I'm here to tell you the truth!"

"The truth about what?" Alex shouted, shoulders squared aggressively. "The truth about you fucking my husband?"

The air went deadly silent. Not a bird chirped, not a leaf rustled. Even Noah sat mute in his carseat.

Jenna's mouth moved, but no sound came out for several seconds. "I don't - I'm not," she finally sputtered.

"Bullshit. I found your fucking underwear in his bag." She stepped towards her and gave her shoulder a shove. "I found the fucking burner phone he uses to make plans with you."

"I swear to God, Alex -"

"I'm so sick of people I'm supposed to trust lying and stabbing me in the back!" Alex cut her off with a yell.

"You can't possibly think -"

"I don't think," Alex bit out. "I know."

Jenna's eyes welled up with tears as they darted between Alex and Cleo. "Whatever she's led you to believe about me," she pointed at Cleo, "it's a lie. Everything she says is a lie-"

Alex held up a hand to silence her. "I think I know who's lying here."

Jenna took in a shuddering breath and let out a mirthless laugh. "Fine," she spat as she swiped her sleeve under her nose. "If you really believe that about me, you deserve whatever happens next." She got in her car and slammed the door so hard the sound echoed through the canyon behind Alex's house. She peeled out with a squeal, leaving two dark skid marks on the sandstone pavers lining Alex's driveway.

Her dramatic exit was compromised when she had to wait at the bottom of the driveway for the gate to open.

When she turned back to Alex, she saw that she was pale and shaking. Cleo came to her side and put her arm around her waist. "Let's walk. It will help you flush the adrenaline out." She guided her down the driveway to the pedestrian gate that opened onto the trail that ran past her house.

"I can't believe it," she kept saying over and over as they walked with no particular route in mind. "I can't believe she would do that to me. That she would betray me that way."

Cleo shrugged. "Who knows. Her life is kind of a shit show right now. And it's not like Mark is some Adonis. Maybe she just wanted a little taste of what you have."

"I guess all that talk about her and Mark's amazing sex life is total bullshit. All I know is that even when I was broke and desperate, I would have never fucked a married man just to cheer myself up."

A wave of rage roared through her, so intense it turned her vision red. Her fingers curled against the urge to wrap themselves around Alex's throat. How dare she so casually throw out words like broke and desperate. Cleo considered herself restraint to be legendary, but even she had her limits. "Oh please," she snapped with disdain she couldn't fully disguise. "As if you've ever been even remotely close to being broke and/or desperate."

Alex stopped short and turned to her with a furrowed brow. "You haven't known me my entire life. You don't know my story."

I know all about your fucking story. She bit back the retort, forcing herself to rein in her hostility. She had conned Alex into thinking she was her closest confidante, that she could trust her more than anyone on earth. Even one of her best friends of three years. She couldn't risk pushing her away. Especially not now when she was so close to achieving what she'd come to Oak Valley to do. "You're right. I'm sorry. I don't know everything you've gone through. I know you talked about some challenging times when Ethan was starting his company, but I just assumed that most people at Stanford business school don't come from the most humble of backgrounds."

"There's such a thing called student loans," Alex huffed as she started down the trail again. Faster this time, as her irritation gave her a boost of energy.

Cleo hurried after her. It made sense that Ethan paid his tuition through loans. The fact that he grew up on a ranch without much money and was a self made man was a major part of his brand as an entrepreneur. But everything she knew about Alex and her upbringing screamed a fully funded education. And then some.

"What are you talking about?" Cleo said, trying to keep the derision from her tone. "You grew up in one of the wealthiest suburbs of Chicago. You told me about your lake house and going with your parents to the country club."

Alex turned to look at her, her lips pressed into a tight line. "Yes, for the first fourteen years of my life, we were very, very well off. But after my father died, everything changed."

As they continued walking, Cleo felt like her entire world was spinning off of its axis, as she began to realize that so much about what she believed about Alex and her charmed life were lies.

34

Alex

"I knew your father had passed. I didn't realize it happened when you were so young."

Alex's chest constricted and her stomach felt queasy like it did any time she allowed herself to think about her father's death and its aftermath. "I don't really talk about it much. It was a really dark time for us. Not that leading up to that had been a cake walk."

"But you just said up until then you were very well off."

"The saying money doesn't buy happiness exists because it's true. My dad made a boatload of money, but no one in that house was happy. He and my mom fought all of the time. I'm pretty sure he cheated on her for most of the marriage. I guess what they say about marrying your parent is really a thing," she laughed mirthlessly. "Anyway, the money was the only good thing, I guess, and probably the only reason my mom stayed with him."

"That must have been really hard for you."

Alex shrugged. "I threw myself into school and did every activity I could. I would go to my friends 'houses after school as many days as they would have me. I learned very early on to pretend nothing bad was going on. But then, a few months before he died, things started getting worse. My dad was already a big drinker, but his consumption increased dramatically. I even caught him spiking his coffee in the morning before work. He would rage at me and my mom for not appreciating how hard he worked to provide this great life, and how we just viewed him as a walking ATM."

"Right before he died, I found him at the kitchen table, drinking a glass of bourbon, staring into space. I asked him what he was doing. He gave me this blank look and said, 'my best. Please remember I always tried to do my best.'" She shook her head and shivered at the memory. "To this day, every time Ethan pours himself a bourbon, I have to stop myself from gagging. Anyway, the next day while I was at school and my mom was at some charity luncheon, he went out to the garage, climbed in the car, and turned on the engine."

"I thought you told me he died of a heart attack."

Alex let out a harsh laugh. "That's what my mother wanted everyone to think. She even went so far as to bribe the medical examiner to put that on his death certificate. She couldn't bear the scandal if people knew he'd committed suicide. Not to mention, his life insurance policy would have had a suicide clause. Not that it mattered in the end."

"Because there was so much other money the life insurance payout was superfluous?"

Alex wasn't completely sure, but she thought she heard a sarcastic edge in Cleo's voice. She stopped in the trail, turned to face her friend and put her hands on her hips. "Actually, it was quite the contrary. After he died, when my mom was finally able to access his accounts, we realized that not only was there no money, he had gotten us nearly half a million dollars in debt."

Cleo's complexion went ashen, her mouth agape in shock. "How could that happen without your mother knowing?"

Alex waved a hand in exasperation. "She had no interest in finances. My dad ran all of our money through his business for tax reasons, and as long as the mortgage was paid and my mom could buy herself and me whatever we wanted, she didn't care."

"So what did you and your mother do?"

"My mother did what many women who haven't worked in over a decade and have grown used to a certain lifestyle do: she found another wealthy man to marry. Within six months of my father's death, my mom was engaged to a son of one of the wealthiest families in Chicago."

"So it sounds like everything worked out for you pretty quickly?"

Alex pulled out her phone to check the time, unable for a moment to speak around the choking sensation that overtook her whenever she thought about those years in her step father's house. "We should turn back," she finally choked out, and turned back toward her house.

They walked in silence for several moments before Alex finally said, "We were once again in great shape financially, and my mother loved the meteoric rise of her social standing. So much so that she didn't care that my step dad's twenty year old son started molesting me when he came home from college that Christmas." She steeled herself at Cleo's horrified gasp, which was the typical response the few times she'd shared this part of her life with anyone. When she spoke again, her voice sounded oddly distant, as though she was listening to someone else tell the story.

"When I told my mother, she slapped me across the face and told me not to make up such malicious lies. She warned me I was going to ruin his future, saying things like that about him."

"What about your future?" Cleo exclaimed, her voice full of righteous anger.

"My future was apparently acceptable collateral damage as long as it kept my mother in a mansion on the lakeshore and an unlimited budget at Marshall Fields. So when it happened again when he came home for the summer, I knew I was supposed to shut up and take it." Pain and fury burned in her chest as memories she kept locked away flooded her brain.

"Oh, my God, I'm so sorry." Cleo reached for her and pulled her into an embrace so tight she almost couldn't breathe. When she loosened her grip and stepped back, Alex could see tears shimmering in her eyes. "I will never understand how a mother could treat her daughter so horribly."

"I know," Alex's voice trembled and tears rolled down her cheeks. "I mean, I love Ava so much, I can't imagine a scenario where I'd sit by and let someone hurt her." She wiped her nose on the sleeve of her jacket as they continued walking. "As soon as I turned eighteen, I packed up the BMW they bought me for my sixteenth birthday and never looked back. I never asked for a dime. Not even if it meant giving up my spot at Princeton. So yeah, I do know how it feels to be broke and desperate."

As Cleo absorbed the truth about Alex's past, guilt, grief, and anger twisted in her gut, threatening to overwhelm her. Her body trembled as she struggled to hold back her sobs as she finally saw Alex for who she really was. Beautiful, yes, but flawed too. Privileged, wealthy, entitled, even. But also a woman who had welcomed a stranger into her life and into her heart, never suspecting that the stranger was here to destroy her.

And most of all, Alex, like Cleo, was a daughter whose parents had failed to love her and protect her when she needed them most.

"Cleo? Are you ok?"

Cleo shook her head and realized she'd frozen in the middle of the trail. Tears blurred her vision so much she could barely make out Alex's concerned expression. She took a shuddery breath and swiped at her cheeks. "I'm sorry, it just makes me so sad and so angry for you. None of that should have ever happened to you. None of it."

"It's okay. I've had a lot of years and a lot of therapy to help me work through it," said Alex, clueless to the fact that Cleo was referring to what she herself had done to wreak havoc in Alex's life. Alex reached out and pulled Cleo in for another hug. Guilt stabbed at her chest at Alex's efforts to comfort her. "Come on, we both need to pull ourselves together and go pick up the girls."

Alex gave her one last squeeze and started on the path back home. Cleo walked behind her, wondering how she could have gotten everything so wrong.

She gave herself a mental shake, Alex was right, she thought. She needed to pull herself together. She still had lives to ruin. Alex's, however, was no longer one of them.

35

Morgan

"So as you can see their sales are projected to double in the next two years, so I think it's critical that we get in on this next round." Morgan was presenting at Acorn's weekly partner meeting, making what she thought was a compelling case to invest ten million dollars in a real estate investing platform.

Katherine Sheldon, who, until Morgan was promoted, was the only female senior partner at Acorn, pursed her lips and shook her head. "There are so many other startups coming into this space. The landscape is changing so quickly, I don't think you can trust those numbers."

Morgan resisted the urge to level her with a glare. Rather than embracing the philosophy of women supporting other women, Katherine viewed younger, more attractive Morgan as a threat, and never missed an opportunity to undermine her.

"Interesting you should bring that up, because on my next slide you'll see that I've done a comprehensive market analysis," she nodded to her assistant to click to the next slide. "What I've found is that even though there are several companies trying to get into this space, RealtyWise's unique technology gives them -"

She was interrupted by a loud gasp. She turned to see Katherine, her mouth agape as she stared at her phone.

"Katherine, do you need to step out?" She said, irritated.

Katherine dragged her gaze from her phone and regarded Morgan with a look that was undeniably smug. "No, but you may want to."

Morgan furrowed her brow as several gasps echoed Katherine's, many of them followed by furtive glances. She darted a look at Ethan. He stared at his phone, his skin so pale it was gray.

She felt her stomach bottom out and her heart thud against her ribs as she scrambled for her own phone. There were several text alerts, the most recent being from a number she didn't recognize. She thumbed open the message app and saw that there were photos attached. She opened the first picture. A low buzz started in her head as she saw a man, who was unmistakably Ethan, and a woman, who was unmistakably her, walking out of a restaurant holding hands. They were friends, she thought frantically. Surely they could explain away the handholding.

However, as she swiped through the other dozen or so photos, each one more graphic than the last, she knew there was no way she was going to be able to explain this away.

###

"Hey, it's me," Cleo said as Alex's phone once again sent her to voicemail. "I just wanted to see how you're doing. At least shoot me a text to let me know you're okay." It had been nearly twenty four hours since Cleo had used a spoof number to send the pictures to everyone at Morgan and Ethan's office, as well as to every parent in the Wyndham School directory. She had waited nearly half an hour to call her the first time. The shock and horror in her voice in that first message wasn't difficult to summon up. She was still writhing in the throes of her own pain and guilt over her misdirected campaign to take Alex down.

Alex hadn't responded to any of her texts or calls. As far as Cleo could glean at drop off, where the playground was abuzz with gossip about the shocking affair, Alex hadn't reached out to anyone. Neither Ava nor Jack were at school that morning, which didn't surprise Cleo at all.

But Alex's lack of response was starting to worry her. Cleo knew how social she was and how much she loved and relied on her friends. It didn't make sense that she wouldn't reach out in the face of such devastation.

As more time passed with no word, Cleo's sense of dread grew. What if she had miscalculated? What if, instead of showing Alex the truth about the people she loved so she could cut them out of her life and move on, this sent her so deep into despair that she did something to hurt herself?

She thought of the Xanax in Alex's medicine cabinet and the wine in her refrigerator. Even if Alex didn't mean for anything to happen…

Unable to wait any longer, she asked Clara to pick Izzy up from school, grabbed her car keys, and sped over to Alex and Ethan's house. She keyed in the code for the gate and parked in front of their garage. She rang the bell and waited several moments but there was no answer. She tried the knob, found it unlocked as usual. It always baffled her that they had taken the time to install a state of the art security system, only to leave their front door unlocked even when they weren't home.

She let herself in and called for Alex but there was no answer. She called again, and finally heard a faint, "In here," coming from the kitchen. She found Alex there, staring zombie-like out at the pool. Even though it had been only a day, Alex looked diminished, her face pale and gaunt, as though she was withering away.

Cleo put her purse down on the kitchen island and rushed to her side. "I was so worried," she said as she pulled Alex into her arms. "When you didn't return any of my messages, I was so scared maybe you had done something to yourself," she said as she stepped away.

Alex grimaced. "Believe me, I've spent most of the last twenty four hours trying to figure out how I can escape the reality that is my life, but I would never leave Ava like that."

Cleo gave a sigh of relief, led Alex to the island and urged her to sit in one of the bar stools. "Speaking of Ava, I noticed she wasn't at school today."

"Neither of us was up for drop off, for obvious reasons," she gave a mirthless laugh.

"I would have been happy to take her."

Alex shook her head. "I wasn't ready to talk to anyone. Not even you. It's fine though. Sylvia picked her up about an hour ago and took her to the kids museum."

Cleo pulled two glasses out of the cabinet and filled them with water. She put one in front of Alex, who looked at it like she didn't know what to do with it. "Where's Ethan?" She said in a low voice, in case he was anywhere nearby.

"He had to go to the office. As you can imagine, HR doesn't love the fact that two of their employees are fucking."

"Are they going to get fired?"

Alex shrugged. "I'm not sure. I mean, neither of them are each other's superior, so there's no issue there. But having a picture of her sucking Ethan's dick sent to anyone remotely involved in their industry is not going to help Morgan's reputation."

"Good. She deserves that kind of humiliation. They both do, assholes," Cleo snarled. "What did Ethan have to say for himself?" She continued.

"He said he still loves me, and that he's sorry. And he doesn't want to lose our family."

Cleo sneered. "If you don't want to break up your family, keep your dick out of your wife's best friend. How long has it been going on?"

"He says it's only been a few weeks, but I suspect it's been going on longer."

"I'm sure it has." Cleo knew it had, but she couldn't tell Alex that.

"I hope you told him he could take his 'sorries and I love you's 'and shove them up his ass."

Alex's lips quirked in a feeble grin. "I didn't use those exact words but the sentiment was the same. I told him to go fuck himself and that I wanted a divorce."

"Great. Let's start researching attorneys. I'm going to find you the most vicious pit bull of a lawyer who's going to make sure you get everything you deserve."

"Not so fast. When I told him that, he reminded me that his company was incorporated two days before we got married."

"Meaning?" Cleo's stomach clenched. She wasn't completely studied up on California divorce laws, but she knew the clock on communal property didn't start ticking until a couple was officially married.

"Meaning all of those shares, all of the proceeds from selling the company are his. If I were to leave, I'd get nothing. I've lived through that. I can't do it again. I can't do that to Ava."

No, Cleo thought, this wasn't what was supposed to happen. This was where Alex was supposed to strike out on her own as a gorgeous, wealthy, divorcee who men with more character in their pinkies than Ethan had in his entire body would line up to show her what real love was.

"It can't possibly be nothing, I mean, he's a venture guy-"

"He's only worked there for a year. Besides, he's an entrepreneur in residence, which means he just earns a salary. The best I can hope for is alimony and decent child support, all of which are based on his current salary."

Cleo desperately wanted to ask how much that number was, but Alex obviously wasn't inclined to say. But from the look on her face, Cleo knew it wasn't nearly enough to keep her luxuriously ensconced in Oak Valley.

"What about the house? Your name is on the deed, right? He would have to buy you out," Cleo said, grasping for a way to get Alex to extricate herself from marriage to a narcissistic bully.

"When I mentioned that, he pointed out that whether my name was on the deed or not, since the house had been purchased with funds that were solely his, the only thing I can claim is half of how much the house has appreciated since we bought it. Which, if Redfin estimates are to be believed, leaves me with around a million dollars."

"That's not nothing," Cleo said.

Alex leveled her with a deadpan stare. "Around here, that's like pocket change and you know it."

"Obviously I'm not a lawyer, but I thought that in California, unless there's a prenup, everything is community property."

"Even if it's not technically legal, people can fight for whatever they want to in court. He can drag it out for years if he wants to and drown me in legal fees. And then there's custody to consider. Can you imagine how ugly it could get for Ava? And for me?"

Her shoulders slumped heavily as she sighed. "I can't believe he's put me in this position," her lip quivered as she swiped a tear away with her thumb. "I always trusted him to take care of me."

Cleo slid her arm around her shoulders and gave her a comforting squeeze. "Unfortunately, sometimes it's the people who are supposed to take care of us who are the ones who end up causing the most pain."

Alex huffed out a mirthless laugh. "Something I should know better than most. Regardless, I'm stuck. For now anyway. But I still have my MBA to fall back on, so it's not like I don't have good work prospects if I do leave. I'm going to take the next few years to get back into paid work, so that I'll be in a better position depending on what happens. But who knows," she turned to Cleo and gave her a watery smile, "maybe in the end, this is what our marriage needed. Maybe this is a chance to tear it down and rebuild it, so it can better than ever."

"Maybe." Cleo didn't believe that for a second. She knew Alex didn't either.

Cleo couldn't leave her like this. She wasn't going to let her waste another week of her life with Ethan, never mind years. After everything Alex had already gone through, and everything Cleo herself had put her through, a new beginning was the least she could provide.

36

Alex

"How was school?" Alex knelt down with open arms as Ava bounded through the front door. She was followed closely by Sylvia, who Alex had enlisted to pick Ava up from Wyndham for the fourth time this week. She still couldn't force herself to face everyone's prying stares. Thank God for Cleo, who had taken her to school the last few mornings, because Ethan had been leaving well before preschool drop off this week.

She hugged Ava hard and tried not to dwell on why he was leaving so early and who he might be seeing. She had decided to stay, at least for the time being. She couldn't spend all her time ruminating and worrying about what Ethan might be up to when he wasn't in her presence.

"Let's get you some lunch," she said as they proceeded into the kitchen. She pulled out ham and cheese from the refrigerator as Sylvia got to work slicing strawberries. Once Ava was settled into her booster and tucking into her sandwich, Alex pulled out her phone.

She had over a dozen unread messages. She didn't have the energy to sift through them to separate those who actually cared about her from those who only wanted to marvel over the dumpster fire her life had become.

One person, however, remained painfully silent. After the commotion over the pictures died down a bit, Alex had called Jenna and left a long, heartfelt voicemail expressing how sorry she was. It went unanswered, as did the handful of follow up texts in which she apologized again, said she never should have suspected her, that she should have trusted her.

Morgan, on the other hand, had sent her own flurry of texts to Alex, apologizing, begging for a chance to try to explain herself.

Alex had finally sent a curt reply:

There is no excuse or explanation for fucking my husband. You're a disgusting human being. I saw you jogging down Eastridge yesterday. You're lucky I didn't run you over.

She slumped next to Ava, feeling like someone had draped a wet wool blanket over her shoulders. It was bad enough to discover Ethan was cheating on her. But to have to get through this without the help of two of her closest friends made it seem all but unbearable.

Thank God for Cleo. She was just about to call her to make a plan for later when the buzzer for the gate went off.

She and Sylvia exchanged a curious look, as she wasn't expecting anyone. She got up and went to the intercom panel mounted by the front door. "Hello?"

"Yes, ma'am, are you the wife of Ethan Drake?"

Alex's stomach clenched. Was this an angry husband of some other woman Ethan had fucked? "Yes," she said warily. "How can I help you?"

"Ma'am this is Deputy Marcos with the San Mateo County Sheriff's department. I'm afraid there's been an accident."

###

As soon as Cleo heard the frantic grief in Alex's tone, she knew she'd been successful. She listened as Alex cried hysterically, explaining between sobs that Ethan had been in a car accident, that they didn't know what happened, but he appeared to have lost consciousness at the wheel. She needed to go to the morgue to identify his body and she didn't think she could drive herself.

"I'll be right there," Cleo said. She left Izzy in Clara's care and drove as quickly as she could to Alex's house. She stifled a pang of guilt when Alex opened the door, sobbing and trembling in obvious distress. Yes, she was hurting now, but it would be better for her in the long run. She hoped it wouldn't take Alex too long to realize that.

Her heart squeezed at the sight of Ava, eyes wide with fear, lip trembling as she clung to her mother's skirt and leaned against her thigh. She, too, would be fine. She was young enough that she wouldn't have too many memories of when Ethan was alive. She would never have to see her mother diminish herself or tolerate her father's unsavory behavior. In the event Alex did eventually leave, she would never have to endure what Cleo had no doubt would be a nasty divorce.

"I'm so sorry," Cleo said and pulled Alex into her arms. She held her for a long time, trying as best she could to absorb her grief. "I'm here for you. I'm going to help you get through this."

She waited as Alex got Ava, who was uncharacteristically reluctant to be left with Sylvia, settled and playing with her dolls.

They got in Cleo's car and she asked Alex where they were going.

"I have no idea," Alex said. "I've never had to go to a morgue before," she said and broke down in tears.

Cleo made some reassuring sounds and looked the address up on her phone and set out under Siri's direction.

"I don't understand how this could be happening. How can Ethan be dead?" Alex said as a fresh wave of sobs overtook her.

"Do they think he was on something? How could he just lose consciousness?"

"I don't know. They'll do a tox screen of course. But it's also possible that he had an aneurysm or a heart attack or something like that."

"Incredibly fit thirty four year old men like Ethan don't have heart attacks," she scoffed.

"His heart condition puts him at a higher risk, especially when he's under stress. And god knows we're both-" she cut herself off. "I'm still talking about him like he's alive. I can't believe he's really dead."

Cleo could. And not from a heart attack either. Heart condition or no, men of Ethan's age and health didn't have sudden massive heart attacks. However, if he were to ingest ten milligrams of a tincture of oleander, he would shortly thereafter experience a life ending event that strongly resembled a heart attack.

Once she'd determined her course of action, Cleo knew she had to work quickly. Jenna might have still been stonewalling Alex, but she knew it was only a matter of time before they made up. Which meant it was only a matter of time before Jenna told Alex what she'd discovered in Cleo's past.

She decided on oleander because not only was it easy to process and lethal in small doses, it would never be detected on even an expanded tox screen. Detecting it would require a separate test that the ME would have to know to ask for. Ethan's heart condition made a heart attack plausible, if unlikely. She was confident no one would bother to dig any deeper.

Once the tincture was ready, she kept her eyes open for an opportunity to deploy it. Such a one had presented itself earlier this morning when she had stopped by Alex and Ethan's to take Ava to school. Ethan was in the kitchen, finishing his coffee while Alex was in Ava's room getting her ready.

She gave a curt smile in greeting, surprised to find him at home since every other morning he had been gone by the time she arrived to take Ava to school. He smiled sheepishly back, and she fought the urge to slap it off of his lying, cheating face. She accepted Ethan's offer of coffee. After he handed it to her, he stood there, uncharacteristically awkward.

"Listen," he said after a moment. "I just wanted to say thank you, for being so helpful, so supportive of our family right now."

"Alex is one of the best friends I've ever had," she replied. "I'm here to love her and support her through anything." Anything but her being forced to stay in a marriage with a cheating asshole like Ethan.

"Well, like I said, I appreciate it." He pulled a water bottle out of the gym bag resting on the seat of one of the bar stools, and filled it with water from the refrigerator.

"What I hope you appreciate is that she's even willing to stay and work it out with you," Cleo snapped. "If I found out my husband was fucking my best friend, I can't say I'd make the same choice."

Any trace of friendliness disappeared from his face. His eyes went cold, lifeless. *Shark eyes,* she remembered Alex saying.

As tough as she was, Cleo's skin prickled.

"Alex knows exactly what's at stake if she leaves," he said as he set his water bottle on the island. "She knows better than to leave me over one mistake." The cold threat of menace in his tone sent ice coursing through her veins.

Before Cleo could point out that having sex with another woman several times over the course of months was more a deliberate choice than a mistake, Alex called from Ava's room. "Ethan, can you please bring me the Aquaphor from Ava's bathroom?"

He shot Cleo a look like he was so put upon and left to fulfill Alex's request.

Which left Cleo all alone with Ethan's water bottle.
###
On the way home from the morgue, Alex was silent, almost catatonic. Cleo needed to attend to her own business, but she wasn't about to leave Alex uncared for.

Once they got back to Alex's house, she settled her on the living room couch with a blanket over her lap and a mug of tea in front of her. Then she called the one person who she knew Alex could really trust.

Of course, Jenna let her go straight to voicemail. Cleo left a curt message asking her to call her back, that it was important. She then sent a text to the same effect.

"What do you want?" Jenna snapped as soon as Cleo answered the phone. She gasped in horror as Cleo explained what had happened. "I need to get home to Izzy, but I don't want to leave her alone."

"Of course," Jenna said, her voice thick with tears, "I'll be over as soon as I can."

Fifteen minutes later, a teary eyed Jenna was at the door, with Noah on her hip and Liam at her side. Sylvia took Noah from her and guided Liam to the playroom where she was keeping Ava occupied.

Jenna gave her a wary look, but let the subject of Cleo's past and the other information she'd dug up rest for now. "How is she?"

"Bad," Cleo said as she led her to the living room. "She hasn't said anything since we left the coroner's office. It's like she's shutting down."

They found Alex in the living room in the same position Cleo had left her. She stared blankly at the wall as her tea sat untouched.

"Oh, honey, I'm so sorry," Jenna sat on one side of Alex and put her arm around her shoulder as Cleo sat on the other.

At first Alex didn't respond, but after a few seconds she lifted her head and gave it a little shake as though waking from a nap. "Jenna? You're here." She started crying, and flung her arms around her shoulders.

A din of sobs and muffled apologies filled the room, and Cleo knew Alex was in good hands. "I need to go now," she said, as her own eyes filled with tears. She leaned over to give Alex one last hug.

"I love you, and I know it doesn't feel like it now, but I promise you everything will be ok."

She released Alex and met Jenna's gaze. "Thank you for coming to look after her."

"Of course," Jenna said as she rested her hand on Alex's thigh. "I wouldn't let a misunderstanding keep me from helping her in something as awful as -" her voice cracked and she trailed off.

Cleo's chest hitched. "I know. But I'm still glad you can be here for her."

Soothed by the knowledge that Alex was in the best of hands, she said goodbye and walked out of Alex's house for the very last time.

37

Alex

The next morning, Alex woke up, head fuzzy from the Xanax Jenna had forced on her along with several glasses of chardonnay. She felt a presence stirring beside her. She reached out, confused at first to feel not Ethan's brawn, but Ava's small body curled in on itself. In that moment reality crashed over her like a tsunami. It had been hard enough waking up to face her life knowing that Ethan was cheating on her. Now that he was dead, going on with her life seemed not just unbearable, but impossible.

Feeling like she had a two ton weight slung around her shoulders, she rolled over and grabbed her phone. There were dozens of messages and voicemails left throughout the evening. The first one she opened was a text from Cleo, written and sent shortly after four in the morning.

Flying to Singapore on the first flight I can get. Hate to leave you right now but Scott is having a medical emergency. I'll be back as soon as I can. Love you and sending you strength.

Alex quickly replied, *OMG how scary. I hope he recovers soon. I'll miss you but I understand. XOXOXO.*

The next several days passed in a grief soaked haze as a steady parade of friends and relatives came to the house. There were a few policemen as well, as it wasn't lost on them that Ethan's affair had recently been revealed to everyone they knew. However, suspicions of foul play were quickly put to rest as Ethan's tox screen came back completely clean.

Through it all, Jenna was her rock, barely leaving her side while Sylvia worked overtime watching the kids. And thank God, because Ethan's mother, who was usually so helpful and a delight to have around, was overcome with grief. Since their arrival two days ago, she and Ethan's father had spent all their time weeping inconsolably and railing at God for taking their son from them.

Alex couldn't claim to be any more useful. Jenna handled it all like a pro, seeing to her visitors, keeping them fed, and forcing Alex into the shower at regular intervals. She even told Morgan to go fuck herself in the ass with her Louboutins when the other woman had the gall to show up to offer her condolences.

Still, she missed Cleo. Jenna had raised a skeptical brow when Alex showed her the text she'd sent. "I'm still not convinced he even exists. I haven't told you this yet, but I had my brother look into her-"

"Don't!" Alex cut her off. "Just don't. I have too much to deal with already to deal with your ridiculous theories."

Instead of getting defensive, Jenna nodded and gave her a sad smile. "You're right. This isn't what you need right now." And then she'd given her a long, hard, hug and set to work helping Alex keep herself somewhat together as her entire life continued to fall apart.

She was such an incredible friend, Alex felt a little guilty for how much she wished Cleo were there as well. There was something about the way they had bonded, so quickly and so deeply. Her absence, especially at a time like this, left her feeling like she was missing a limb.

She tried not to take personally how infrequently the other woman had been in touch. Not only was her husband hospitalized with a life threatening infection, there was a sixteen hour time difference between here and Singapore.

Tox screens came back negative, she wrote to Cleo four days after Ethan's death. *I'm no longer a suspected black widow. I have to go down to the morgue to release his body to the funeral home.*

When is the service? Cleo replied hours later.

Next Thursday at Valley Pres. Will you be back by then?

Again, Cleo's reply came hours later. *Can't say for sure. I'll do my best.*

But by the morning of the funeral, not only was Cleo nowhere to be found, she hadn't replied to Alex's texts for three days.

The service was lovely. I'm sorry you missed it, Alex messaged after.

Again, no reply. Grief and anger roiled in her chest. How could Cleo do this? How could she just abandon her in the wake of such a devastating loss? *I get it that you've got a lot going on over there, but you could at least reply to your friend whose husband just fucking died.*

She sent it and immediately felt guilty. Scott was very sick. Cleo said his infection was so virulent the first two antibiotics didn't work. What if he had died too? And Alex was ripping her a new asshole for not looking out for her.

Her phone buzzed in her hand. She looked down, dreading what Cleo might have read. But instead of a reply from Cleo, it was an automated reply from her cell phone carrier. *The number you have reached is no longer in service...*

It had to be a mistake, maybe something to do with Cleo being out of the country. She tried to text again and got the same reply. Then she tried to call. *The number you have reached is no longer in service...*

"Alex, Aunt Violet and Uncle Jim are looking for you to say their goodbyes." Marion, Ethan's mother, stood in the doorway of Alex's bedroom, where she had retreated. She would have to try to solve the mystery of Cleo's disappearing phone number later. For now she had to put on a brave face and endure hugs and words of condolences from dozens of relatives, friends, and business acquaintances. All of which had a particular sort of awkwardness when the recently deceased had been so publicly revealed as a cheater.

She didn't have much time to think about Cleo until the next day, when she shared what happened with Jenna.

"What exactly did your brother find out about her?"

Alex felt like she'd been dropped into some bizarro universe as Jenna told her about the assumed identity, the partying with billionaires, and the probability that she'd been a prostitute or at least prostitute adjacent.

"That's insane," Alex said. "But I guess I can understand why she would want to have a fresh start."

Jenna shook her head. "You give people way too much of the benefit of the doubt."

"Why? You think there was some malicious intent?"

Jenna shrugged. "I always got a weird vibe off of her. I would catch her watching us sometimes and it felt very calculating. Like she was trying to figure out how we could be of use to her."

Alex felt a swell of unease as she thought about how open she had been with Cleo, how many secrets she had shared. It grew in force as she reflected on how little in comparison Cleo had revealed about herself. "I wonder who she really is, and how she ended up in Oak Valley."

The weeks went on as Alex tried to settle into the dramatically changed landscapes of her home and social lives. As if the grief she felt for Ethan, complicated by his betrayal, wasn't enough to bear, she was burdened with the knowledge that yet another person she loved and trusted lied to her. Had lied to her from the very first hello. She did her best to navigate daily life and spoke twice a week to her therapist. She feared there wasn't enough therapy in the world to help her heal from all of this.

One day, about a month after Ethan died, Alex received an email. Her heart skipped several beats when she saw the address. CleoB@gmail.com. She braced herself against the kitchen island and began to read.

Dear Alex,

I'm sorry I haven't been there for you though all of this. I don't know how to say this, so I'll just cut to the chase. Jenna was right when she said I'm not who you think I am. While I can't tell you who I really am, I feel like I owe it to you to tell you a little more about myself. I owe it to you to explain why there was a time when I wanted to ruin your life.

I was told from a young age that my father had abandoned my mother when she was pregnant, and that he wanted nothing to do with her or with me. Understandably, I grew up hating him, and by association, the wife and family upon whom he lavished his vast wealth. By the time I discovered his identity, he'd been dead for over a decade. But his daughter was very much alive, and appeared to be living a life that I could only dream of. All of the hatred I held for him became focused on her. On you, Alex, my half sister.

Alex swayed as blood roared in her ears. She read on, feeling her skin go icy with shock as she read on about how the half sister she never knew she had came up with a plan to ruin her life.

Four Years Earlier...
Nicole surveyed the empty rooms of her mother's house. Though the movers had hauled everything away yesterday, a faint medicinal odor lingered in the bungalow. Her mother's last few months had required round the clock care, and the house Nicole had purchased for her shortly after she married Paul slowly morphed into a mini hospital.

You could go, a little voice inside her head whispered, *now that you don't have to worry about your mom having a place to live and proper medical care.*

Having access to her husband's millions had been a godsend when it came to helping her mother, particularly in the last year. But now that she was gone, Nicole wasn't sure that access to those millions was worth what she had to endure. If it were just her...

Her hand strayed to the small bump below her navel.

It wasn't just her, not anymore. She wouldn't give her baby a childhood like her own. Fatherless, penniless, going from place to place and man to man. Her daughter was going to be born in the lap of luxury and never want for anything in her life. Nicole wouldn't deny her that, even if she had to endure some... unpleasantness.

Sun shining through the window of her mother's bedroom sparked off the diamond encrusted Rolex on her wrist. A gift from Paul after he made her fuck two Saudi princes while he watched. Any unpleasantness was always similarly compensated.

If that made her a whore, so be it.

Fortunately, once they had established the baby's paternity, Paul had been uncharacteristically solicitous, treating her with kid gloves, affectionately patting her belly whenever she passed. That, thankfully, was all the physical contact she'd had to endure since she'd told him. She'd stay pregnant for the next decade if it meant keeping his and any others 'hands off of her.

"Miss?" It was Celia, a member of the cleaning crew she'd hired to deep clean her Mother's house. She was holding a shoe box in one hand. "I found this under the sink in the powder room."

"Just throw it away with everything else," Nicole waved her off. She wasn't surprised at another errant piece of junk. Her mother had packed every cabinet in the house with a collection of odds and ends. The shoe box was probably full of hotel toiletries or half full tubes of toothpaste.

"But it's full of letters people wrote to your mom. You should look through it before you throw it out."

She took the box with a shrug. Other than her grandmother, she couldn't imagine who her mother would have corresponded with. She burned nearly every bridge with every person she'd ever known, and never mentioned any childhood friends or other family. She opened the box and saw her grandmother's familiar perfect cursive on the top envelope. She read the note describing the planting she was doing in her garden and how the neighbors needed to mow their lawn. She ended by reminding her that Nicole was welcome to come back to stay with her any time for as long as she needed.

Her heart squeezed at the memories of living with her grandmother. It was the last time she ever felt truly safe and loved.

She blinked back tears and shoved the sentimental thoughts aside as she sifted through the dozen or so envelopes in the box. More from her grandmother, as expected.

There was one towards the bottom addressed to her mother in handwriting she didn't recognize.

Dear Stella,

I don't understand why you are being so difficult regarding my involvement in our child's life. I know you are upset that I am going forward with my marriage to Andrea, but that doesn't mean that I can't be a father to our baby. I hope you will come to your senses soon and allow me to be a part of our child's life. It truly is in his or her best interests, both emotionally and financially.

Robert

She struggled to catch her breath as the paper trembled in her hand. The envelope fluttered to the floor. She stooped to retrieve it. Sure enough, there was a return address, neatly printed in the upper right corner.

Robert Bradford
224 California St. 2b
San Franciso, CA 94111

After thirty years, she finally knew her father's name. And she knew that her mother had been lying to her about the fact that he'd wanted nothing to do with her. She should have known her mother had lied. She lied about everything, especially if it could make her look like a bigger victim.

Her father had wanted to be part of her life.

Really? Her mother's voice echoed in her head. *People can say anything they want in the moment, but actions speak louder than words. If he really wanted to be part of your life, he could have tracked you down. It's not like I took great pains to hide.*

No, but moving every six months or so pre internet made it harder to keep tabs on someone. But it was true, if he'd really wanted to find them, or more specifically her, he could have done. She imagined that once it dawned on her father that being in her life meant putting up with her mother's brand of crazy for the next eighteen years, he'd been happy enough to wash his hands of Stella and their unborn child.

After all, as she discovered back at her hotel room via an internet search, Robert had gone on to marry a beautiful, accomplished woman named Andrea Sullivan. And she had given him another daughter, Alexandra.

Her father had died of a heart attack nearly sixteen years ago. His wife had gone on to remarry a wealthy Chicago businessman. Judging by her social media, Alexandra, or Alex as she called herself, was happily married to a gorgeous tech millionaire named Ethan. Photo after photo featured them on lavish vacations, hanging out in their beautiful home in a wealthy suburb of Silicon Valley. When she wasn't with her adoring husband, she was surrounded by dozens of friends.

Fuck her, Nicole thought at the time. *Fuck her and her girls' nights and her pussy whipped husband. What do I need with any of that when I'm married to a guy who can buy and sell her and her husband ten times over?*

But as much as she tried to pretend Alex didn't exist, she kept going back to her social media. It was like picking at a scab, making herself bleed anew every time, deepening the wound in the process.

She watched as Alex announced her pregnancy and gave birth to a daughter only a few months after Nicole's was born. She watched, seething, as she posted photos and videos of Ethan lovingly cradling their daughter in the hospital.

Despite his doting during her pregnancy their daughter, Elizabeth, or Lizzy, hadn't met her father until three days after her birth. Nicole had gone into labor during Burning Man, and Paul couldn't be bothered to tear himself away. Not that Nicole wanted him around anyway. Before he hopped on the private jet to California, he'd looked at her swollen body and told her she better have a plan to get back into shape, because he was expecting some special visitors in the coming months.

As months went by, a plan took root. She began selling her jewelry and siphoning the money into an offshore account. She figured out how to get into Paul's accounts and transfer funds in a way that wouldn't raise any flags. She stayed quiet, she stayed compliant, and she endured. All the while she continued to monitor Alexandra Drake's idyllic existence.

Then Paul had nearly killed her in front of her daughter, and she knew she could no longer wait to put her plan into action.

She didn't know when she decided that not only did she want a new life for herself and her daughter, she also wanted to destroy the woman who had the life that Nicole should have had. Soon after, Nicole became Cleo Baird. And Cleo set off on her mission to blow Alexandra Drake's life apart.

Alex's legs buckled under her and she slid to the floor as Cleo's email continued.

...Now I realize I had no idea what the truth really was. The truth is that you didn't deserve any of it, not what happened when you were younger, not how Ethan treated you, and certainly nothing that I did to you. I am so deeply sorry for my part in your suffering. I will never forgive myself for how terribly I wronged you. I know there is nothing I can do to make it up to you, but I did what I could to make things right for you. I know you are devastated right now, and never would have wanted things to end this way. I hope, sooner rather than later, you will see that this is all for the best. As your big sister, I should have been looking after you all along. I can't undo the past and I can't make your husband a better person, but I can give you and Ava a new beginning. I hope you seize it with both hands and create a life that is truly and authentically happy. You and Ava deserve it.

Love,

Your Sister

Alex's vision blurred and she felt like she was going to pass out as she absorbed the meaning of Cleo's words. "Oh, my God, she killed him."

38

Alex

Six Months Later

You're Invited to the Wyndham Preschool Potluck Picnic!

When: Saturday, August 31, 12:00 pm

Where: Wyndham Preschool Playground and Courtyard

Hello Wyndham Friends! The school year is almost upon us. Join us for a fun afternoon and get to know the pre-k families. Bring a favorite dish to share (Please no nuts. Gluten free preferred, and an assortment of vegan dishes are most welcome). Teachers Annie, Olivia, and Jennie can't wait to see our old friends and meet our new ones!

Alex pulled her Mercedes SUV into the nearly full parking lot. "Ready?" She said, as though asking Ava who was strapped in her carseat in the back. But really, she was asking herself. And honestly, she wasn't sure. She wasn't sure she would ever be ready to face this big of a group since Ethan's funeral.

"Yes!" Ava yelled, already fumbling with the buckle on her carseat. Unlike Alex, who had been content to keep her social circle very small for the last several months, Ava was beyond excited to get back to school to see her friends.

Alex took several deep breaths in an attempt to ease the tightness in her chest.

"Mommy, come on!" Ava urged as she scrambled out of the carseat and tugged at the doorhandles. Fortunately, the child locks were on so Ava couldn't go careening into the parking lot.

"Okay, okay," Alex sighed. She got out of the car and went around to the passenger side to retrieve her tote and a tray of sushi. She opened Ava's door and snagged her hand before she could run off unattended. "Just hold my hand until we get out of the parking lot," she said when Ava tried to tug from her grip. Ava gave an exasperated sigh that made her sound more like she was fourteen rather than four. But she held Alex's hand until they got to the school's entry, then took off like her hair was on fire.

Alex followed more slowly, feeling like her feet weren't quite steady. It was a feeling that had dogged her ever since she found out about Ethan's affair. Like she'd been blown apart and put together wrong, and now she was destabilized at a molecular level. She lingered at the edge of the playground, watching the other parents chat and sip wine while they kept one eye on their kids tearing around. They all looked so normal, so stable, like they didn't have a care in the world. She'd probably looked just like that last year, the first time Cleo laid eyes on her.

"Alex, is that you?" She turned towards the voice and pasted on a smile for Melanie Parker, who stood in a cluster with Lena Umanski and Rose Wilson. Melanie beckoned her, and even though she didn't really want to join them, she was too polite to refuse.

"Alex it's so good to see you!" She pulled her into a hug. Alex returned it as best she could while balancing a tray of sushi in her hand. "It feels like I haven't seen you in months."

"I've been out of town a lot. Ava and I spent most of the summer in our new place in Carmel."

She'd bought the sweet little cottage near the beach right before the school year ended. Ethan had always hated Carmel, disdaining the golfers, tennis players, and idle retirees. Alex had always loved the artsy, low key vibe. And now that she only had herself and Ava to consider, she could buy houses anywhere she goddamn pleased.

"Well it must agree with you," Lena said. "You look amazing. What have you lost, like, twenty pounds? What have you been doing?"

Alex gave a mirthless chuckle and brought her hand up to rest on her now prominent collarbone. "I've found infidelity and widowhood to be incredibly effective weightless plans."

Lena's face flooded with color as the other two grimaced. "I'm sorry," Lena sputtered, "that was incredibly insensitive of me-"

Alex held up a hand to cut her off. "Don't worry about it. It's been long enough that what I went through isn't at the top of everyone's mind. But my life falling apart is apparently a good look, so I've got that going for me."

She took their awkward laughs as her cue to retreat. "I'm just going to go put this down," she gestured to her tray of sushi. She set it down next to a bowl of what looked like quinoa and kale salad.

"I see Matthew and Ava found each other." Alex turned and smiled down at Tricia, and followed her gaze to where Ava and Matthew sat in the sandbox, meticulously mixing sand with water into the perfect consistency to make a sand castle. Tricia reached up and pulled her into a hug, which Alex returned enthusiastically.

If someone had told Alex a year ago that Tricia would become one of her closest, most trusted friends, she would have told them they were batshit. But Tricia had been so kind and supportive in the months since Ethan died. Alex had discovered that under her uptight exterior, she had a wicked sense of humor. And it didn't hurt that Ava and Matthew had become best friends.

"She had the best time with him last weekend. I'm so glad you were able to come visit," Alex said. Tricia and Matthew were among the few people Alex had invited to Carmel over the summer. "I brought Matthew's favorite," she gestured to the sushi. "And of course I remembered this," she pulled a bottle of Tamari sauce out of her tote. "Gluten free," she said with a wink.

Tricia gave a little laugh and gently elbowed her. "Let's get you a glass of wine," Tricia said and started to lead her toward the drink table.

Though she would love nothing better than a plastic cup full of cold chardonnay, between passing out at the fundraiser last year and the DUI last spring, she knew it wouldn't look good for her to be swanning around the playground with a drink in her hand. People were already whispering and giving her furtive looks. "I'm going to stick to seltzer today."

Tricia gave her a look of silent understanding. "I'm happy to be unfunzie with you today."

There was a sudden commotion, and they looked over to see that Jenna, Mark, and their boys had arrived in typical chaotic fashion. Liam made a beeline for the climbing structure while Jenna kept Noah in a desperate grip on her hip as he tried to hurl himself to the ground. They made their way over to Alex and Tricia. Alex hugged Mark, then Jenna. Jenna set Noah down, who immediately took off. Mark gave Tricia a brief squeeze and followed him.

"God, that kid is fast," Jenna sighed. From the moment he could stand on two feet, Noah's regular gait was a sprint.

"At least Mark is here to chase him for you," Alex said.

"I know. Ever since he finally hired a VP of operations, he's been able to be around so much more." A few months ago, Mark's company had received a significant investment from a well renowned VC firm. As a result he'd been able to make several key hires, as well as give himself a significant pay raise. Jenna looked happier and more relaxed than she had since before Noah was born.

"Oh, there's David," Jenna said in a hushed voice as she looked over Alex's shoulder. Alex turned, and felt her heart squeeze. She hadn't seen David since the beginning of summer. She had tried to get him and Jack down to Carmel to visit, but between his older kids' schedules and what was turning into a very messy divorce from Morgan, they hadn't been able to make it work.

She made her way over, fighting a grimace as she took in his appearance. Like her, he'd lost a substantial amount of weight. Unlike her, he hadn't had much, if any, to lose in the first place. Now his face was gaunt, and his polo and shorts hung off his near skeletal frame. Deep lines of stress were carved into either side of his mouth, and his smile did nothing to banish the look of utter misery in his eyes.

Alex and Jenna both hugged him then bent down to squeeze Jack. "Liam's over there," Jenna said, pointing at her older son. Jack gave his dad a questioning look. David nodded in approval, and Jack slowly made his way over. Alex's heart squeezed at the way Jack, who was always such a ball of unconfined energy, seemed diminished. "How is everything going?" She asked cautiously.

David shrugged. "Not great. Morgan told me yesterday that she's been offered a job in Boston. She wants to take Jack with her."

"She can't do that," Alex protested.

"That may be true, but that doesn't mean that she and that pitbull she hired won't try to make it happen."

"I don't understand why she thinks that would even work," Jenna said. "She works all of the time. Jack would be raised by his nanny."

"She knows that. I know that. But she's a selfish bitch who only cares about herself. Why should we expect her to think about what's best for her son?"

Alex patted his shoulder in sympathy even as she felt a surge of relief. If Ethan had lived, and she had tried to divorce him, she would have been in this exact situation.

The relief was followed by an immediate wave of guilt. What kind of mother wished for the death of her daughter's father? Regardless of how he had treated Alex, Ethan had loved Ava with every cell in his body. His death left a hole in Ava's life that no one would ever completely fill.

"It's understandable," Jenna had said months ago, when Alex had first dared to utter the truth that part of her was glad she was widowed rather than having to go through an ugly divorce. "As hard as this is, in a way his death did make things easier. And it's not like you had anything to do with it. It was a freak accident."

Of course, she couldn't tell Jenna, or anyone else for that matter, the real reason she felt so guilty. She couldn't tell Jenna why she felt like she shouldered a little bit of the blame for Ethan's death. She hadn't told a soul about the email Cleo has sent last spring. No one else on the planet, besides Cleo herself, knew that she was Alex's sociopathic half sister who started out to ruin her life, then murdered Ethan out of some twisted sense of justice.

Alex had briefly considered going to the police, but she knew it would only generate more salacious interest in her and her life than she'd already experienced. Besides, Ethan had been cremated. There was no evidence of any crime left. And Cleo Baird and her daughter had disappeared into the ether. So Alex kept it to herself hoping the guilt, along with the grief, would ease over time.

"There's the new family that bought the house on Oak Grove," Jenna said, in an attempt to distract David from another expletive laced tirade about Morgan. "Mark met the husband at Oakwood and says he'd nice. Should we go introduce ourselves?"

Alex looked over at the petite blond in a pink sundress. Her tall, dark haired husband held the hand of a boy with mop of brown curls.

Alex thought about the last time she'd actively tried to make a new friend. "You go ahead," Alex said. "I'm going to get Ava some food."

"I'll get some for Jack too," David said.

"Be sure to get some for yourselves too," Jenna said as she eyed them. "You're both wasting away." She left them to go greet the new family.

They got plates for the kids and settled them at one of the picnic tables. Alex picked up a piece of sushi from Ava's plate, started to lift it to her mouth, then thought better of it as her stomach squeezed in protest. "Did you ever think we would end up like this?" She asked David as she put the sushi back.

"Never in a million years," he sighed, shoulders slumping.

"But here we are. It's not what we want, but we have to get through it and make the best of it." There really was no other choice. All she could do was be the best mother to Ava she knew how to be, and to take advantage of the fresh start Cleo had forced upon her.

"To making the best of it," David lifted his plastic glass full of wine and tapped it against Alex's seltzer.

"To making the best of it," Alex repeated. "And to staying away from liars."

About the Author

Jami Worthington is the author of the domestic thriller The Playgroup. She previously authored over twenty contemporary romance and romantic suspense novels under a pen name. Jami is a graduate of Stanford University and still lives in the San Francisco Bay Area with her teenage sons and crazy cattle dogs. When she's not writing, she enjoys running, hiking, reading, cooking, and listening to live music.

Printed in Great Britain
by Amazon